John Torrey Morse, Oliver Wendell Holmes

# Life and Letters of Oliver Wendell Holmes

In Two Volumes. Vol. I

John Torrey Morse, Oliver Wendell Holmes

**Life and Letters of Oliver Wendell Holmes**
*In Two Volumes. Vol. I*

ISBN/EAN: 9783337016081

Printed in Europe, USA, Canada, Australia, Japan

Cover: Foto ©Raphael Reischuk / pixelio.de

More available books at **www.hansebooks.com**

# LIFE AND LETTERS

OF

# OLIVER WENDELL HOLMES

BY

JOHN T. MORSE, Jr.

IN TWO VOLUMES

VOLUME I.

LONDON
SAMPSON LOW, MARSTON & COMPANY (Limited)
St. Dunstan's House
FETTER LANE, FLEET STREET, E. C.
1896

*The Riverside Press, Cambridge, Mass., U. S. A.*
Printed by H. O. Houghton & Company.

# PREFACE

To the reader I have only a word to say: I fear his criticism that these volumes have too much Memoir, too little Correspondence. To this complaint, if it be made, I must plead in " confession and avoidance." The fact is that letter-writing was to Dr. Holmes an irksome task. Except to Motley and to Lowell, during their absences in Europe, he very rarely wrote spontaneously and in the way of friendship. His letters, it will be observed, were almost always written because some correspondent could not courteously be left unanswered, or under the more or less mild compulsion of some special occasion. Therefore his letters were few. Every effort has been made to collect them, and the result is spread very fully before the reader. Nothing has been omitted which, by any liberality of judgment, could be supposed to have any interest; on the contrary, notes and letters are printed, which would hardly have been selected had there been an *embarras de richesses*. Now " occasional " letters often demand an explanatory setting; and besides this it was to be considered that Dr. Holmes's life was so retired that those who care for him have not that knowledge of it and of him which they naturally desire to possess. For these reasons, a narrative apparently disproportioned to the space allotted to the letters seemed inevitable.

It is right for me to say that my friend and cousin, Mr. Justice Holmes, has been most patient and liberal in aiding me; so that the faults of the book, at least, are all my own.

JOHN T. MORSE, JR.

16 FAIRFIELD STREET, BOSTON.
*February 17, 1896.*

# CONTENTS

# CONTENTS

## CHAPTER X



## CHAPTER XI



## CHAPTER XII

# LIST OF ILLUSTRATIONS

## VOLUME I

# MEMOIRS AND CORRESPONDENCE

## CHAPTER I

### GENEALOGY AND BIRTH

WHEN this memoir was in an early stage of preparation, a thoughtful friend read aloud to the writer these ominous words from *Temple Bar :* "There is a common complaint against the biographies of men of letters, that they are, with few exceptions, insufferably dull reading. And the cause of this is not far to seek. If an author has put the best of himself into his books, he has, as a rule, left his biographer little to tell."

" With few exceptions," — there was scant comfort in these words, and even that was immediately taken away by the explanation that they covered only the cases of those authors who had *not* put the best of themselves into their books ; whereas in point of fact Dr. Holmes had not only put the best, but absolutely *all*, both of and about himself, into the volumes with which he had amused and instructed the English-reading world.

It was further not unknown to the biographer that Dr. Holmes himself had uttered sundry pungent, discouraging sentences : —

" I should like to see any man's biography with corrections and emendations by his ghost. We don't know each other's secrets quite so well as we flatter ourselves we do."

"There are but two biographers who can tell the story of a man's or a woman's life. One is the person himself or herself; the other is the Recording Angel. The autobiographer cannot be trusted to tell the whole truth, though he may tell nothing but the truth, and the Recording Angel never lets his book go out of his own hands."

"Think what a horrid piece of work the biographers make of a man's private history! Just imagine the subject of one of those extraordinary fictions called biographies coming back and reading the life of himself, written very probably by somebody or other who thought he could turn a penny by doing it."

Yet in spite of all this, it is certain that Dr. Holmes expected that some Life or Memoir would be given to the public; and it is hardly doubtful that he desired this; and if he has told so freely of himself, yet, as he says of Carlyle: "He remains not the less one of the really interesting men of his generation, a man about whom we wish to know all that we have a right to know."

His life was so uneventful that the utter absence of anything in it to remark upon became in itself remarkable. He passed two years of his youth in Europe studying medicine; in his old age he went there again for three months; otherwise he lived all his years, almost literally all his days, in or near Boston, within tethering distance, so to speak, of that State House which he declared to be "the hub of the solar system,"—and by the phrase made true his accompanying words: "You could n't pry that out of a Boston man, if you had the tire of all creation straightened out for a crowbar." All his intimate friends lived within a few miles of him, save when some one of them went abroad, as Motley and Lowell did. He was not, like so many English and a few American men of letters, connected in any way with political affairs; he never held any office; nothing ever happened to him. Fortunately the picturesqueness of poverty was never his, nor the prominence of wealth. Days and years glided by with little to distinguish them from each other, in that kind of procession which those who like it call tranquil, and those who dislike it call monotonous. Such is the panorama which awaits the reader.

In view of the fact that a large part of Dr. Holmes's literary work was devoted to the enforcement and illustration of the controlling influence of inherited tendencies, one would expect to find him making careful inquiry concerning his own ancestors. Yet so far was this from being the case that he seemed almost indifferent about them. Other persons, perhaps desiring to establish relationship with him, or instigated by mere genealogical curiosity, from time to time sent him information and pricked him with queries; and by these means he gradually acquired a more accurate information than he would ever have been at much trouble to obtain by original effort. In truth, the facts that A begat B, and that B begat C, and so on, were wretched dust for him, and he was entirely satisfied with the fragmentary knowledge which showed that he himself, as he said of Emerson, " came of the best New England stock." But since it was "the best New England stock," the memorial of it is worth preserving, especially since the name of New England is now a mere geographical title rather than, as it used to be, an implied expression of racial and social characteristics.

When Dr. Holmes died, his friend, Mr. John Bellows, an Englishman, wrote to the *Gloucestershire Chronicle* a statement that Dr. Holmes "was descended from a Sheriff Hoar, of this City, and from Richard Hoar, the donor, in 1607, to our corporation of three houses at the Cross, the rents of which were to go to certain charities." He added that lately, upon the demolition of these buildings, a piece of the old oak therefrom had been carved with the city arms, and sent to Dr. Holmes.

Thomas Holmes, a lawyer of Gray's Inn in the sixteenth century, was the earliest ancestor, of the name, of whom there is any record. A letter which the Doctor wrote to Mr. Emra Holmes, also an Englishman, may fairly be construed to imply that he supposed himself to have English ancestors who had been men of some note, and also that he had never been at the trouble to assure himself on the subject; indeed, it appears by this letter that he "mistook the Admiral Charles Holmes, Wolfe's contemporary, for his great ancestor, Sir Robert Holmes."

TO EMRA HOLMES.

BEVERLY FARMS, MASS.

MY DEAR SIR, — I thank you for the interesting notices you have sent me of the family with which I may suppose myself connected through my ancestry. Most of the settlers of New England were too poor and too hard worked in fighting famine and the Indians to think much of their genealogical trees. My own great-great-grandfather was one of the first settlers of the town of Woodstock, Conn., where my father was born. He probably carried an axe on his shoulder, and thought himself lucky if he could keep his scalp on his crown. His grandson, my grandfather, fought the French and Indians in Canada, in what we used to call the "Old French War," the same in which Wolfe fell, and in which Admiral Sir Robert Holmes took a part, as the *Gentleman's Magazine*, among other authorities, will inform you. My father was a clergyman and an author, his *Annals of America* having made him a reputation as an accurate and trustworthy writer. I, too, have made a number of books, some of which are not unknown in England. My eldest son, who bears my own name, has very recently published a work on the Common Law, which you may see noticed at considerable length, and in a very flattering way, in a late number of the *Saturday Review*. So we are trying to keep the name of Holmes respectable on this side of the Atlantic; and I thank you for what you have done on yours. I remember, by the way, the statue of Sir Robert Holmes, in Westminster Abbey, one of the most pleasing that I can recall. If you ever look in Camden's *Britannia*, you will find our old family name as we spell it, and its derivation.

The first Holmes who appeared upon this side of the Atlantic was John. He came to the village of Woodstock, Conn., with the first settlers, in 1686, not as an original proprietor or grantee of the township, but "taken in on the way by the company of 'Goers,'" because he was "the kind of man they wanted," since "he knew something of surveying." He is reported to have become "generally useful," to have set up a saw-mill and a fulling-mill, and to have given for the public use the land which is now South Woodstock common. One of his sons, David, comes down to us simply as Deacon Holmes. In the next generation, the second David was a captain in the "Old French War," and a surgeon of the army in the Revolutionary War. He married Temperance, daughter of John and Temperance Bishop, of Norwich, Conn. His tombstone states that he "fell on sleep March y⁰ 19th, 1779, Aetatis 57." His son, Abiel, the father of Oliver Wendell Holmes, was born at Woodstock, December 24, 1763, and graduated from Yale College "with honour and a respectable part at Commencement," September, 1783. He married for his first wife Mary, daughter of Rev. Ezra Stiles, D. D., president of Yale College; embraced the ministry, went to Georgia, and was settled over a parish there until 1791. Then he returned to Cambridge and became the pastor of the First Congregational Church. March 26, 1801, he married his second wife, Sarah Wendell, only daughter of Hon. Oliver Wendell, of Boston.

Twice his lecturing journeys brought Dr. Holmes to the neighborhood of Woodstock, and he made some little exploration there, apparently to gratify his sister Ann (wife of Charles W. Upham,[1] of Salem), who seems to have cared more than he did for matters genealogical. Some of his notes are as follows : —

"While I was in the burial-ground an old man and his daughter drove up to the fence in a wagon. His staff lay by him. He had come, as his daughter afterwards told me, to mark out with his staff the place where he was to be buried. His name was Jacob Lyon and his age 88." With this couple the Doctor visited the "Old Holmes place." There he found a

---

[1] A clergyman, an author, and a member of Congress, 1854–1856.

well, which "had the aspect of antiquity. This, I
doubt not, was 'old Dr. David Holmes's' well, and
that he 'drank thereof himself and his children and
his cattle.' The brook, which I remember Father's
mentioning, ran at the foot of the mound where the
house was placed. There he went one Sunday morning, when a child, forgetting that it was 'Sabbath
day,' until some horror-stricken person startled and
confounded him by announcing the awful fact. In the
rocky, steep banks of the brook, near his father's
house, he might easily have found the natural pulpit from which he used to hold forth in his tender
years."

"Rode to Muddy Brook, where an old man, *Child*
by name, sat in front of his house. He was nearly
80 years old. Remembered father's brothers. Was
ready to talk, in a mild way, but said: 'I am not
very *flippant.*'

"Old Mr. Lyon spoke well of the Holmeses. Liberty H. was 'a little dissipated,' — went off — thinks
he became a Methodist preacher."

In June, 1866, Dr. Holmes made another visit to
Woodstock, and on this occasion his genealogical
booty was as follows: —

"Visited the old Holmes place. . . . Came upon
Dr. Daniel Lyman, son of the Rev. Eliphalet Lyman,
who was minister of Woodstock from 1779 to 1821.
Dr. Lyman is about 82 years old. His father and
mother, when first married, boarded with Dr. David
Holmes. He told me what here follows: —

"Dr. David Holmes was a pleasant sociable man,
like my father. His wife, whom Dr. Lyman remembers very well, was a nice old lady.

"General David, his oldest son, was a man of

character, — would have been distinguished if he had been living in this last war. Dr. L. told me a story of David's cleverness and boldness in the raising of the Academy steeple.

"Major Sanford H. was a humorist. Story about his talking of 'land-eels,' meaning *snakes* thereby. He tried a great many things, as Deacon Sanger had told me, — a saw-mill — a pepper-mill — tavern, etc., — then went to Vermont.

"Captain Leonard H., a worthy man, went to Muddy Brook, lived there.

"Hartwell H. was an ingenious mechanic.

"Dr. Lathrop H. sold out slaves, etc., in Georgia. Lost the proceeds and his life by shipwreck, but left a good deal of property to his daughter, Tempe [Temperance].

"Tempe married Barstow. Had two daughters. The first married Stoddard, and died. The second married Wilkinson, and was divorced (after some scandal); then married Stoddard, deceased sister's husband."

Among Dr. Holmes's papers, I also find the following "Extracts from the Diary of my father:" —

"August, 1790. Rode to Coventry with my sister Tempy, lodged at my Uncle Coleman's, find my much respected and very pious Grandmother Hewet much debilitated, etc., will be 88 years old if she lives till the 6th September. August, 1791. My Grandmother Hewet departed this life in the 88th year of her age at Coventry July, 1791, — paid the following tribute of respect : —

"MRS. TEMPERANCE HEWET.

"'T is done, O Death ! thy well-aim'd dart hath sped —
Swift from the clay-cold corse the spirit fled ;
Nor deem the triumph thine — SHE, she did gain
The palm of victory on the ethereal plain —
All calm and placid as the unruffled sea
She met thy dart, and own'd a Friend in thee."

[Several more stanzas follow, in the same strain.]

"1803.  On Thursday the 4th day of August, at 4 o'clock in the morning, I was awakened by a messenger from Woodstock, who brought me the melancholy tidings of the death of my much honored and beloved MOTHER.  She died very suddenly the preceding day, August 3d, between 11 and 12 o'clock, A. M. . . .

"Mrs. Temperance Holmes, my much honored and beloved Mother, was born at Norwich in Connecticut, A. D. 1733.  She was the daughter of John and Temperance Bishop.  Were I to attempt a delineation of her character I should probably betray the Son.  I will, however, minute a few things, in indulgence to my present feelings, and in aid of my future recollection.  She was, in my estimation, a woman distinguished for vigour of mind, and energy in action. . . . Eight children, the eldest of whom was not at that time seventeen years of age, were devolved, under Providence, on her entire care.  She was left sole Executrix of my Father's Will (a proof of *his* high estimate of her judgment and ability), and had therefore, in addition to the cares of her family, the sole care of settling the estate. . . . To the affairs of her household she was assiduously and unweariedly attentive, and never *ate the bread of idleness*. . . . Although I entered College in less than six months after my father's death, I do not recollect the time when I was not seasonably supplied with suitable clothes, and money for my college expenses, so far as to enable me to be punctually present with my class.

"My Mother was an admirer of learning. Though she received her education in a part of the town of Norwich (Newent Parish) which did not probably furnish her any signal advantages at school, yet she had a Mother who was at once a school and a library to her. My Grandmother Hewet possessed very superior accomplishments. I seldom, if ever, have seen a woman at so advanced a period of life as hers when I knew her, so comely in countenance, so polite in address, so graceful in mauners, so pleasant and improving in conversation, so pious and exemplary in deportment. She had a thirst for knowledge ; so desirous was she of knowing something of Virgil in the original, that, with some little instruction and the aid of a dictionary, she examined that classical author for herself. The writings and the character of Watts she greatly admired. . . . I do not mean that [my mother] read extensively, but she read more than was usual for her sex at that day, and what she did read was judiciously selected, attentively perused, and faithfully retained. Milton's *Paradise Lost* and Young's *Night Thoughts* were her very favorite authors. . . . The loss of a most estimable husband had occasioned that temperament of mind which I know not how better to describe than by the *Penseroso* of Milton. Hence the writings of the pensive and contemplative Young were now more congenial to her than ever. . . .

"I cannot forbear to mention another instance, of her resolute refusal to change her state of life, — a refusal which seemed to me grounded on her delicate respect to the memory of her deceased husband, which she would not suffer to be violated, together with a devoted care for her children, which she seemed determined neither to relinquish nor divide. A very worthy man, whose years somewhat exceeded her own, made her several visits and appeared evidently inclined to make proposals of marriage. As Young was commonly near at hand and she had occasionally read some paragraphs in his hearing, she took care seasonably to select one with the intention that it should be understood, and the end was completely answered without offence : —

"'Though gray our heads, our thoughts and aims are green,
Like damaged clocks, whose hand and ball dissent,
Folly sings six, while nature points at twelve.'"

.   .   .   .   .   .   .   .   .   .   .

"She always commenced the Sabbath at sunset on Saturday, as did my father in his lifetime, and in the observance at home and at the house of God was highly exemplary. In the disposal of her children she consulted their genius and inclination, and had the happiness to see them reputably established in different occupations and professions.

.   .   .   .   .   .   .   .   .   .   .

"Her dissolution was at last sudden and surprising to us, it was probably without any premonition to her."

"1800. A few weeks since I visited a Mrs. Prentiss, at Newton, aged about 91, who was originally from Woodstock, and whose maiden name was *Bacon*.

She was at Woodstock in the time of Mr. Dwight, and sat under his ministry. She says (what I have often heard of Mr. D.) that he was very *singular* in his manner of preaching, and added this anecdote: That one winter, he dwelt so long upon the oppressions of the Israelites in Egypt, and mentioned such strange and incredible things (as that the streets in Egypt were paved with the skulls of the Israelites, etc.) that Mrs. Holmes, my great-grandmother, *refused to write after him.* It was her custom (said Mrs. P.) to write after the minister, at meeting, for she was a learned woman, and wrote short-hand."

"Of my paternal ancestors," wrote Dr. Holmes, in 1889, "I know little compared with what I know of those on my mother's side." His mother's name was Wendell, and the first Wendell came, in 164?, from Friesland to Albany. "In speaking of Holland," wrote the Doctor to Mr. Motley, "and my maternal ancestors, it was from Emden, in East Friesland, which as you know is — now at any rate — in the kingdom of Hanover, that my progenitor came, — Evert Jansen Wendell, — about 1640, to Albany. I suppose if I were there and found Mynheers of the name grand people I should claim their acquaintance, but if the descendants of the Regicenden Diaconen whose arms were emblazoned on the old Dutch Church window were come to be poor devils, — I don't know just what I should do."

And again he said, in his usual odd tone, half interested, half indifferent, concerning his ancestry: —

"I wonder if you ever heard my maternal name *Wendell* in Holland. It came from Emden, and was then honorable; but they may be all rogues now for aught that I know. *Vondel*, 'the Dutch Shakespeare,' comes pretty near it."

TO GEORGE W. VAN SICLEN, SECRETARY HOLLAND SOCIETY, NEW YORK.

BOSTON, *January* 10, 1887.

MY DEAR SIR, — The very kind and cordial invitation you send me, on behalf of the Holland Society of New York, warms every drop of Batavian blood in my veins. I heard a great deal of my Dutch ancestors in my early years. There was a Dutch family Bible in the family, which was to be the property of the first of us children who could read a chapter in it. My sister Mary had the start of me by half a dozen years or more, and so I lost my chance of trying for the Bible.

My forefather Evert Jansen Wendell was among the early settlers of Albany, and his arms, as I have often mentioned with a certain satisfaction, were stained on one of the windows of the old Dutch Church of that city. I never meet a Schuyler, or a Cuyler, or a Van Rensselaer, without claiming relationship with the owner of that name.

TO THE SAME.

BOSTON, *January* 22, 1889.

MY DEAR SIR, — If I were in the flower instead of being in the brown leaf, I could hardly resist your appeal. I have no doubt that I should sit down at once and write a ballad of the Schenectady Wendell who, when the town was burned and the inhabitants were massacred, had a horse and a blanket brought him by a friendly Indian, and escaped in the darkness of that terrible night.

But from me, just now, you can hardly hope for anything more than kind wishes and cousinly greetings; you may be assured that these are with you, warmed by all the drops of Holland blood that run in my veins.

Another line of good blood came as follows: Thomas Dudley, governor of Massachusetts Bay,[1] had a daughter Anne, who married Simon Bradstreet, who also was twice governor of the province.[2] This lady published, in London, in 1650, a volume of Poems under the droll title of *The Tenth Muse, lately Sprung up in America*, wherefore she herself has ever since been spoken of as "the tenth muse." The nickname has done more to immortalize her than ever her rhymes did, for they were poor stuff, and would not have made the original nine jealous.

Her grand-daughter, Mercy Bradstreet, married Dr. James Oliver (whereby that name came into the family); and Sarah Oliver, the daughter of this couple, married Jacob Wendell, who "came to Boston from Albany early in the last century." His son, the Hon. Oliver Wendell, married Mary Jackson, and their daughter, Sarah, was the mother of Oliver Wendell Holmes.

It may be remarked that the Mary Jackson above named was the daughter of Edward Jackson (son of Jonathan Jackson) and Dorothy Quincy, his wife, celebrated in the fascinating verses "Dorothy Q.;" and Dr. Holmes's own wife was also in the direct line of descent from this same couple.

Thus at last the patient reader is brought within

[1] 1634–1640 and 1645–1650.
[2] 1679–1686 and 1689–1692.

one generation of Dr. Holmes himself! The Doctor's father, the Rev. Abiel Holmes, was a clergyman who taught the old-fashioned Calvinism, with all its horrors, and yet apart from his religious creed was a gentleman of humanity and cultivation. Colonel T. Wentworth Higginson calls him " that most delightful of sunny old men." A portrait of him at the age of thirty-one years, by Edward Savage, shows a refined and pleasing face, of regular and handsome features. The Doctor wrote of it: " Everybody remarks on the beauty of the countenance. Richard Dana Sen[r] told me that when Father first came to Cambridge he was considered very handsome, and the girls used to say ' There goes Holmes — look ! ' " He had a weakness for writing poetry, and offered to the world a volume of verses; but his gifts were not great. If he could have managed to be a contemporary of his son, he would probably have received the sound advice: not to publish. His *Annals of America* was more in the line of his capacity; it was a careful, accurate, and useful history.

Sarah Wendell, his second wife, was born December 30, 1768. She well remembered that, when she was a little girl, six years old, she was hurried off from Boston, then occupied by the British soldiers, to Newburyport, and heard the people saying that " the redcoats were coming, killing and murdering everybody as they went along." Her traits were very different from those of her husband. She was a bright, vivacious woman; of small figure, and sprightly manners. Being also very cheerful and social, and fond of dropping in upon her neighbors, and withal of sympathetic and somewhat emotional temperament, so that she readily fell in with the mood of her friend, whether for tears or for laughter, she was a very popular lady whom every one greeted kindly. Dr. Morrill Wyman, of Cambridge, who knew her well, wrote to Dr. Holmes: "Your mother's age, her pleasant ways, her gentleness, her never-failing inquiries for others, all impressed me with a reverential love, like that for my own mother." Those who knew somewhat about the old couple say that in Dr. Holmes there was much more of the intellectual quality of the mother than of the father.

One day, in 1868, Colonel T. Wentworth Higginson happened upon a letter, which had been written by his mother in her girlhood, and which contained the following passage, which he copied and sent to Dr. Holmes: —

"Now, Mamma, I am going to surprise you. Mr. Abiel Holmes, of Cambridge, whom we so kindly chalked out for Miss N. W. is going to be married, and, of all folks in the world, guess who to. Miss Sally Wendell. I am sure you will not believe it; however, it is an absolute fact, for Harriot and M. Jackson told Miss P. Russell so, who told us; it has been kept secret for six weeks, nobody knows for what. I could not believe it for some time, and scarcely can now; however, it is a fact they say.

"Mamma must pay the wedding visit."

To this the doctor replied as follows: —

TO COL. T. WENTWORTH HIGGINSON.

164 CHARLES ST., July 7, 1868.

MY DEAR MR. HIGGINSON, — I thank you for the curious little scrap of information so nearly involving my dearest interests, — whether I should be myself or somebody else, — and such a train of vital facts as my household shows me.

How oddly our antenatal history comes out! A few months ago my classmate Devens told me, that he had recently seen an old woman who spoke of remembering me as a baby, and that I was brought up on the bottle, — which has made me feel as tenderly every time I visit my wine-cellar as Romulus and Remus did when Faustula carried them to the menagerie and showed them the wolf in his cage.

Our life is half underground — *Quantum vertice*, etc.

Here are two rootlets of mine that accident has brought to light, not very important to the race, but having an odd sort of interest for one at least.

From the foregoing pages the reader, assuming that he has had the patience to plod through them, has learned that Dr. Holmes, to use his own words, had "a right to be grateful for a probable inheritance of good instincts, a good name, and a bringing up in a library where he bumped about among books from the time when he was hardly taller than one of his father's or grandfather's folios." He was fortunate in having social — or genealogical — antecedents precisely to his taste. For such a lineage as his was of the best that could be had in New England; locally speaking, it was aristocratic; and every one who knew the Doctor, or his writings, must admit that, in his feelings, he was an aristocrat. The Autocrat admits openly: "I go for the man with the family portraits against the one with the twenty-cent daguerreotype, *unless* I find out that the latter is the better of the two. I go for the man who inherits family traditions, and the cumulative traditions of at least four or five generations." He also originated the phrase, or name, of "the Brahmin Caste" of New

England, which was a household word for quarter of a century, and is now only dying out through a sad necessity. But of course the New England aristocrat is to be widely differentiated from the American aristocrat, or plutocrat, from " the untitled nobility which has the dollar for its armorial bearing." " Chryso-aristocracy," as the Doctor called it, was not to his taste ; yet of course he was obliged to recognize that wealth brings opportunity, and that opportunity improved for a sufficiently long time produces what is called an aristocrat. On this perilous and delicate subject the Autocrat ventures to utter one of his most gravely humorous sentences : —

" We are forming an aristocracy, as you may observe, in this country, — not a *gratiâ-Dei*, nor a *jure-divino* one, — but a *de-facto* upper *stratum* of being, which floats over the turbid waves of common life like the iridescent film you may have seen spreading over the water about our wharves, — very splendid, though its origin might have been tar, tallow, train-oil, or other such unctuous commodities."

' But any ill-starred reader, who cannot account for his own existence or justify his own respectability by showing a first-rate New England ancestry, may find comfort not only in the curt sarcasm of the afore-quoted passages from Dr. Holmes's writings, but also in this paragraph from a letter which he wrote, July 22, 1865, to Mrs. Caroline L. Kellogg, of Pittsfield : —

" We have such cases here, some of them really pleasant to look upon as illustrating the fair chance everybody runs here.  ——, who lived with us seventeen years and whom you have seen at Pittsfield, has a house on Pinckney Street hard by, and is now at her country seat a few miles out of town.  The sons of a deceased citizen go to our fashionable assemblies, whose father I remember a boy that 'lived out.' B.B. is A.A. in point of wealth and stylish residence. You remember how he began. I like it; I like to see worthless rich people have to yield their places to deserving poor ones, who, beginning with sixpence or nothing, come out at last in Beacon Street and have the sun come into their windows all the year round."

Such were the variously tinted threads which were to furnish the warp and woof for the weaving of the pattern of man to be shown as well as may be in this book.

No doubt the reader thinks that it is time that Dr. Holmes should be born; in good truth, so it is; and the occurrence shall be delayed no longer. Though Dr. Holmes's own example excuses my prolixity, for he only gets Emerson born upon the thirty-seventh page of his life of that philosopher, — conceiving it important to show fully " of what race he came, and what were the conditions into which he was born." For, he says, " The nest is made ready long before-hand for the bird which is to be bred in it and to fly from it. The intellectual atmosphere into which a scholar is born, and from which he draws the breath of his early mental life, must be studied, if we would hope to understand it thoroughly."

" In the last week of August used to fall Commencement day at Cambridge. I remember that week well, for something happened to me once at that time, namely, I was born." It was on the twenty-ninth day of August, 1809, that this event befell. Nature was active that year, like a stirred volcano, casting forth also upon the world Gladstone, Tennyson, Darwin,

and Abraham Lincoln.  An hundred years earlier
Samuel Johnson was born, or, as Dr. Holmes put it:
"The year 1709 was made ponderous and illustrious
in English biography by his birth.  My own humble
advent to the world of protoplasm was in the year
1809 of the present century."  And it used to amuse
the Doctor somewhat to lay his own progress in life
alongside that of the great lexicographer, as though
the two were passing through the world like a pair of
oxen with the yoke of just a century between them,
which would keep them swaying alongside each other,
never letting them either separate farther or draw
nearer together.  He used to take down his Boswell
and see what Johnson was about, in that year of his
age to which he himself had then come.  Johnson,
however, died in 1784, and when the Doctor came to
1884, he said that he felt as though he had had his
allotment of time and ought to die out of respect to
the long parallel.  Another occurrence, connected with
his birth, gave him much amusement, as indicating
what a very trifling incident his coming into existence
had seemed to his father.  "I will tell you," he wrote
to Mrs. Emma Hubbard, "what my real birthday is,
with a circumstance.  Looking over a pile of old
almanacs belonging to my father, I took up that for
the year 1809, — opposite a certain date was an aster-
isk, and a note below consisting of four letters thus, —

August  27<br>
"       28<br>
"       29*<br>
"       30<br>

    * son b.

My father thus recorded my advent; and after he wrote

| M | W | Observable Days, &c. | r ⊙ s | | r ☾ s | | H. Sea |
|---|---|---|---|---|---|---|---|
| 1 | 3 | C. S. Plym. —flying | 4 | 51 8 | 10 | 11 | 8 35 |
| 2 | 4 | clouds, | 4 | 52 8 | 10 | 43 | 4 22 |
| 3 | 5 | with | 4 | 53 8 | 11 | 21 | 5 8 |
| 4 | 6 | 7*s rise 11h. signs of | 4 | 54 8 | morn. | | 5 54 |
| 5 | 7 | rain. ☾ apo. | 4 | 55 8 | 0 | 1 | 6 41 |
| 6 | A | 10th Sun. past Trin. Transf. | 4 | 55 8 | 0 | 43 | 7 28 |
| 7 | 2 | Low tides. | 4 | 57 8 | 1 | 34 | 8 16 |
| 8 | 3 | C. P. Plym. Hazy, but | 4 | 59 8 | 2 | 27 | 9 4 |
| 9 | 4 | very warm | 5 | 0 7 | 3 | 23 | 9 52 |
| 10 | 5 | St. Lawrence. for | 5 | 1 7 | 4 | 22 | 10 40 |
| 11 | 6 | some days. | 5 | 2 7 | ☾ sets | | 11 28 |
| 12 | 7 | Some rain | 5 | 3 7 | 7 | 34 | ev. 15 |
| 13 | A | 11th Sund. past Trin. this | 5 | 5 7 | 8 | 4 | 1 2 |
| 14 | 2 | C. P. Castine. time | 5 | 6 7 | 8 | 35 | 1 50 |
| 15 | 3 | C.P. & S. Mach. C.P. Aug. | 5 | 7 7 | 9 | 7 | 2 40 |
| 16 | 4 | Comm. Middlebury Col. | 5 | 8 7 | 9 | 43 | 3 30 |
| 17 | 5 | Grows cooler, | 5 | 9 7 | 10 | 22 | 4 24 |
| 18 | 6 | with clouds. | 5 | 11 7 | 11 | 7 | 5 19 |
| 19 | 7 | Middling tides this month. | 5 | 12 7 | morn. | | 6 17 |
| 20 | A | 12th Sund. past Trin. ☾ per. | 5 | 13 7 | 0 | 2 | 7 16 |
| 21 | 2 | Fine | 5 | 15 7 | 0 | 58 | 8 16 |
| 22 | 3 | 7*s rise 9h. 50m. weather | 5 | 16 7 | 2 | 4 | 9 15 |
| 23 | 4 | Comm. Dartm. Col. N. H. | 5 | 17 7 | 3 | 12 | 10 10 |
| 24 | 5 | St. Bartholomew. again | 5 | 19 7 | 4 | 22 | 11 8 |
| 25 | 6 | Signs of a | 5 | 20 7 | ● rise | | 11 55 |
| 26 | 7 | N. E. storm. | 5 | 21 7 | 7 | 12 | morn. |
| 27 | A | 13th Sund. past Trinity. | 5 | 23 7 | 7 | 43 | 0 44 |
| 28 | 2 | C.P. Nor.ha. Topf.C.P. & S. | 5 | 24 7 | 8 | 15 | 1 32 |
| 29 | 3 | Pleasant [Lenox. | 5 | 25 7 | 8 | 48 | 2 19 |
| 30 | 4 | Comm. Cambridge Col. | 5 | 27 7 | 9 | 24 | 3 6 |
| 31 | 5 | again. | 5 | 28 7 | 10 | 4 | 3 53 |



LEAF FROM ALMANAC SHOWING RECORD OF
DR. HOLMES'S BIRTH

the four letters, according to his wont, he threw black sand upon them to keep them from blotting. I am looking at it *now*, and there the black sand glistens still."

The " old gambrel-roofed house " in Cambridge, the birthplace of Dr. Holmes, would seem to-day a picturesque relic of bygone times. It was not a " colonial mansion," but it was sufficiently spacious, and far enough withdrawn from the high road, to have the air of a gentleman's residence ; there was a generous expanse of quasi-public greensward beside it, and tall American elms overshadowed it. In the Doctor's writings are many affectionate references to it : —

Let me, he says, remind the reader, "that the old house was General Ward's headquarters at the breaking out of the Revolution; that the plan for fortifying Bunker's Hill was laid, as commonly believed, in the southeast lower room, the floor of which was covered with dents, made, it was alleged, by the butts of the soldiers' muskets. In that house, too, General Warren probably passed the night before the Bunker Hill battle, and over its threshold must the stately figure of Washington have often cast its shadow."

Elsewhere he admitted his " doubts about those ' dents ' on the floor of the right-hand room, ' the study ' of successive occupants, said to have been made by the butts of the Continental militia's firelocks ; but this was the cause to which the story told me in childhood laid them."

In this house the Doctor lived until, in his maturity, he left it for independent quarters ; in his own phrase he struck his tap-root deep down into the soil, and the radicles of affection and association entwined themselves about everything there, even to the " stone with a whitish band" in the pavement of the back yard. "Our hearts are held down in our homes by innumerable fibres, trivial as that I have just recalled; but Gulliver was fixed to the soil, you remember, by pinning his head, a hair at a time."

At last, after the Doctor's mother had died in the house, and it had then become one of the investments of Harvard University, it was torn down. "The slaughter," said the Doctor, "was, I am ready to admit, a case of justifiable *domicide*. Not the less was it to be deplored by all who love the memories of the past." "Alas," wrote Lowell, "for the Holmes House, so dear and sacred in my memory;" and if he felt thus, it was natural enough that Dr. Holmes should exclaim: "You will see how much I parted with which was not reckoned in the price paid for the old homestead." He spoke of the tearing down as of a death: —

"The 'Old Gambrel-roofed House' exists no longer. I remember saying something, in one of a series of papers published long ago, about the experience of dying out of a house, — of leaving it forever, as the soul dies out of the body. We may die out of many houses, but the house itself can die but once; and so real is the life of a house to one who has dwelt in it, more especially the life of the house which held him in dreamy infancy, in restless boyhood, in passionate youth, — so real, I say, is its life, that it seems as if something like a soul of it must outlast its perishing frame."

To Lowell he wrote: "Our old house is gone. I went all over it, — into every chamber and closet, and found a ghost in each and all of them, to which I said good-by. I have not seen the level ground where it stood. Be very thankful that you still keep your birthplace. This earth has a homeless look to me since mine has disappeared from its face."

Dr. Holmes's schooling began early, as was the fashion of those times, at a dame's school. No special traditions are preserved save the memory of Mrs. Prentiss's long willow wand, a "reminding rather than a chastening" weapon, says the Doctor. From ten to fifteen years of age he was at school at Cambridgeport, and thence of course was sent to that factory for the manufacture of good Orthodox, Phillips Academy, at Andover, then presided over by Mr. John Adams. There he established a friendship with a lad named Phineas Barnes; and though they were soon separated, because Barnes did not go to Harvard College, the friendship was maintained with a tenacity which, in view of their youth and the brevity of their actual contact, was very singular, and at last it was severed only by death. The Doctor referred to him affectionately in the *Pages from an Old Volume of Life:* —

"My especial intimate was a fine rosy-faced boy, not quite so free of speech as myself, perhaps, but with qualities that promised a noble manhood, and ripened into it in due season. His name was Phineas Barnes, and if he is inquired after in Portland or anywhere in the State of Maine, something will be heard to his advantage from any honest and intelligent citizen of that commonwealth who answers the question. This was one of two or three friendships that lasted."

The only incident of Holmes's school-days which has survived oblivion is referred to in this letter concerning an article which he had published.

TO PHINEAS BARNES.

*December* 28, 1868.

MY DEAR BARNES, — I was delighted to find that
you were pleased with the way in which I mentioned
your name, — the one that comes up first, when I remember my school-days at Andover.

.    .    .    .    .    .    .    .    .    .

I meant to have these cinders warm, **not** burn,
those who stooped over them. I touched the **tender**
points lightly, I hope, remembering that there **were**
children and grandchildren of some of our old professors and teachers who might be wounded by too
searching recollections. My article stirred the memories of my old room-mate, N. S. Dodge, who wrote
me a letter saying that he was pleased with my mention of him. He spoke of some things I might have
recalled; for instance, my famous feruling, which I
suppose you have not forgotten. He did **not know**
the sequel — forty years afterwards — which I will
tell you. A year or two ago, a gentleman **entered my**
study, an elderly man, tall, slender, or bent a little
with a natural stoop, light-complexioned, with pale
gray or blue eyes, and a somewhat peculiar smile. He
stood facing me for a moment, and then said : —

"Do you know me ?"

"C—— ?"

"The same."

So I received him courteously, and we talked of
various matters. I knew what had **got** to come out,
and sure enough, after a time, there was **a** pause, and
he brought up the old story of the feruling and all
the regrets it had caused him from that day to this.

**Well, somehow or other, I did not feel as expansive**

as I should have expected, but I was kindly enough,
and we parted, he I hope more at ease and I in good
feeling enough toward the poor man. It was a sad
mistake he made, — one a boy never gets over, but as
for malice, it rusts soon out with me, if it belongs to
my nature. I should not have referred to the feruling in this article certainly, at any rate, and especially
after this scene with old C——.

It is fair to infer that a lad who got through his
school-days with only one chastisement, in that time
when the rod was never spared, must have been well
behaved, and the evidence of one or two school-fellows
has been given to the like purport concerning Holmes.
Nothing else, so far as I know, can be said concerning
his stay at Andover. But a letter sent to him at that
place by the Rev. Abiel Holmes must not be omitted;
for it suggests the life of the times and the surroundings of the lad more vividly than could be done by
many descriptive paragraphs.

ABIEL HOLMES TO O. W. H.

CAMBRIDGE, 5 *January*, 1825.

MY DEAR SON, — We received your letter of 30th
Dec. and thank you for the wish of a happy New
Year. We cordially reciprocate the wish, and our
desire is, that you may improve your time and talents,
and be attaining those virtues and graces, which will
make *all* time pleasant and profitable to you. The
commencement of a New Year is a suitable time to
review the past for the correction and improvement of
the future. Whatever we find to have been wrong in
thought or feeling, in word or action, let it be our aim
to correct it; whatever we find to have been favorable

to an improvement in knowledge and virtue, let us cherish it. Your opportunities for such improvement are very much greater than those of most others, and we shall expect the more accordingly. Be diligent in your studies; punctual in your attendance at the Academy; and strictly observant of its rules. Avoid bad company, and choose the virtuous only for your companions. I need not enlarge. You know my wishes and advices on the subject, and trust you will regard them. Remember daily to ask the guidance and blessing of your heavenly Father.

We are all in good health — and all send love to you. M—— often inquires about you. — We had a letter from her a short time since, in which she affectionately inquires for you. Ann is well and going into town with me this morning. John is also well — and pleased with the new school-house, which is now occupied. I saw Mr. Farrar, of Andover, yesterday, and expecting to see him in Boston, I write this to forward by him — not forgetting "its attendant benefit," ($2.) Be prudent. Be more particular when you write next, and let us know all about you. Our united regard to your aunt Cooper, and Dr. Murdock's family.

I was in hopes that your mother would have added a line, but I must unite her love with mine to you, and close.

Andover did not make a clergyman of young Holmes, though his father had exposed him to clerical infection not without a willingness that the chance should so fall out. It is hard to fancy Holmes as the incumbent of a pulpit; yet he says: "I might have been a minister myself, for aught I know, if [a certain] clergyman had not looked and talked so like an undertaker." In fact the lad had seen a great number of specimens of that calling at his father's house, and though he drew his distinctions between them somewhat shrewdly even in early youth, and though he was greatly pleased and attracted by some of them, yet he seems from the outset to have regarded the ministry as a perilous profession, in which no man could embark without great danger of becoming exceedingly disagreeable to others, and even personally unwholesome and distasteful in himself, — one " of those wailing *poitrinaires* with the bandanna handkerchiefs round their meagre throats and a funeral service in their forlorn physiognomies." " The middle-aged and young men," he says, " have left comparatively faint impressions in my memory, but how grandly the procession of the old clergymen who filled our pulpit from time to time, and passed the day under our roof, marches before my closed eyes! . . . But now and then would come along a clerical visitor with a sad face and a wailing voice, which sounded exactly as if somebody must be lying dead upstairs, who took no interest in us children, except a painful one, as being in a bad way with our cheery looks, and did more to unchristianize us with his woebegone ways than all his sermons were like to accomplish in the other direction."

# CHAPTER II



IT has been somewhat widely believed that Dr. Holmes, for some time prior to his death, had been engaged upon an autobiography. In point of fact he left only some disjointed notes and memoranda, in which he had not advanced beyond the period of youth, nor even covered that period thoroughly and consecutively. They were dictated at odd moments, without method, connection, or revision. Naturally, therefore, they are rambling, disjointed, entirely fragmentary, and often overlap and repeat each other. It might be regarded as the biographer's duty to treat them as material out of which to construct a narrative; but the charm of reminiscences of early days is gone when they lose the form of reminiscences, and therefore I have decided to give these jottings, the amusement of an old man's leisure hours, just as they were left by him, with some omissions but no changes.

"*General Considerations*. The life of an individual is in many respects like a child's dissected map. If I could live a hundred years, keeping my intelligence to the last, I feel as if I could put the pieces together until they made a properly connected whole. As it is, I, like all others, find a certain number of connected fragments, and a larger number of disjointed pieces, which I might in time place in their natural connection. Many of these pieces seem fragmentary, but would in time show themselves as essential parts of the whole. What strikes me very forcibly is the arbitrary and as it were accidental way in which the lines of junction appear to run irregularly among the fragments. With every decade I find some new pieces coming into place. Blanks which have been left in former years find their complement among the undistributed fragments. If I could look back on the whole, as we look at the child's map when it is put together, I feel that I should have my whole life intelligently laid out before me."

" The mysteries of our lives and of ourselves resolve themselves very slowly with the progress of years. Every decade lifts the curtain, which hides us from ourselves, a little further, and lets a new light upon what was dark and unintelligible. I have never until very recently thought out fully all the elements which I can perceive went to the shaping of my character. They were somewhat singularly mingled."

" *Early Period.* When the chick first emerges from the shell, the Creator's studio in which he was organized and shaped, it is a very little world with which he finds himself in relation. First the nest, then the hen-coop, by and by the barnyard with occasional predatory incursions into the neighbor's garden — and his little universe has reached its boundaries. Just so with my experience of atmospheric existence. The low room of the old house — the little patch called the front yard — somewhat larger than the Turkish rug beneath my rocking-chair — the back yard with its wood-house, its carriage-house, its barn, and, let me not forget, its pig-sty. These were the world of my earliest experiences. But from the western window of the room where I was born I could see the vast expanse of the Common, with the far-away 'Washington Elm' as its central figure — the immeasurably distant hills of the horizon, and the infinite of space in which these gigantic figures were projected — all these, in unworded impressions — vague pictures swimming by each other as the eyes rolled without aim — threw the lights and shadows which floated by them. From this centre I felt my way into the creation beyond."

" *Boyhood.* My boyhood had a number of real sensations. . . . An inspiring scene, which I witnessed many times in my early years, was the imposing triumphal entry of the Governor attended by a light horse troop and a band of sturdy truckmen, on Commencement Day. Vague recollections of a 'muster,' in which the 'pomp and circumstance of glorious war' were represented to my young imagination. But my most vivid recollections are associated not with war, but with peace. My earliest memory goes back to the Declaration of Peace, signalized to me by the illumination of the Colleges in 1815. I remember well coming from the Dame school, throwing up my 'jocky,' as the other boys did, and shouting 'Hooraw for Ameriky,' looking at the blazing College windows, and revelling in the thought that I had permission to sit up as long as I wanted to. I lasted until eight o'clock, and then struck my colors, and was conveyed by my guardian and handmaidens from the brilliant spectacle to darkness and slumber.

"Like all children, I began to speculate on the

problems of existence at an early age. I remember thinking of myself as afloat — like a balloonist — in the atmosphere of life. I had come there I knew not how, but I knew I had got to come down sooner or later, and the thought was not welcome to one who enjoyed the present with all the keenness of lively boyhood. As for the government of the universe to which I belonged, my thoughts were very confused. The Deity was to me an Old Man, as represented in some of the pictures I had seen. Angels and Demons were his subjects, and fellow-inhabitants with myself in the planet on which I lived. A most striking example of my notions of the supernatural might be seen in the way in which I conceived of the two great painters, Michael Angelo and Raphael. Their names, which I had heard of as belonging to supernatural beings, of course suggested the idea that these human creatures were exceptional natures, though commonly considered as men. A story I heard of unmarried maternity completely confounded my teachings as to the birth of the Son of Man. I was not without apprehensions of the dangerous presence of malignant spirits. . . . The bare spots known as the ' Devil's Footsteps,' one of which was near Mt. Auburn, another in a field very near our own, were objects of serious contemplation in my childish thoughts; and even the irregular breach in one of the College buildings through which the Evil One was said to have made his exit from a circle of profane youths, who had raised him in their unhallowed orgies, was, to me, full of ominous and appalling suggestions. The garret, by the door of which I sometimes passed, but whose depths I never explored until later in life, was full of unshaped terrors. There was an out-house where old and broken furniture had been stored, which I shunned as if it were peopled with living bipeds and quadrupeds in the place of old chairs and tables. My theology was to the last degree vague. If I might say it without irreverence: The Deity was to me the Jewish *Jehovah — Jahveh* — tamed from his barbarous characteristics into a civilized kind of Deity.

"Two spectres haunted my earliest years, the dread of midnight visitors, and the visits of the doctor. I hardly know when I was not subject to fears when I was left alone in the dark. These terrors were vague, and different at different times. I could not say that I believed in ghosts, nor yet that I disbelieved in their existence, but the strange sounds at night, the creaking of the boards, the howling of winds, the footfall of animals, voices heard from a distance and unaccounted for, — all such things kept me awake, restless, and full of strange apprehensions. These fears lasted until, on the approach of adolescence, I became greatly ashamed of them. I do not say that I have got rid of these feelings, and to this day I sometimes fear a solitary house, which I would not sleep alone in for the fee simple of the whole deserted farm. I cannot describe the amount of worry I have had from this source. Perhaps the stories I heard from the country-bred inmates of our kitchen kept this feeling alive. I can remember being told by one of the bucolic youths, with the most serious air, that the Evil One was wandering around every night, and that if one wrote his name in his own blood, and left it, the prowling agent of Satan, if not Satan himself, would pocket it, if there were pockets in his asbestos suit, and the writer would from that day forth become his servant and slave. . . . The other source of distress was, as I have said, the visits of the physician. The dispenser of drugs that embittered my boyhood was Dr. William Gamage. He was an old man, associated principally in my mind with two vegetable products, namely: the useful though not comforting rhubarb, and the revolting and ever to be execrated ipecacuanha. The dread of the last of these two drugs was one of my chronic miseries. He designated it by a monosyllable, the sound alone of which is almost equal to . . .! Such causes of unhappiness as those I have mentioned may seem trivial to persons of less sensibility than myself, but they were serious drawbacks to the pleasures of existence, and, added to the torture of tooth-drawing, made a considerable sum of wretchedness."

" *School-Days.* My first school-master, William Biglow, was a man of peculiar character. He had been master of the Boston Latin School for a number of years, and seems to have found his pupils an unmanageable set in the early part of his reign. I can easily understand how he found difficulties in the management of a large collection of city boys. He was of a somewhat Bardolphian aspect, red in the face, and was troubled from time to time with headaches, which led to an occasional absence from the place of duty. He was a good-natured man, a humorist, a punster; but his good-nature had something of the Rip Van Winkle character. He had something of a literary talent, and on the occasion of the second centennial of Harvard University, he wrote an ode in macaronic Latin verse. He signed [it] *Gulielmus magnus humilis.* . . .

" I do not remember being the subject of any

reproof or discipline at that school, although I do not
doubt I deserved it, for I was an inveterate whisperer
at every school I ever attended.   I do remember that
once, as he passed me, he tapped me on the forehead
with his pencil, and said he 'could n't help it, if I
would do so well,' a compliment which I have never
forgotten.   After a while, what with his headaches
and other hindrances, he gave up school-keeping and
became corrector of the press."

"*Domestic Inmates.*   We used to receive into the
family as 'help,' as they used to be called, young
men and young women from the country.   From the
men and boys, young persons of both sexes, I learned
many phrases and habits of superstition, and peculiarities characteristic of our country people.   They did
not like to be called servants, did not show great
alacrity in answering the bell, the peremptory summons of which had something of command in its tone,
which did not agree with the free-born American.
. . . Many expressions which have since died out were
common in my young days, — 'haowsen' for houses,
'The haunt' for Nahant, 'musicianers' for musicians.
They had their *Farmer's Almanac*, their broadsheets
telling the story of how the 'Constitootion' took the
'Guerrier,' and other naval combats.   They had their
specific medicines, of which '*hiry pikry*' (*hiera picra*
— sacred bitters) was a favorite.   Some of the country customs were retained.   'Husking' went on upon
a small scale in the barn.   The habits of parlor and
kitchen with reference to alcoholic fluids were very
free and hazy.   In the parlor cider was drunk as
freely as water; wine was always on the table at
dinner, and not abstained from; and, in the kitchen,

cordial, which was simply diluted and sweetened alcohol, whatever was its flavor, was an occasional luxury ; while 'black strap,' or rum and molasses, served in mowing time or a 'raising.'   One of the greatest changes of the modern decades has been in the matter of heating and lighting.   We depended on wood, which was brought from the country in loads upon wagons or sledges.   This was often not kept long enough to burn easily, and the mockery of the green wood fire was one of my recollections, the sap oozing from the ends and standing in puddles around the hearth.

" Some of my pleasantest Sundays were those when I went with my father, who was exchanging pulpits with a neighboring clergyman.   I remember my visits to Dorchester, to Burlington, sixteen miles from Cambridge, to Watertown, Brighton, Lexington, and other places.   We jogged off together in one of the old-fashioned two-wheeled chaises, behind a quiet horse, for the most part.   I remember the house at Lexington, at which we stayed, had a sanded floor instead of a carpeted one.   The clergymen with whom my father exchanged in those days were, most of them, nominally Orthodox, but weak in the theological joints. They were pleasanter to meet with, so it seemed to me in my boyhood, than were those whom I afterwards heard of as *Evangelicals*, most of them smitten with the Sabbath paralysis which came from the rod of Moses and killed out their natural spirits, and was apt to make them — to childhood — dreary and repulsive.

"To one of the most distinguished leaders of the Orthodox party I had an instinctive dislike from early childhood.   I was told that I laughed when I went to church and heard him preach.   I remember upsetting his inkstand, which left a very black spot in my memory. Another had a twist in his mouth that knocked a benediction out of shape, and proved afterwards to have a twist in his morals of a still more formidable character.

"I never wanted for occupation. Though not an inventor, I was always a contriver. I was constantly at work with tools of some sort. I was never really a skilful workman, — other boys were neater with their jackknives than I. I had ingenuity enough to cut a ball in a cage, with a chain attached carved out of the same wood ; but my tendency was to hasty and imperfect workmanship. I was always too much in a hurry to complete my work, as if finished when only half done. My imagination helped me into immense absurdities, in which, however, I found great delight. Thus, before I had a pair of skates, I had made one skate of wood, which I had fastened on to my foot, and experimented with ' on the ditch,' a narrow groove which one could step across, but where I served my first apprenticeship in the art of skating. But the strongest attraction of my early 'teens' was found in shooting such small game as presented, more especially small birds and squirrels. It sounds strangely now to say that my achievements as a sportsman were performed, not with a gun, such as is carried by the sportsman of to-day, not even with the percussion lock in use during the greater part of my manhood, but with the old flint lock, such as our grandfathers used in the Revolution. I do not think I ever used a percussion cap, but many a flint have I worn down in service. . . . An old 'king's arm' had been hanging up in the store closet ever since I could remember. This I shouldered, and with this I blazed away at every living thing that was worthy of a charge of the smallest shot I could employ."

"*Religious and Literary Education.* Its conditions were quite exceptional. My father, — coming from the land of steady habits, the grandson of an Orthodox deacon bred at Yale College in intimacy with the distinguished President Ezra Stiles, whose daughter he married, after becoming thoroughly imbued with the doctrines of Calvinism, modified by the kindly nature in which they were received, — after living in the polite society of New Haven and spending seven years in the South, most of it in Midway, where he had charge of a church and congregation, found himself obliged to return to the North on account of his health. Here he became settled in the year ——? over the First Church in Cambridge. He married the daughter of a much respected citizen of Boston, — a man of some property and high social connections, — a member of the Committee of Safety in the time of the Revolution, — a graduate and a Fellow of Harvard University. Sarah Wendell, his wife, — mother of myself and my brother and sisters, was a lady bred in an entirely different atmosphere from that of the straight-laced puritanism. Most of the families around me, those of the professors and preachers in the neighboring towns, were of 'liberal' ways of thought. The influence of his surroundings on my father was that which has always been noticed where Unitarianism comes into contact with the dehumanized creeds of the churches. It is not so much in making converts to its organization as it is in softening the harsh beliefs of those with whom it comes in contact, as was long ago pointed out by Mosheim, the great historian of the church. My father felt that he did his duty in expecting my mother to hear me recite the shorter Westminster Catechism. My mother, like a faithful wife as she was, sobered her pleasant countenance, and sat down to hear us recite of 'justification,' 'adoption,' and 'sanctification,' and the rest of the programme. We learned nominally that we were a set of little fallen wretches, exposed to the wrath of God by the fact of that existence which we could not help. I do not think we believed a word of it, or even understood much of its phraseology. I am quite sure that my father found the application of these doctrines very difficult as a matter of personal explanation. I was given to questionings, and my mind early revolted from the teachings of the Catechism and the books which followed out its dogmas.

In the number of my father's exchanges with the neighboring clergymen there was a great diversity of character in the individuals who occupied his pulpit. There were pleasant old men, like Dr. Osgood, of Medford, Dr. Forster, of Brighton, who had a cheerful look and smile in spite of its being the Sabbath day; and there were others of sad and despondent mien, whose presence lent additional gloom to the Puritan solemnity of the holy day. There were two classes of preachers, as there are to-day, — though one of these classes is comparatively rarely met with. One class preached, in their own language, 'as dying men to dying men.' The other, of whom Henry Ward Beecher was a typical example, 'as living men to living men.' Children are wonderfully sagacious in detecting their natural friends and enemies. The little creatures, whom Jonathan

Edwards described as 'vipers, and worse than vipers,' had never quite recovered from the anathema pronounced upon them by this great exponent of New England theology.

"My notions respecting the Deity — the future, the relations of man to his Maker — shaped themselves as they best might in the midst of conflicting opinions. I had an old worn-out catechism as my text-book on the one hand, and a Unitarian atmosphere on the other, surrounding me as soon as I stepped out of my door, for I was born close to the colleges, and the benignant smile of President Kirkland had so much more of heaven in it than the sour aspect of certain clergymen of the type I have referred to, that it went far towards making me a 'liberal' thinker. An instinct was working in me which could not be choked out by the dogmas of the Assembly's Catechism. Much of its language was mere jargon in my ears, — I got no coherent idea from the doctrine of transmitted sinfulness, and the phrases of 'adoption,' 'justification,' and 'sanctification' had as little meaning for me as the syllable by the aid of which we counted ourselves 'out' in our games. When it came to the threats of future punishment as described in the sermons of the more hardened theologians, my instincts were shocked and disgusted beyond endurance. Bunyan's *Pilgrim's Progress* — that wonderful work of imagination, with all its beauty and power — seemed to me then, as it does now, more like the hunting of sinners with a pack of demons for the amusement of the Lord of the terrestrial manor than like the tender care of a father for his offspring. No child can overcome these early impressions without doing violence to the whole mental and moral machinery of his being.

He may conquer them in after years, but the wrenches and strains which his victory has cost him leave him a cripple as compared with a child trained in sound and reasonable beliefs.

" I had long passed middle age before I could analyze the effect of these conflicting agencies, and I can truly say that I believe I can understand them better now than when I was at the comparatively immature age of threescore years and ten. There are many truths that come out by immersion in the atmosphere of experience; which reminds me of an old experiment in the laboratory: an irregular lump of alum being placed in water dissolves gradually in such a way as to expose the crystal in form underlying the shapeless outline. It seems to me that hardly a year passes over my head in which some point or angle, some plane, does not start out and reveal itself as a new truth in the lesson of my life. This experience is more common than most people would suppose. The great multitude is swept along in the main current of inherited beliefs, but not rarely under the influence of new teachings, of developing instincts; above all, of that mighty impulse which carries the generation to which we belong far away from the landmark of its predecessors.

" I read few books through. I remember writing on the last page of one that I had successfully mastered, *perlegi*, with the sense that it was a great triumph to have read quite through a volume of such size. But I have always read *in* books rather than *through* them, and always with more profit from the books I read *in* than the books I read *through*; for when I set out to read *through* a book, I always felt that I had a task before me, but when I read *in* a book it was the page or the paragraph that I wanted, and which left its impression and became a part of my intellectual furniture. . . . Besides, I have myself written a great many books, — there are a dozen or more of them bound, upon my shelves, — but my mental library is full of books that I have written and never reduced to outward form. These books would no doubt contain a vast amount of repetition, but they would also present a great variety of fresh illustrations and incidental comments furnished by the experience of each successive day. . . . My father's library may have held between one and two thousand books; among them were the great English classics, historians, and poets, and many volumes of sermons, and odd volumes of periodicals, especially of the *Annual Register* and the *Christian Observer*, but above all Rees's *Encyclopædia*, the American reprint of which was finished during my boyhood. In that work I found a very considerable part of my reading. My father intended to keep from me all books of questionable teaching. I remember that many leaves were torn out of a copy of Dryden's Poems, with the comment *Hiatus haud deflendus;* but I had, like all children, a kind of Indian sagacity in the discovery of contraband reading, such as a boy carries to a corner for perusal. Sermons I had had enough of from the pulpit. I don't know that I ever read one sermon of my own accord during my childhood. *The Life of David*, by Samuel Chandler, had adventure enough, to say nothing of gallantry, in it to stimulate and gratify curiosity. If I remember right, Kimpton's *History of the Bible* was another book that presented some green patches among the deserts.

"Biographies of pious children were not much to

my taste. These young persons were generally sickly, melancholy, and buzzed round by ghostly comforters, or discomforters, in a way that made me sick to contemplate. I had a great preference for wholesome, rosy-cheeked children, satisfied in the main with the enjoyments of nature suited to their time of life.

"I think my readers ought to be told that one of the books that has most influenced me, but not in the direction which the author intended, was the Rev. Thomas Scott's Family Bible. The narrowness and exclusiveness of his views waked me up more than anything else to the enormities of the creed which he represented. Starting from the fable of Paradise and the Fall of Man, as a fact, it represented the unfortunate race to which I belonged as under the curse of its Maker, — disinherited by its Father, — given over in the main to that other being, who seemed to have the vastly larger portion of the human race as subjects to his irresponsible treatment. . . . The effect of Calvinistic training on different natures varies very much. The majority take the creed as a horse takes his collar ; it slips by his ears, over his neck, he hardly knows how, but he finds himself in harness, and jogs along as his fathers and forefathers had done before him. A certain number become enthusiasts in its behalf, and, believing themselves the subjects of divine illumination, become zealous ministers and devoted missionaries. Here and there a stronger-minded one revolts with the whole strength of his nature from the inherited servitude of his ancestry, and gets rid of his whole harness before he is at peace with himself. A few shreds may hold to him. . . . I must own that the effect of reading *The Pilgrim's Progress*, — that wonderful work of genius, which captivates all persons of active imagination — made the system, of which it was the exponent, more unreasonable and more repulsive, instead of rendering it more attractive. It represents the universe as a trap which catches most of the human vermin that have its bait dangled before them, and the only wonder is that a few escape the elaborate arrangement made for their capture. The truest revelation, it seems to me, which man has received is that influx of knowledge brought about by astronomy, geology, and the comparative study of creeds, which have made it a necessity to remodel the religious belief of the last few thousand years.

"Thus, though fond of society at times, I have always been good company to myself, either by day or night. The 'I' and the 'me' of my double personality keep up endless dialogues, as is, I suppose, the case with most people, — sometimes using very harsh language to each other. One of them, I am sorry to say, is very apt to be abusive and to treat the other like an idiot, with expressions which, if uttered, would make a very bad figure in these pages."

"The process of extricating ourselves from those early influences which we are bound to outgrow is a very slow and difficult one. It is illustrated by the phenomena of waste and repair in the physical system.

"It is fortunate for our civilization that our early impressions are got rid of with such difficulty. The conservative principle is always (except at brief intervals) largely in excess of the destructive and renewing tendencies which go hand in hand with the task of improving society. The process is like that of respiration. The oxygen taken into the system preys upon its effete material, which is carried out by exhalation

and secretion, at the same time that it adds the vivi-
fying element to the forming tissues.  New ideas act
upon society as oxygen does on the body, attacking its
errors, which pass away from the lists of human beliefs, and strengthening the new truth which is building
in its place.  Born near the beginning of the century,
my mind was early impregnated with beliefs which,
in the minds of those whom I consider the best think-
ers of the present, are utterly extinct, and replaced by
newer thought.  The change in my own mind, like
those of many others born in similar circumstances,
has been gradual, and to a large extent insensible. . . .
It was a New England doctrine that a child must re-
pent of, and be punished for, not only his own sins
but those of his first parent.  This was the foundation
of the condemnation of unborn and unbaptized children, as taught in the *Day of Doom*, the celebrated
and most popular poem of Michael Wigglesworth, the
minister of Malden (?).  The doctrine of inherited
guilt, held up to scorn in the fable of the ' Wolf and
the Lamb,' was accepted by the church as in perfect
harmony with the human reason and the divine character.  This doctrine of the fallen race was incorporated into the food of the New England child as truly
as the Indian corn, on which he was fed, entered into
the composition of his bones and muscles.  During
his early years, if he was possessed of an active intelligence, he struggled against this doctrine contrary to
all the instinctive convictions which belonged to his
nature, and which were embodied in the old fable
referred to.  The doctrine of the Fall of Man, and
all connected with it, was not only wrought into
the intellectual constitution of a New England child,
coloring his existence as madder stains the bones of

animals whose food contains it, but it entered into his whole conception of the universe. The early years of a thinking child, who was not subjugated by this doctrine, and those allied with it, were spent in conflict enforced by the threat of eternal punishment.

" What is to become of the reason of a child taught to repeat, and believe that he believes, the monstrous absurdity which he reads in the lines of the *New England Primer*, —

> ' In Adam's **fall**
> We sinnéd all ' ?

Doctrines like that, introduced into the machinery of a young intelligence, break the springs, poison the fountains, dwarf the development, ruin the harmony, disorganize the normal mechanism of the thinking powers."

" Ever since I paid ten cents for a peep through the telescope on the Common, and saw the transit of Venus, my whole idea of the creation has been singularly changed. The planet I beheld was not much less in size than the one on which we live. If I had been looking on [this] planet [from] outside its orbit, instead of looking on Venus, I should have seen nearly the same sight as that for which I was paying my dime. Is this little globule, no bigger than a marble, the Earth on which I live, with all its oceans and continents, with all its mountains and forests, with all its tornadoes and volcanoes, its mighty cities, its myriads of inhabitants? I have never got over the shock, as it were, of my discovery. There are some things we believe but do not know, there are others that we know, but, in our habitual state of mind, hardly believe. I knew something of the rela-

tive size of the planets. I had seen Venus. The
Earth on which I lived has never been the same to me
since that time. All my human sentiments, all my
religious beliefs, all my conception of my relation in
space for fractional rights in the universe, seemed to
have undergone a change. From this vast and vague
confusion of all my standards I gradually returned to
the more immediate phenomena about me. This little
globule evolved itself about me in its vast complexity
and gradually regained its importance. In looking at
our planet equipped and provisioned for a long voyage in space, — its almost boundless stores of coal
and other inflammable materials, its untired renewal
of the forms of life, its compensations which keep its
atmosphere capable of supporting life, the ever growing control over the powers of Nature which its inhabitants are acquiring, — all these things point to its
fitness for a duration transcending all our ordinary
measures of time. These conditions render possible
the only theory which can 'justify the ways of God
to man,' namely, that this colony of the universe is
an educational institution so far as the human race is
concerned. On this theory I base my hope for myself and my fellow-creatures. If, in the face of all
the so-called evil to which I cannot close my eyes, I
have managed to retain a cheerful optimism, it is because this educational theory is the basis of my working creed. The churches around me are based upon
the Fall of Man, a dogma which has spread its gloom
over the whole world of Christendom. This supposed
historical fact, based upon what our venerated Bishop
Brooks called the parable of Eden, is gradually losing
its hold on the intellects it has so long enslaved. The
great truths contained in our sacred legends are the

stones laid in a cement of human error.  The object
of what is called the higher criticism, which is only
another phrase for *honest* criticism, is to pick out the
mortar from between the stones, — to get the errors
from between the truths which are embedded in them.
The stones will remain, for the eternal laws of gravity
are the basis of their stability."

" *Poetical Influences.*   My early attempts at rhyme
were very few and slight, not as good as those on the
duck which Sam. Johnson trod on.  I remember repeating heroic lines to myself, which were imitations
of Pope or Goldsmith ; but I never wrote them down,
— perhaps for the reason given by the French poet,
' Je fis mes premiers vers sans savoir les écrire.'
Now and then I made a fanciful comparison, which
pleased my sisters, who made a note of it.  Such was
that which compared our pretty visitor, A. L., for the
beauty of her complexion, to the most delicately white
object with which I was familiar, — *slack lime*, — by
which name I always spoke of her.  Singularly
enough many years afterwards I found the same
similitude had been used by a Welsh poet.  A slim
and stooping theological student, whose hair was of
a *blonde ardente*, I remember likening to a slender
shoot tipped at the end with a red blossom.  I have
often been asked what were the first verses I printed.
I can't be quite certain on this point ; but of one
thing I am quite certain, that, so far as I know, no
vestige of talent is found in any one of them. . . . .
My acquaintance with poetry was principally derived
from the pieces for recitation and elocution contained
in the school-books of my day.  The lines attributed to John Rogers, the martyr, and printed in the

*New England Primer*, always touched me almost to tears, especially those in which he sends his portrait to his children, 'that you may see your father's face, when he is dead and gone.' Such poems as Cowper's 'The Rose had been washed, just washed in a shower' were presented to my youthful appetite, — literary confections not favorable to the growth of sound and wholesome taste ; but I had Gray's 'Elegy,' and 'The Spacious Firmament on High,' and, by and by, *The Galaxy of American Poets*, Bryant shining among them, and lesser lights, such as Percival, Drake, Halleck, and others, twinkling to the best of their ability. But my favorite reading was Pope's Homer ; to the present time the grand couplets ring in my ears and stimulate my imagination, in spite of their formal symmetry, which makes them hateful to the lawless versificators who find anthems in the clash of blacksmiths' hammers, and fugues in the jangle of the sleigh bells.

> ' Aurora now, fair daughter of the dawn,
> Sprinkled with rosy light the dewy lawn '

thrills me with [its] splendid resonance, just as the lines from John Rogers's letter touched me with tender emotion. The low, soft chirp the little bird hears in the nest, while the mother is brooding over him, lives in his memory, I doubt not, through all the noisy carols of the singing season ; so I remember the little songs my mother sang to me when I was old enough to run about, and had not outgrown the rhymes of the nursery. I have been recently asked how such and such a poem was born into my consciousness, and I have answered, it was a case of spontaneous generation or *abiogenesis*. If it was a good poem, I did not write it, but it was written through me. I can only refer it to that 'inspiration of the Almighty which giveth understanding' to all His thinking creatures, and sends His spiritual messengers to them with thoughts, as He sent the ravens with food to Elijah in the wilderness.

"I have written so much verse, amidst which I hope there is some fraction of poetry, that I feel bound to give an account of the influences which tended to make me a poet. In the first place, the infancy of every human being born under favorable conditions is full of inspiration, which acts in the consciousness long before it has found words to express its exalted and excited emotions. The blue sky overhead, the green expanse under foot, the breath of flowers, the song of birds, the smile of a mother, the voices of loving guardians and friends, the changes of day and night, the roll of the thunder, the blaze of lightning, — all that makes up the scenery and orchestra of Nature, as yet uninterpreted by language, sink into the consciousness, to be remembered only in the effects they have produced. All this, I believe, is much more literally true than the poetic assertion of Wordsworth about the clouds of glory that we come trailing from a previous existence. Substitute for the 'Heaven which is our home' the unremembered world of our existence before we have learned to label our thoughts and emotions with words, and the child may be said to possess a wonderful inheritance derived from his infancy before the time of their articulate expression. Although the spot of earth on which I came into being was not as largely endowed by Nature as the birthplaces of other children, there was yet enough to kindle the fancy and the imagination of

a child of poetic tendencies.   My birth-chamber and
the places most familiar to my early years looked out
to the west.   My sunsets were as beautiful as any
poet could ask for.   Between my chamber and the
sunsets were hills covered with trees, from amid which
peeped out here and there the walls of a summer
mansion, which my imagination turned into a palace.
The elms, for which Cambridge was always famous,
showed here and there upon the Common, not then
disfigured by its hard and prosaic enclosures ; and
full before me waved the luxuriant branches of the
‘ Washington Elm,’ near which stood the handsome
mansion then lived in by Professor Joseph McKean,
now known as the Fay House, and the present seat of
Radcliffe College.”

“ *College-Days*.   There were two societies which
held convivial meetings while I was in college, to one
of which I belonged.   These were the Porcellian
Club and the Knights of the Square Table.   I did
not belong to the first of these while in college, but
was afterwards made an honorary member.   The two
at last were joined and became a single association.
It was a great change from the sober habits of a quiet
clergyman’s family to the festive indulgences and
gay license of a convivial club.   The Goddess of
Wisdom did not always preside at the meetings, but
undoubtedly there was refreshment, and possibly a dis-
guised use in the unrestrained freedom of these occasions ; sooner or later there was a chance that a young
man, who had to face the temptations of the wine that
was red in the cup, or sparkled in the tall wineglass,
would be betrayed into some degree of excess which
might lay the foundation of evil habits, but more

probably would pass away like the bubbles on the beaker's brim. Fortunately, there were no reporters at those meetings, for many tongues forgot the lessons they had been taught at the sober family board, and indulged in wit, or what passed for it, which would have borne chastening to advantage. Oh, this was the period of illusions! The supper-table and the theatre seemed lively as compared with the Assembly's Catechism and Saurin's sermons, which I remember my father placing in my hands with commendation. Wine was very freely drunk in those days, without fear and without reproach from the pulpit or the platform. I remember, on the occasion of my having an 'Exhibition,' that, with the consent of my parents, I laid in a considerable stock, and that my room was for several days the seat of continuous revelry; but we must remember what an immense change opinion has undergone since my time in regard to the use of alcoholic stimulants. It was still worse in my father's day, for when he went to college his mother equipped him with a Dutch liquor-case containing six large bottles filled with the various kinds of strong waters, probably brandy, rum, gin, whiskey, doubtless enough to craze a whole class of young bacchanalians."

# CHAPTER III



## 1828–1831

*January* 31, 1828.

DEAR BARNES, — I know very well that I am a lazy fellow and a procrastinator, — I am in a terrible fright lest the letter you spoke of should arrive before I have got this fairly dispatched. Your letter came just at the beginning of a term, when I had so many things to think of that I could hardly remember to get my lessons. At last, though, I have sprung into a chair, slapped down a sheet of paper, grasped my trustworthy silver pen, and will soon have a good sheet of my ideas ready for you. I would have you remember, if you happen to find an ill-chosen word or a badly constructed sentence or a few ungraceful sweeps of the pen, that I have not time now to attend to the graces of style or the elegance of chirography, because in truth I have snatched a hasty moment from the time when I expected to be skating, and, urged by the motive I have before mentioned, I am determined to do as much as possible in a certain given time. I am glad you liked the catalogue of the Medical Faculty; its aim is not so much, however, to caricature absurdities as to produce amusement by its mock solemnity, and the contrast between its pompous titles and its real nature. I shall send you something else in the humorous line, but you must not conclude yourself, nor let others conclude, that there is any bad spirit existing between the students and the officers who were the objects of its satire, — a mock theatre bill, which was got up some time ago under the auspices of our old friend F. W. Crocker of blessed memory. There were two published before this, quite equal to it in wit, though not in execution. Of course you cannot understand all the allusions, like us who are naturalized to Harvard. Mr. Sykes is the old and established nickname for Dr. Ware; the women mentioned are the college chamber-maids, and those who play the part of "mob, watch, etc." comprise a college servant, two negroes, and a proctor. I think it may be an object of curiosity to you, though it cannot have much interest to one who does not know the characters concerned.

You seem quite a politician for an undergraduate. We are almost all here Adams men, except the Southrons, and consequently rather down in the mouth, as the saying is.

We are going to have a new president, Mr. Quincy, the late mayor of Boston, unless the Overseers reject him; and we shall have great times at his inauguration, I suppose, with the illumination and the balls and all that sort of thing.

I will try to give you an account of some of our societies some of these days, if you would like to hear about them. I had like to have forgotten to tell you that I received the paper you sent me containing the obituary of Bartlett, which I suppose you wrote. Tell me if ever you write in *The Yankee* — some of our fellows have written in it. I should think your rival societies would be great sport. What are you going to study?

*March* 28, 1828.

DEAR BARNES, — I am in a great hurry, for I must go into Boston this forenoon; but if I do not say something now, I cannot this term, I am afraid. My vacation begins next Wednesday, the first of April, so that if you come here in yours it will be in my term time. I will do my best to show you the lions and make it pleasant to you, but you need not expect to find me any such great things. I am afraid you over-rate me on your scale. I have been busy lately in getting ready two poems which were assigned me, one by the government for a college exhibition, and the other by the class for our valedictory exercises. . . . We are going to have a grand time at the inaugura-tion [1] (you see I think of that notwithstanding your exclamation at my puerility), — they say that the gov-ernment is going to give a dinner to all the students and I don't know how many other people. We talked of getting up a ball, but could not find a convenient place, and so we shall confine our demonstrations of joy to the eating of meat, the drinking of wines, the smoking of segars, and the lighting of tallow candles. I suppose the whole college will be gibbeted in the next week's *Recorder* for the immorality and impiety of a public dinner.

I never wrote for *The Yankee* in my life, and therefore I am not " Clarence." Our people round here have got rather sick of it, I believe, and I myself am almost tired of the peculiarities which were at first amusing. The numbers I have seen lately were dull and uninteresting.

When you come here you must not expect to see in me a strapping grenadier or a bearded son of Anak,

---

[1] Of President Quincy.

but a youth of low stature and an exceeding smooth
face. To be sure I have altered a little, since I was
at Andover. I wear my gills erect, and do not talk
sentiment. I court my hair a little more carefully,
and button my coat a little tighter; my treble has
broken down into a bass, but still I have very little of
the look of manhood. I smoke most devoutly, and
sing most unmusically, have written poetry for an
Annual, and seen my literary bantlings swathed in
green silk and reposing in the drawing-room. I am
totally undecided what to study; it will be law or
physick, for I cannot say that I think the trade of
authorship quite adapted to this meridian. Do you
ever go mineralizing? You have a fine country for it,
and a celebrated professor to direct your studies. I
would give a good knock about the rocks in Maine
for some of their excellent specimens. I have paid
considerable attention to Chemistry and Mineralogy,
and think them both very interesting studies. The
towns around Cambridge are utterly destitute of interest to the mineralogist. C—— has not left our college,
nor is he like to until we all go together; he behaves
very well, though rather exclamatory, to speak moderately, in his language. Good-morning; I will go to
Boston now.

August 15, 1828.

DEAR BARNES, — I suppose I must begin with an
apology for not writing sooner. I have been away
from home about a month, or I would not have been
guilty of such neglect. Your letter was the first token
of remembrance that I have received from any of my
old Andover friends or acquaintance, saving certain
catalogues of the different colleges, in which article I
have kept up quite a brisk correspondence. . . . With

regard to myself I am determined that you shall not be so much in the dark. I shall therefore describe myself as circumstantially as I would a runaway thief or apprentice. I, then, Oliver Wendell Holmes, Junior in Harvard University, am a plumeless biped of the height of exactly five feet three inches when standing in a pair of substantial boots made by Mr. Russell of this town, having eyes which I call blue, and hair which I do not know what to call, — in short, something such a looking kind of animal as I was at Andover, with the addition of some two or three inches to my stature. Secondly, with regard to my moral qualities, I am rather lazy than otherwise, and certainly do not study as hard as I ought to. I am not dissipated and I am not sedate, and when I last ascertained my college rank I stood in the humble situation of seventeenth scholar. You must excuse my egotism in saying all this about myself, but I wish to give you as good an idea as I can of your old friend, and I think now you may be able to form an idea of him from this. The class we belong to is rather a singular one, and I fear not much more united than yours. I am acquainted with a great many different fellows who do not speak to each other. Still I find pleasant companions and a few good friends among these jarring elements. I am sorry Bartlett is sick; he used to be an excellent scholar, and I should think him a very promising young man. It seems to me from what little I have heard, and certainly from what I have seen, that our schoolmates have not turned out very well. Of six who were offered here, C—— and I were the only ones who entered without difficulty. O—— was turned by for the year and has entered the class below me, and the others made a sufficiently miserable appearance.

I am sorry you feel so sober for want of friends, but you need not be afraid that I shall think it silly in you to say so, for indeed I have had many such feelings myself. I have found new friends, but I have not forgotten my old ones, and I think I have had quite as pleasant walks within the solemn precincts of Andover as I have ever had amidst the classic shades of Cambridge. I should like to go over some of those places again in the same company ; you remember how we used to wander about all round the old place, and a pretty town it is, too, notwithstanding they are rather stiff and formal on the hill of Zion, as some of the profane used to call it. Dr. M—— has got into hot water, you know: the Board have dismissed him, but the little doctor says he won't go, and so they are going to law about it. . . . I heard of Tom C—— pretty lately. In the words of my informant, he is what he used to be, a lazy little dog, and has not grown any. Tom, however, was one of the prettiest, best, funniest little fellows that ever lived. I have 'most got to the bottom of the page, and I am sure I shall omit something that I wanted to say. I want to know what you did to vex my " peaceable disposition " (I am as cross as a wild-cat sometimes, by the way) when I was leaving Andover. I shall send you a triennial catalogue with this. I have had a part at our Exhibition, an English translation. I would send you an Order of Exercises, but I have lost them all. I will send you an Order of Exercises when I have my next part, if I ever get one. I will not read this over, because I shall find mistakes. Take it with all its imperfections on its head.

*October* 23, 1828.

DEAR BARNES, — It is Saturday afternoon — the wind is whistling around the old brick buildings, in one of which your humble servant is seated in the midst of literary disorder and philosophical negligence. . . .

You ask me sundry questions, which I will try to answer. I have been to the delectable town of Andover and witnessed their last Exhibition, and I will tell you what I saw. Imprimis — I saw children in petticoats running to and from Phillips Academy; next I saw A—— M—— that was, who has been sick nigh unto death, but is better. Next I saw old John Adams in his old blue surtout, and Clement in his old cloak, like "a shirt on a handspike." I saw Phillips Academy and the Theological Seminary and lubberly Academites and long-faced Seminarians, and C—— D—— and J—— V——, and Ann S——, and the rest of the cattle, and the Mansion Hotel and a good dinner and a bad segar. As for hearing, I heard the Academy bell, and I went to the Exhibition and heard the boys speak, and then I heard some most execrable singing and fiddling, and then a long, prosing address from Dr. Dana. I believe the little reprobate Abraham M—— is in a store in Boston; he was a sad young scapegrace. I won't send you any of the Harvard Registers, I believe; I don't think they were very great.

Wednesday — yesterday — was our Exhibition; on the whole it was very poor; sometimes fellows will get high parts who cannot sustain them with credit. Our Exhibition days, however, are very pleasant; in defiance of, or rather evading, the injunctions of the government, we contrive to have what they call "festive entertainments" and we call "blows." A fine body of academic militia, denominated the "Harvard Washington Corps," parades before the ladies in the afternoon, and there is eating and drinking and smoking and making merry. I wish you would tell us more particularly about our old school-mates, and how you get along at your college. We have not any President yet, — there is some talk of making Dr. Ware. I ought to have written sooner, — have a great many excuses too tedious to mention. I would send you a catalogue, if it would do you any good.

CAMBRIDGE, December, 1828.

DEAR BARNES, — I am going to answer part of the fifty questions, and I suspect I shall not have much room to ask anything in return. And so here I am, with your two last sheets before me, like a sheep about to be sheared, or a boy to be catechised.

Imprimis (letter 1st, page 2d). "What do I do?" I read a little, study a little, smoke a little, and eat a good deal! "What do I think?" I think that's a deuced hard question. "What have I been doing these three years?" Why, I have been growing a little in body, and I hope in mind; I have been learning a little of almost everything, and a good deal of some things.

I have heard nothing of the Social Fraternity, but I should imagine that it could not be well supported by a parcel of overgrown lubberly rustics and a flock of unweaned bantlings, who now constitute the greatest part of Phillips Acad. In my own opinion —— is one of the most bigoted, narrow-minded, uncivilized old brutes that ever had the honor of licking into shape the minds of two such promising youths as P. B. and O. W. H.

They are going to have a High School for girls at Andover. What a pity it was not instituted when we were there; there are very pretty walks and very shady groves in the place.

If ever you come to Boston you will, of course, come out to Cambridge. Our town has not much to boast of excepting the College; it contains several thousand inhabitants, but there are three distinct villages. Our Professors are several of them perfect originals. . . . I have studied French and Italian, and some Spanish. We have been studying this year Astronomy, Good's *Book of Nature*, Brown's *Philosophy of the Mind*, and attended Dr. Ware's Lectures on the Scriptures. We have themes once a fortnight, forensics once a month, and declamation every week.

I have seen and read a good many numbers of *The Yankee*, and certainly it is an entertaining paper. At the same time that you allow X to be a man of some talent, you cannot deny that he is one of the most egotistical, impudent, conceited fellows that ever lived. Indeed, I believe that his paper owes half its popularity to the singular audacity and effrontery of its editor. A is a booby indeed. I cannot conceive what induced B to tack him to his skirts, unless it is on the same principle that the lion enters into partnership with the jackal. I will send you a catalogue of the officers and students, and one of the Medical Faculty. This will need some explanation. It is a mock society among the students, which meets twice a year in disguise, and, after admitting members from the junior class, distributes honorary degrees to distinguished men. The room where they meet is hung round with sheets and garnished with bones. They burn alcohol in their lamps, and examine very curiously and facetiously the candidates for admission. Every three years they publish a catalogue in exact imitation of the Triennial Catalogue published by the college. The degrees are given with all due solemnity to all the lions of the day. I thought it might afford you a little amusement, although it was not intended for wide circulation. Remember, it is only a private thing among the students. Perhaps I will send you a Harvard Register some time or other.

September je ne sçais pas quoi, 1829.

DEAR BARNES, — I suppose you are looking about as much for a roll of papyrus from Memphis, or a waxen tablet from Pompeii, as for any communication from this lazy latitude of Cambridge. I would make a sort of Hibernian request to you, then, that you would open this letter, and not take it for granted that it comes from some bore of a classmate, or some member of a parish school committee gifted with the art of shaping interpretable characters, or some miserable victim of your too fickle erotic propensities, who "takes this opportunity" to send you a lock of her golden hair and four pages of her bad grammar, or some suckling of a Southern college, that sends you a doctorate because you are a graduate and a schoolmaster, or appoints you a professor in five-and-twenty branches of literature and science. It is from none of all these. It goes to my heart to think that, not knowing where to find you, my poor letter may come to no better end than to amuse the Jackson clerks in the post-office at Washington.

I am settled once more at home in the midst of those miscellaneous articles which always cluster around me wherever I can do just as I please, —

Blackstone and boots, law and lathe, Rawle and rasps, all intermingled in exquisite confusion. When you was here, I thought of going away to study my profession; but since Judge Story and Mr. Ashmun have come, the Law School is so flourishing that I thought it best to stay where I am. I have mislaid your last letter, and my not being able to find it has been one reason, in addition to my procrastinating disposition, why I have not written sooner. And now, young man, I have no more conception where you are, or how you are situated, than I have of the condition of the ear-tickler to his majesty the Emperor of China. I can imagine, however, that you are in some queer little outlandish Eastern town, with a meeting-house the timbers of which bore acorns last autumn, that you live in the only painted house in the village, and that at this present time you are seated in magisterial dignity, holding the rod of empire over fourscore little vagabonds, who look up to you as the embodied essence of all earthly knowledge. I might go farther and fancy some houri of the forest welcoming you home from your daily labours with a kiss and a johnny-cake and all other sweet attentions that virgin solicitude can offer to the champion of education. Alas! I [fear] too much that, where you had fondly anticipated a blushing maiden of sixteen, you have a good-natured dowdy of forty, or an ill-natured walking polygon of fifty. You must write and tell me all about these things, if you have indeed persisted in your plan of school-keeping. As for Cambridge, nothing great has happened here, and even what seems great to us can have little interest for you. I will just tell you that the Law School has increased from one solitary individual to twenty-six. I was much pleased to learn that you received the first appointment in your class.

Did you ever see such a squabby little lump of a letter?

[Addressed to Phineas Barnes, A. B., Brunswick, Maine, [changed to] "China," and bearing this memorandum: —]

Oct. 24. Brunswick. My dear Son: Samuel came home last night with the intelligence that there was a letter in the office for me. Not doubting but it was from you, I borrowed nine pence and dispatched him for it with all possible speed; when, to my inexpressible regret, it was *to* you. Excuse me for opening it. Why don't you write me? Do write soon; we are all well.　　　　　Yours,　　　　S. BARNES.

The following letter to James Russell Lowell also may be inserted, as relating to this period, and having, perhaps, some little interest: —

#### TO JAMES RUSSELL LOWELL.

296 BEACON STREET, *January* 28, 1875.

MY DEAR JAMES, — I can tell you about two classes, and I am afraid no more.

Our class Orator was George H. Devereux, of Salem. The opposition candidate was Ben Curtis. I was chosen class poet over James Clarke.

In my son Wendell's class he was poet and N. P. Hallowell orator.

Our class did not cheer the buildings or the professors, so far as I remember. There was some talk about planting a tree in the new president's garden, and I think one was planted.

We had a great talk about wearing gowns either on Class Day or Commencement, I forget which. It was all going on swimmingly in that direction, when —— got up, and, in a speech which gave us a higher idea of his cleverness than anything else ever had, blew the whole project sky high.

Our class made a fuss about taking a degree of A. M. It cost fifteen dollars, they said, and signified nothing at all. So a large number of them did not take it at the usual time. Some came in afterwards, — I never did, and never missed it much. I do not remember about dancing round the liberty-tree, — I think that must have come in later. There used to be punch-drinking in a group of elms between Professor Pierce's house and Holworthy, but whether that was a regular institution or not I do not know. . . . .

TO PHINEAS BARNES.

*January* 13 [1830], **Wednesday evening,**
immediately after receiving your letter.

DEAR BARNES, — If doing a thing that I never did before is any atonement for unpardonable negligence, I am wiping off some of the purgatory I deserve by sitting down instantly to answer you.

I am inclined to think that you are a little disposed to be what the ladies call "blue," and the doctors "hypochondriacal," and old women "notional." What else could have put it into your head to mention such a vulgar project as getting your brains blown out for the sake of those everlasting Greeks, or to go teaching your "vermicular" to hard-eyed foreigners. You are really such a thorough-bred, grumbling, discontented Yankee that I expect to hear of you on a mission to Cochin China, or colonizing the

North Pole, before you have done with your vagaries.
That plan à *la* Goldsmith, though, I like very much ;
to tell the truth it has always been a favorite hobby
of mine, and if I could scrape catgut and my countrymen liked music well enough to pay for it, I should
try a small tour through a State or two to begin with.
And now I suppose that you are brooding over your
involuntary retirement, and thinking what a fine time
I must have in this focus of literature and refinement.
Nothing is easier than to make disadvantageous comparisons between ourselves and our neighbors. I will
tell you honestly that I am sick at heart of this place
and almost everything connected with it. I know not
what the temple of the law may be to those who have
entered it, but to me it seems very cold and cheerless
about the threshold. And another thing too ; I feel,
what one of the most ill-begotten cubs that ever entered college when he was old enough to be a grandfather most feelingly lamented, " the want of female
society." If there was a girl in the neighborhood
whose blood ever rose above the freezing point, who
ever dreamed of such a thing as opening her lips without having her father and her mother and all her little
impish brothers and sisters for her audience, — nay,
if there was even a cherry-cheeked kitchen girl to
romance with occasionally, it might possibly be endur-
able. Nothing but vinegar-faced old maids and drawing-room sentimentalists, — nothing that would do to
write poetry to but the sylph of the confectioner's
counter, and she — sweet little Fanny has left us to
weep when we think of her departed smiles and her
too fleeting ice-creams. I do believe I never shall be
contented till I get the undisputed mastery of a pet-
ticoat. . . . There 's nothing like the pathetic. The

girls used to tell me I wrote very pretty verses in their good-for-nothing albums. I will give you a chronicle in rhyme now, if I can, and go back to prose if I can't: —

The Præses has a weekly *row*,[1]
I think they call it a *levee*,
And people say it 's very fine ;
I 'm sure it 's flat enough to me.
Judge Story 's bought a horse in town ;
The law school every day grows bigger ;
And Sukey Lenox — I forgot,
I 've told you all about the nigger.
One fellow lately came from Maine,
And now there is another comer ;
And one is Upton called by name,
And t' other one is christened Dummer.
The undergraduates have made
Proposals for a monthly paper,
Which I am very much afraid
Will end in something worse than vapor.

I wish I had a little room, —
It makes my heart feel very sadly,
When I have so much news to tell
To crowd it up so very badly.
The folks have bolted up the doors,
And I have bolted down my supper.
My pony threw me t' other day
And very nearly broke my crupper.
Get *Blackwood's Magazine* and read
The story of the modern Gyges ;
And if you ride a coltish steed
Be careful of your " os coxygis."
The college servant took some books
And laid the mischief to the students,
But as it happened to be false
We thought him guilty of impudence.

[1] " Row : " " a scrape — a kicking up of the dust." — *Johnson.*

I have forgotten all the philosophy about contentment I intended to bore you with. I have nothing to
say about not writing before, but that I am an inveterate lazybones.

CAMBRIDGE, May 8, 1830.

DEAR BARNES, — If you know as much about me
as I think you do, you are not surprised that I have
been so long in making my voice heard among the
antipodes. But I will just tell you that I have been
very busy for some time past with one kind of non-
sense and another, and you know the laxity that
always follows this tension of a man's sinews. In the
first place I have been writing poetry like a madman,
and then I have been talking sentiment like a turtle-
dove, and gadding about among the sweet faces, and
doing all such silly things that spoil you for anything
else. And now I have subsided into that lethargy of
soul which with us men of talent comes as periodically
as calms upon the ocean. This month of May is too
good for anything but love, — the air whispers of
sighs, and the sky looks down upon you like a great
bright blue eye, and the motion of every leaf is as
soft as the step of a barefoot beauty, and our pulse
begins to beat with all the warmth and more than
all the freshness of summer. If that had been put
into an ode, it would have run from Maine to New
Orleans, but I cannot take the trouble to string my
pearls. Have your icebergs melted? Have your girls
begun to thaw out of their wintry iciness? Have you
seen such a thing as an opening bud or a flaunting
fan? Fill your next letter with sentiment, and seal
it with a Cupid. What a ridiculous notion that was
of yours about my amativeness, and your patriarchal
wish of success in getting a pretty wife and a numer-

ous offspring, or some such antediluvian benediction.
If I am in love now, I had not seen the lady when I
last wrote to you; I told you I had been scribbling,
and now you shall hear the whole of it. The collegers
got up a little monthly concern called *The Collegian*,
and I wrote poetry fiercely for the four numbers which
have been published. It was silly stuff, I suppose,
but the papers have quoted some of it about as if they
really thought it respectable. It is not absolutely impossible but that you may fall in with it somewhere
or other, and so I will give you a catalogue of what I
wrote, just as if you wanted to see them. You need
not look for philosophy or technical " poetry " among
the lists, perhaps with the exception of one or two
abortive attempts. Here they are.

RUNAWAY BALLADS.
THE TOAD-STOOL,
An Enigma.

THE LAST PROPHECY OF CASSANDRA (DOLEFUL).
ROMANCE.
*Scene from an unpublished play.*
Another Enigma.

TO A CAGED LION.
THE CANNIBAL.

TO MY COMPANIONS (NOT LIVE ONES).
THE DORCHESTER GIANT.
*Another scene from an unpublished play.*

THE SPECTRE PIG.
REFLECTIONS OF A PROUD PEDESTRIAN.
An invocation, from the Arabic (which was a lie).

I call that quite savage for an incipient rhymester.
You will excuse my silly vanity in supposing that
you care a snap about so insignificant a thing as a
college periodical. I should like to have sent you the

numbers, if the vagabonds that conduct it had the grace to send me a single copy, — but the world is ungrateful, as the sonneteers say.

The people are crowding in so to the Law School that we begin to apprehend a famine. . . . Nothing is going on but murder and robbery ; we have to look in our closets and under our beds, and strut about with sword-canes and pistols. The first thing a fellow knows is that he has a rap over his head, and a genteel young man fragrant with essences is fumbling with white-gloved fingers in his pockets, and concludes his operations with kicking him into a jelly or dropping him over a bridge. Poor old Mr. White was " stabbed in the dark," and since that the very air has been redolent of assassination. The women have exhausted their intellect in epithets and exclamations, the newspapers have declared it atrocious, and worst of all the little poets have been pelting the " villain or villains " with verses.

There is nothing to tell you of here. The president's levees have stopped, parties are no longer dreamed of, and society seems sinking into annihilation. Kiss the pretty girls all round for me on the left cheek, if you please, and do not sermonize, or find fault, or wish me a wife and a numerous offspring, — but write me a letter.

March, [1831].

DEAR BARNES, — I should violate the unity of my character if I did not open my communication with an apology. What a busy world we live in ! The turmoil of those bustling around us, the ebb and flow, the dash and recoil, of the unceasing tide within us, — but I begin to talk fustian. I suppose now that whenever you take the trouble to think about me

your fancy sketches a twofold picture. In the front
ground stands myself, on one side sparkle the fountains of Castalia and on the other stand open the
portals of Nemesis (if that be the name of Law).
My most excellent romancer, it is not so! I must
announce to you the startling position that I have
been a medical student for more than six months, and
am sitting with Wistar's Anatomy beneath my qui-
escent arm, with a stethoscope on my desk, and the
blood-stained implements of my ungracious profession
around me. I do not know what you will say, — but
I cannot help it. I cannot tell what *she* will think, —
but I cannot help it. I know I might have made an
indifferent lawyer, — I think I may make a tolerable
physician, — I did not like the one, and I do like the
other. And so you must know that for the last
several months I have been quietly occupying a room
in Boston, attending medical lectures, going to the
Massachusetts Hospital, and slicing and slivering the
carcasses of better men and women than I ever was
myself or am like to be. It is a sin for a puny little fellow like me to mutilate one of your six-foot men
as if he was a sheep, — but *vive la science!* I must
write a piece and call it records of the dissecting-
room, so let me save all my pretty things, as plums
for my pudding. If you would die fagged to death
like a crow with the king birds after him, — be a
school-master ; if you would wax thin and savage, like
a half-fed spider, — be a lawyer; if you would go off
like an opium-eater in love with your starving delu-
sion, — be a doctor. Whenever I undertake to write
to you, — and you are the only single person to whom
I write except my brother-in-law, — I cannot help
thinking how few things, in which I am interested,

can have any meaning to you, — how each is girded by his own horizon and played upon by his own lights and shadows.  (A)——————(B)  Let A stand for yourself and B for me, time and space draw a line between our circumferences, and through that void must pass the solitary ray from the world of one to that of the other.

There is a murderer of melody on the piano-forte in the next room who plays the deuce with my metaphysics.  To change the subject — I have just now a ruse in my head which I am in hopes to put in execution this summer.  You must be aware, then, that there is a young lady, or what sounds sweeter, a girl, in Maine — I do not say where.  Well, perhaps I am in love with her, and perhaps she is in love with me.  At any rate I made a strapping fellow bite his nails, who had the impertinence to think she was pretty.  I quizzed the caitiff in his remarks, anticipated his gallantries, and plagued him till he went about his business.  Now I have a sneaking notion of coming down to Maine to see *you*, as I shall tell the folks, and take a cross-cut over to her log house.  I can find it.  She had so much the air of a human being while she was here that I have a curiosity to see her wild.  Keep quiet.  Do not write sixteen pages of cross-questions about her name and home and such sublunary things.  When I am married you shall come and see us, and show her this letter.  We shall breakfast at eight and dine at two precisely.

I shall come if I can, but you need not positively expect me.

About writing for you, — I have too many million things to do here with studying and scribbling to be able to do it at present.  By the way, if you find any floating scraps with O. W. H. to the tail of them, set them down to the owner and, I believe, the only one, of those preposterous initials. . . . I cannot write on corners and edges, — and so. . . .

BOSTON, *July* 14, 1831.

DEAR BARNES, — Swear at me two or three times, if you please, for not answering you before, and bite your bearded lip at the meagreness of my tardy communication, — but keep your temper, if you can, in consideration of my very numerous engagements and very forgetful habits. If I have been very negligent to you, I have at the same time been putting off for almost three months answering an invitation from a learned society in Boston to become one of their members, to say nothing of a thousand little acts of forgetfulness and procrastination which have won me but too many ill looks for my gentle spirit. This is the way I always have begun, — it is the way I always shall begin, — it seems as if the genius of preconcerted harmony had left me out of his calculations and I was limping in the rear of his neatly marshalled phalanx. It is past eleven o'clock in the evening, — I am sitting in solitude and almost unbroken silence, though in the heart of a busy metropolis, and ever and anon turning up my eyes from the sheet before me and thinking of the pretty little hand which I held so quietly but a very little while ago — and the girl who was silly enough to let me.

Pooh! some impish interruption broke me off three evenings ago just as I was going on so prettily. It is now ten minutes after ten, — at five to-morrow morning I set out for the South, — as I indefinitely tell my neighbors, — meaning perhaps Philadelphia.

I know, good soul as you are, you will not blame
me for stopping in my second page when I tell you
that I have all my things to pack before I go to bed,
and that I am one of the most somnolent fellows you
ever met with. . . .

I shall not come down to Maine probably this season, for a reason which implies neither faithlessness
nor anything else naughty. It is possible that one
who has been in Boston might make another visit,
you know.

Your letter was sent in to me as an appendix to
some of those villainous necessaries that old families
are always sending in to young colonies, and so I did
not see the gentleman who brought it, if indeed he
came with it, for I have inquired for him and have
not heard of him.

I will begin my third page out of spite, although I
have little to say, and that little hurried enough when
my empty trunk and my most multitudinous investments are staring me so full in the face. I may be
coming "down your way," as I threatened, another
time, and just keep quiet for the sake of mercy.

P. S. Don't take an inventory of all the country
girls that have come to Boston — there 's a good
creature.

February 22, 1832.

DEAR YOUTH, — Of all the days in the year this
patriotic anniversary is the worst calculated for a man
to sit down at his writing-desk. They have been
making such an uproar with their processions and
stuff that I almost wish we had paid the tea tax and
remained a colony. But as I am going off to-morrow
to Providence (to cut up a child), and as I never
can write with comfort anywhere but in my own

room, I shall contrive to slice a little parenthesis out of this day of tumult. What in the world did you make such a fuss about your writing for? I shall always be glad to hear from you at reasonable intervals, not too thick, as I told my lady love when she spoke of writing once a fortnight, — but I do not think you have been very culpable in frequency.

It is a lamentable fact that I am pretty much in the same situation with you and the scissors-grinder, — I have no story to tell. If I am engaged, I shall not tell you anything about it. However, about this taking wives, I think a man who has to swim without a cork jacket had better not put lead into his breeches' pocket. (Quite apothegmatic.) I wish to mercy I could only get on to my hooks. I am not tired of studying, and I expect to be no more idle certainly when I begin to practice; but I am tired of being a dependent and an underling, a mere appendage to the wheels of society. I am tired of living here among folks, some of whom are disagreeable and some loathsome, — reading just so much medicine, eating just so much dinner, writing just so much trash. There is a confounded tendency in a man to get into a routine every few months, that he hates for its sameness. I expect to trot off to Europe some of these days, for that reason as well as some better ones. In the mean time if you come to Boston I cannot promise you much, but I will give you a good dinner and a glass of wine somewhere or other, and some good cigars, if you smoke, and say "Come in" when you knock at the door of my attic. If you stay any time, you can board here where I do at a reasonable rate enough, if you would like it. But I must go to the Hospital and to the Eye Infirmary, and I must dissect, if you bring the Governor and Senate with you.  I have met Professor Longfellow, one of your "down East" folks, two or three times lately, and a very nice sort of a body he seems to be.  I should be ashamed to send you an unfilled letter if I had not a hundred things to do before I go to Providence.

You shall have three pages next time.

# CHAPTER IV



From Andover Holmes came, in the summer of 1825, to Harvard College, thus becoming a member of the class of '29, — "the famous class of '29," as it used to be called, and I hope the distinction does not seem invidious; at least it is safe to aver that no *more* distinguished class ever emerged from the nursery of that productive mother.

Of his college career there remain only scant memoranda, which have been already given in the paragraph of his own reminiscence, and in the few letters to his friend Barnes.

After graduation his membership in the "famous class" became a life-long source of pleasure to him. Those were the days of "class feeling;" the jarring elements, to which he refers, and the quarrels among the lads while undergraduates were merely after the foolish fashion of adolescence, and as transitory as the youth which they indicated. A strong sentiment of fellowship succeeded, became the permanent condition, and effected a solidarity that few individuals ever repudiated. To-day one hears that the loyalty of the student is to his club; then it was to his class; the class and the college remind one of the relationship which the Southerner used to establish between his State and his country, — the class first, the college next. Probably the authorities would laugh now at the idea of treating a class as a unit upon any public question; but in that era, to treat a class otherwise than as a unit would have been a course gravely perilous. And the union became closer after graduation than before; a man expected his classmates to befriend and even aid him in his journey through life, and he was rarely disappointed.

As was usual, the graduates of '29 soon began to have annual dinners in Boston, for which there certainly was rare social material, — George T. Davis, a member of Congress, whom Thackeray declared the most agreeable dinner-companion whom he met in the United States; B. R. Curtis, of the Supreme Court of the United States, one of the greatest lawyers whom this country has ever produced; George T. Bigelow, Chief Justice of Massachusetts; James Freeman Clarke, than whom none was more charming; Professor Benjamin Pierce; Rev. Samuel May, kindliest of abolitionists; S. F. Smith, who had the good luck to write "America;" Rev. Joseph Angier, who was supposed to sing precisely like an angel; with others less publicly known, yet hardly less agreeable mates for the annual festival.

Dr. Holmes naturally enough enlivened one of their meetings with an ode, whereof the result was that he was expected to do the like ever after. Some of his most pleasing "occasional" verses, sometimes convivial, later on pathetic, were written for these class gatherings. Mr. May was custodian of the "Class Book," which gradually became valuable by its annals and its contributions. In reply to a query from Dr. Holmes in January, 1874, he said: " I find . . . that you regularly began to furnish us a poem in 1851, — ' The summer dawn is breaking.' "    And in another letter he says, " And from that day (1851) to this, no class meeting of ' 1829 ' has been without a poem from you, — not one ; and several of them have had two, — the better luck for us." Generally Dr. Holmes read these odes, but we have the word of Mr. May that on some occasions he sang them. The following letter, also written by Mr. May, in the year after the Doctor's death, gives vivid evidence of how deeply Dr. Holmes cared for these meetings : —

SAMUEL MAY TO F. J. GARRISON.

LEICESTER, *September* 11.

DEAR FRANK, — " After the Curfew " was positively *the last.*  " Farewell ! I let the curtain fall." [1] The curtain never rose again for " '29." We met once more — a year later — at Parker's. But three were present, Smith, Holmes, and myself. No poem — *very quiet* — something very like tears. The following meetings — all at Dr. H.'s house — were quiet, social, *talking* meetings — the Doctor of course doing the *live* talking. Smith so hard of hearing that most things had to be said, or shouted, over again at his very ear ; and yet he clearly gathered much by his eye, for his face constantly moved in expression, and the Doctor ever kept his face towards Smith, raising his voice slightly ; yet seldom making S. hear him, I think. At one of these meetings four were present, all the survivors but one; and there was more *general* talk. But never another *Class Poem.*

When Holmes graduated he was still in some doubt as to what should be his calling in life. He went, in a tentative way, into the Dane Law School, and stayed

---

[1] See *Over the Teacups*, p. 69.

there for a year.  But he did not take to his studies with any ardor, and scanty trace of any influence of this twelvemonth is to be noted in his writings.  If he had cared for it at all, this would not have been the case.  In fact, however, he had not started on the right road; he soon found it out, and stopped at the first milestone.  In a few fragmentary words in his reminiscences he attributes to "the seductions of verse-writing" the fact that his year "was less profitable than it should have been."  *The Collegian*, edited by John O. Sargent, of the class of 1830, was alluringly ready to receive all the poetry which Holmes would contribute.  Having tried both pursuits, he alleged: "The force which is required for continuous and prolonged application is rapidly dissipated in the act of poetical composition.  The labor which produces an insignificant poem would be enough to master a solid chapter of law, or a profound doctrine of science.  I mean, of course, if the poem is written with any amount of lyric passion.  The mere stringing of rhymes together, as is done by so many young persons, is hardly an intellectual employment."

Holmes had already tried his hand at writing poetry, or, as he would have preferred to have it said, at scribbling verses; for he was very severe upon these *Juvenilia*.  In later years he absolutely forbade the republication of most of them, and it was really with some difficulty that even such bits as "The Mysterious Visitor," "The Spectre Pig," and others escaped his remorseless condemnation.  One genuine lyric outburst, however, done in this year of the law, almost made him in a way actually famous.  The frigate Constitution, historic indeed, but old and unseaworthy, then lying in the navy yard at Charlestown, was condemned by the Navy Department to be destroyed. Holmes read this in a newspaper paragraph, and it stirred him. On a scrap of paper, with a lead pencil, he rapidly shaped the impetuous stanzas of "Old Ironsides," and sent them to the *Daily Advertiser*, of Boston. Fast and far they travelled through the newspaper press of the country; they were even printed in hand-bills and circulated about the streets of Washington. An occurrence, which otherwise would probably have passed unnoticed, now stirred a national indignation. The astonished Secretary made haste to retrace a step which he had taken quite innocently in the way of business. The Constitution's tattered ensign was *not* torn down. The ringing, spirited verses gave the gallant ship a reprieve, which satisfied sentimentality, and a large part of the people of the United States had heard of O. W. Holmes, law student at Cambridge, who had only come of age a month ago.

In his farewell address to the Medical School, delivered in 1882, Dr. Holmes reverted to these early days : —

"Let me begin with my first experience as a medical student. I had come from the lessons of Judge Story and Mr. Ashmun in the Law School at Cambridge. I had been busy, more or less, with the pages of Blackstone and Chitty, and other text-books of the first year of legal study. More or less, I say, but I am afraid it was less rather than more. For during that year I first tasted the intoxicating pleasure of authorship. A college periodical, conducted by friends of mine, still undergraduates, tempted me into print, and there is no form of lead-poisoning which more rapidly and thoroughly pervades the blood and bones and marrow than that which reaches the young author through mental contact with type-metal. *Qui a bu, boira,* — he who has once been a drinker will drink again, says the French proverb. So the man or woman who has tasted type is sure to return to his old indulgence sooner or later. In that fatal year I had my first attack of author's lead-poisoning, and I have never got quite rid of it from that day to this. But for that I might have applied myself more diligently to my legal studies, and carried a green bag in place of a stethoscope and a thermometer up to the present day.

"What determined me to give up law and apply myself to medicine I can hardly say, but I had from the first looked upon that year's study as an experiment. At any rate, I made the change, and soon found myself introduced to new scenes and new companionships."

So from law Holmes turned to medicine. He says, in his reminiscences : —

"At the end of the first year in the Dane Law School, I took up the new study which was to be my final choice. There is something very solemn and depressing about the first entrance upon the study of medicine. The white faces of the sick that fill the long row of beds in the hospital wards saddened me, and produced a feeling of awe-stricken sympathy. The dreadful scenes in the operating theatre — for this was before the days of ether — were a great shock to my sensibilities, though I did not faint, as students occasionally do. When I first entered the room where medical students were seated at a table with a skeleton hanging over it, and bones lying about, I was deeply impressed, and more disposed to moralize upon mortality than to take up the task in osteology which lay before me. It took but a short time to wear off this earliest impression. I had my way in the world to make, and meant to follow it faithfully. I soon found an interest in matters which at the outset seemed uninviting and repulsive, and after the first difficulties and repugnance were overcome, I began to enjoy my new acquisition of knowledge.

"The head of the private school at which I studied was Dr. James Jackson,[1] a very wise and a very good man, whose influence on the minds of the students who followed him in his visits to the hospital, and who listened to his teaching as professor, was of the soundest and best character. . . . Dr. Jackson never talked of *curing* a patient except in its true etymological sense of *taking care* of him. I think we may say, in general, that the doctor who talks of curing his patients belongs to that class of practitioners known in our common speech as 'quacks.' It is in medicine as in surgery, — nature heals, art helps, if she can; sometimes hinders, with the best intentions; oftener is entirely ignored by the great remedial agencies ordained by the shaping intelligence which gives form and life to mortal organization."

Holmes attended two courses of lectures in this private school. But of course if he was to be anything better than a rural dispenser of pills and powders, he had to pass at the very least two years in the European hospitals. Practically this must have been incorporated in the programme when his choice of the medical profession was made. Yet so large a part of the "consideration" received by clergymen in those days was "good" rather than "valuable," that this

[1] See *Medical Essays*, p. 424.

foreign education would have been wholly impossible had it not fortunately so happened that the daughter of the prosperous Boston merchant had brought with her into the clerical household a purse not altogether empty; and even with this aid, it would seem that some effort had to be made in order to send the young student to Paris with funds enough in his pocket to enable him to live comfortably and becomingly, — "like a gentleman," as he jealously expressed it. But his father and mother, like true New England parents of that day, came gallantly to the mark, made such sacrifices as they had to make, and equipped him.

On March 30, 1833, Holmes was in New York, seeing for the first time in his life a real city, and awaiting the sailing of the packet Philadelphia. "I do believe," he writes, "that half Boston is going out in the packet: Dr. and Mrs. Bigelow, Mr. and Mrs. Whitwell, Mrs. John Gray, Mr. and Mrs. Curtis, Bob Hooper, Tom Appleton, and Mr. Young, and Mr. Nobody-knows-who-besides. . . . You cannot imagine the pleasure which my falling into this little party has given me. . . . Last night I went to see Fanny Kemble, the daughter of Charles Kemble (who also played) and the niece of Mrs. Siddons. She was a very fine affair, I assure you."

On April 26th, from the "neat parlour of the Quebec Hotel" in Portsmouth, he reported his arrival after a passage of twenty-three days in the "superb ship," during which he "was not seasick very badly." Stormy weather was holding him back from crossing the Channel, but the ill wind blew him the good of enabling him to get to Salisbury. There, he says, "on Sunday we attended service at the Cathedral, and had the luxury of a benediction from a lord bishop who receives £15,000 a year." Such was the first news sent home to the worthy clergyman who was dispensing the red-hot truths of Calvinism at a price suited to the shortest purses, and snugly paring the family expenses in order to educate his son! Fortunately, however, that clergyman knew full well that, in a world which was sure to come, the great principle of compensation or average would be at work with vindictive efficiency.

Holmes also made report of a visit to the ruins of Carisbrook Castle, and to "the Earl of Radnor's seat, Longford Castle, where Queen Elizabeth stayed once and left some of her duds, which they showed us." " In a fly (as they call it) with two mules " the lads went out to visit Stonehenge, which " stands on Salisbury Plain where once lived a shepherd, according to Hannah More." One of the party "had a letter to Mr. McAdam, son of the Colossus of Roads," and by virtue of this they were "carried over the estate of the Earl of Pembroke." During their stay in Portsmouth, Dr. Holmes says: " We passed ourselves off for Englishmen (!) and went all over the dock-yard, which no foreigners are allowed to visit." Then, the storm abating, the youths went over to Havre, and there resumed their proper nationality, of which they had so artfully — or artlessly — divested themselves at Portsmouth. " By giving the custom-house officers a hint that we were Americans, our baggage was passed over very lightly," says the young traveller, who later in life might not have found these officials so amiably accepting a " hint " as a *douceur !*

The annals of the stay in Europe are somewhat scanty, — a few allusions in Dr. Holmes's published

writings, a page in the reminiscences, and a bundle
of the letters which were sent home pretty regularly
by the weekly mail packet to the parents in the
gambrel-roofed house. The earlier letters are not
especially interesting, being largely taken up with
descriptions of the common sights. Thus, he draws
a map of the "odd vehicle" called a *diligence*, and
describes the *conducteur* as "a man dressed up like
a jackanapes, who sits on top." His next letter begins like Cæsar's Commentaries *De Bello Gallico*, —
"Gallia est omnis divisa in partes tres," — "the Seine
divides Paris into two parts," and so on, guide-book
like. He talks about the narrow, dirty, sidewalk-less
streets, the *chiffonnières*, the shops, — "the windows of
many are very large, of fine plate glass, and crowded
as if the clouds had hailed jewelry upon them."
"There are shops of engravings, countless — of old
books, innumerable — of skulls and skeletons and
small children in bottles, and nobody knows what,"
and so on. But erelong, of course, this phase passes,
and the letters become more entertaining. He very
soon found lodgings in the Latin quarter, Numéro
55, Rue M. le Prince, where "many of the old nobility
and most of the scientific people," and "of course all
the medical students," resided. But though he enu-
merates the public buildings with conscientious accuracy, he certainly gives to the good people at home
a description of this famous neighborhood much less
vivacious and entertaining than may be found in the
pages of some of our novelists.

He had not been a fortnight in Paris before he
wrote that he was "at last quietly established and
almost naturalized;" and in a short time he asserted
that he was "quite absorbed" in study. This was

straightforward and satisfactory enough, and for that matter so were all his letters. Yet his father had the natural parental misgivings, and conceived of Paris not alone as a seat of learning where Louis, whom young Holmes reassuringly declared to be "one of the first pathologists in the world," gave priceless lectures, but also as a place where the Devil, about whom he had a much fuller knowledge than he had of Louis, gave gratuitous instruction with alluring illustrations. But the young man was compounded of good spirits and good sense in very fortunate proportion; he took his work and he took his pleasure, but he took his work with all his might, and his pleasure very moderately. At half past seven o'clock every morning he was at the hospital of La Pitié, and generally stayed there until ten o'clock, when he went to breakfast. On June 6th he writes, as of a specimen day: "It is no trifle to be a medical student in Paris. I had attended a lecture of an hour and a half, and gone through a tedious dissection this morning before breakfast, — that is, I left my bed at half after six, and did not sit down to breakfast till after eleven."

After breakfast study continued until five o'clock in the afternoon. Then came a pleasant dinner with a knot of fellow-students, Bostonians all, at some café, and many a time he refers with much gusto to the tasteful viands and the pleasing wines. They undoubtedly were different from the crude joints, the massive puddings, the depressing pies, and the hard cider or Medford rum, which marvellously nourished New England and tempered it, not sweetly, in its era of development. Then sometimes of course came the theatre, yet not so very often, for he does not seem especially addicted to this amusement. Indeed, he

writes : "I must own that I feel rather guilty in not
having attended the theatres more than I have — first,
because it betrays a want of taste, and second because it argues a neglect of the best means of learning the language."   But he pleads, as if in extenua-
tion, that at the opera "he has heard some famous
singers and seen some famous *figurantes.*"   He has
also seen "another amusement of a ruder nature, . . .
essentially a vulgar exhibition, and of course to be
seen by everybody except *petits maîtres* who travel in
white gloves ; and so Hooper, Warren, and I took a
box one day at the Combats des Animaux, which
take place twice a week just in the outskirts of the
city.   A great number of bull-dogs fought with each
other in succession, each pair fighting until one was
killed or fairly beaten ; and, of course, I suppose,
bets being laid upon them.   Then a wolf was tied
to a post and worried by bull-dogs, and afterwards a
bear — and a wild boar — and a bull — and last of all
a jackass.   The wolf and bear were poor concerns
and got worse than they gave ; the wild boar ran
round the ring making a great noise and trying to get
out ; the bull had his horns sawed off, but he tossed
the dogs up into the air after each other like so many
coppers ; and the poor jackass got into a corner and
kicked the dogs and jumped upon them with real
ferocity.   And in the middle of my description I am
obliged to break off in order to get my letter in, in
season " — which sudden snapping off may account for
the absence of comment upon this singular display.
The packet sailed only once a week, and it was the
age of " mail days."

In his reminiscent notes occurs the following passage : —

"I was busy enough during the time I spent in Paris, but saw little outside hospital and lecture rooms. If I had known how much literature would occupy my time in later years, I should have taken the pains to meet the historians Thiers and Guizot, — Balzac, Victor Hugo, Lamartine, Béranger, — George Sand, Comte, and others of the celebrities in politics, letters, and science. I saw the great actors, singers, and dancers, Mlle. Mars, Ligier, Frederick le Maître, Lablache, Tamburini, Grisi, and Taglioni. The Déjazet was the particular star at the Palais Royal. I remember her well about the middle of her perennial existence, the stability of which was the keenest satire on the perpetual changes of the government under which she lived. I remember Arago, a man of singularly fine presence, Poisson the mathematician. . . . But I never went lion-hunting as I might have done.

"I wish I could have foreseen the future clearly enough to induce me to lay up a store of memories which would have been precious to me in after years. One of my delights in Paris was to *flaner*, as the French call it; to roam about the streets using my eyes to see everything that life had to show on the *quais* or on the bridges. To stand on the Pont Neuf and look in the yellow waters of the Seine, with the barges and boats; with the patient anglers on its margin, who lived in hopes, apparently as happy as if they had been sharers in a miraculous draught of fishes; to watch for the priest, the soldier, and the white horse, who were said always to be passing on the bridge — was occupation enough for an idle hour. But I had an especial pleasure in hunting among the books exposed for sale on the wall of the *quais*, and for prints in the portfolios open at the doors of the

small dealers.  Now and then I would see at the road-
side, sitting with her household goods about her displayed for sale, a pathetic little show which oftentimes
excited my sympathies."

The truth certainly was that Holmes was absorbed
in the study of his profession, and that his interest in
it increased as he advanced in knowledge.  By way
of an example of the vein in which he often wrote,
here is a passage from a letter of November 14,
1833 : —

"I am more and more attached every day to the
study of my profession, and more and more determined to do what I can to give my own country one
citizen among others who has profited somewhat by
the advantages offered him in Europe.  And let me
tell you, this they have not all done who might have
done it, partly because they were contented with an
equality or a moderate superiority to those they left
behind them, and partly because they found other
things pleasanter than following hospitals and lectures
and autopsies.  The whole walls round the Ecole de
Médecine are covered with notices of lectures, the
greater part of them gratuitous ; the dissecting-rooms,
which accommodate six hundred students, are open ;
the lessons are ringing aloud through all the great
hospitals.  The students from all lands are gathered
together, and the great harvest of the year is open to
all of us.  The consequence is that I am occupied
from morning to night, and as every one is happy
when he is occupied, I enjoy myself as much as I
could wish."

It is entertaining also to come across the following
passage : —

"The young men, and especially young students,

perhaps were never so important a part of the community as at the present time. The arbitrary governments are occupied half their time in checking that class of their subjects, — the same class which excited the insurrection in Poland and headed the revolution in France. To tell the truth, the young men here are more feared and perhaps more respected than with us. I can say more particularly in scientific matters that there is nothing at all resembling the patriarchal authority which so often has held, and has such a tendency to acquire, the place of sound reason. There is this misfortune about it, that a man who lives to an advanced age in Paris, however great may have been his eminence during his prime, is very certain to be exploded, to be considered as used up, the moment that he falls behind the improvements of his time ; whereas with us, when a man has once acquired a reputation, it is still sustained by a kind of *vis inertiæ* twenty [years] after a new impulse has carried another generation in advance."

" How strange it is," he remarked in his later days, " to look down on one's venerated teachers, after climbing with the world's progress half a century above the level where we left them."[1]  He himself, in thus looking backward, gave a few happy sketches of some of the instructors of his youth. Easily the foremost among these was, of course, the famous Louis, who, however high was his place in the knowledge and practice of medicine, held a yet higher place as an inspirer of youth. In a rare degree he had this priceless quality of an instructor, so that those who followed him among the beds of the hospitals became filled with an ardent ambition. Holmes says that he

[1] *Hundred Days*, p. 164.

was " of serene and grave aspect, but with a pleasant
smile and kindly voice for the student with whom he
came into personal relations ; " he was the " object of
our reverence, I might almost say idolatry," and he
adds : " Modest in the presence of nature, fearless
in the face of authority, unwearying in the pursuit of
truth, he was a man whom any student might be happy
and proud to claim as his teacher and his friend."
But the result of this personal charm was admitted to
be that his students gave themselves up perhaps too
exclusively to his methods and theories.  " I devoted
myself too exclusively," said Dr. Holmes in his reminiscences, " to the teachings of Louis.  No one man
could perhaps have been so useful to me ; but I wish
I could have better remembered the *nullius addictus
jurare in verba magistri* of Horace.  Many a long
and wearying hour I have passed on the stone floor of
the autopsy-room at La Pitié, wasting my time over
little points which, a few years later, would have been
easily settled by the microscope."

Less attractive but more picturesque were others,
among whom " Andral was by far the most eloquent
and popular.  He lectured in the same room, immediately after Broussais.  Towards the close of Broussais's
lecture, the doors began to bang as the audience
expecting Andral began to gather.  The old man was
savage and looked almost carnivorous at these interruptions ; but that is the way the new theory treads
on the heels of the old, and the new generation crowds
upon the retreating forms of that which is passing
from the stage."  In his remarks on " Some of my
Early Teachers," he says that " Broussais was in those
days like an old volcano, which has pretty nearly used
up its fire and brimstone, but is still boiling and bub-

bling in its interior, and now and then sends up a
spirt of lava and a volley of pebbles."

And Lisfranc, "I can say little more of him," says
Dr. Holmes, "than that he was a great drawer of
blood and hewer of members.  I remember his ordering a wholesale bleeding of his patients, right and left,
whatever might be the matter with them, one morning
when a phlebotomizing fit was on him.  I recollect
his regretting the splendid guardsmen of the old
Empire, — for what? — because they had such magnificent thighs to amputate.  I got along about as
far as that with him, when I ceased to be a follower
of M. Lisfranc."

Then there was " the short, square, substantial man
with iron-gray hair, ruddy face, and white apron ; "
this was " Baron Larrey, Napoleon's favorite surgeon,
the most honest man he ever saw, — it is reputed that
he called him.  To go round the Hôtel des Invalides
with Larrey was to live over the campaigns of Napoleon, to look on the sun of Austerlitz, to hear the
cannons of Marengo, to struggle through the icy
waters of the Beresina, to shiver in the snows of the
Russian retreat, and to gaze through the battle smoke
upon the last charge of the red lancers on the redder
field of Waterloo.  Larrey was still strong and sturdy
as I saw him, and few portraits remain printed in
livelier colors on the tablet of my memory."

At the Hôtel Dieu there " ruled and reigned the
master-surgeon of his day, at least so far as Paris and
France were concerned, — the illustrious Baron Du-
puytren.  No man disputed his reign, — some envied
his supremacy.  Lisfranc shrugged his shoulders as
he spoke of *ce grand homme de l'autre côté de la
rivière,* — that great man on the other side of the river ;

but the great man he remained, until he bowed before
the mandate which none may disobey." He was, as
the Doctor recalled him, " a square, solid-looking
man, with a fine head. With his white apron girt
around him, he marched through the wards of the
Hôtel Dieu like a lesser kind of deity, — soft-spoken,
undemonstrative, unless opposed or interfered with,
when he would treat his students, I have heard, as a
huntsman does his hounds. But of this I never saw
anything, except, when they piled up on his back as
he overlooked a patient, he would shake them off
from his broad shoulders like so many rats and mice."

There was also " the vivacious Ricord, whom I
remember calling the Voltaire of pelvic literature, —
a skeptic as to the morality of the race in general,
who would have submitted Diana to treatment with
his mineral specifics, and ordered a course of blue
pills for the vestal virgins."

And there was " the famous Baron Boyer, author of
the great work on surgery in nine volumes; " and
Velpeau, who looked " as if he might have wielded
the sledge-hammer rather than the lancet."

So many famous professors of medicine or surgery,
with others less well remembered, or less temptingly
lending themselves to description, were bringing their
contributions of knowledge to the Yankee student, —
and he, a quick-witted, keenly observant, earnest youth,
slackened not, but fatigued himself with incessant
gathering. In his reminiscences he says that much
of his " time in Paris was lost in ill-directed study.
Still I gained the same familiarity with disease which
the keeper of a menagerie does with the wild beasts
he feeds and handles. I there learned the uncertain-
ties of medical observation. The physician is like a

watchmaker having charge of watches that he cannot open ; he must make the best guess he can, yet it is fair to say that the exploration of the interior of the human body has reached a degree of perfection which was not dreamed of at the time when I was a student."

Holmes says that the students, becoming admirers of one or another of these several teachers, created a condition of things like that which subsisted in the cities of the Middle Ages, when each baron had his following ready in feud on his behalf.

In the spring and summer of 1834, the courses of medical instruction being over, Holmes and some of his friends started forth to travel. Before leaving the Continent they took the conventional trip down the Rhine, and devoted a liberal allowance of time to the Low Countries. Thence they crossed to England. In his earlier letters Holmes had spoken very disrespectfully of that country. In June his friend " Tom Appleton, son of Nathan," came from London to Paris, bringing such tales of the former capital that Holmes was moved to declare : " If what he says of London is true I almost hate to go there, — exorbitant expense and little comfort are no temptation after the paradise of Parisian life."

In October, 1833, he wrote: " As for the science of England and France, or rather Paris and London, — to judge by their books and their students, and the reports of the intelligent young men who have seen both, — the Frenchmen have half a century in advance."

I think his letters from England, and upon his return to France, do not show that his personal experiences dissipated this prepossession. He stayed a few weeks in London, saw something of English hospitals, and got some idea of English teaching. Then the party moved northward, saw Edinburgh and liked it, and of course visited and enjoyed those neighborhoods which owe a little to nature and a great deal to Walter Scott, — Abbotsford, Melrose, Loch Katrine, Loch Lomond, The Trosachs, and so on. There is no doubt as to how young New Englanders in the year 1834 were affected by these scenes. From them the travellers came down to the English Lakes, and saw somewhat more of the English country, before the mill began to grind again in Paris. But I think that Holmes preferred working in Paris to amusing himself in England; he was young; later in life the opposite would have been true, at least as regards the localities; though for the matter of labor and amusement he was deeply infected with the feverish industrial propensity of his native State.

About this time money matters began to exhibit those symptoms familiar to the memories of most persons who have been young in Europe. The purse was nearly empty, not because Holmes had been extravagant, but because it had never held any very great sum. The letters which he wrote asking for reëstablishment were very dignified, sensible, and self-respecting, though they held some strenuous pleading, certainly, and showed, perhaps, a person rather self-centred and absorbed in his own strong purpose. But unfortunately it so happened that just at this time there developed between France and the United States a relationship so strained that war might ensue at any moment. France had agreed by treaty to pay our "French claims," but the legislature would n't find the money, and General Jackson was raging furiously, and flinging epithets which sounded like cannon-balls. England kindly pulled us out of the scrape, or there would have been bloodshed.

The parents at home were evidently greatly disturbed by conditions which might endanger the safety of their son, besides of course breaking up those studies which were costing so much beyond the forecasting. Betwixt alarm and economy they began to think that he might as well come home. He was thrown into despair by the suggestion. His sense of the loss which he would suffer is really heart-rending, even at this distance of time, and when we know that ultimately he escaped it. But while the decision hung uncertain, and seemed likely to go against him, his letters are very intense and pathetic.

Moreover, he had been looking forward eagerly to a trip to Italy, with all that it promised of pleasure and education; he expected to take it as a fairly earned reward at the end of a winter of hard study. "All the other fellows did," and every one who remembers his own youth knows what a sledge-hammer argument that is.

Discussion moved tardily to and fro during the winter passages made by the weekly packets across the stormy Atlantic. Holmes would send a burning, anxious letter, well knowing that its ardor must be chilled during storm-tossed weeks before it could reach his parents; and then their reply would be as long in reaching him. The suspense was a severe ordeal. All the winter he worked desperately hard, under pressure of the apprehension that the end of his opportunity might be brought by any incoming packet. Apparently it was not until the middle of

*Rev. Abiel Holmes*

June that he was assured of the Italian journey.
Then right joyfully, early in July, he packed for
shipment to Boston all his accumulated belongings, a
select little professional library, a modest stock of
instruments, and a box, " with two skeletons and some
skulls, etc.  One of the skeletons is for Dr. Parsons.
I paid 135 francs for the large one and 90 for the
little one, — which last I bought for myself, as I
supposed the Doctor would like the more showy one."

In the autumn of 1835 he returned home.  His
voyage was a long one, forty-three days, and he landed
in New York on December 14th.  Besides the skeleton in the box it is probable that he brought no other
skeleton.  He had used time and money conscientiously, had gathered memories both useful and pleasant, knew the French language almost like his own,
and had as much professional knowledge and skill as
hard work could master in two winters.  This was
much, yet it was not quite all.  It is reasonable to
presume that when the young man left home, the
relationship between his father and himself was like
that between most fathers and sons in that generation.  This relationship may be represented by a per-
pendicular line, having the Rev. Abiel Holmes at the
top and the lad O. W. Holmes at the bottom, each
accepting his position as a matter of course.  But
Europe had disturbed this line, had made it pivot
upon its central point, and had even given such an
impetus to its gyration that O. W. Holmes seemed to
have come round to the top, while the good clergyman
of Cambridge had swung to the nether end.  In a
trifle less than quarter of a century moral and intellectual independence had been achieved, — fortunately without any disturbing conflict, for respect
and affection survived subordination.

# CHAPTER V



### TO HIS PARENTS

PARIS, June 14, 1833.

DEAR FATHER AND MOTHER, — James Jackson
has just come up to my room to write home a letter,
and reminded me that I must have one ready for the
next packet. My weeks run along now in a pretty
uniform manner. The hospital, — breakfast, —
study, — a walk of an hour or two, — dinner at five
o'clock, and evening sometimes bringing my French
master, and sometimes some amusement or other, —
make up a day which is pleasantly and not unprofit-
ably spent. Well, here we are, Jackson at my desk
and I at my table, both of us in a little hurry, but not
willing to let the day pass without our weekly tribute.
I must as usual sketch off a little description of something which I have seen, and among these objects are
many with which I already feel as familiar as I do
with the gate of our front yard, or the little shelf at
the right as you go into the upper wood-house.

*The Palais Royal.* You have heard of this very
often, but have probably no idea of it at all. The
building which forms its boundary is of this figure.
. . . A is the courtyard of the palace, formerly occupied by the Duke of Orleans (citizen Egalité), and
B is the courtyard of the larger division called the
gallery of the Palais Royal, — in the centre of which

is a garden with a fountain, and around which are the
most brilliant shops, cafés, and restaurants of Paris.
You are to know, then, that what Paris is to France
the Palais Royal is to Paris. It is the radiating centre of novelty, which in one word comprises almost
everything that is interesting to Parisians. The
most splendid articles of dress, the richest jewelry,
the rarest delicacies and the most delicate rarities
crowd to profusion the broad and glaring windows of
this immense amphitheatre. The area, if I might
form a conjecture, would contain a hundred thousand
people, and it is always gay with the multitude of
strangers and Parisians that go there to dine or to
walk or to game, — or any of the thousand occupations or amusements which give to this Vanity Fair
its unceasing stir and glitter. I find that I cannot
describe this place, simply for the reason that I have
no terms of comparison or illustration. It is essentially Parisian, — it could not exist perhaps were it
peopled by any others, — and lastly, if enjoyment is
the object of life, as many old and modern philoso-
phers have believed, no one spot in the world offers
more varied sources than may be found within its
precincts.

*The Louvre.* I went to see it for the first time
yesterday, —and as I have made an engagement to
go and see it again to-day, I must hurry my letter a
little for the sake of keeping my engagement. The
gallery of the Louvre extends from the palace of the
Louvre to that of the Tuileries, and is more than a
quarter of a mile long. It is full, I suppose you
know, of paintings, and was the storehouse of the
spoils of Napoleon. When I went yesterday it was
almost the hour for the gallery to shut, and I had

scarcely an opportunity to walk from one end to the other before the soldiers hinted that it was time to retire. Besides the pictures of the French school, — among which are those of Poussin and Claude Lorraine, — there are nearly one thousand by the old masters of the Flemish, Dutch, German, and Italian schools. Among them are a large number by Raffael and his master — by Titian — by Rubens — Guido — Salvator Rosa — in short, paintings by all the masters of celebrity with whose names we are familiar — transmitted from the times of Francis I, Henri IV, and Louis XIV. I have hitherto seen nothing which seemed to me so royal as this gorgeous hall. Its extent is so great that the eye can hardly appreciate it, and yet from the oaken floor to the arched and gilded ceiling there is not a spot which the eye of a king might not repose upon with pleasure. There are more than 900 pieces of statuary in the hall beneath this gallery. This collection of paintings and statues is open to the public every Sunday; but strangers are admitted every day — except Monday — from ten to four, by showing their passports. So you see that I, like all foreigners, have treasures enough thrown at my feet, for delight as well as instruction, to make me forget in some measure that I am in the land of strangers. I have not as yet had any letter. I shall mention this whenever I write, to let you know if your letters come when you write, and to make you more attentive to this part of your duty. Love to all.

TO HIS BROTHER JOHN.

PARIS, June 21, 1833.

DEAR JOHN, — I just send you two words by Sullivan Warren, who went so much sooner than I expected that I had only a moment to write to James Russell and Park Benjamin, — and have just a minute left for you. This will be of little consequence if you have got my letters, for I have written every week since I have been in Paris. I admire the French so far as I have seen them, — indeed the only very disagreeable people one meets with are generally Englishmen. I had observed one fellow, who attended at the same hospital with me, for his vulgar, bustling air, and because he had his sleeve turned up in an important and business-like kind of way. He was a man about thirty years old, and resembled so much one of our own conceited country practitioners, in the confidence of his remarks as well as their stupidity, that I might have mistaken him for a Berkshire County luminary. I found out afterwards that he was *Sir* —— ——. And I can tell you that a man with a title may be just as great a booby as a republican, — and as for the English students here, so far as I can learn and observe, they cannot compare with the American.

I hope by this time you have taken hold of law or some business. When a body has got to your age he should give up all his idle fancies and notions and apply himself to some practical use, pleasantly if he can — odiously if he must. In about thirty years he will have money and character, and then he may go again to his cat's-cradles and speculation. But just put off the age of action a little too long, and there is a great chance that you evaporate into " general knowledge," or dribble down into a half intellectual harlequin like ——. I say it once more, that I have found no difficulty whatsoever from not having my degree. They are not taken the least notice of, —

nobody uses the title of Doctor, and I would not give a
copper for any advantages it would give me.  In this
as in many other things I have found that my own
opinion, after examining the evidence of things, is a
much better guide for me than anybody's advice.
Take no clothes to Paris, said some wiseacre or other
to me.  I did so, and was of course made a fool of,
— for people dress here with the same variety that
they do with us, and for my own part I was much
more of a dandy in Boston than I am here.  For instance, if I had brought that black coat, it would have
saved me twenty dollars, and so of many other things.

Well, I feel now as if I had known Paris from my
childhood.  I am as much at home, day and night, in
the streets as in Boston, or almost so.  I am so completely naturalized that it seems as if Boston must be
only about twenty miles to the west, and I feel as if
some of you would be calling up at my room some of
these mornings.  M. Breschet, to whom Mr. Warden
gave me a letter, has been very useful to me.  I hope
you have remembered certain little matters which I
spoke to you about, — such as the Sydenham, which
Hook has, — and my notes at the Hospital.  I intend
to write expressly some of these days to Dr. Parsons
— and to Mr. Upham.  With regard to professional
advantages I can only say that, great as I had supposed them to be, the standard of medical instruction, the opportunities to embrace every variety of
[illegible], the facility with which all is obtained, and
the rapidity with which instruction is acquired, convince
me that the attentive student may return a sounder
physician at twenty-five than many who slumber till
sixty in our own languid scientific atmosphere.

I understand my French lectures almost as perfectly as English. So on the whole I am getting accomplished. — I have had no letter yet.

Give my love to Father and Mother, — and all their descendants and connections.



PARIS, *June* 29, 1833.

DEAR FATHER AND MOTHER, — Not a sign of a letter from home yet, and I have been away three months! I go on one invariable principle, that nobody who leaves many friends behind him need be worried in such circumstances ; for if anything happens to one, that is the very reason why another should write immediately. If you have received all my letters, there have been seven, I believe, or eight, — and I am just sitting down to this in surprise to find the week come round so soon again. The truth is, I live at Paris just as if I had been there all my life, and indeed I can hardly conceive of anybody's living in any other way, so completely have I naturalized myself. It seems hideous to think of more than two meals a day ; how could I ever have dined at two o'clock ? How could I have put anything to my mouth but a silver fork ? How could I have survived dinner without a napkin ? How could I have breakfasted without drinking white sugar and water ? It is very narrow and ridiculous, and yet it is very common, to hear people taking the standard of their own fancy for that of necessity. One will tell you that he prefers a separate plate from his neighbor, but has no idea of any napkin but the tablecloth, — another would shudder at an iron tumbler, but is astonished that his neighbor has an aversion to an iron fork. Now as for napkins and silver forks, the most ordinary, meanest eating-houses in Paris consider them as indispensable, — and so with regard to many things which we consider as luxuries, they make a part of ordinary existence with the Parisian. And yet a young man goes abroad, and perhaps lives for years among strangers, at that part of his life when tastes and habits are forming; but if, when he returns, he would modestly adopt a foreign custom at his table, or venture an opinion even that his countrymen want refinement in such or such a point, sober people shake their heads at the travelled monkey, and old people draw the corollary that their gawky offspring will be made a puppy by crossing the Atlantic. The more I see of French character, the more I am delighted with it. I have hardly heard an — As I was writing this, Waldo Emerson came up to see me. He had been sitting some time when I heard another knock, and in walked — James Russell! I never was so astonished in my life; but as he is here, and I must attend to him, without ceremony I shall take the liberty to conclude my letter. . . . Give my love to everybody.

PARIS, July 14, 1833.

You will not say or think anything hard of me for omitting to write the last time the packet went, because on the whole I have set you an example of punctuality which unhappily has not been followed. Not a sign of a letter from any living body. . . . I will rake for a little Parisian news. James Russell has been here for the last fortnight, and he and Tom Appleton set out a day or two ago for Switzerland. James Jackson left Paris for England day before yesterday, where he will stay a week or two and then return home. Hooper and Mason Warren go in about a month to Italy, and I remain quiet for the present. The Americans had a dinner as usual on the Fourth of July, where that inextinguishable old gentleman M. Lafayette and his progeny stirred up our patriotism with their presence. The partridges stuffed with truffles were good, no doubt, and the fifty wines worthy of praise, but the toasts were stale and the speeches farcical, to say nothing of the scrape's costing seven dollars to each enthusiastic republican. There was an incident which threatened mischief. After a few toasts had been drunk, there jumped up a naval officer at one end of the table. " Mr. President," said he, " I should like to know if this is a meeting of the Hartford Convention or of citizens of the United States?" He went on to say that the health of the President of the United States had been drunk without the requisite number of cheers! He was interrupted with hisses and other noises. But loudest and fiercest was Russell, who sat next to me but one. He got up — his moustaches curling like a sultan's — hissed in his very eyes — called on the company to cut off the buttons of his uniform and turn him out ; and this to an officer, a dead shot, who had killed his man already. He expected, and all those about him expected, that he would be challenged for the next morning ; but the table was very long, and the lieutenant's attention was taken up by another gentleman directly opposite him, whom he did challenge, and who refused on the score that he was a blackguard. The fellow was not in fact considered a gentleman, as we found out afterwards, and Russell got much credit for his spirit in resisting such an atrocious insult to the company.

The French are a restless people, — perhaps not

more so than others, but they are never quiet. Notwithstanding they made the government of Louis Philippe, there is no lack of grumblers against it. There is a notion that the old gentleman, who is said to be a cunning fellow, has slackened a little in his zeal for liberal principles. The papers talk without the slightest ceremony about his defection from the principles of the revolution of July. But nothing has excited more remark than the project of the government for erecting a large number of detached forts around the city. It appears from the plan that has been submitted that these forts, which are pretended to be for the defence of the city, are to be so placed as to command all its principal quarters, so that in the event of what kings call insurrection and people revolution, they may knock Paris to pieces with her own cannon. The king is caricatured without mercy. If you have ever seen his portrait you know that he has a narrow forehead and large fat cheeks. This has been ingeniously imitated by the outline of a pear; so that on half the walls of Paris you will see a figure like this, done in chalk or charcoal, with inscriptions, etc. In a more elaborate caricature, the people, under the shape of a porter, is represented as groaning under an enormous pear. I saw one the other day where the pear was cut open, — there was a great hollow, in which were the favorite ministers. These, however, are nothing, for they caricature everything and everybody. It is very likely that in the course of time they will have a sober revolution and a republic.

I do not think of anything of particular interest in the last week or two except what I have mentioned, and indeed Paris is the most retired place in the

world to live in if a man is busy. I think it strange
you have not written, but I should not think of worrying myself about it. . . . Love to all.

PARIS, *August* 13, 1833.

I cannot conceive why I have had no letters. I
suppose you must have written; be sure and direct
right, for I should really love to have a few words
from home. I am going on as usual, except that for
the present I dine in a French family, breakfasting
at the Café Procope, — the café of Voltaire, Rousseau, and Fontenelle. It is said that Rousseau used
to go there twice a week when his funds were in good
order, and once a week when he was low in the
pocket. Voltaire used to affect a particular table,
the place of which is pointed out. You must know
that the cafés are filled with little tables covered with
marble slabs and fixed to different parts of the room,
some for one person, some for two, some for four.
My most pleasant and original classmate, Morse, of
New Orleans, is living close to me at present — he and
a Philadelphian by the name of Stewartson, whom
Jackson introduced me to, and I frequently breakfast
together. I attend Louis at the Hospital of La Pitié
regularly at half after seven every morning. Monsieur, seeing me taking notes this morning, did me
the compliment to say, "Vous travaillez, monsieur,
c'est bien ça," — "you are working, sir, it is well,
that," whereat I was pleased. I showed him, a week
or two ago, a little medical contrivance of John
Jackson's which he requested me to mention, and
which pleased him so much that he has used it every
morning since. Our physicians of the old school
have not the slightest idea of the confidence and cer-

tainty with which such a man as Louis speaks of his
patients. If I was asked: Why do you prefer that
intelligent young man, who has been studying faithfully in Paris, to this venerable practitioner who has
lived more than twice as long? I should say: Because
the young man has experience. He has seen more
cases, perhaps, of any given disease; he has seen
them grouped so as to throw more light upon each
other; he has been taught to bestow upon them far
more painful investigation; he has been instructed
daily by men whom the world allows to be its most
competent teachers; by men who know no master and
teach no doctrine but Nature and her laws, pointed
out at the bedside for those to own who see them, and
for the meanest student to doubt, to dispute, if they
cannot be seen; he has examined the dead body
oftener and more thoroughly in the course of a year
than the vast majority of our practitioners have in
any ten years of their lives. True experience is the
product of opportunity multiplied by years, until we
come to a certain point, when years become a minus
quantity. The product is in proportion to both elements: If I have enjoyed opportunity (and improved
it) = 10 for ten years, my product may be stated at a
hundred; if for forty years, it will be greater, but not
four hundred; if my opportunity = 100, and I have
enjoyed it five years, I have five hundred for my
product, minus a slight discount, if you are very mathematical. I have written a page to show that it was
worth while in a professional point of view for me to
come to Paris. If I say more, I may get technical.
But merely to have breathed a concentrated scientific
atmosphere like that of Paris must have an effect on
any one who has lived where stupidity is tolerated,

where mediocrity is applauded, and where excellence is deified. The only difference between my present opinions and those I have often expressed on this subject before I left America is that I compared many of our physicians with what they ought to be, and now with what I see others are. There is not so much as might seem at first to be angry at; we are too far from the scientific centres of Europe, and the impulse given thirty years ago by the French pathologists to the severe study of medicine, accumulating up to the present moment, falls more fully on us than on our fathers, as it may leave us behind when it falls redoubled upon our children. These remarks are *sub rosâ*, and I expressly exclude from them a small number of individuals, among whom are more than one of " my very worthy and approved good masters." However, I have more fully learned at least three principles since I have been in Paris: not to take authority when I can have facts; not to guess when I can know; not to think a man must take physic because he is sick.

I am getting more and more a Frenchman. I love to talk French, to eat French, to drink French every now and then (these wines are superb, and nobody gets drunk, except as an experiment in physiology); and I do believe, if Napoleon was alive, and I stayed here much longer, I should want to fight a little ; but he is at St. Helena, and I must take off cases at the ward St. Charles. I meant to have given you a formidable account of some of the oddities of Paris, but I have no room. I was driven into a shop in a shower this morning, where I picked up three exquisite old engravings of Madame de Maintenon, Rousseau, and Molière. One's taste soon becomes refined here about such matters; I think myself quite a connoisseur.  I pique myself on not cramming my letters with French words.  Give my love to all, collateral and descending.

PARIS, *August* 30, 1833.

I begin this letter as I have all of late with a complaint of not receiving letters.  I cannot suppose but that you write, and am entirely unable to conceive why I hear nothing from you.  Although I go on the principle of not worrying myself, I confess it is not comfortable to be so long without one word from home.  I like the family where I dine very well indeed.  A good many of the Americans have boarded there before me, — Jackson, Greene, Warren, Hooper, and others.  Morse has left Paris for Spain within a few days.  Stewartson, the Philadelphian I have mentioned, is the only civilized countryman I see much of at present.  The Englishmen we meet at the hospital every morning have grown quite communicative and civil, and Sir —— ——, who appears as honest and profound an ass as is extant, extends his sagacious remarks in the most paternal manner to us untitled republicans.  There are two or three incidental advantages in living in Europe that are not to be forgotten, particularly by promising young men not exactly on a level with the information of the times.  One must pick up some notions on geography, for instance, and on politics.  One must get a few scattered ideas on history.  And a foreigner has this advantage, that when he is cornered on a weak point he cannot " shift his trumpet and only take snuff " — but find a difficulty in understanding the voluble Frenchman and shelter himself under an amiable ignorance of the language.  As for politics, as the journals make a part of breakfast universally at the cafés, it is impossible not to become gradually interested in their daily current. At the present moment the affairs of Portugal of course are absorbing the attention of everybody, and as we have the accounts every few days in Paris, our sensations are almost as vivid as mine used to be when I stood on the Common and heard the guns rattle and felt the air shake in those formidable sham fights that echoed from the plains of Watertown and Waltham. I have told you before that the present government of France was by no means free from opposition. The legitimists are for putting the young duke of Bordeaux, grandson of Charles X, on the throne; the young men are republicans; the polytechnic students want to fight; the people count up more than thirty thousand arrests that have taken place under Louis Philippe, and scowl at the power that decimates its own creators; every day fires squibs at the government from the journals and fills the windows with caricatures. Well, it is fortunate for me that I do not happen to take a revolutionary turn, or I might have had the pleasure, like a young man who boards at the same place with me, of being kept under lock and key at St. Pélagie through all the fine doings of July, and of having my room entered and finding myself and my friends in the guard-house under the name of a political association, as he did a few days ago.

The peaches, grapes, apples, and pears are as plenty as pebbles in Paris. It is a luxury to a Bostonian to find at one season the finest apricots and at another the most beautiful grapes at the corner of every street. They have a little sweet purple grape, which I saw selling this morning at three sous (or cents) the

pound.   The large white grapes, like those we have
at home, are getting every day more abundant; in
their full season they are not considered a luxury, but
form part of the food of the laborers.   You have no
idea of the use or necessity of bread at home, but
here it is the principal food of a large part of the
population.   They bake it in loaves of about a yard
long, which would be no despicable weapons in the
case of an invasion, for they are almost as strong as,
and larger than, the clubs of the New Zealanders.   I
must again express my surprise at not receiving any
letters, and if you have written, assure you that there
is some error in your way of directing or sending.
Give my love to all.

PARIS, September 28, 1833.

I am unwilling to let the packet go without taking
advantage of it, and I shall therefore send you a few
lines, the principal object of which is to let you know
that I am well, and to inquire again why I hear
nothing from you.   If the post has done its duty, you
have received more than a dozen letters from me, and
I have not had the shadow of an answer.   I am
entirely unable to account for it.   I cannot but suppose you have written several times, and what is the
reason I receive nothing is beyond my comprehension.
Everybody else is having news almost weekly from
home, and I am left as destitute of them as if I were
going to the North Pole out of the region of post-
offices.   There is no reason in the world why I should
not have letters every week with as much certainty as
if I were at New York.   The consequence is that I am
obliged to insist upon it, time after time, that every
letter may remind you how far my patience has been
taxed.   If I could only have news from home I should
be perfectly contented.

The more I become acquainted with the advantages
and the comforts of life in Paris, the more I am delighted with it. I have now become familiar enough
with the language to make out a conversation without
much difficulty. I have become acquainted with
some intelligent French students who are of assistance
to me in one way and another, and I acquire every
day the little practical matters of experience which
teach one how to make the most of such a city as
Paris. An American or an Englishman, when he first
comes to Paris, grumbles because his windows open
like folding-doors instead of up and down ; he wakes
up in the morning and frets because his breakfast is
not ready until ten o'clock ; he is unable to compre-
hend the graceful variety of his dinner, which, instead
of gorging him with a single dish until he loathes the
sight of it, presents a succession of pleasures which
it requires some cultivation to appreciate, as do the
results of all the other fine arts. Again, when our
stranger first comes to Paris he is always extravagant, and this for two reasons : first, because he is
under an excitement to find himself in a strange place,
and indifferent to the bare motive of economy ; and
next, because he is totally ignorant of the thousand
expedients for avoiding expense which have sprung
from the philosophy of the Parisians. Thus he pays
his *garçon* (servant) double what he ought to — he
gives money to the little rascally beggars who never
dare to ask it of a Frenchman — he takes a cabriolet
when he should take an omnibus — he calls for twice
as much at the *restaurateur's* as he wants — ignorant,
poor creature, that while the Englishman values everything in proportion to its price, the Frenchman's
eulogy is *magnifique et pas cher !* When I first came

to Paris I found my mind almost entirely dissipated, with my voyage and my trip in England and the new situation in which I found myself. It took me a good while to bring it back to its centre of equilibrum. However, I began immediately to attend my hospital through thick and thin, at first not understanding a word and by degrees getting a little insight into matters, and by perseverance and punctuality at my morning visit I soon found my interest in medicine become even stronger than before I left home. At present I am quite absorbed in my profession. I mean to take advantage of the museum and collections at the Garden of Plants to become somewhat acquainted with natural history.

A week ago we thought the cholera was about to make another serious irruption into Paris, but since it appears to have declined, and has passed out of notice. I am still at the same boarding-house. This living in a French family has had an admirable effect upon my proficiency in the language. I say it once more that I am living in every respect very happily, that I have every advantage of improvement, and that if I could only hear from home I should have nothing to complain of. I feel as if it was in vain to write, for I have no means of knowing whether my letters are received or not, but I shall do it and remind you that there is something a little neglectful in this obstinate silence. If you have written by the post and your letters miscarried, send them in future to Mr. Welles in Boston and he will transmit them. Give my love to all.

PARIS, *October* 22, 1833.

I always find myself in a little hurry when I sit down to write, — partly because I am generally pretty busy, and partly because I always put off writing on purpose as nearly as I can to the time of the packet's leaving.  I have made out in a week to get tolerably over my chagrin at that most intolerable business which prevented me from having my letters.  So I mean to wait in a philosophical spirit until you have got the letter which precedes the one I am writing, and our epistolary diplomacy has arrived at a stable conclusion.  I will explain to you in a few words how it happened.  When I called on Mr. Welles, or rather at his counting-room, soon after coming to Paris, I asked for letters ; was told there were none, — that if there were they would be sent to me.  Soon afterwards I changed my lodgings, and it was my impression that I gave them my new address.  However, they say I did not, and they ought to know.  I asked once or twice more for letters and received the same answer, that they would be sent to me.  This put me entirely at rest, because I knew that the other young [men] were receiving letters at their own houses in the same way, — and I went on in perfect confidence that, if they had letters, the men of business would not fail to send them to me ; therefore, as they did not send, there were none.  In the mean time I was going to the counting-room about once every other week, — as I do not draw a great deal at a time, — and they were accumulating letter after letter for me, without ever taking the trouble to mention it to me, or to inquire my address.  At last I became outrageous, went to the general post-office, found nothing, and then determined to go to Welles's and see if it was possible they could have kept letters for me and neglected to mention it, and at any rate to take measures immediately for having some news from

home by their means. What was my astonishment
when the clerk — one of two who speak English —
opened a common drawer and, pulling over a single
pile of letters, took out five for me, — four from home,
and one from James Russell at Amsterdam! I must
have been ten or twelve times at the counting-room
since the first was received, and they had given me
my money and suffered me to go away wondering
what was the reason why I had no letters like others,
and never asking the question — not through carelessness, but because I supposed it a matter of course
that a banker took cognizance of letters as much as
of other property intrusted to him for the benefit of
those who deal with him. I sent for the head clerk
and expressed my astonishment to him; his excuse
was an impudent one, — that it was a matter of favor
on their part to take charge of letters. In other
words, I consider it as a conviction of gross negligence
of the interests which the custom of business has
trusted to the banker's protection. Having read my
letters and found that everything was going on well
and pleasantly at home, I made up my mind not to
worry myself at all about the series of complaining
letters that must necessarily pass between us for a
month or six weeks, but to wait like a martyr until
my first letter should have time to cross the Atlantic
and settle the whole affair quietly.

You cannot have any idea of what a difference your
letters made in my feelings. I labored under a
double difficulty, — I had no news from home, and I
was uncertain whether or not you had received a single
letter from me. I wish to stop all your disagreeable
reflections, and *attendrissements*, as the French say, by
just remarking that time flies so fast here, and I have

been so much occupied, that I have had incalculably
little time to torment myself. So that it is rather
by the general quiet that hearing from America gives
one all day long than by any momentary sensations,
that we owe so much happiness to the packets and
post-office. Our news here does not amount to much.
The cholera has entirely subsided so far as I can see
or hear, — it was very slight in its prevalence. Day
before yesterday I had a letter from Hooper who, with
Mason Warren, was at Rome. I think I must contrive
to get into Italy before I leave Europe, — that is, if it
is in any way possible. I intend, however, to spend a
strictly, studiously, devotedly professional year before
I think of even tripping across the Channel for London. As for the science of England and France, or
rather Paris and London, — to judge by their books
and their students, and the reports of the intelligent
young men who have seen both, the Frenchmen have
half a century in advance. — George Crowninshield
has been here two or three weeks — George Gardner,
my old friend, about a week. I have amused myself
with giving them lessons in the art of eating French
dinners at the restaurants occasionally. The longer I
stay, the more facilities do I find to acquire instruction. When I write to Dr. Parsons, which I will do
when I can write to my own satisfaction, tell him he
may find some new notions, but that they come fresh
from the clinique and the dissecting-rooms of Paris.
I desire my best love to Mr. Upham, to Ann and the
young ones — to Dr. Parsons and Charles.

PARIS, *October* 30, 1833.

My room is all up in a heap, — my *garçon* being in
the commencing stage of an operation he performs

occasionally — that of setting it to rights.  I am sitting here like Marius at Carthage in the midst of my chaotic magnificence.  It is very fortunate for you indeed, for otherwise you might have had a letter with more French in it than you could have managed without the help of old Boyer. — Je me flatte que je suis bien fort là-dessus à présent, mais comme je suis un peu pressé, il faut que je parle cette bête d'Anglais — parole d'honneur, il me fâche, mais, 'cré nom d'un chien ! n' importe.  Everything is going on nicely here. George Gardner, I believe I told you, is here — I see him very often — the fellows are not back from Italy — the winter lectures are just commencing — in a few days.  The king of Belgium and his queen, Louis Philippe's daughter, are here.  I met them both in the rue Richelieu as they were entering Paris — two kings in one coach — the guest, and the host who went out some miles from Paris, and escorted him in. Whereby there was a great military ball at the Tuileries last night, and whereupon George Crowninshield and I, as we were returning from a visit to George Gardner, looked at the illuminated palace and drew invidious comparisons.  However, they say the Belgians hate King Leopold, and perhaps these newly got up kings are not over pleasantly situated.  I have not read the papers much lately ; the last thing interesting I saw was the declaration, or report, of the society of the " Rights of man."  Among the committee whose names were affixed to it was a young man who boarded at the same house I did, and whom I have mentioned to you before as having had solitude and seclusion added to his aids of reflection during the three days of July, by the cares of the *de facto* government, which is rather indifferent to the progress

of political metaphysics.    These good folks — the
society — are the legitimate descendants of the ancient
Jacobins, quote M. Robespierre with respect, reprint
the works of Marat, kicked up a row at the funeral of
General La Marck a year ago, and have a great disposition to disarrange the *ordre des choses*.    Their
last sentence is something like this, — "Kings, Ty-
rants, Aristocrats, whoever they may be, are slaves
revolted against the monarch of the earth, which is
the human race, and against the legislator of the
universe, which is nature."    So you see they have no
contemptible talent at manufacturing aphorisms.

And speaking of such matters, I went the other
night to see Mlle. Mars for the second time, — in
Moliére's Tartuffe.    She is now about fifty-eight years
old and, as you well know, the most celebrated living
actress in her line.    She had left the stage some years
ago, but having lost a good deal of money by specu-
lating in the funds, she returned to it once more.
Although she shows the effects of years, her face has
still great sweetness and dignity, her voice is perfectly
clear and pure, her pronunciation perhaps the best
model of classic French that exists, and all her deportment on the stage such as you might expect from the
unrivalled favorite for thirty or forty years, of the best
judging and most intellectual population of Europe.
There are nearly twenty theatres in Paris, and eight
or ten of them very large and beautiful.    Their prices
are generally moderate — their scenery fine — their
music excellent.    But perhaps in nothing are they
more preëminent than in the richness and truth of
costume, — a branch which has been entirely regenerated by the influence of Talma.    The other night at
the Théâtre Français, for instance, the costumes of

the seventeenth century were exceedingly striking, —
so much so that from that moment I shall date an
accurate idea of the gentleman under Louis XIV.  A
theatre like that is indispensable to the intelligent
foreigner, as an amusement, as giving him just notions
of past and present French manners in the different
classes, and as the best standard of the language.

There is no need of cutting or tearing off this
last page about theatres ; where society is far advanced they must exist and are a blessing ; they are
cherished and improved in proportion as it is enlight-
ened, and the outcry of civilized Europe would ex-
plode their assailants, were they not, in Europe, con-
fined to an inappreciable body of the community.  For
the rest, observe that I have not been zealous to send
home proofs every week that I had ideas different
from many that I love ; but as generations change if
they do not degenerate, you must excuse these little
remarks, and not waste your next letter in refuting
them. . . . I will tell my *garçon* that I have finished
my letter, and that he may go on setting things to
rights.  If George Gardner goes home in a month or
two, I will try to send some gimcracks.  Love to all.

P. S.  Best love to J. Jackson, and respects to his
father.  Can't have letters shown.  I will write a
show letter some day.

PARIS, *November* 29, 1833.

I know you must respect me for writing short letters in a hurry, because it shows that I have my hands
full of business.  It is true enough that I am avari-
cious of my time, because I want to learn more than
—— knows, and beat —— out and out in the nice
scientific touches.  I am, as usual, all medicine, getting up at seven and going to hospitals, cutting up,

hearing lectures, soaking, infiltrating in the springs of knowledge. There is a great deal more to be done than I was inclined to suppose, but the more the better, when one gets into good working trim. I suppose of course you wonder, in looking over my meagre letters, not to find them full of Parisian talk and gardens and statues and such; but to tell the plain truth, I see no more and hear no more of those things than you do. If you get discontented, send me word, and I will give up following the diseases of the skin at the Hospital St. Louis, cut off a slice from my daily anatomy, drop Broussais's lectures, take a fashionable journal, a box at the Italian opera, and become as amusing as possible. Well, you may depend upon it that we never gain without losing, and I suppose if I should make verses nowadays (which heaven forbid!) my readers would think I had not grown much the better poet for crossing the water. . . . Mr. W——— was polite enough; told me he met you, and that you had rather formidable ideas of Paris, and that you had some rather funny anxieties about my not getting money, and all that. Believe me, my untravelled reader, whatever clerk in a post-office you may be, that there is much humbug in the notions which vegetate in the twilight of villages. And, most of all, there is humbug in the notions of the difficulty of travelling and its arrangements. I should never want more than a day's notice to leave America for Europe, so far as *fixing* is concerned. Our fellows here get up from dinner some day and go off to Italy; in a month or two they come back again with their heads full of long stories to tell their grandchildren; or to Russia or Spain, and there is no more fuss about it than a Boston cockney would make about an excur-

sion to Fresh Pond, and about as little risk, if so be
that the cockney become mystified as usual, and has a
horse with the propension of the late Diamond or
Dolly. I shall stop. My letters are crisp, and snap
short off. I shall stop, first because I must breakfast, and, second, because I have a million of things
to do afterwards. . . . Give my love to all, and excuse me for hurrying to the Café Procope.

PARIS, December 13, 1833.

I must send you a few lines by the packet, although, as I have told you, my weeks have now very
little interest about them except such as is connected
with my studies. I received your letter of 7th November, and sympathized with your vexation, which I
hope was quieted before I got it. I told you my resolution, — not to worry or fret, but to wait quietly
until you should find that I had got all your letters
and was receiving them regularly. I have made out
to keep it very well, and as I am now old and tough,
— as the skim milk sentiment of my younger days has
hardened into the white oak cheese of maturity, you
need not suppose I allow myself to be disconcerted by
such matters. However, I was very sorry that you
should have been worried, and very glad that it was
all right at last. We are all very anxious about
James Jackson, whose sickness you have not mentioned, but who was in a very dangerous state when
our last account came. No one could excite a greater
interest in our minds on all accounts, — no young man
could be worse spared by his friends or by science.

The winter here is not very cold, but the streets are
all mud and trash. It is like walking on wet bar
soap. Wood is enormously dear. I have told you

that it was all humbug about living over cheap in
Paris.  I will say now that I cannot get along, and
that none of us do get along, without spending at the
rate of about six or seven thousand francs a year.
But in the mean time I am getting a library which
forms part of my stock in trade.  It is clear that I
shall be obliged to use my letter of credit before the
first year is out.  And what better can be done with
money than putting the means of instruction — the
certain power of superiority, if not of success — into
the hands of one's children?  Besides, economy, in
one sense, is too expensive for a student.  For my
part, I say freely that a certain degree of ease connected with my manner of living, — a tolerably good
dinner, a nice book when I want it, and that kind
of comforts, are in the place of theatres and parties,
for which I have less taste than many good fellows of
my acquaintance.  I can go home, if I must, but
while I am here I will not eat a dinner for twenty-five
sous and drink sour wine at a shabby restaurant.  In
this point I agree with the experience of the first
young men we have had here — Jackson — Gerhard
— Stewartson — all hard, very hard students, but who
utterly exploded the idea of getting along for less
than I have mentioned.  But let me say that I have
no disposition to extravagance, and that probably I
spend less money on pure gratification than most of
the young men with whom I associate.  To speak
definitely, you may consider my expenses as at least
twelve hundred dollars a year — books — instruments
— *private* instruction (which costs a good deal), and
everything included.  I tell you that it is not throwing away money, because nine tenths of it goes
straight into my head in the shape of knowledge.

And once for all I say that you may trust me, and I beg you to remember that, in being in Europe for my good, I am here for yours. If I should think best to go to Italy — let me go. If I should choose to spend a few months in London — let me go. I have told you all this about money matters beforehand, — as I was and am abundantly supplied without touching my letter for several months to come. I will only mention, as folks at home have odd notions sometimes, that I never risked a franc at any game in Europe, and that none of us Boston boys take to that amusement. To conclude, a boy is worth his manure as much as a potato patch, and I have said all this because I find it costs rather more to do things than to talk about them. Love to all. I suppose most of the family see my letters, or part of them.

PARIS, *December* 20, 1833.

I just write to tell you that I am quite well and wish you a happy new year, which will come rather late to be sure for the beginning of 1834. Nothing particular new in Paris. Lectures going on as usual, — new year is coming, and all Paris is getting ready to make presents. The shop windows are full of everything which can do duty as a new year's present. It is really cheerful to see such a tumult of preparation, — the whole city seems to have received an impulse from it. It is the custom here for gentlemen to call upon ladies on the new year's day with some gallant offering or other, and get a kiss for their trouble. Everybody whom you have the habit of employing, — *par exemple* your *garçon* at the boarding - house — at your café — your restaurant — the man that brings you letters, etc., expect to be remembered, and it is said they always make the first advances by offering you sweetmeats or some such matter. The display of bon-bons, that is to say sugar things, is *tout à fait magnifique.* I do not know anything that would be more characteristic to send home, but it is a good deal of trouble. The crack shops in Paris cut out Washington Street; particularly their contents show off — as in several of them — through a window formed of a single plate of glass as big as a moderate sized barn door.

I have no time to write you a letter to-day — but I just learned that it was the day for writing, which I had forgotten, and so I determined to send a sheet of paper at any rate.

I suppose of course at this season you receive my letters very irregularly because the winds are generally unfavorable for ships returning ; but we get our letters from twenty to thirty days after they are written.

I am obliged to go straight to the Ecole de Médecine, and must snip the thread of my document.

Paris, *January* 13, 1834.

I received yesterday your two very nice and kind letters of December 3d and December 13th. This morning I had a letter brought me from Dr. Parsons dated December 8th. I am very happy to find that you are all well and cheerful. I am delighted at several circumstances mentioned in these different communications. First, I am delighted at the mutual charity of the parish and their former minister. I am delighted to hear that the young man and the boys behave themselves and study. . . . I am delighted to hear that they had a slight row in the prints about

phrenology. (This is from the Doctor's letter.) I
am delighted to know that you know, that I have
received your letters — as you will soon be delighted
to know that I know that you know, that I have received your letters. I am delighted at the Doctor's
advice to go to Italy in the spring, for I have thought
for some time of going with Bowditch. There are
many reasons in favor of this: first to refresh my
body and mind after such a campaign of labor and
confinement — next to see the world — and lastly to
go in good company; for Bowditch is an excellent fellow, and there are not probably a dozen young men in
the country whose name is so powerful an introduction in Europe. This is the gay season and lots of
fun going, of course. Did you ever go to the Italian
opera? Did you ever hear Julie Grisi? Or Rubini?
Or Tamburini? Or Santini? Did you ever go to a
masked ball at the Royal Opera? Did you ever see
a row at the Odéon? But I forget, — you are probably not even aware that the *obélisque* of the Luxor is
now lying just beyond the Pont de la Concorde. And
by the way I suppose this is the first great *obélisque*
brought to Europe from Egypt since the time of the
old Romans. The officious *bêtes* here are getting up
a ball to be given by the American gentlemen to the
American ladies. I suppose I shall be pulled in with
the rest to spend some fifty francs for a parcel of
folks I do not know or care much about. . . . I suppose I shall add a few lines to-morrow morning and
hurry off my letter

> . . . but half made up
> And sent into the post before its time.

Morning of the 14th. Must hurry as usual. I
want you to tell me all about J—— F——; try to

get up a match between him and his prototype, widow
———. I think I shall write to John the next time.
I shall have to root up his prejudices as an elephant
might be supposed to twist out turnips. . . . I think
by the time I go to London, after a good training in a
first-rate Parisian *clinique*, I shall be *fort* enough on
pathological anatomy to make myself intelligible to
the *conservatore* of the Hunterian museum. . . .

It rains forever here. . . . The last caricature in
the *Charivari* was as follows: France, as a fair
maiden with a mural crown upon her head, is walking
in a storm, — Louis Philippe holds out over her his
famous revolutionary umbrella (an old-fashioned, re-
publican-looking one, such an one as Dunnum used
to carry his aunt home with) ; she turns mildly
round, — "Vous me crottez, mon cher." You will
hardly believe it, but the universality of the joke
about the pear is such that if you ask for a pear at
a restaurant you are liable to have your head cut off
for high treason, or at least create a stare and a smile
in the whole company. . . . Love to all.

Paris, February 14, 1834.

I have been so idle or so busy that I have not written by the last two packets. But I wrote a monstrous
professional letter to Dr. Parsons a fortnight ago, and
I told him to send you word that he had received
*mes nouvelles*, as the French, my worthy compatriots,
call it. There has been a good deal of fun going
on lately here. I believe I have not told you of the
American ball. Well, I did not go to it ; first, because I did not want to — and second, because I did not
choose to spend seventy-five francs for a parcel of
folks of whom I knew little more than that they were

raised on the same side of the water as I was. Two
things happened : there was a row as usual, — Mr.
Barton, secretary of the legation, was refused admittance because he did not bring his card ; he had his
wife with him ; he saw fit to knock down, which being
translated means to strike, the servant — to talk hard
at the managers — and there were some probabili-
ties of a duel between him and one of the managers.
The next thing was that the managers found their
ball cost more than the subscription amounted to, and
" would be glad of a little assistance," to which the
non-subscribers said they did not encourage mendi-
cants and requested them to apply to the parish.
Some proposed a cent society to be instituted, others
were for a Dorcas sewing association. Speaking of
duels, I suppose you have heard of the famous one
about a fortnight ago between two members of the
Chamber of Deputies, — M. le général Bugeaud and
M. Dulong. One of Dulong's seconds was George
Washington Lafayette. M. Dulong was shot through
the head — the ball striking on the external part of
the orbital process, etc., as said M. Jules Cloquet in
his interesting report *là-dessus*. Dulong was a great
republican ; the government were afraid of mischief
at his funeral, — for they remembered that of La
Marck, — and took their precaution. The procession
was embedded in a mass of soldiery, and at different points artillery-men stood over their cannon with
*lighted matches* in their hands. The people did nothing
but unharness Lafayette's horses and drag his coach
in triumph. You know, I suppose, that he is alienated
from the present government ; but it can hardly seem
credible to you that a man, whose life seems to belong
to a preceding age, is still an idol of the people, and

that, if the circumstances of the nation should require it, he must be called upon once more to act as the dictator in their emergency.

The carnival days have just passed, and I believe it is Lent now, according to the almanack, for the people think a good deal more of the fun that precedes than of the fasting that follows. Last Tuesday was Mardi Gras. On that occasion a fat ox is carried about in a stately procession, and all the world, masked or unmasked, appear in their equipages on the boulevards. It is doubtless one of the most brilliant shows in the world. I suppose several hundred thousand people must have been on the boulevards. Among the masks were two people in a barouche dressed as white bears; but perhaps the best was a caricature of an English lady on horseback; it was annihilating. One coach with four horses had its whole harness and reins richly gilded; some of the barouches were full of masks, who pelted the people with bon-bons. One of the most striking differences in Europe and our own country with regard to little matters is in the appearance of servants. In an English inn the head waiter appears to you sometimes as an elegant and courtly young man; at others with a graver aspect, much that of a professor in one of our higher colleges on a public occasion. The livery servants, as I saw them on the coaches the other day, were fine, tall, handsome men with rich uniforms, *chapeaux bras*, and stately plumes. I saw Mlle. Mars again over here at the Odéon the other evening. A fine old gentleman in one of the boxes, who seemed to be an Englishman, cried like a baby. Oh, if Talma were alive! But all this is nothing to medicine. Lectures are going on as usual, and I am working as hard as ever. In my next letter I must contrive to give you some hints from the hospital St. Louis on certain matters. In the mean time, bad correspondent as I am, you must contrive to prevent any of my dear friends and relations from getting outrageous, by the customary phrases, "much engaged in his profession," "time entirely occupied," and the rest. Love to all.

PARIS, *April* 30, 1834.

As there is not any packet for the first of this month, I shall leave these few words to go by the next. To-morrow, Hooper, Mason Warren, and myself set out for Strasbourg to make a little tour in Belgium, Holland, perhaps Prussia, and then to England. I have only time to say a few words. I have spent a year, within a few weeks, in Paris. In that time my expenses have been seven thousand francs, — that is to say, about as much as those of my companions. I have lived comfortably, liberally if you please, but in the main not extravagantly. I have employed my time with a diligence that leaves no regrets. My aim has been to qualify myself so far as my faculties would allow me, not for a mere scholar, for a follower of other men's opinions, for a dependent on their authority, but for the character of a man who has seen, and therefore knows; who has thought, and therefore has arrived at his own conclusions. I have lived among a great, a glorious people; I have thrown my thoughts into a new language; I have received the shock of new minds and new habits. I have drawn closer the ties of social relation with the best-formed minds I have been able to find from my own country; and, few though they have been, I think I may say that I have friends in at least two of our cities and a home at least in one. I hope you do not think your money wasted. For my own part, I am perfectly certain that I might have lived until I was gray without acquiring the experience I have gained in part, and hope still farther to improve by changing the scene of my life and studies.

The papers will have told you what the tumult in Paris after the affairs in Lyons amounted to. A few barricades were raised, but no general movement was made by any party. The rioters were all killed up without ceremony. On the Sunday morning, when they were anticipating some formidable occurrence, there was a review of the troops, who were mustered around the Tuileries. The soldiery make a most superb appearance. It is something I never expected to find realized in my own sight, something of which a militia muster can give you no idea, to see the long line of cuirasses glittering on the bosoms of tall, broad, stately Norsemen, and the lancers with their little tri-colored pennons floating from their unamiable weapons, and those dense masses of infantry with their bayonets undulating and sparkling under your window; and all this with the music of a hundred instruments ringing and rolling around you. There are other ideas to be got of the French people and the French soldiers besides those in Hogarth's pictures, or Goldsmith's poor soldier, or Mr. Coleridge's cockneyisms.

Mais c'est assez, je m'en vais, et il faut finir. I shall write next from London, perhaps; perhaps from Strasbourg; I do not know.

It is late, and I am sleepy. I must ride three days and three nights in succession to get to Strasbourg, and I therefore bid you good-night.

Love to all. Much letter-writing is out of the question except for gentlemanly young folks that do not get tired with study before evening. I am not half as communicative as I expected to be.

LONDON, June 13, 1834.

Although I have not quite finished my continental story, I must put off the sequel and tell you what I have been about in London. We arrived on Sunday, somewhere about the 20th of May, I suppose, for I scorn chronology, and having piled our baggage upon that beast of burthen which men call a porter, we trudged to find St. Paul's coffee-house, where we were advised to go by an erratic Dutchman we twice fell in with on our travels. Of course after the gayety of a Parisian Sunday, there was somewhat of the austere, not to say the repulsive, in the bald streets and set faces which form such a contrast with the exhalation of happiness that hovers around the sister capital when the seventh day dawns, — rather jocundly, but welcomed in their fashion by a great people, who have as much right to their opinions as this nation of sulky suicides. Now with London you are perfectly familiar. You know the Thames runs east and west, as one may say, and I will gorgeously illustrate the matter on the top of the next page, if you will forgive my " flare-up " about Sunday in London. . . . The London of story-books is the city, but the London of fashionable novels nowadays is Westminster, and only the west part of that. In the city proper are the Tower and St. Paul's, and shops, and counting-houses, and everything vulgar. Finally, on the southern side, or in Southwark and the neighboring parts, I suppose there may be something interesting, but I have not heard of anything but Vauxhall, I believe. . . . Well, of course you understand that the distinctions of these different parts are more in name than reality, for the whole is one " tarnation lot of housen."  So under the shadow of St. Paul's, in that saint's coffee-house, did we depose ourselves on that memorable Sunday, choosing to make our début in that humble spot rather than in the saloons of the Clarendon, or beneath the pillared domes of Regent Street.  After abiding in the same place a day or two we proceeded to look for lodgings, and having looked at several, and being in a paroxysm of the economical, we at last subsided upon the floors of the interesting Mrs. Peters, beneath whose wings we have remained until now, so much pleased that we present her with two pounds ten a week, conjointly, and intend to do so while we remain with her. For this money we have our sty — but we must fill our own trough — or to speak less irreverently, we pay besides for the abominable breakfast we insult ourselves with, and we dine at some hotel or chop-house. For a fortnight, I believe, we did nothing but grumble.

Well, now it is enough to say that, in a great measure through the kindness of Mr. Clift, which I owe to Dr. Parsons's letter, we have entrance to almost all the hospitals, and attentions from their physicians. At the present moment my letter is clipped by being obliged to whistle down to St. Thomas to see Mr. Green operate, and my letter must go, clipped or not clipped.  However, I shall write somewhat liberally while I am here, and I will try to send you two letters while I am here. . . . Though I am living pretty reasonably, I should feel comfortable to know that I had a little longer credit on this side the water ; but this I have told you, and I have no doubt you will do your best.  Love to all.

*June* 21, 1834.

I have no very particular story to tell of the last week. I have been at different hospitals looking at the different manifestations of the English spirit of quackery. I will say that some of the medical people have been very polite to us — and indeed without the personal interest of somebody it is impossible to see anything in this country. . . . About medical matters you do not much care, I suppose; so I will say what sights I have seen, and then briefly bring up the history of my late travels. . . . And, first, let me tell you that one soon acquires a wonderful apathy to sights, and that one, after a while, goes still farther and avoids all sightseeing where he has no particular fancy for the thing to be seen, and where he dares to leave it unseen.

*Sights I have seen. Westminster Abbey.* A great gothic church, not half as handsome as Nôtre Dame outside, but finer in the interior, — the gothic arches remarkably narrow, — fine monuments, — Poet's Corner, — 1s. 3d. to pay, etc. See all tourists. One of the finest monuments is to the memory of an Admiral Holmes, — not the Dryden one, I think. . . . Henry the 7th's chapel, — a piece of stone filigree work as big as Holden Chapel, — surpassingly fine. Do you know what a flying-buttress is? Well, on the flying-buttresses of this chapel are figures of animals, — lions, bears, and hippogriffic monsters, as if crawling down. This is the oddest thing about it, — the most wonderful is the extent and delicacy of the carving all over the outside of the building. . . . I heard the Bishop of Gloucester preach a stupid sermon the other day in Westminster Abbey.

*Mr. Irving.* I heard this notorious preacher the

other Sunday. He is a black, savage, saturnine, long-haired Scotchman, with a most Tyburn-looking squint to him. He said nothing remarkable that I remember, and I should suppose owes much of his reputation to a voice of great force and compass, which he managed nearly as well as Macready. The charlatan he most resembles is Mr. ——, whose yell is, however, instinct with a profounder expression of vulgarity and insolence. Mr. Irving and his flock have given up the unknown tongue, and confine themselves to rolling up their eyes so as to show the whites in a formidable manner. I would ask for no better picture than has been presented by these poor enthusiasts, drunk with their celestial influences and babbling paltry inanities.

*The royal family.* I went last night to the royal opera, where they were to be in state. I had to give more than two dollars for a pit ticket, and had hardly room to stand up, almost crowded to death. The Duchess of Kent and the Princess Victoria — a girl of fifteen, and heir of the throne — came in first on the side opposite the king's box. The audience applauded somewhat — not ferociously. . . . The princess is a nice fresh-looking girl, blonde, and rather pretty. The king looks like a retired butcher. The queen is much such a person in aspect as the wife of the late William Frost, of Cambridge, an exemplary milkman, now probably immortal on a slab of slatestone as a father, a husband, and a brother. The king blew his nose twice, and wiped the royal perspiration repeatedly from a face which is probably the largest uncivilized spot in England. . . . I have a disposition to tartness and levity which tells to the disadvantage of the royal living and the plebeian defunct, but it is accidental and must be forgiven. . . .

*St. Paul's.* Admittance two pence, but additional fees required by the banditti who show the different parts of the house, — "but ye have made it a den of thieves." I suppose it is necessary; so I took two pence worth of the magnificence. It is monstrous high to look up to the interior of the dome. The triumphal flags are no great things, and I thought the statue of Nelson rather a poor concern, but I will look again. The outside is very fine, which is more than can be said of most of the public buildings. . . .

*Bridges.* These are the finest structures of the metropolis, "worthy of the days of Semiramis and Ninus," or Cheops, as somebody says. The Tower and the tunnel I have not yet seen. I am off for Scotland or Ireland about the first of July to make a little excursion, which I shall render as short and cheap as I can, for otherwise I shall get out of money. . . . I shall try to get back to Paris as soon as I can, where I hope I shall find something to replenish my pockets, which are melting away somewhat. Travelling is necessarily an extravagance. Some remarks on Dutchmen in my next letter may be expected. I have only had one letter for the last month, but I expect a packet from Mr. Welles before long. . . . Give my love to all.

LONDON, *July* 25, 1834.

In my history of our late tour we had got to Rotterdam, which was the first place we arrived at in Holland, and to which we returned from Amsterdam in order to sail for London. Though possessing great interest, the history of our Dutch experience may be brief.

*Scenery.* Alike throughout, — wide plains, cut as

true as if made by a spirit level, bursting with a most riotous vegetation, intersected by dikes of all sizes, and sprinkled with cattle, the most beautiful from their shape and their almost invariably mixed or calico colors I have ever seen. In the background windmills *ad libitum*, — here and there a boat that seems as if it were pushed along on the grass, as you are unable to distinguish the ditch it is in.

*Windmills.* In immense numbers; I counted *fifty* from the coach window in a single part of the landscape, and it is said that around Saardam, or in it, are several thousand.

*Canal-Boats.* Very neat things, and may often be seen in a canal parallel to the road, but are soon left out of sight by the coach. The horse draws them by an awfully long rope.

*Flower Gardens.* We saw some pretty ones, but the best sight of that kind was the collection of tulips at Haarlem, which were very fine. Every now and then at the side of the road we saw a country-seat with a lawn separating you from the house, which looked very beautiful and English. The aspect of a Dutch town is much as I expected, and of course quite peculiar. Brick houses with sharp roofs, green blinds, generally small and not more than two or three stories high, with remarkably pretty iron fences before them, — odd names and signs up at the windows, — here and there the inscription, "Dis haus is te huur," which we supposed meant : this house is to let, — at intervals the figure of a man opening his jaws as if to bolt a score of pills, the sign of the apothecary shops, — here a street and there a canal, — here a hackney coach on wheels, and there one which is dragged over the smooth flagstones on runners, —

such are the images that rise to my mind when I think
of Rotterdam or Amsterdam.

*Dutchmen and Dutchwomen:* they do not differ so
much from other folks as one might suppose, — they
are not much broader or shorter. We did not see
half so much smoking as in Germany. Our opinion
with regard to the attractions of the Dutch *vraws* or
*fraus* was far from unfavorable. Their style of beauty
is more like that of the English than the French, —
and indeed the Dutch folks look generally somewhat
like them.

While at Amsterdam we made two excursions, — or
rather both in one, for it was all in one ride. The
first was to a village called *Broek*. This place contains between one and two thousand souls, who, or
their bodies, are engaged principally in making cheese
and butter and in scrubbing down. No vehicle ever
is allowed to enter this town. You leave your equipage at a tavern just outside, and walk into the village. The streets are every day washed and look like
a clean brick hearth. In every house you perceive a
door of rather a large size for the building, and generally ornamented with architectural decorations. This
door is never opened except at christenings, marriages,
and funerals, and the room into which it opens is only
visited to be kept in order, excepting on the same
occasions. In this room are collected the valuable
furniture — the pictures and memorials of the family.
We had the good fortune to have admittance to one
of these — a blind being partially opened to throw a
dim religious light on the solemn chamber, with its
broad and bright tables and stately wardrobe, its
dainty chairs, its quaint china, and all its unsunned
relics.

It is a sweet village — still as the tomb, for the jar
and noise of wheels cannot reach it, — and all that
is not luxuriant greenness is pure and still water,
with a little boat here and there on it, — and then
the arbors, with strange wooden figures to cheat the
stranger — of a parson with his book, of an old
woman at her spinning-wheel, — it is a rum place to
look at and an odd one to live in.

Well, one thing more and I must be off to St. Bar-
tholomew's Hospital. This is Saardam. It was here
that Peter the Great worked as a ship carpenter for
some years, and his room and the closet where he slept
are still shown, and indeed were visited a few years
ago by the Emperor Alexander, who had a brick building put around the wooden house, and commemorated
his visit by a tablet in the walls of Peter's room.
Well, as I said, I must be off to the hospital, and try
to find something more interesting for the next time.
Love to all.

PARIS, September 3, 1834.

Me voilà revenu. Once more in the gay, the glorious city, where I have passed so many happy days.
I wrote you last, I believe, from Liverpool. I strolled
about the city in the evening, and next morning got
upon the coach for Birmingham. However, as I am
not certain whether I told you, I will say once more
that I arrived at Manchester, intending to go straight
to London, but the idea of the railway was so tempting that I ordered a hasty dinner, clapped my luggage and myself upon one of the steam carriages, and
was in Liverpool in an hour and a half, having gone
considerably more than twenty miles an hour, and not
making a very short passage either, for they have been
the whole distance (thirty-two or thirty-four miles) in

an hour. Well, then, after seeing Liverpool, the next day I rode about a hundred and twelve or fourteen miles to Birmingham, and the next day a hundred more to London. I always ride, you know, on the outside. This is much cheaper and pleasanter. The coaches carry but four inside passengers, and eleven outside. But the macadamized roads are so perfectly hard and smooth that coaches rarely overturn or break down. In going down hill they always *shoe* one of the hind wheels. *Eh bien!* I was once more at London. I stayed three days, and was delighted beyond measure at finding two letters for me, for I had begun to feel desolate at remaining so long without any news from home. I was set at ease at once by finding all were well and cheerful, and I have got another letter of July 24th since my arrival which was equally pleasant. I took it into my head to return to Paris by the Dover and Calais road. So on the first day I rode to Dover. As we passed by Gravesend we saw the royal yacht, escorted by two steamboats, returning up the Thames with the Queen on board, who had been on a visit to her cousins of Germany. We passed through Canterbury, too, when, in defiance of the coachman's orders, I took a peep at the cathedral. I slept that night at Dover, and the next morning got into the steamboat, which carried us across the Channel in a couple of hours. There was quite a heavy swell, so that the poor wretches round me said their breakfast backwards — many of them, — but we old sailors, who have seen whales and icebergs and such like, are not so extravagant of our victual. Now I, who have read Sterne's *Sentimental Journey*, determined to see the scene of his adventure at Calais. And, sure enough, M. Dessein keeps the same hotel that Sterne has immortalized; therefore, I had my luggage carried to the Hôtel Dessein, and, inquiring for the *remise*, etc., I got upon a coach-box, and read the " Preface in the *désobligeante*." M. Dessein, who is a meek-looking little man, answered all my questions very civilly, which plainly accounted for the wine's costing just three times as much as in the Palais Royal.

> Once more upon the *diligence*; once more
> The horses jog before me like a flock
> That knows no leader.

The cathedral at Amiens was the only remarkable thing upon the route. After riding two days and two nights, the morning found us close to Paris. But before we reach Paris, at a distance of five or six miles, we pass through St. Denis, where is the church which has received for centuries the remains of the French monarchs. There is the spire that so sickened the heart of Louis XIV that he left his palace of St. Germains and founded that of Versailles, in a spot where he might look from his window without seeing his sepulchre in the horizon. And now we are on the road which St. Denis, the headless martyr, walked over, to lay his mutilated body on the spot where the church now stands, and over which St. Louis bore the body of his royal father to its burial-place, and over which passed the footsteps of that fierce multitude who tore the relics of their kings from the tombs, and tossed side by side into a single pit the bones of Carlovingian, Merovingian, and Capetian. . . . And there is the Dome of the Invalides, and to the left is the Panthéon, and there rise the square, solemn towers of Nôtre Dame. N'est-ce pas que c'est

très bien fait tout celà?  Voilà une description vrai-
ment magnifique.

I hope Mr. Upham is not seriously out of health.
Give my love to all.  Mr. Welles let me have what
money I wanted, but I do not like to borrow.

P. S. . . . As for abridging my stay in Paris, a few
reasons will soon convince you on that matter.  I am
just going to become a member of a society of medical
observation, which comprehends some of the most intelligent young French and foreign students.  I have
free access to the wards of M. Louis, a favor which he
has granted only to a few; James Jackson was one of
them; and, besides, there are subjects which I have
scarcely touched, and which I *must* study in *Paris.*
It is not a selfish matter; I am devoted to my profession, and I wish to return second to no young man
in it.  I think I shall be much more moderate in my
expenses; I will try, at any rate.

PARIS, *October* 6, 1834.

I know you will not find fault if I send a short
letter now and then, when you know that it shows I
am occupied.  Paris is full of good news just now.
Hooper and Warren have got back from England,
and so I am no more alone; and yesterday John's
classmate, or sophomore, Inches, who has taken his
degree, arrived in Paris, and we all dined together in
jubilee at the Café de Paris.

Everything is now perfectly favorable to my progress in my studies.  I am master enough of the language to take a case from a patient, write it off, read
it uncorrected, and defend it against criticism, in a
society of Frenchmen.  There will be no difficulty in
my obtaining any advantages I may desire here.  My

belonging to the society I have mentioned brings me into contact with young men in confidential stations in most of the hospitals, lays their experience before me, and puts me under the obligation to be exact, methodical, and rigorous. Besides, as I told you before, I have undisputed entrance at all times to two wards, containing together a hundred beds, generally full, where I examine and pound and overhaul the patients before even Louis or his *interne* have seen them. Nothing but private personal favor would give anybody this extraordinary privilege. I owe it in a great measure, perhaps, to the favorable introduction given me by poor Jackson, and to the very high character which he and one or two others of a similar stamp have established for the better class of American students. . . .

I wish you would tell me something of my most excellent and very dear instructor, Dr. Jackson. Next to my own family, there is no one in the world that I long so much to see. I beg, if you should see any of the family, you would offer them the kindest remembrances from one who has lost one of his most esteemed friends in the son, and who can never forget and never repay the advantages he has derived from the inestimable instructions of the father.

I have not heard of Mr. Upham for a good while, and Dr. Parsons has not written to me. But give my love to them and all.    .

*October* 22, 1834.

Short letters, — jammed, crowded like an ill-packed portmanteau with a few things of consequence so hustled together as to seem to fill it. These are all you are like to get at present from your most obedient and occupied correspondent. We have two accessions to our Parisian society, — Inches, whom I believe I mentioned before, and the individual commonly designated as the elder B——.  He began, the first day of his arrival, to rectify our opinions on the French wines, — of which he had just thirty-six hours' experience, — and will probably soon establish a school for the education of children in the French language. This is only a scandal — the youth no doubt is estimable, and besides when only three of us dined together we did not eat up all the soup — so it is a great pleasure to have a fourth corner of our table filled up.  There is no very particular news except the burning up of parliament, and a terrible quarrel between some doctors, with a duel or two, and three pamphlets *là-dessus* — which dropped from the press in as rapid succession as leaves from the forest.  I had no particular interest in any of the parties concerned, much to my satisfaction.

I received this week a letter from my old friend John Sargent, which I shall answer *tout de suite.* He wants me to write in the *New England Magazine* which he and Dr. Howe — the Grecian and blind-compelling Dr. Howe — have bought.  I have entirely relinquished the business of writing for journals and shall say No, though Minerva and Plutus come hand in hand to tear me, the Cincinnatus of Science, from the ploughtail she has commanded me to follow. How much I must learn — how hard I must work, before I have wrought this refractory ore into good tough, malleable, ductile, elastic iron.

Have you got any news — any scandal — any fun, from the ancient seat of learning ?  How come on the *bourgeoisie* of the community?  What offspring of the classic soil has been baptized in Castaly, through

the munificence of the departed Hopkins? How
flourish the red and white roses of orthodoxy and het-
erodoxy? What is the success of ——? How are
the numerous wall-flowers, or rather stock-gilly flowers, that garnish the trim garden edges of Cambridge
society? — Answer such questions and similar such.

Give my love to all, and tell Dr. Parsons that he
has not written to me. Say to Mr. Upham that
when I think of the Japan cigar box and the slight
indisposition which used to justify him in his unusual
indulgence in its luxuries, — when I think of the long
talks over the fire and all the doctrines therein held,
I should like to have something to remind me of them
in the shape of a letter.

Tell Ann to measure exactly the height of the principal children, and send it to me, together with that of
Charles, that I may mark them against the wall. Do
not make the children study too hard, and remember
that if they grow up stout and healthy they can learn
as much as they will want by and by, if they have the
proper habits of acquiring knowledge, which are
better than any quantity of ill-packed knowledge
itself — as is well remarked by Zoroaster.

### TO JOHN O. SARGENT.

PARIS, *November* 2, 1834.

DEAR JOHN, — I am sorry that a year and a half of
absence, in the midst of circumstances which are very
favorable to some faculties of the mind, have so
weaned me from some of my old habits that I may
be less useful, I hope not less agreeable, to one who
has so often borne me company — shoulder to shoulder
— quill to quill — paragraph to paragraph — in more
than one aspiring periodical. Alas, my dear editor!

the blossoms of my flaunting youth have fallen, and
I am watching day and night over the cold, green,
unripened fruit that must supply their places.  The
nature of the studies which I am pursuing, the singular advantages which I am at present enjoying, and
the number of the objects which absolutely require
my attention have induced — have forced me rather,
to forbid myself any diversion from the path of my
professional studies.  I am very unwilling to desert
you, and I will not do it without giving you the best
reasons for doing it, even at the double risk of over-
rating the importance of any literary services I could
render, and of trumpeting my own ardor of application.  I am at the present moment living not merely
the most laborious, but by far the most unvaried and
in its outward circumstances most unexciting mode
of life that I have ever lived.  Nearly five hours in
the day I pass at the bedside of patients, and you
may imagine that this is no trifling occupation, when
I tell you that it is always with my note-book in my
hand; that I often devote nearly two hours to investi-
gating a difficult case, in order that no element *can*
escape me, and that I have always a hundred patients
under my eye.  Add to this the details and laborious
examination of all the organs of the body in such cases
as are fatal — the demands of a Society of which I
am a member — which in the course of two months
has called on me for memoirs to the extent of thirty
thick-set pages — all French, and almost all facts
hewn out one by one from the quarry — and my out-
of-door occupations have borne their testimony.

You may suppose, then, that if I can devote three
or four hours every day to my books — which I always
endeavor to do — the electricity for that day is pretty

thoroughly drawn off, and in fact if I, who somewhat labor in literary parturition, were to attempt that which invariably exhausts my powers, I should wrong myself for too small a matter. No, John, a heavier burden from my own science, if you will, but not another hair from the locks of Poesy, or it will be indeed an ass's back that is broken. I am not ashamed of the ambition of being distinguished in my profession; but more than that, I have become attached to the study of truth by habits formed in severe and sometimes painful self-denial. For, trust me, the difficulties in the investigations of our profession, the carelessness and stupidity — often the obstinacy — of patients, the cold and damp and loathsomeness of the dissecting-room, are exceedingly repulsive to the beginner; and I am sorry to say are sufficient to prevent the great majority of students from becoming properly acquainted with the science they profess to cultivate. I have said enough, and I am afraid too much, and you will do as I have done in running over the leaf before you. If some poor feeling of vanity should appear in my justification, remember that there are waters enough between us to wash it out.

I promised myself, when I left America, to write a great many letters to my friends, and you among the first, and I write none except to my own family. All the novelty of European life soon dies away upon the eyes and ears of those long in the midst of it, assimilated to the mind of the individual as his daily food is assimilated to his body, with like ease whether it be bun or *brioche*, roast chicken or *poulet à la Marengo;* and so one soon has lost the power of writing a letter of impressions — it becomes a matter of analysis — of reflection — and that is study, a study

which I shall not attempt until I write a rigmarole
for my children or the family library. I desire all
manner of success to your enterprise, and regret that
I must not participate in it. You have taste and
talent. If you have calculated your chances, and if
you have perseverance, I have no doubt that you will
do well.

TO HIS PARENTS.

PARIS, November 4, 1834.

DEAR FATHER AND MOTHER, — I write, because I
suppose you love to see a sheet of paper with the
Paris postmark upon it, rather than because I have
anything very particular to say. In short, if I depended on the incidents only that surround me, I
never passed a time more without excitement than
the present. Hard work — " digging," as we used to
say — oscillation from three or four fixed points backwards and forwards — make up my existence. As
for all of the great city that I trouble myself with,
you might almost put it in a vignette. But I am getting formidably wise, and that is the main thing.
Lectures are just beginning, and all the gigantic
machinery of the Parisian Ecole de Médecine is
about to shake the " quartier Latin " with its thrill
of activity. French is a second mother tongue to me
almost. On many subjects I not infrequently think
in it, — and how can it be otherwise when a man is so
immersed in the atmosphere of it, and when so many
of his ideas come through its mediation? It is quite
pleasant to multiply in this way the medium of solution for one's thoughts — and, to express an idea to
yourself with exactness, to be able to make change as
it were by means of two different metals. . . .

Our little set here are on the most amiable terms

together, and, as you know, the Boston party is the predominant one so far as there is any such division. If I should class the young men who have been out here from our three great cities, I should say that I consider that Boston went first, Philadelphia second, and after a long, long interval comes limping in New York. However, Philadelphia may dispute us the palm, and I for one will try to make her work for it. One of the greatest pleasures of living abroad is to meet in such an easy, pleasant sort of a way people from all quarters of the world. Greek and Barbarian, Jew and Gentile, differ much less than one thinks for at first, and this you never learn from books — or never believe. They know it well here, and you may see what we should call nigger people — that is, young black Egyptian students, of a shade between ink and charcoal, arm in arm with God's image cut in ivory.

I have not had any new letters since my last to you, — but I am on the lookout. Love to all.

PARIS, December 28, 1834.

I am afraid it is a prodigious while since you have heard from me, but I am so occupied that the weeks slip by me almost unperceived. However, as I wrote a long letter to Dr. Parsons last week, in which I requested him to let you know that he had heard from me, I trust you will not be in despair. I believe I told you I had received your letter of October 28th — I do now at any rate. My studies are going on magnificently. I have every opportunity, and try to make all possible use of them. I had the pleasure two or three days ago of a *tête-à-tête* dinner with the gentleman whom Dr. Marshall Hall, of London (a professor in one of their medical institutions, and a man whose name is well known in our country), has called the " first physician of the present day " — M. Louis. He even has trusted me with the analysis of a work which he is going to make use of in a publication he is employed upon. . . .

I say nothing about coming home. It is the invariable precedent to stay at least until the autumn of the second year, — and I told you that Dr. Warren sent out word to Mason to finish his third winter, — a great self-denial, under the circumstances, and an additional opportunity which will make the imp doubly dangerous. — If I had my own way, I own I would never return until I could go home with the confidence of placing myself at once at the head of the younger part of the profession, — as much for your sake as my own, for I am not only ambitious, but I long to pay for my tedious and expensive education. — I need not say that I have the fondest desire to see my parents and my relations and friends — but I keep my heart light in keeping my mind busy, and you must do the same. . . .

PARIS, May 14, 1835.

I hardly know how I have contrived to miss writing for a fortnight, but I have been so occupied that the days passed away without my counting them. I have received no new letter from you since the one in which you spoke of my coming home sooner than I had expected. Since that letter one of the ideas that troubled your imagination — that of war — is removed, and I suspect a little uneasiness on your part has been alleviated by the complaisance of the French ministry. And in the mean time I cannot give you an idea of the zeal and profit with which I have been applying myself to certain branches which I had hitherto neglected. Among other things I have turned my attention to operating, and in the course of a few weeks I have become an expert and rapid operator. To give you an idea of how this is possible, I will tell you how I have occupied my time during this time. On the site of the ancient cemetery of Clamart, about a mile from my room, there now stands another receptacle for the defunct, where they are consigned to the open hands of science. This establishment is not one of the little infernal suffocating holes in which the unhappy native of our uncivilized land is often obliged to pursue his labors, but a spacious courtyard with several neat white halls, and a garden and fountain in the middle. In these precincts hundreds of students dissect during a part of the year and operate during another. After having taken our lessons in operative surgery, a Swiss friend of mine, — whose intimacy has been enjoyed successively by poor Jackson, by Bowditch, and now by myself, — the Swiss student and myself, I say, bought a few cheap instruments together, and began to make ourselves operators. It is an odd thing for anybody but a medical student to think of, that human flesh should be sold like beef or mutton. But at twelve o'clock every day, the hour of distribution of subjects, you might have seen M. Bizot and myself — like the old gentlemen one sometimes sees at a market — choosing our day's provision with the same epicurean nicety. We paid fifty sous apiece for our subject, and before evening we had cut him into inch pieces. Now all this can hardly be done anywhere in the world but at Paris, — in England and America we can *dissect*, but rarely operate upon the subject, while here one who

knows how to use his hands, and who gives his attention exclusively to the subject for a time, may, as I
have said I have done, become an expert operator in
a few weeks.  I have told you all this to let you know
that I am not staying at Paris for nothing ; and my
letter must stop, for it is time to go to the hospital St.
Louis, which is a couple of miles off — and I am here
writing in bed like the author of the *Seasons*. . . .

MILAN, *August* 16, 1835.

Since I wrote you from Geneva I have been
through a large part of Switzerland and crossed the
Splügen — a pass over the Alps — into Italy.  This
tour we have made partly in carriages, partly on
mules, and a good deal on foot.  At Geneva we bought
knapsacks, and having filled them with the most
necessary articles, we sent our trunks on to Milan by
the baggage-wagon.  In walking we generally had a
guide who carried two of our knapsacks, and took the
other alternately on our own shoulders.  I have been
of course very much delighted with the novel aspect
of the wonderful country we have passed through, but
glad to finish this part of my trip in order to get
through with Italy the sooner.  You do not ask from
me a description of all I have seen, because I am not
a professed traveller, and such only have the time and
inclination for this kind of labor, which requires a
great deal of elaboration to offer any peculiar value.
The majesty and beauty of the scenery of Switzerland,
as you know, have made it a thoroughfare of travelling
Europe, and especially of the English, who swarm in
it to the most outrageous extent.  And yet so vast
and so varied, so savage in some regions and so lovely
in others, is the country we have been through, that

the steamboats on the lakes, and the great hotels and splendid roads, which one meets with from time to time, leave too slight traces on the face of Nature to take away the sense of freshness and wildness that characterize it. From the peaks of the mountains down into the fertile valleys you meet with all climates; the shores of the lakes offer every variety, from bald and broken rocks to the softest green of the southern vineyards; their waters vary from the deepest green to a blue as clear as that of the brightest sky, and all along their shores are scattered the little villages which seem shut out from all the world, like Rasselas's happy valley, by walls that lose themselves in a region too ambitious for the clouds to make any pretensions to reach. I have seen more than a dozen such lakes. I have been at the top of the Righi, where I could see down to more than a dozen at once, even. I have clambered up mountains and sat down to rest on a moss-bank. I have walked nine leagues in one day, and ten in another. I have been to the famous monastery of St. Bernard, where they keep the dogs that pick up people lost in the snow, where the monks give everybody that comes a dinner and a bed for nothing, with monstrous Catholic bottles of good wine. I counted twenty skulls of poor wretches that had been lost in the snow, in their charnel-house, besides some cartloads of odd human bones. I have been at Goldau, where a slide of the mountain sponged out a village of four hundred and fifty inhabitants in a single moment, some thirty years ago. I have seen the falls of the Rhine at Schaffhausen, and these and a thousand other recollections are all set in my mind in a gigantic frame of snowy summits and arrowy peaks, which close around the picture still warm

in my memory.  And here I am at Milan, and all day
to-day and all day yesterday I have been seeing sights,
the most tedious of occupations, whatever one thinks
at home.  Oh! but this marble cathedral, which
the labors of four centuries have not fully completed,
with its hundreds of spires and its thousands of statues, is the most glorious piece of embroidery in stone
that man might wish to see.  They talk of Henry the
7th's chapel in Westminster Abbey; it would make a
very pretty pigeon-house for the Milan cathedral,
and that is all.  I saw the original of Leonardo da
Vinci's Last Supper yesterday, but it is [illegible].
I have met the Channings three times since we were
at Geneva.  I found no letters here, but shall probably get some at Florence, where I expect soon to be,
as I mean to do Italy as fast as I can.  I shall write
next from Venice or Florence.  Love to all.

ROME, *September* 8, 1835.

I have seen almost all there is to be seen in the
Eternal City, and mean to leave it in a few days.
Since I wrote you from Milan, I have seen Venice,
Bologna, and some less important, but interesting
cities, and I have now been a week in Rome.  I hope
we shall get back to Paris early in October, and I
shall take my passage for New York immediately
after returning.  You have no idea of the infinite
wealth of Italy in architecture, painting, and sculp-
ture.  All that elsewhere is most rare and precious is
found here in such profusion that the eye is fatigued
and the susceptibility worn out with over exercise.
Venice prepares one very well for the riches of Rome
by the fine churches and rich paintings it possesses,
but after all nothing at all approaches what we have

seen here. If modern Rome did not exist, still the
world would come here to look at the monuments of
antiquity, and if all the traces of ancient Rome were
effaced, the great masters of the arts in modern times
would have been enough to have made it a centre of
the schools of all Europe. It is not until seeing
Rome that one gets the perfect idea of having seen
the very noblest objects of art; but now I can say I
have seen the Colosseum and the Pantheon — and the
most splendid cathedral of modern times — and the
Laocoön and the Apollo Belvidere and the Dying
Gladiator and the Transfiguration. And after studying these grand works of art one's taste and notions
are essentially different from ——

September 12th.

Something interrupted me the other day, and I have
been so occupied since that there my sentence rested.
This morning I have been to see the baths of Titus,
— which were built on the ruins or site of Nero's
golden palace. The arabesques executed in fresco on
the ceilings are so beautiful in their design that they
quite surprised me — but I did not know that Raphael himself did not disdain to copy them in painting the Vatican. I saw also this morning the beautiful little antique group of Cupid and Psyche, of which
I remember that there are three engravings in Rees's
Encyclopædia, — and the famous Venus of the capi-
tol. As I was saying when I left off, one's taste and
notions become essentially different after seeing the
best works of the old masters. But I can say with
regard to statues that I found the ideas given me by
copies and casts essentially correct, whereas it is but
here and there that the finest copies or engravings

come at all up to the standard of a splendid painting.
With regard to the magnificence of the ancient
Romans, it surpassed all the ideas I had entertained
so far that I can hardly yet believe my own eyes.
The immense numbers of pillars of precious marbles,
of polished granite and porphyry — the gorgeous
vases and gigantic baths sculptured often from a
single mass of jasper or granite or porphyry — the
innumerable statues and busts — the tremendous ruins
of the Colosseum — of the baths of Caracalla — the
triumphal pillars and arches, astonish altogether any
one who has formed his ideas of antiquity from a few
old copper coins and a collection of broken earthen-
ware.

We have pretty much done up Rome, and intend to
leave it as soon as possible.  I have, as I said, only
one plan in this journey, — to see as much and as fast
and as cheap as I can.  I have not received any letters since I left Paris, but I hope I shall shortly.
Love to all.

New York, December 14, 1835.

I have just arrived, after a passage of forty-three
days from Havre, sound and safe.  I have only time
to tell you that I am nicely, and that I shall come on
directly, — that is, to-morrow or day after.  I am
delighted to see my own country again, and if I
can only find all well shall have every reason to be
thankful.  Love to all.

# CHAPTER VI



AT last, with the opening of the year 1836, it was time for Dr. Holmes to set his foot upon the initial rung of that ladder to the top of which he had expressed his ambition to climb. His sign duly indicated to the diseased among his neighbors their opportunity to assist his ascent; but it is safe to suppose that one of the earlier uses made of that publication of his presence was not altogether gratifying; for the Autocrat's friend, the Professor, is said to have had this provoking experience: "Behind the pane of plate-glass which bore his name and title burned a modest lamp, signifying to the passers-by that at all hours of the night the slightest favors (or fevers) were welcome. A youth who had freely partaken of the cup which cheers and likewise inebriates, following a moth-like impulse very natural under the circumstances, dashed his fist at the light and quenched the meek luminary."

In May, 1836, he invested himself with professional respectability by joining the Massachusetts Medical Society; and if membership in that body helped him at all, he repaid the debt, with great accumulations of usury, in later years. But well equipped, ambitious, trustworthy as was this young aspirant, he did not escape the lot of youth, — youth that has enough pleasures without that only one which is reserved for maturer years, — success. He had not that flattering experience which we are told was enjoyed by the angel who came to work miraculous healing at the pool of Bethesda; for when Dr. Holmes came to Boston he did not find "a great multitude of impotent folk, of blind, halt, withered, waiting for" him. To tell the truth, a brilliant career in the way of practice not only did not begin with him early, but it never developed at all. He built up a very fair business (if the word is permissible), but hardly more. For this there were many reasons. Probably he did not find the toil of the visiting physician quite so consonant to his taste as he had anticipated; I have been told that he never could become indifferent to the painful scenes of the sick-room, and of course when friends and neighbors were the sufferers he did not find his heart hardened. In after life he admitted that he did not "make any strenuous efforts to obtain business." He acknowledged, in his gay way, that, after all, the thing which pleased him best about practising medicine was, that he had to keep a horse and chaise. In this he found indeed much joy, and his friends found not less fear. In one of the clumsy great vehicles of that day, swung upon huge C springs, vibrating in every direction, the little gentleman used to appear advancing along the road, seeming at once in peril and a cause of peril, bouncing insecurely upon the seat, and driving always a mettlesome steed at an audacious speed. Furthermore, it was of course a hindrance to be a wit and a poet; for some reason, or no reason, the wise world has made up its mind, that he who writes rhymes must not write prescriptions, and he who makes jests should not escort people to their graves. In Nux Post-Cœnatica he wrote plaintively: —

Besides — my prospects — don't you know that people won't
    employ
A man that wrongs his manliness by laughing like a boy ?
And suspect the azure blossom that unfolds upon a shoot,
As if wisdom's old potato could not flourish at its root ?

.   .   .   .   .   .   .   .   .   .   .   .   .   .

It's a vastly pleasing prospect, when you're screwing out a
    laugh,
That your very next year's income is diminished by a
    half,
And a little boy trips barefoot that your Pegasus may go,
And the baby's milk is watered that your Helicon may
    flow.

His students he forewarned more gravely: "Medicine is the most difficult of sciences and the most laborious of arts. It will task all your powers of body and mind if you are faithful to it. Do not dabble in the muddy sewer of politics, nor linger by the enchanted streams of literature, nor dig in far-off fields for the hidden waters of alien sciences. The great practitioners are generally those who concentrate all their powers on their business." I think that he never did this act of concentration, or at least not very persistently. He had learned the truth of these rules not by the practice of them, but by suffering for the breach of them. When he said that the smallest fevers were thankfully received, the people who had no fevers laughed, but the people who had them preferred some one who would take the matter more seriously than they thought this lively young joker was likely to do. In this they were in error; for a more anxious, painstaking, conscientious physician never counted pulse nor wrote the mystic ℞. To this the writer has earned the right to bear personal testimony, having in years long gone by made wry faces over many a nauseous drug administered by the orders of Dr. Holmes.

If anything could be worse even than being a wit, that worse thing was being a poet; better to be a libertine or a hard drinker, which might seem a valuable experience, or bond of sympathy, with not a few patients. So it militated seriously against this respectable and abstemious physician that he had actually published a volume of poetry. This reckless act was perpetrated in the latter part of the year 1836, only about twelve months after his return from Europe. The book contained " Old Ironsides," of course, and " The Last Leaf " (of which latter I shall have a word to say later on), and the Φ B K poem which he delivered at the meeting of the society that summer. For the most part, however, the short poems were marked by little else than the exuberant jollity of youth. The natural ear for melody, the happiness of expression, the just feeling for proportion, might be noted; but the impression left was that the writer regarded life as a sort of rosary of the gayest kind of jokes, the most absurd extravaganzas of wit. There was abundant and wholesome provocation to rollicking laughter, but only a very prescient critic would have seen much else. Unfortunately the Doctor's avowed function was not to amuse but to heal his fellow-citizens; doubtless he felt a youthful thrill of gratification at seeing his name on the back of a printed book, — not quite so commonplace an affair in those days as it is now; but worldly wisdom would have dictated suppression as the shrewder part. It was flattering, in a certain way, of course, to be invited to deliver the Φ B K poem; but it was a poor advertisement. For hindrances thus incurred Holmes consoled himself by reflecting that Haller lost his election as physician to the hospital in his native city of Berne, principally on the ground that he was a poet. But, then, was he himself going to be another Haller? If not, he must seek some other consolation to which he could more logically lay claim.

His active mind and industrious temperament would not permit him to be idle; and the hours which were left to his free control were busily employed. For three seasons he was one of the physicians at the Massachusetts General Hospital. But now, in looking back, it is easy to see that he was predestined more for the academic than the practical side of his profession. In 1838 he was "mightily pleased," as he said, to receive the appointment of Professor of Anatomy at Dartmouth College; it called for his presence there only during August, September, and October, and he held the place for the years 1839 and 1840. He busied himself also with writing for the Boylston and other prizes, and he recorded the smile of Fortune in this note to his brother-in-law.

TO CHARLES W. UPHAM.

BOSTON, August 4, 1836.

MY VERY DEAR SIR, — The lesson of humility which you were anxious I should receive has found some other customers. The Boylston prize was almost unanimously awarded to my dissertation. The committee, however, have determined to pay for and publish two others, which they were anxious the public should see, — they are by Dr. Haxall, of Virginia, and Dr. Bell, of New Hampshire. This is what they have never done before, and it is somewhat pleasant to have cut out a fifty-dollar prize under the guns

of two old blazers, who have each of them swamped
their competitors in preceding trials.

In the following summer he again notified the same
friend, more briefly: —

BOSTON, *August* 3, 1837.

DEAR MR. U——.   Both prizes unanimously.
All very well at Cambridge yesterday.

Of these essays the one on "Intermittent Fever in
New England" still retains value as a careful collection of all the evidence concerning malaria in that
region up to that time.   It represented very great
labor in inquiry and investigation; the Doctor even
examined the works of the old colonial writers page
by page (by reason of the imperfection of the indices),
save, as he said, the sermons and theological treatises
of Cotton Mather, which he passed by, on the ground
that they were "more likely to cause a fever than to
mention one."

Probably enough, the mere existence of the volume
of *Medical Essays* is a fact unknown to the "general
reader," — that ill-starred being who is to the book-
sellers what the refuse-barrel is to the household, a
receptacle for all transitory rubbish, whither the silver fork or other article of value finds its way rarely
and by accident.   Yet this collection of papers is
delightful reading, sparkling with cleverness in the
Doctor's best vein.   The earliest papers, two lectures
on homœopathy, bear the date of 1842; they cannot
fairly be recommended to believers in that art, for
their wit and wisdom are administered in by no means
homœopathic doses; but the rest of the world may
rejoice in them.   The good Doctor hated homœopa-

thy with a whole-souled hatred, and from an intellectual standpoint he regarded it with utter contempt. He spoke against it as one speaks who feels that he is rendering good service to his fellow-men. It led him, in his earnestness, to utter some of the happiest of his brilliant sentences, however distasteful they may be to some readers. He always spoke of it as a "pseudo-science."[1] He admitted that some patients might "have been actually benefited through the influence exerted upon their imaginations," which must also be conceded "to every one of those numerous modes of practice known to all intelligent persons by an opprobrious title." But "the argument founded on this occasional good would be as applicable in justifying the counterfeiter in giving circulation to his base coin, on the ground that a spurious dollar had often relieved a poor man's necessities."

The defensive argument which homœopathists drew from the action of the tiny particle of vaccine matter, and which they applied to some of their minute preparations of minerals, he disposed of as follows: "The thoughtlessness which can allow an inference to be extended from a product of disease possessing this susceptibility of multiplication when conveyed into the living body, to substances of inorganic origin, such as silex or sulphur, would be capable of arguing that a pebble may produce a mountain, because an acorn can become a forest."

Later on, the French Academy gave out as the result of an experiment, that the ten-trillionth part (or

---

[1] Later, in *The Professor at the Breakfast-Table*, he said : "So while the solemn farce of over-drugging is going on, the world over, the harlequin pseudo-science jumps on to the stage, whip in hand, with half-a-dozen somersets, and begins laying about him."

thereabouts!) of a drop of septicæmic poison would kill a guinea-pig. This was naturally turned into an argument in favor of the homœopathic dose. But Dr. Holmes wrote: "The argument from the effect of animal poisons in small quantities to medicinal substances in general, is like saying that because a spark will burn down a city, a mutton chop will feed an army."

In 1843 he published his essay on the "Contagiousness of Puerperal Fever." Upon this, preëminently if not alone, rests his claim to having made an original and a greatly valuable contribution to medical science. There had already been suspicions of the fact rather than belief in it, with consequent sporadic assertions and suggestions, which had fortunately led to the recording of a useful amount of evidence. Dr. Holmes now announced his theory, carefully but very positively, in an article published in a short-lived periodical of little note, the *New England Quarterly Journal of Medicine.* That the paper, thus ill placed, was not overlooked or forgotten was due to the indignation which it excited. Dr. Holmes was handled with something worse than the fair severity of hostile argument by "the two leading professors of obstetrics in this country,"[1] both of Philadelphia, Hodge (the elder) in 1852, and Meigs in 1854. The latter especially used language so abusive that the medical discussion might easily have lost itself in a personal quarrel. But fortunately for multitudes of women who were to become mothers, — fortunately, too, for these assailants, though they do not deserve sympathy, —

---

[1] Letter of Dr. Holmes, quoted by Professor Osler in his *Remarks made at the Johns Hopkins Medical Society,* October 15, 1894, p. 9.

the Doctor had the good sense to keep his temper. He knew that "every real thought on every real subject knocks the wind out of somebody or other. As soon as his breath comes back, he very probably begins to expend it in hard words." Therefore he contented himself with reprinting his essay in 1855, with an introduction which held no anger, but an appeal, earnest to the point of being touching, that his arguments might be fairly considered. He said, very beautifully: "I take no offence, and attempt no retort. No man makes a quarrel with me over the counterpane that covers a mother, with her new-born infant at her breast. There is no epithet in the vocabulary of slight and sarcasm that can reach my personal sensibilities in such a controversy." "Let it be remembered that *persons* are nothing in this matter; better that twenty pamphleteers should be silenced, or as many professors unseated, than that one mother's life should be taken." The odds of prestige and authority were heavily against him. Medical students, he said, "naturally have faith in their instructors, turning to them for truth and taking what they may choose to give them; babes in knowledge, not yet able to tell the breast from the bottle, pumping away for the milk of truth at all that offers, were it nothing better than a professor's shrivelled forefinger." "The teachings of the two professors in the great schools of Philadelphia are sure to be listened to, not only by their immediate pupils, but by the profession at large. I am too much in earnest for either humility or vanity, but I do entreat those who hold the keys of life and death to listen to me also for this once. I ask no personal favor; but I beg to be heard in behalf of the women whose lives are at stake, until some stronger voice shall plead for them." His argument had been prepared with such care that he could add little to it by entering into controversy; if it were a seed of truth it would grow, while the assaults watered it. Thus very soon it did grow, and in good season became an accepted and familiar principle; and then the Doctor was accorded enrolment among the practical benefactors of mankind. He gathered a natural satisfaction from the reflection. He doubted much whether he should "ever again have so good an opportunity of being useful;" and in *The Professor at the Breakfast-Table* he said: "When, by the permission of Providence, I held up to the professional public the damnable facts connected with the conveyance of poison from one young mother's chamber to another's, — for doing which humble office I desire to be thankful that I have lived, though nothing else good should ever come of my life, — I had to bear the sneers of those whose position I had assailed, and, as I believe, have at last demolished, so that nothing but the ghosts of dead women stir among the ruins."

These essays indicate some mental traits which are not often associated with Dr. Holmes. Wit and poetry, a capacity to write novels and a fitness for the production of entertaining literature in many varieties, are not customarily regarded as naturally coordinating with powers of constructing close, clearly put, well-proportioned arguments, weighing and stating evidence, and generally doing in a very skilful and forcible manner that which lawyers call "presenting a case." But Dr. Holmes achieved precisely this sort of work in the papers which have been mentioned, and he did it with an ability which would have been

marked even among distinguished members of the
rival profession.   If instead of having homœopathy
on trial before the bar of public opinion on the charge
of being a counterfeit science, there had been going
forward the trial of J. S. for uttering forged notes,
and conducted before one of the established high tribunals of justice, Dr. Holmes, as prosecutor, would have
won the distinction of having made one of those mas-
terly forensic efforts which pass into history, or rather
into tradition.  In the paper on " Puerperal Fever," the
reader will be not less struck by the Doctor's admirable clearness and accuracy of statement, by his signal
skill in marshalling his evidence, by his appreciation
of the just weight of the several items, by his accurate
perception of precisely what logical conclusions could
be drawn from them, of how far some of them went in
establishing probability, and of how near the whole
came to sustaining the severer burden which is called
proof.   Later, in an introduction to a re-publication
of the essay, the Doctor excused himself for stating
a few points so simple that they might have been
deemed superfluous, by saying : " It affords a good
opportunity, as it seems to me, of exercising the un-
trained mind in that *medical logic*, which does not seem
to have been either taught or practised in our schools
of late, to the extent that might be desired."   After
reading these *Medical Essays* one can understand
the impulse which at first led Holmes to enter the
Law School.   One can also see the influence of his
beloved teacher, Louis, whose chief and favorite motto
Dr. Holmes was never tired of repeating : —

> " Formez toujours les idées nettes.
> Fuyez les à peu près."

"No better proof of his spirit can be given than that, just a year from the time when he began to practise as a physician, he took that eventful step, which, in such a man, implies that he sees his way clear to a position; he married a lady blessed with many gifts, but not bringing him a fortune to paralyze his industry." Thus spoke Dr. Holmes concerning Dr. James Jackson, the uncle of the lady whom he himself was soon to marry; and his own action was like unto that which in another he thus highly commended. In fact, he had the domestic instinct very strongly developed, and was as sure to woo and wed as any man could be. The following, to his old school-friend, contains premonitions: —

TO PHINEAS BARNES.

*February* 3, 1838.

MY DEAR BARNES, — I received your letter yesterday, and contrary to my usual procrastinating habits I will give you a prompt answer, — a little hurried, perhaps, for I am a busy mortal, and I am just now agonizing between my patients, clamorous for their morning doses, and a poem with which I have been saddled for an approaching medical dinner.

And first, with regard to my book, I have two or three questions to ask you. Did you suppose that, after my boring you with letter after letter, taking advantage of your good-nature to lead you from your proper pursuits into the region of miasms and fevers, quoting whole pages from your communications, and reprinting the letters you obtained from others,[1] —

---

[1] Mr. Barnes had collected a great deal of evidence for use by Dr. Holmes in writing his essay on " Intermittent Fever in New England," which took the Boylston prize.

you must make a fuss about asking me for a paltry
volume which, but for you and a few other kind
friends and professional brethren, would not have
been worth writing?   And in the next place, did you
think me such an ungrateful vagabond as to forget
not only past friendship, but recent kindness? and
such a calculating miscreant as to grudge a friend a
book, although I could have made up my mind to let
him have a pamphlet?   The truth is this, that having
been much occupied since my Essays were published,
— two or three weeks ago, — I have but just had time
to distribute a few copies to a few friends in the neighborhood, and have hardly yet thought how to get
them to such as live at a distance.   You may be very
certain that one shall go to Gould, Kendall & Lincoln's, for you, this very morning; and instead of
taking it as such a mighty favor, please to remember
that the obligation is altogether and a hundred-fold
on my side.   Your information was of great value and
assistance to me; especially as I had no other means
whatsoever of getting at many parts of your State to
which it referred.

And so you are married.   I wish I were, too.   I
have flirted and written poetry long enough, and
I feel that I am growing domestic and tabby-ish.   I
have several very nice young women in my eye, and
it is by no means impossible that another summer or
so may see my name among the hymeneal victims. . . .

I do indeed congratulate you on changing your iso-
lated condition into the beatific state of duality.   The
very moment one feels that he is falling into the old
age of youth — which I take to be from twenty-five
to thirty, in most cases — he must not dally any
longer; the first era of his life is not fairly closed,

and he may live half his bright days over again if
"woman's pure kiss, sweet and long," comes only to
his lips before it is too late.   If he waits till the next
epoch of life begins, there is great danger lest he
marry his wife as a jockey buys a horse, — sensibly,
shrewdly, and merely as a convenience in his domestic
operations.   Such are my sentiments on this matter;
and two years will give me — a certain age, I shudder to repeat.   My best respects to your lady, — and
may the state into which you have ventured prove to
you a prolific source of happiness.

That "certain age" which Holmes "shuddered to
repeat" found him, of course, in the matrimonial
way.   On June 15, 1840, he married Amelia Lee
Jackson, the third daughter of Hon. Charles Jackson, of Boston, an Associate Justice of the Supreme
Judicial Court of the Commonwealth.   This lady,
whose memory is enshrined in my affection and admiration, I shall not attempt to depict, lest the reader
should suspect me of extravagance, and refuse to give
credit to the praise which I should utter.   Every estimable and attractive quality of mind and character
seemed to be hers; all who knew her loved her, and
respected her not less than they loved.   The kindest,
gentlest, and tenderest of women, she had the chance
given her, when her eldest son was three times
wounded in the civil war, to show of what mettle she
was; and she did show it, as all who knew her would
have foretold of her.   For Dr. Holmes she was an
ideal wife, — a comrade the most delightful, a help-
mate the most useful, whose abilities seemed to have
been arranged by happy foresight for the express purpose of supplying his wants.   She smoothed his way

for him, removed annoyances from his path, did for
him with her easy executive capacity a thousand
things, which otherwise he would have missed or
have done with difficulty for himself ; she hedged
him carefully about and protected him from dis-
tractions and bores and interruptions, — in a word,
she took care of him, and gave him every day the
fullest and freest chance to be always at his best,
always able to do his work amid cheerful surroundings.  She contributed immensely to his success, as
all knew who came near enough to have any knowledge of the household.  If in thus ordering all things
alike within and without the daily routine with such
careful reference to the occupations and the comfort
of her husband, she often gave herself in sacrifice, —
as no doubt she did, — she always did so with such
amiable tact that the fact might easily escape notice,
and the fruit of her devotion was enjoyed with no dis-
quieting sense of what it had cost her.  She eschewed
the idea of having wit or literary and critical capacity; yet in fact she had rare humor and a sensitive
good taste, which could have been infallibly counted
upon for good service, if on any occasion these qualities could bring assistance to the Doctor, — and as to
this no man probably knows.

Though this lady had not "a fortune," her father
was very "well off," as the Boston people of his day
would have said.  Otherwise Dr. Holmes's nuptials
would hardly have taken place so soon.  Yet even
thus he had committed himself to a life of hard work,
and to a moderate scale of living for some time to
come.  The children of this marriage were three.
The eldest, Oliver Wendell, has since had an illustrious career; entering the twentieth Massachusetts

Regiment among the early volunteers in the civil war, he was severely wounded in three engagements, but each time returned to the field. He became a lieutenant-colonel in the service. He afterward studied law, won distinction by his writings, and has now been for many years an Associate Justice of the Supreme Judicial Court. The second child, a daughter, named after her mother, married Mr. Turner Sargent. After his death she was the companion of her father during his "Hundred Days" in Europe. She died in 1889. The third child, Edward Jackson, inherited much of his father's wit and humor; but unfortunately also inherited the asthma; this hampered him in the practice of the law, gave him, in fact, no chance at all in life, and finally so undermined his constitution that he died, untimely, in 1884. He left a son, who alone represents the name in the third generation.

# CHAPTER VII



In 1847 Dr. Holmes received the appointment of Parkman Professor of Anatomy and Physiology in the Medical School of Harvard University. Occasionally also he overstepped the strict boundaries of these departments to give instruction in microscopy, and to dabble in psychology or in matters akin thereto. The variety of his functions led him to say that he occupied not a professor's chair in the school, but a whole settee. In 1871, however, the overloaded condition of the chair, or settee, became so apparent that a separate professorship was established for physiology, and Dr. Holmes thereafter had charge only of anatomy. The position was of moderate emolument, but he felt great pride and interest in it, and held it for thirty-five years. So long an incumbency in such an office had serious perils, which fortunately the Doctor fully appreciated, and appreciating avoided.

"The professor's chair," he said, "is an insulating stool, so to speak; his age, his knowledge, real or supposed, his official station, are like the glass legs which support the electrician's piece of furniture, and cut it off from the common currents of the floor upon which it stands." Further, in this connection, may be quoted an entertaining passage in one of the Doctor's letters to his friend Dr. Weir Mitchell, the distinguished Philadelphian: "I am much pleased to find that you are going on in that path of research which you entered so auspiciously. I could have wished that you had obtained the place we tried to aid you in obtaining; but such labors as yours will sooner or later find their reward. Perhaps it is hardly desirable that an active man of science should obtain a chair too early; for I have noticed, as you doubtless have, that the wood of which academic *fauteuils* are made has a narcotic quality, which occasionally renders their occupants somnolent, lethargic, or even comatose. Hoping that you will get *seated* soon enough for your comfort, and not too soon for your reputation, and thanking you very sincerely for your admirable essay, I am," etc.

Of Dr. Holmes as a medical instructor I do not, of course, feel myself competent to speak from my own knowledge. But by taking the liberty of using freely what has been well said by eminently competent judges, I hope to present a fair sketch of him in this part of his life. His death, of course, called forth many articles in the way of reminiscence and criticism from the physicians who had sat under his instruction, or had worked with him at the school. Notable among these were articles by Dr. David W. Cheever, who had been one of Dr. Holmes's "demonstrators," and by Dr. Thomas Dwight, also one of his "demonstrators" and his successor as Professor of Anatomy. By the kind permission of these gentlemen I shall slash freely with my scissors into their excellent papers.

Doctor Cheever writes:[1] —

"It nears one o'clock, and the close work in the

---

[1] *Harvard Graduates' Magazine*, vol. iii. No. 10, December, 1894.

demonstrator's room in the old Medical School in
North Grove Street becomes even more hurried and
eager as the lecture hour in Anatomy approaches.
Four hours of busy dissection have unveiled a portion
of the human frame, insensate and stark, on the
demonstrating-table.  Muscles, nerves, and blood-
vessels unfold themselves in unvarying harmony, if
seeming disorder, and the ' subject ' is nearly ready
to illustrate the lecture. . . . The room is thick with
tobacco smoke.  The winter light, snowy and dull,
enters through one tall window, bare of curtain, and
falls upon a lead floor.  The surroundings are singularly barren of ornament or beauty, and there is
naught to inspire the intellect or the imagination,
except the marvellous mechanism of the poor dead
body, which lies dissected before us, like some complex and delicate machinery whose uses we seek to
know.

"To such a scene enters the poet, the writer, the
wit, Oliver Wendell Holmes.  Few readers of his
prose or poetry could dream of him as here, in this
charnel-house, in the presence of death.  The very
long, steep, and single flight of stairs leading up from
the street below resounds with a double and labored
tread, the door opens, and a small, gentle, smiling
man appears, supported by the janitor, who often has
been called on to help him up the stairs.  Entering,
and giving a breathless greeting, he sinks upon a
stool and strives to recover his asthmatic breath. . . .

"Anon recovering, he brightens up, and asks,
' What have you for me to-day?' and plunges, knife
in hand, into the ' depths of his subject,' — a joke he
might have uttered.  Time flies, and a boisterous
crowd of turbulent Bob Sawyers pours through the

hall to his lecture-room, and begins a rhythmical stamping, one, two, three, and a shout, and pounding on his lecture-room doors. A rush takes place; some collapse, some are thrown headlong, and three hundred raw students precipitate themselves into a bare and comfortless amphitheatre. Meanwhile the professor has been running about, now as nimble as a cat, selecting plates, rummaging the dusty museum for specimens, arranging microscopes, and displaying bones. The subject is carried in on a board; no automatic appliances, no wheels with pneumatic tires, no elevators, no dumb-waiters in those days. The *cadaver* is decorously disposed on a revolving table in the small arena, and is always covered, at first, from curious eyes, by a clean white sheet. Respect for poor humanity and admiration for God's divinest work is the first lesson and the uppermost in the poet-lecturer's mind. He enters, and is greeted with a mighty shout and stamp of applause. Then silence, and there begins a charming hour of description, analysis, simile, anecdote, harmless pun, which clothes the dry bones with poetic imagery, enlivens a hard and fatiguing day with humor, and brightens to the tired listener the details of a difficult though interesting study. We say tired listener because — will it be believed? — the student is now listening to his *fifth* consecutive lecture that day, beginning at nine o'clock and ending at two; no pause, no rest, no recovery for the dazed senses, which have tried to absorb Materia Medica, Chemistry, Practice, Obstetrics, and Anatomy, all in one morning, by five learned professors. One o'clock was always assigned to Dr. Holmes because he alone could hold his exhausted audience's attention.

"As a lecturer he was accurate, punctual, precise, unvarying in patience over detail, and though not an original anatomist in the sense of a discoverer, yet a most exact descriptive lecturer; while the wealth of illustration, comparison, and simile he used was unequalled. Hence his charm; you received information, and you were amused at the same time. He was always simple and rudimentary in his instruction. His flights of fancy never shot over his hearers' heads. ' Iteration and reiteration ' was his favorite motto in teaching. ' These, gentlemen,' he said, on one occasion, pointing out the lower portion of the pelvic bones, ' are the tuberosities of the ischia, on which man was designed to sit and survey the works of Creation.' But if witty, he could also be serious and pathetic; and he possessed the high power of holding and controlling his rough auditors. . . .

"And how he loved Anatomy! as a mother her child. He was never tired, always fresh, always eager in learning and teaching it. In earnest himself, enthusiastic, and of a happy temperament, he shed the glow of his ardent spirit over his followers, and gave to me, his demonstrator and assistant for eight years, some of the most attractive and happy hours of my life."

Professor Thomas Dwight[1] bears testimony to the same purport as Dr. Cheever: —

"During that autumn I frequently recited to Dr. Holmes, and saw the great patience and interest with which he demonstrated the more difficult parts of the skeleton. In November began the dreary season of perpetual lectures, from morning till night, to large classes of more or less turbulent students. The lec-

[1] *Scribner's Magazine*, vol. xvii. No. 1, January, 1895.

tures began usually at nine, sometimes at eight, and
continued without interruption until two, old students
and new for the most part attending all of them.
The lecture on anatomy came at one o'clock five days
in the week.  I lack power to.express the weariness,
the disgust, and sometimes the exasperation, with
which, after four or five hours of lectures, bad air,
and rapid note-taking had brought their crop of headaches and bad temper, we resigned ourselves to another hour.  No one but Dr. Holmes could have been
endured under the circumstances."

Professor Dwight describes the older quarters much
as Dr. Cheever does: —

"The amphitheatre, the seats of which were at a
steep pitch, was entered by the students from above,
through two doors, one on each side, each of which
was approached by a steep stairway between narrow
walls.  The doors were not usually opened until some
minutes after the hour.  The space at the top of
these stairs was a scene of crowding, pushing, scuf-
fling, and shouting indescribable, till at last a spring
shot back both bolts at once, and from each door a
living avalanche poured down the steep alleys with an
irresistible rush that made the looker-on hold his
breath.  How it happened that during many years no
one was killed, or even seriously injured, is incom-
prehensible.  The excitement of the fray having
subsided, order reigned until the entrance of the professor, which was frequently the signal for applause.
He came in with a grave countenance.  His shoulders
were thrown back and his face bent down.  No one
realized better than he that he had no easy task before him.  He had to teach a branch repulsive to
some, difficult for all; and he had to teach it to a

jaded class which was unfit to be taught anything.
The wooden seats were hard, the backs straight, and
the air bad.   The effect of the last was alluded to by
Dr. Holmes in his address at the opening of the new
school in 1883: —

"' So, when the class I was lecturing to was sitting
in an atmosphere once breathed already, after I had
seen head after head gently declining, and one pair of
eyes after another emptying themselves of intelligence,
I have said, inaudibly, with the considerate self-re-
straint of Musidora's rural lover, " Sleep on, dear
youth; this does not mean that you are indolent, or
that I am dull; it is the partial coma of commencing
asphyxia.'

"To make head against these odds he did his utmost
to adopt a sprightly manner, and let no opportunity
for a jest escape him.   These would be received
with quiet appreciation by the lower benches, and
with uproarious demonstrations from the ' mountain,'
where, as in the French Assembly of the Revolution,
the noisiest spirits congregated.   He gave his imagination full play in comparisons often charming
and always quaint.   None but Holmes could have
compared the microscopical coiled tube of a sweat-
gland to a fairy's intestine.   Medical readers will
appreciate the aptness of likening the mesentery to
the shirt ruffles of a preceding generation, which from
a short line of attachment expanded into yards of
complicated folds.   He has compared the fibres con-
necting the two symmetrical halves of the brain to the
band uniting the Siamese twins. . . .

"One would think, from Dr. Holmes's wonderful
facility of expression, that lecturing year after year
on the same subject, the lectures would have been as

child's play.   But I am convinced that this was not
so.   'You will find,' said he to me at the time that
I succeeded him, 'that the day that you have lectured
something has gone out from you.'   To his sensitive
organization I imagine that the trials incident to the
tired, and in early years more or less unruly, class
were greater than his friends suspected.   I remember
once his telling Dr. Cheever and myself, how exceedingly annoying it is to the lecturer to have any one
leave the room before the close.   I often marvelled at
the patience he displayed."

That Dr. Holmes should have selected anatomy
and dissection as his province of labor may seem a
little odd to the reader who has just been told that he
was too tender-hearted to practise medicine.   Here is
what the two good witnesses, who have been placed
upon the stand, depone as to this point.   Dr. Cheever
says: "Too sympathetic to practise medicine, he soon
abandoned the art for the science, and always manifested the same abhorrence for death and tenderness
for animals.   When it became necessary to have a
freshly killed rabbit for his lectures, he always ran
out of the room, left me to chloroform it, and be-
sought me not to let it squeak."

Professor Dwight says: —

"In spite of the attention bestowed on dissection,
I do not think that he much fancied dissecting, himself, though our Museum still has some few specimens
of his preparation.   Once he asked me which part
of anatomy I liked best, and on my saying: ' The
bones,' he replied: ' So do I; it is the cleanest.'
Still he usually gave the class the time-honored joke
that bones are dry. . . . Almost the only topic on
which he could not speak with patience was the cruelty

often practised in vivisection.  Like all sensible men, he recognized the necessity of vivisection.  He has called it ' a mode of acquiring knowledge justifiable in its proper use, odious beyond measure in its abuse,' but I am sure that in his heart he hated it bitterly.  But if in physiology he eschewed vivisection, believing, perhaps, with Hyrtl, ' that nature will tell the truth all the better for not being put to the torture,' he did some work which now would be dignified with the name of experimental psychology. ' I have myself,' he writes, ' instituted a good many experiments with a more extensive and expensive machinery than I think has ever been employed, — namely, two classes each of ten intelligent students, who had joined hands together, representing a nervous circle of about sixty-six feet, so that a hand-pressure transmitted ten times around the circle traversed six hundred and sixty feet, besides involving one hundred perceptions and volitions.  My chronometer was a horse-timer, marking quarter-seconds.' He varied these experiments by having the transmissions made from hand to foot and from hand to head."

An Englishman, writing a very good article in the *Quarterly Review*, says: "Into all his professional studies he carries the same kindly, tender heart.  He utters his Laus Deo that he assisted at no scientific cruelties; and thirty years afterwards there is still a sob in his throat when he speaks of the little child in the hospital cot, whose fresh voice yet rang in his ears like ' the reedy trill of a thrush's evening song.' "

In *The Professor at the Breakfast-Table* Dr. Holmes himself says: "You may be sure that some men, even among those who have chosen the task of pruning their fellow-creatures, grow more and more thoughtful and truly compassionate in the midst of their cruel experience. They become less nervous, but more sympathetic. They have a truer sensibility for others' pain, the more they study pain and disease in the light of science. I have said this without claiming any special growth in humanity for myself, though I do hope I grow tenderer in my feelings as I grow older."

Concerning Dr. Holmes's scheme of instruction Professor Dwight says: "Any one who has experience in lecturing recognizes that he must decide whether he will address himself to the higher or lower half of the class. Dr. Holmes lectured to the latter. It was a part of his humanity to do so. He felt a sympathy for the struggling lad preparing to practise where work is hard and money scarce. 'I do not give the best lectures that I can give,' he said on several occasions; 'I should shoot over their heads. I try to teach them a little and to teach it well.'" As to this Dr. Holmes's own testimony is: "My advice to every teacher less experienced than myself would be, therefore: Do not fret over the details you have to omit; you probably teach altogether too many as it is. Individuals may learn a thing with once hearing it, but the only way of teaching a whole class is by enormous repetition, representation, and illustration in all possible forms. Now and then you will have a young man on your benches like the late Waldo Burnett, — not very often, if you lecture half a century. You cannot pretend to lecture chiefly for men like that, — a Mississippi raft might as well take an ocean-steamer in tow. To meet his wants you would have to leave the rest of your class behind, and

that you must not do.  President Allen, of Jefferson
College, says that his instruction has been successful
in proportion as it has been elementary.  It may be
a humiliating statement, but it is one which I have
found true in my own experience."

To know really and with thoroughness *something*,
be it more or less, seemed to him the thing chiefly
desirable.  It was a reminiscence of the old influence
of Louis, who had impressed on his pupils that accuracy was the first and highest of what may be called
the virtues of the intellect.  Smatterings, and the con-
ceit of half knowledge, were odious to Dr. Holmes;
and as in this country they rise to the dignity of a
national characteristic, he had to wage unresting war
against them.  He said: "Our American atmosphere
is vocal with the flippant loquacity of half knowledge.
We must accept whatever good can be got out of it,
and keep it under as we do sorrel and mullein and
witchgrass, by enriching the soil, and sowing good
seed in plenty; by good teaching and good books,
rather than by wasting our time in talking against it.
Half knowledge dreads nothing but whole knowledge."
And again: "The difference between green and sea-
soned knowledge is very great."

Dr. Holmes was one of the early microscopists, and
was a very good one.  The instrument was not among
the tools of the instructing physicians when he was
studying in Paris, but soon afterward it came into
general use.  He brought one home with him from
Europe.  It fascinated him, as indeed it did many
another.  He had a great taste for everything ingenious, and playing with this new machine devoured
many an hour.  He was forever taking his own to
pieces and putting it together, and trying all sorts of

experiments with it, both as to the mechanism itself,
and as to the subjects of examination.    How well I
recollect the intense absorption with which he would
thus pass long hours! — hours which were not wasted,
for "he was no mean authority on this subject in his
day," says Dr. Cheever.

The Doctor was a great lover of the old writers upon
medicine; those men, of whom the better educated
physicians knew the names and the less educated ones
knew nothing, were familiar to him.    They appealed
doubtless to his literary sense by their quaintness;
but he justified his study of them by stoutly maintain-
ing that the study of anatomy had undergone no great
change since they wrote.    The venerable folios which
embalmed their wisdom gladdened his eyes.    "He
cuddled old books, and hugged them close," says Dr.
Cheever; and the purchase of them sometimes led
him to the verge of extravagance, or even beyond that
annoying frontier.    The excellence of the old illustrations charmed his skilled eye; such work, he said,
could not be had in these days, when big editions are
cheaply prepared.    He handled his volumes affectionately, turned to these engravings with delight, and
dilated upon them in the spirit of the bibliophile,
which he really was in the matter of medical books.
This dearly loved collection — "965 volumes and
many pamphlets" — he finally gave to the Boston
Medical Library, an institution which, Dr. Cheever
says, "was largely due to his name and influence."
For thirteen years he was its president, and upon re-
signing his office he made the gift.    "These books,"
he said, in his tender way, "were very dear to me as
they stood upon my shelves.    A twig from some one
of my nerves ran to every one of them. . . . . They

marked the progress of my studies, and stood before me as the stepping-stones of my professional life.   I am pleased that they can be kept together, at least for the present ; and if any of them can be to others what they have been to me, I am glad to part with them, even though it costs me a little heartache to take leave of such old and beloved companions."[1]

The period of Dr. Holmes's incumbency in his medical professorship was, of course, one of change and advancement.   When the younger men demanded novelties, and were sustained by the new President of the University, Dr. Cheever tells us that Dr. Holmes "was at heart favorable to advance, but he was timid as to the losses and dangers of radical changes, although not a violent opponent."   Among Dr. Holmes's letters there are some passages which state clearly that he was pleased with the ways of Mr. Eliot, and that he contemplated with amused satisfaction the rattle and clatter with which that vigorous gentleman knocked the respectable antiquities about, and threw out of the collegiate windows and thrust out of the doors the comfortable old habits, customs, and prejudices, — let us stop short of adding abuses, because there had hardly been time for real *abuses* to establish themselves.

During his day there took place a famous and desperate engagement between the friends and the foes of the admission of women to the Harvard Medical School.   His friend Dr. Henry J. Bigelow led with characteristic strenuousness the opponents.   But, though Dr. Holmes was so situated that he could not be altogether a neutral, he would not become an active combatant.   Dr. Cheever says that his "kindly

---

[1] *Medical and Surgical Journal,* vol. cxxxi. No. 24, p. 584.

nature inclined him to the claims of the other sex, but he voted with the majority [in the negative] for prudential reasons." It is "interesting as an index of his delicacy and purity, that he affirmed that he was willing to teach women anatomy, but not with men in the same classes; and, above all, that he should insist on two dissecting-rooms, which should strictly separate the sexes." Dr. Dwight says that Dr. Holmes had "inclined to the losing side," but does not "remember that he ever showed much enthusiasm in the cause."

A short time afterward, when the smoke of this battle was lifting, if not quite all gone, at the opening of the new building of the Harvard Medical School, Dr. Holmes delivered an address, and Professor Dwight tells the following anecdote: —

"On this occasion, after speaking in his most perfect style on woman as a nurse, with a pathos free from mawkishness which Dickens rarely reached, he concluded: ' I have always felt that this was rather the vocation of woman than general medical, and especially surgical, practice.' This was the signal for loud applause from the conservative side. When he could resume he went on: ' Yet I myself followed the course of lectures given by the young Madame Lachapelle in Paris, and if here and there an intrepid woman insists on taking by storm the fortress of medical education, I would have the gate flung open to her, as if it were that of the citadel of Orleans and she were Joan of Arc returning from the field of victory.' The enthusiasm which this sentiment called forth was so overwhelming, that those of us who had led the first applause felt, perhaps looked, rather foolish. I have since suspected that Dr. Holmes, who always knew his audience, had kept back the real climax to lure us to our destruction."

Dr. Cheever and Professor Dwight ought to be better informed than I am on this subject, therefore I hardly venture to say that I should think Dr. Holmes "inclined" against the practice, at least the general practice, of medicine by women. In 1871 (before the great marshalling of hosts and arguments, it is true) he wrote to Professor Arthur M. Edwards: "Accept my thanks for the pamphlet you have sent me, . . . and the interesting address of Miss Dr. Ward. I go for women in women's diseases and midwifery, and am always glad to see a real expert, like yourself, helping them in his department." So likewise in *A Mortal Antipathy* he writes: "I am disposed to agree with your friend, that you will often spoil a good nurse to make a poor doctor. . . . I am for giving women every chance for a good education, and if they think medicine is one of their proper callings, let them try it. I think they will find that they had better at least limit themselves to certain specialties, and always have an expert of the other sex to fall back upon. The trouble is that they are so impressible and imaginative that they are at the mercy of all sorts of fancy systems," — with more, which I refrain from quoting, lest the women should take offence! [1]

Literature never really weaned Holmes from the science of medicine, though in time it put a conclusive end to his practice as a physician. I think that it was by no means alone the salary which induced him to continue his lectures at the Medical School so long as he did; but that he would not sever the connection which kept him still a genuine member of that profession, which had won the love of his youth and still held the loyalty of his mature, even his declining

[1] See, also, *Medical Essays*, Riverside Ed., pp. 299, 317.

years. Pleasant evidence of the respect in which he held it, and the faith he had in its elevating influence, is furnished by his remark that "Goldsmith and even Smollett, both having studied and practised medicine, could not by any possibility have outraged all the natural feelings of delicacy and decency as Swift and Zola have outraged them." His brethren of the calling appreciated and returned his feeling, and always warmly and rightly counted him as one of their brotherhood. Professor William Osler [1] said: "He will always occupy a unique position in the affections of medical men. Not a practitioner, yet he retained for the greater part of his active life the most intimate connection with the profession. . . . The festivals at Epidaurus were never neglected by him; and as the most successful combination which the world has ever seen of the physician and the man of letters, he has for years sat amid the Æsculapians in the seat of honor."

From 1847 to 1853 he was Dean of the Medical School. In 1852 he was Anniversary chairman at the annual meeting of the Massachusetts Medical Society. In 1860 he was the orator at the annual meeting of the same society.

During the early years of Holmes's married life the famous lecture-habit of the country, of New England and New York more especially, was in its prime and heyday. It is difficult for persons, who know that system only in its later development, to picture to themselves what it then was. Now some third-rate

---

[1] Professor of Medicine at Johns Hopkins University, — in some "Remarks" made before the Medical Society of that University, October 15, 1894.

person is "managed" about the country, not himself
illustrious, but with an illustrated lecture, like an
itinerant picture-book with simple text for good people not too much grown up.  In those days, on the
other hand, the best men of the time gave out their
best thoughts upon the lyceum platform.  Emerson
tried his finest wisdom upon many audiences before
he offered it in print; for many years James Russell Lowell found his way to the minds of his countrymen through their ears not less than through their
eyes; the scholarly eloquence of Wendell Phillips
and the strenuous iconoclasm of Theodore Parker
were familiar far and wide; Dr. Kane thrilled many
a listening crowd with his tales of Arctic adventure
before he printed his exciting volumes; even Thackeray came from England to talk about the "Four
Georges;" and in a lighter strain Alfred Bunn, the
Englishman, with his reminiscences of the English
stage, and Gilman, with his droll dissertations on
Yankee humor, gave more entertainment if less instruction than the graver talkers.  These were a few,
only; how long and varied a list will the old lecture-
goers recall !  Everybody went to the lectures in
those days; they were fashionable as well as popular.
Not a few of the more conservative citizens still looked
askance upon the theatre, and entered it not at all or
rarely; but the lecturer always found the benches
before him full, and if he were a man of any note
from whom really good things could be expected, his
audience was a gathering of the men and women whom
it was best worth while to address among all the
community.  The demand was not less throughout
the smaller cities, the country towns, and even the villages.  Thus there was working an immense educa-

tional machine, which produced great and valuable results.

Among the lecturers Dr. Holmes was a favorite with the bureaus, and had no lack of engagements. Physically he certainly lay under some disadvantages upon a first introduction; but these were quickly forgotten. His voice was not good in sound, but it had much variety, was very expressive, and was skilfully controlled; his countenance responded with apt and lively change to each passing phase of thought; and his whole air, bearing, and presence were visibly permeated by a quick attractive sympathy with the audience, and with what he was saying to it.

The most important work of this kind which he did was the delivery of a course of twelve lectures on the English poets, before the Lowell Institute. I remember these well; the hall was crowded with the best auditors that Boston could furnish, and the lecturer was most cordially received. He ventured at once on the novel scheme of closing his lecture with some verses of his own, which were so kindly taken that he continued it, and afterwards he extended the idea to the Breakfast-Table Series. This sort of lecturing was all very well; for, after the legitimate labor of composition was over, he had only to walk comfortably round from Montgomery Place into Washington Street, and talk for an hour or two to the *élite* among his friends and neighbors, and receive their generous applause. But this came like an oasis amid the dreary waste of country lecturing. No one who tried that, in those days, is upon record as liking it. First there was the stifling super-heated railway car, devoid even of modern pretences at ventilation; next, the cold darkling drive, usually about the dreary sunset hour; then the chilly "best bedroom," perchance fireless, or perchance heated with an air-tight stove. For sustenance, to fortify one's self against these ills, there was that dyspepsia-breeding meal called "tea," with its glutinous breadcakes, its viscous pastry, all its various awful sweetened impossibilities. Bad enough for any one, these discomforts were especially bad for Dr. Holmes; his sensitive constitution suffered from the meals; and his dreaded asthma, stimulated by the exposure, often kept him painfully awake a good part of the long and desolate night. James Russell Lowell spoke of this sort of thing, as he experienced it at the West, with some acerbity: "To be received at a bad inn by a solemn committee, in a room with a stove that smokes but not exhilarates, to have three cold fish tails laid in your hand to shake, to be carried to a cold lecture-room, to read a cold lecture to a cold audience, to be carried back to your smoke-side, paid, and the three fish tails again — well, it is not delightful exactly." In New England, the hospitality of some ambitious villager usually displaced the inn; nevertheless it wasn't pleasant. "Family men," said Dr. Holmes, "get dreadfully homesick. In the remote and bleak village the heart returns to the red blaze of the logs in one's fireplace at home.

'There are his young barbarians all at play,'

— if he owns any youthful savages. No, the world has a million roosts for a man, but only one nest." It was of her creator, of course, that the Autocrat's landlady said, that he generally came home from a lecturing excursion "with a cold in his head as bad as a horse distemper."

Then, too, the country audiences, though usually intelligent, were rarely either genial or congenial, and in time their "awful uniformity" begat a deadly weariness. "I have sometimes felt," the Doctor said, "as if I were a wandering spirit, and this great unchanging multi-vertebrate, which I faced night after night, was one ever-listening animal, which writhed along after me wherever I fled, and coiled at my feet every evening, turning up to me the same sleepless eyes which I thought I had closed with my last drowsy incantation!" There are several charming pages about this lecturing business in this sixth paper of *The Autocrat*, of which these remarks are a part; but it is significant that, with the exception of these passages, Holmes referred rarely and charily to his lecturing experiences, though it was his wont otherwise to use freely all the incidents of his life. It is evident that the reminiscences of the travelling and touring about the towns and villages had a flavor too disagreeable for toleration. Nevertheless, in spite of those sleepless nights, those dyspepsias and colds and aching joints, and although he might reasonably prefer "nateral death to puttin' himself out of the world by any such violent means as lecterin'," the work had to be done. For worse than any or all these ills was that old classic difficulty, with which he was afflicted, the *urgens egestas*, which was epidemic in New England in those days, and could only be cured by very hard work; and though this "lecture-peddling," as he called it, "in competition with the cheapest itinerants, with shilling concerts and negro - minstrel entertainments," was indeed "a hard business and a poorly paid one," yet one "could get a kind of living out of it if he had invitations enough." In this

point of finances Dr. Holmes was in the like condition
with pretty much all his friends and neighbors; the
few who were called rich were only less poor than the
others, and all alike, rich gentlemen or poor gentlemen, took work for granted as the inevitable lot of
man and entirely in accord with the highest pretensions to gentility.   Those who were lazy only worked
a little less hard than the others.   It is true that the
lecturing part of Dr. Holmes's work, in addition to
being hard, was disagreeable; and the pay certainly
was meagre, — ridiculously meagre, by any modern
standard.   Still he had no right to consider, and did
not consider, his lot an especially bad one in comparison with the average of his compeers.

Here is a letter sketching his family matters at this
time: —

TO PHINEAS BARNES.

*December 4, 1842.*

MY DEAR BARNES, — I am sorry to have to say in
reply to your kind invitations on behalf of the Committee of the Lyceum, that I have felt obliged to
decline all invitations to lecture during the present
season, on account of my other occupations.   If I
had not made up my mind on this point, I should
have [been] tempted to Portland by the desire to see
an old friend and what would be to me a new city.

I will not let my answer go without taking the opportunity to give a rub at that old chain which was
once bright enough, but which in the lapse of time
has got a little rusted, as everything must that is not
in daily use.   Can you believe that it is almost twenty
years since we took our strolls together beneath the
trees, and dipped our slender limbs in the waters of

Andover? What a difference between the micro-
scropic view of years at fifteen and the telescopic look
of them at thirty! I believe you learned, when you
were here, that there was a second edition of your old
acquaintance, an o. w. h., who now numbers the
goodly period of twenty months. I think, too, that
you are more abundant in olive branches than myself
— if I remember your domestic record. I may, perhaps, come on an exploratory tour to your oriental
regions some time or other, and ascertain for myself.

When you were here, I believe I was living as a
temporary bachelor, and so you only saw the worse
half, or third rather, of my interior. The time has
gone away very fast, and with the exception that my
then rusticating companion is scribbling fearfully in
a great book of visiting accounts at my side, everything goes on much as it did then. I am getting a
little more practice as I grow older, but rather slowly,
— taking rather more interest in my profession, —
gradually depositing the turbid particles of juvenility,
— not sitting up quite so late, — drinking, singing,
smoking in a more subdued vein, but on the whole
cheerful and comfortable. I am afraid you will not
meet our friend Roby in your quarter of the globe
very soon, for two reasons: one that he is sitting in
a professional chair at Baltimore, — the other that he
has in the calmest and quietest manner possible gone
and engaged himself to a fine, rosy, buxom, and delightful young lady who will, I suspect, make him
rather more stationary in his habits.

So if you wish to know anything about me or mine,
you must come and ask me, as the Spartans said —
or pretty near it. The great book is shut up, and
the silk gown is put on, and the bonnet is forthcoming

for an evening sally to an aunt's of that name, and in
order to avoid that most severe trial of woman's affection, — ten minutes' delay after she is armed and
equipped for a tea fight or other social struggle, — I
shall bid you good-night with a thousand good wishes
and kind recollections.

When Dr. Holmes was married he bought a house
in Montgomery Place, No. 8.   But the shrine-hunter
will now look for it to little purpose; for well did the
Doctor say: "We Americans live in tents." January
1, 1885, he wrote to Mrs. Kellogg: "Yesterday morning I passed through Montgomery Place, and found
workmen tearing out the inside of No. 8, where we
lived for eighteen years, and where all my children
were born. — Not a vestige is left to show where
our old Cambridge house stood. — We must make ourselves new habitations — that is all; and carry our
remembrances, associations, affections, all that makes
home — under the new roof."   Montgomery Place
afterward became Bosworth Street, a purlieu not sa-
vory, though much given over to eating-houses; it is
now for a third time being revamped.
From this house the Doctor moved to Charles
Street, on the river-side, near Cambridge bridge.
The house had a beautiful outlook over the estuary of
the Charles to the range of hills which made the
western horizon, and the Doctor greatly enjoyed the
years spent here; he was in the heyday of his fame,
and life seemed full of happiness.   In time, however,
never-ending "progress," the fell destroyer of all
comfort in the United States, "improved" him out
of this place also; and Charles Street became a noisy
thoroughfare for business traffic.   So in 1870 the

Doctor pulled up his tent-stakes again, and fled far down Beacon Street, still, however, clinging to the river-bank.   In this third house he lived the rest of his days; for "improvement" was only threatening, not achieved, at the time of his death.   He became much attached to this house, which was much larger and handsomer than its predecessors.   He told, with glee, how the sun lay all day long in its front windows, and what a grand view he had from his library in the rear.   He wrote to Motley: "We have really a charming house, and as I turn my eyes to the left from this paper I seem to look out on all creation, Bunker Hill, and the spires of Cambridge, and Mount Auburn, and the wide estuary commonly called Charles River, — we poor Bostonians come to think at last that there is nothing like it in the *orbis terrarum*. — I suppose it sounds, to one who is away, like the Marchioness with her orange-peel and water."

It is an interesting circumstance that many long years before Dr. Holmes came to live in this house, its site was a small patch of dry land rising amid the waters of the Charles River estuary, which no one had then dreamed of "filling" and using for building purposes; and the Doctor in his early days used to look at the little island and say to himself that he should like to have a house on it.   This reminiscence was one of the motives which led him to select this especial situation.

Every one who saw Dr. Holmes in Boston would have had difficulty in imagining him as other than a city-denizen, so completely did he look and seem that character.   Yet he almost indignantly repudiated the idea, as though an incapacity to enjoy country life indicated a shortcoming in character.   He said that his city life was a necessity by reason of asthma, and the exactions of labor. For a while he owned a place at Pittsfield, to which he went in the spring of 1849, and where he passed the next seven summers. He wrote to Mr. Holker Abbott: "The place on which I lived during seven summers, 1849–1856, was in Pittsfield on the road leading to Lenox. The place contained 280 acres, and was the residue of a section six miles square bought of the State — or Province, more properly — by my great-grandfather, Jacob Wendell. The Province held it directly from the Indians. All of the present town of Pittsfield, except one thousand acres, was the property of my great-grandfather, whose deed used to hang in the entry of my house. It was dated in 1738."

The Doctor constantly referred to his life at Pittsfield, not only in his letters but in his writings, and always with affection. He made many friends there, especially Mrs. Caroline L. Kellogg, whose pleasant letters of reminiscences cheered him in his old age, and called forth lively responses so long as he could write. The place bore the old name of Canoe Meadow. "From those windows at Canoe Meadow," he says in *Elsie Venner*, "among the mountains, we could see all summer long a lion rampant, a Shanghai chicken, and General Jackson on horseback, done by Nature in green leaves, each with a single tree." And in *The Autocrat* he speaks of "that home where seven blessed summers were passed, which stand in memory like the seven golden candlesticks in the beatific vision of the holy dreamer." In 1885 he wrote to Mrs. Kellogg: "When you meet any one who you think remembers me, tell them that I am loyal to the place where I passed seven blessed summers of my life, and that

the very stones of it are precious to me as those of
Jerusalem to an ancient Hebrew." This letter to his
mother gives a pleasant glimpse of the daily life: —

TO MRS. ABIEL HOLMES.

PITTSFIELD, August 17, 1849.

MY DEAR MOTHER, — I received a very pleasant
and facetious letter from mine ancient brother John,
full of right merrie quips and jollities, for the which
he will please accept my best thanks and acknowledgments, with the request, in the words of the razor-
strop man, for a few more of the same sort. Since I
wrote you we have had a week of weather, which, if
we were not interested greatly in the greenness of
grass and clover, would have been hard to bear. But
mark you — *no east winds* — and after a very gentle
touch of dog-days it has come out clear and cool, the
mountains sharply defined, and my lawn (that is to
be) so amazingly restored, regenerated, and rejuve-
nated, that my eyes can hardly believe the change.
In the mean time we have been reading and doing
indoor work. I work in the woods sometimes, for
they are habitable in all weather, — and have even got
so far as a quiet game of backgammon, in which it
proves that the grey, etc., etc., is the better, etc., etc.

To-day Amelia went out in the forenoon with the
"kerridge," while I rode my little horse over to
Lenox to see Mr. —— and Dr. Neil. Mr. ——'s
place, which we propose to visit again soon in proper
style, is one of the most beautiful spots I ever saw
anywhere. I visited it some years ago when it was
building, and it appeared to me perfect almost to a
miracle. One of Mr. ——'s daughters — a great
lover of the picturesque and beautiful — the celebrated

Miss "——," having married a young slip of philosophy and poetry whose terrestrial name is ——, is about to build another house alongside of ——; and Mrs. Butler — the tragedy queen herself — has selected another spot, on the margin of the same lake which he overlooks, as the seat of her future residence. All this is within an hour's ride of where I am, and many of the same beauties they come so far to seek are round me here in Canoe Meadow, with others peculiar to this place.  So that I am contented enough with my own locality, though I can do homage to the marvellous charms of the more remote and secluded nook which they have chosen. . . . .

This letter to his sister also has pleasant references to the place : —

TO MRS. CHARLES W. UPHAM.

8 MONTGOMERY PLACE, *October* 16, 1849.

MY DEAR ANN, — It gave me more pleasure to find that you were pleased with my versicles than you can have had in reading them.  I was all the more gratified because I liked them myself, and could not help thinking beforehand that others might also. They were written at one sitting, and I, who am apt to be a slow coach, have rarely done so much without a break or two in the work of composition. —I cannot promise, but I hope we shall be able to run down to Salem in the course of a week or two. We shall be very glad, you may be sure, to see you all after so long an absence, which has been indeed singularly happy to us in everything but separation from our friends.  I hope some time we shall see you at Pittsfield, where we have better appliances for hos-

pitality than in town, and where it takes a great deal
less to make a visitor contented than in Boston. I
must say it comes a little hard to take up the burden
of work and obligation which has been so long laid
down, — but here I am — the hills, the green fields,
the streams, the magnificent woods, all beyond the
sunset, and my table covered with papers, my hand
at this moment cramped with writing, and everything
in bustling preparation for a new campaign of lecturing. Well, I have earned a right to a share of labor
by a long and glorious vacation of ease, and I mean
to go at it as my ploughmen went at their patches the
other day.

I have a great many things to tell of country experience and pleasures, which I can do better by word
of mouth than on this scrap of paper, and so, till I
see you, good-by, with many thanks for your praises
and kindest wishes to all.

In 1883 he wrote to John O. Sargent: "I am
glad, my dear John, to know that you are taking your
comfort in the midst of your own acres in my dear
old Berkshire, where I once thought I should have a
permanent summer home. I have never regretted
my seven summers passed in Pittsfield, and never had
the courage, though often asked, to visit the place
since I left it. I have one particularly pleasant remembrance about my place, — that I in a certain sense
created it. The trees about are all, or almost all, of
my planting, — many of them not more than a foot
high from English nurseries, others transplanted by
myself and my tenant. Look at them, as you pass
my old place, and see how much better I have deserved
the gratitude of posterity than the imbecile who only
accomplished a single extra blade of grass."

And later still, to Mrs. Kellogg: —

"A happy New Year, my dear Mrs. Kellogg, and as many such as you can count until you reach a hundred, and then begin again, if you like the planet well enough.

"But how good you are to send me all those excellent and to me most interesting photographs! I delight in recalling the old scenes in this way; changed as they are, I yet seem to be carried back to the broad street — East Street, down which I — we — used to drive on our way to the ' Four Corners ' and 'Canoe Meadow,' as my mother told me they used to call our old farm. I wonder that Pittsfield is not a city by this time. It seems almost too bad to take away its charming rural characteristics, — but such a beautiful, healthful, central situation could not resist its destiny, and you must have a mayor, I suppose, by and by, and a common council, and a lot of aldermen. But you cannot lose the sight of Greylock, nor turn the course of the Housatonic. I can hardly believe that it is almost thirty years since I bade good-by to the old place, expecting to return the next season. We passed through the gate — under the maple which used to stand there, and is probably in its old place, took a look at the house, and the great pine that stood, and I hope stands, in its solitary beauty and grandeur,— rode on — passed the two bridges, reached the station — the old one, — I think you have a better since — and good-by, dear old town — well, that is the way."

Probably the reason why the Doctor left Pittsfield is indicated by this extract from a letter published by Mrs. Fields in her article in the *Century Magazine:* "But a country house, you will remember, has been

justly styled by Balzac *une plaie ouverte*.   There is
no end to the expenses it entails.   I was very anxious to have a country retreat, and when my wife had
a small legacy of about two thousand dollars a good
many years ago, we thought we would put up a perfectly plain shelter with that money on a beautiful
piece of ground we owned in Pittsfield.   Well, the
architect promised to put the house up for that.   But
it cost just twice as much, to begin with; that was n't
much !   Then we had to build a barn; then we
wanted a horse and carryall and wagon; so one thing
led to another, and it was too far away for me to look
after it, and at length, after seven years, we sold it.
I could n't bear to think of it or to speak of it for
a long time.   I loved the trees, and while our children
were little it was a good place for them; but we had
to sell it, and it was better in the end, although I felt
lost without it for a great while."

In 1870 Miss Harriet Putnam (now Mrs. H. J.
Hayden, of New York), sent him an apple "*stolen*"
from a tree which overhung the road in front of his
old house, and he replied thus: —

> We owe, alas ! to woman's sin
>   The woes with which we grapple ; —
> To think that all our plagues came in
>   For one poor stolen apple !
> And still we love the darling thief
>   Whose rosy fingers stole it ; —
> Her weakness brought the world to grief,
>   Her smiles alone console it !
> — I take the "stolen" fruit you leave, —
>   (Forgive me, Maid and Madam,)
> It makes me dream that you are Eve,
>   And wish that I were Adam !

The " Pine-Tree " at Pittsfield

The " Pine-Tree " at Pittsfield

# CHAPTER VIII



THUS the years drifted along until only a couple more were required to bring Dr. Holmes to the sobering line of the half-century, to the "five-barred gate," as he called it. He wrote afterward of Dudley Venner, that "he had entered that period which marks the decline of men who have ceased growing in knowledge and strength: from forty to fifty a man must move upward, or the natural falling off in the vigor of life will carry him rapidly downward." He himself was near the exit from the period which he thus described, and his name had scarcely been heard outside of the small town of Boston. There his friends knew him only as a clever man, a medical professor who lectured creditably, a poet whose lines were good enough to have been once or twice gathered into a volume, a shrewd humorist, a merry wit, delightful in the chance encounter, not to be surpassed at the dinner-table, and of much usefulness upon so-called "occasions." It was a sufficiently pleasant and satisfactory life, from day to day and year to year, if one had no especial ambition; and, for this matter, nothing indicates that Dr. Holmes had been disturbed in his contentment by any notion that he had in him unexploited value. Yet the discovery was about to be made, as unexpectedly to himself and others as when the ordinary pasture is suddenly discovered to be pregnant with gold.

The country was without a first-rate, purely literary magazine. *Putnam's Magazine*, which by its merit had deserved to live and prosper, had unexplainably died. Now the publishing firm of Phillips, Sampson & Co., established in Winter Street in Boston, undiscouraged by the fate of this predecessor, gallantly resolved to renew the experiment, and invited James Russell Lowell to act as editor. He accepted, but "made it a condition precedent" that Dr. Holmes should be "the first contributor to be engaged."[1] "I," said the Doctor long afterward, "who felt myself outside of the charmed circle drawn around the scholars and poets of Cambridge and Concord, having given myself to other studies and duties, wondered somewhat when Mr. Lowell insisted upon my becoming a contributor." "I looked at the old Portfolio, and said to myself, ' Too late! too late. This tarnished gold will never brighten, these battered covers will stand no more wear and tear; close them, and leave them to the spider and the bookworm.' " But Lowell, with shrewd insight, pertinaciously applied a friendly pressure, and Holmes yielded. As he afterward said: Lowell "woke me from a kind of literary lethargy in which I was half slumbering, to call me to active service." His usefulness began at once, for he christened the unborn babe; and the name of *The Atlantic*, since so famous, was his suggestion. That he engaged thus early in this undertaking was most fortunate, not only for himself and for the reading world, but for the enterprise, which had been projected in a most unpropitious time, — the disastrous year of 1857. Only once before, in 1837, had the country

---

[1] Letter to Holmes, December, 28, 1884. Lowell's *Letters,* ii. 292.

been tried by such financial ruin. Even the twenty-five-cent piece, which was the price of a single number of the new magazine, was now jealously regarded by many a one, who had heretofore spent his dollars carelessly. That the craft launched into such stress of weather survived the storm was by many attributed to the attraction of Holmes's spirited and witty papers, which brought cheer and liveliness to worn minds sadly in need of such wholesome influences. Howells well said that Dr. Holmes "not named, but made, *The Atlantic.*"

The *nom de plume*, under which the new writer appeared, was happily chosen. *The Autocrat of the Breakfast-Table*, now for more than a generation a household word, was odd enough to attract curiosity when it first struck upon the public ear. "L'Autocrate à la table du déjeuner, titre bizarre!" exclaimed a puzzled Frenchman, writing in a land where they have no breakfast-tables. And it was a joke, which may have been also a truth, that "the proprietor of a well-known religious weekly" assumed it to be a cookery-book. But the writers for the religious papers depreciated it from the start, and indicated an opinion that its writer might himself in the dread hereafter become the subject of cookery.

Yet though the Autocrat seemed a new birth, he was in fact already past his majority. "I was just going to say, when I was interrupted," he now began. The interruption had lasted somewhat more than quarter of a century; for in the *New England Magazine*, which lived briefly from 1831 to 1835, Dr. Holmes had published two papers under this same name and of much this same plan, — papers which he would never afterward permit to be reprinted. Now,

he said, "the recollection of these crude products of
his uncombed literary boyhood suggested the thought
that it would be a curious experiment to shake the
same bough again, and see if the ripe fruit were better
or worse than the early windfalls."

It is not worth while to discourse in the vein of
the literary critic concerning *The Autocrat;* if all the
discussions which have been written concerning the
book should be gathered together, they would make
another volume as large as itself, and anything which
can be said now can be only commonplace repetition.
To speak of the "epigrammatic wisdom and tender
fancies of *The Autocrat*" would be quotation; to
dwell upon the abundance and the rare originality, the
wit, beauty, and infinite variety of its similes, would
be like calling attention to the logic of Plato or the
dramatic gift of Shakespeare.  George William Curtis said, with his wonted skill: "The index of *The
Autocrat* is in itself a unique work.  It reveals the
whimsical discursiveness of the book, the restless
hovering of that brilliant talk over every topic, fancy,
feeling, fact; a humming-bird sipping the one hon-
eyed drop from every flower, or a huma, to use its
own droll and capital symbol of the lyceum-lecturer,
the bird that never lights.  There are few books that
leave more distinctly the impression of a mind teem-
ing with riches of many kinds.  It is, in the Yankee
phrase, thoroughly wide-awake.  There is no languor,
and it permits none in the reader, who must move
along the page warily, lest in the gay profusion of the
grove, unwittingly defrauding himself of delight, he
miss some flower half-hidden, some gem chance-
dropped, some darting bird."  After all the literary
dissectors had had and used their chance, as best they

could, Dr. Holmes himself said, as usual, the best thing: "This series of papers was not the result of an express premeditation, but was, as I may say, *dipped from the running stream of my thoughts.*"

Let it not, however, be supposed that the admiration for the essays of the Autocrat was a stream which broke against no stone, encountered no snags. The critics, that strange class of men who never cease from pronouncing opinions, wholly undiscouraged by the fact that in a large percentage of cases they prove to be wrong, suggested various reasons for holding the new writer cheap. Some cried out that he was undignified; others would have it that he was nothing more than an "inordinate egotist;" another did n't think that his puns were very good; another was offended at his use of slang; and some one suggested that the poems, which were scattered among the pages, though brilliant, "showed as ill as diamonds among the spangles of the court fool."[1] But after all, the critic is only the mosquito of the literary world, he may sting an author into momentary discomfort, but he can't kill a book. And by the way it is pleasant to think that Dr. Holmes, though often thereto solicited, as the gentlemen of the law like to express it, obstinately refused to become a critic and reviewer. He said that he disliked such work. He did, indeed, review *The Light of Asia*, but his paper consisted wholly of sentences of praise and quotations from the poem; and if he did other work of the kind it has escaped me. Perhaps in criticism he encountered the same difficulty which had interfered with

---

[1] See the article by Francis H. Underwood, writing as a good witness from his own knowledge, in *Scribner's Illustrated Magazine*, May, 1879, vol xviii. No. 1, p. 121.

his professional practice, — an antipathy to cutting up people.

The majority vote has long ago established it that *The Autocrat* is the best of Dr. Holmes's prose work. It is somewhat uneven; the two or three numbers which followed the brilliant opening one were hardly equal to it; the writer seemed not quite settled to his new work; but immediately thereafter he caught the pace again and held it steadily to the finish. It is probably true that the best things in *The Autocrat* are the best things that Holmes ever wrote. Yet it is difficult to judge accurately in such a matter. When a writer makes a genuinely new departure in literature, gives the world something which, however it may be compared in any one or another single point to something which has gone before, yet is as a whole original, the atmosphere of freshness and piquancy will seem always thereafter to cling around it, so that a reader will fancy that he would single it out as the first-born of genius even if he were ignorant of the chronology.

One thing Dr. Holmes's neighbors could allege with pride and with truth: The book could have been written only in New England, and by a New Englander. The audience which was present to the mind's eye of the writer, whom instinctively he addressed, was made up from the people whom he met daily in the streets of the town. The flavor was as local, as pungent, as unmistakable, as that of a cranberry from the best bog on Cape Cod. It was not even "American," in any possible meaning of that most vague and perplexing of national adjectives; it belonged to the little northeastern corner of "America;" and was almost as local as the "pudding-stone"

of that neighborhood, which had once been the topic
of some of the Doctor's lively stanzas.[1]  It is said!
and *litera scripta manet,* — although that dread word
"provincial" fills the air with its damning sound.   I
know that some excellent men have been in a great
taking of late about this matter of provincialism; they
say that the people of the United States were "provincial" until somewhere about the time that Rich-
mond fell and Lee surrendered, — events which, it
would seem, wrought a change in this particular and
eliminated the unpleasant quality; yet they are so
worried lest this elimination should escape the notice
of Europe, nay even of the very people of this country, that they cannot open their mouths or take their
pens in hand, without proclaiming the glad tidings of
our emancipation with that surplusage of protestation
which is always so disturbing.  Was, then, Dr.
Holmes indeed "provincial"?  He was so in precisely
the same way in which — let us say, for example —
Sir Walter Scott was so.  In fact, he was *racial.*

When the first settlers came to Massachusetts, they
were, as everybody knows, the Lord's "peculiar people," and tolerably, or intolerably, peculiar in worldly
ways also.  During the many generations which succeeded, they lived in much isolation; immigrants
rarely invaded the uninviting region; it is true that
the Irish invasion had set in before Dr. Holmes began
to write; but at that time these new-comers had been

---

[1] An Englishman, though so far removed from the *locus,* got
an inkling of this, and wrote in the *Spectator:*  "The Autocrat of the Breakfast-Table, besides his perfectly marvellous
insight into the good side of his countrymen — not the Americans, understand, but the born New Englanders — had in him,
in a full degree, the power of expressing their drift, of revealing
to themselves the line upon which their minds are travelling."

chiefly laborers and servants; their gifts in the way
of statesmanship were not suspected, and the condition of Hibernocracy was not yet foreseen. All this
time the descendants of the Puritans had had New
England to themselves, had been free to develop along
such lines as their idiosyncrasies suggested, and had
availed themselves of the opportunity. If they were
a little less picturesquely singular at the end of two
centuries, if they had lost some traits which were dan-
gerously near to the grotesque, they were not the less
individual. In religion and in thought, in a philosophy of life, in their views of what men should strive
to do and to be, they had moved very independently
according to views of a quite local scope, working out
theories and principles which were all their own.
Morally and intellectually they were easily to be differentiated from all other communities of the world;
they were even supposed to have developed a new
physical type; they were tolerably homogeneous; they
had for many generations kept for themselves a considerable territory. Not ethnologically or in a scientific sense of the word, of course, but for all social,
moral, and intellectual purposes they had thus become
a *race*. Dr. Holmes now appeared as one of their
best exponents. He was a New Englander from the
central thread of his marrow to his outermost rind;
he could have made himself nothing else; he knew
this, and accepted it not as a limitation, but with a
just pleasure, and sense of power. He believed that
it was worth while — that it could fill any reasonable
ambition — to give expression to New England, the
place and the people. They were in him and he in
them. He has had co-laborers rather than competitors in the same field, a few of whom have done truth-

ful and vivid work. *The Autocrat* is not a picture of New Englandism; it is an actual piece of New England, a sample cut solidly out of the original body. *Elsie Venner* and *The Guardian Angel* are different in this respect: they contain pictures; they are more like the work of other writers distinguished in arraying the like scenery and *dramatis personæ*.

Such, as it seems to me, was Dr. Holmes's real literary relationship to mankind; he certainly was not cosmopolitan — fortunately, for after Shakespeare has been excepted, what creative genius in fiction, who has been cosmopolitan, has really made himself a place in the hearts of mankind? Some critic will perhaps reel off half-a-dozen names of writers who seem to him to contradict this position; but still I believe that to be cosmopolitan in the literature of fiction is perilous. A writer in *The Atlantic* seems to agree with this view, saying that Holmes is "another witness, if one were needed, to the truth, that identification with a locality is a surer passport to immortality than cosmopolitanism is."

If Dr. Holmes was not even national, it is probably because there was such a lack of moral, intellectual, and social solidarity in the United States that the quality of nationality was not reasonably within reach; the South, the West, New England, the middle seaboard States, differed too widely for any one person to give expression to them all in the manner in which Dr. Holmes gave expression to one of these four quarters; for it would, of course, have been impossible to do this by bringing together characters from different neighborhoods, like specimens in a museum. So it may be said that Dr. Holmes's function in literature was to present New England to the rest

of the world in his own day, and to all the world in
future days.   He did it admirably, so as to leave
nothing to be desired.   So far as New England was
worth presenting and preserving, his work merits cor-
responding eulogy.

In this same connection a word may be given to, or
wasted upon, sundry persons who have busied themselves in writing about Dr. Holmes, apparently with
little other purpose than to maintain that he was like
somebody else.   This began as soon as *The Autocrat*
had fairly made his success.   There are those who,
whenever any one in the United States does anything
noteworthy, find out and publish that he is "an American somebody-or-other."   For these people, Cooper
has been "an American Scott," Bryant, "an American Wordsworth," and so on; every American is
some European, and is expected to accept the pseudo-
nym as a compliment.   So at once the friendly critics
began to say that Dr. Holmes was "an American
Goldsmith," and regarded the likeness as exceedingly
striking, because Goldsmith once studied medicine in
a perfunctory sort of way.   Later on, when this comparison became stale, some one remembered that
charming old physician Sir Thomas Browne, who was
then forced to do service for some time.   By degrees
the list was extended; I cannot pretend to remember
it in full, but a small percentage includes Burton,
Addison, Steele, Sterne, Dr. Johnson, Smollett, Dr.
Brown, Father Prout, Praed, Hood, Sydney Smith,
Hazlitt, Leigh Hunt, Cobbett, Dryden, Pope, Moore,
Wilson, Horace Walpole, Gay, Rogers, Thackeray,
Montaigne, Goethe, Lamb, Coleridge, even Renan,
and — may it be believed! — one writer has discovered
a resemblance to Macaulay!   One would think that

Dr. Holmes was, in modern literature, what *croute-au-pôt* is in a French peasant's ménage, — scraps of everything boiled together. Could one who had so many prototypes have furnished anything at first hand? Yet one of the few sentences worth remembering, which the critics have written, was this: that Dr. Holmes "was in no sense a writer inspired by his culture." The unknown newspaper writer who said this expressed the truth very cleverly. If these suggested likenesses amuse any one, they are for the most part as harmless as they usually are absurd; and yet it does excite a certain amount of indignation to see the fair reputation for individuality, which is as much an author's property as his hat or his coat, thus whittled away, and pared off until there seems little left of that which nevertheless we all know to be a real thing and fact. Nevertheless, while no one of the multitudes of comparisons which I have read ever struck me as having the slightest value, I must come under my own ban, and confess that one day, reading what Emerson said of Montaigne (after I had passed the first half-dozen words), the thought of Dr. Holmes at once arose in my mind: "There have been men with deeper insight, but, one would say, never a man with such abundance of thought; he is never dull, never insincere, and has the genius to make the reader care for all that he cares for. The sincerity and marrow of the man reaches to his sentences. I know not anywhere the book that seems less written. It is the language of conversation transferred to a book. Cut these words, and they would bleed; they are vascular and alive. Montaigne talks with shrewdness; knows the world and books and himself, and uses the positive degree," — with more almost equally applicable.  In spite, however, of the fact that all this, which is said of Montaigne, might be said of Holmes, if any one says that Holmes is "an American Montaigne," he must be contradicted, absolutely. *Holmes was Holmes!*

In speaking of Dr. Holmes's individuality it may be worth while, in passing, to remark upon his literary solitude.  He has told us that, when *The Atlantic* was founded, he felt himself "outside the charmed circle drawn around the scholars and poets of Cambridge and Concord."  In fact, he never in any part of his career allied himself with any school, and never had any comrades pledged, by fellowship in aim or purpose, to sustain and praise him.  As has been remarked (by George William Curtis, if my memory is correct), the waves of abolition and transcendentalism, which for a time swept through the land, did not carry him along with their tide.  Neither had he followers or imitators.  To a degree which was singular, considering the somewhat peculiar surroundings, habits, and influences of the time, he stood by himself.  Thus, whatever of success and commendation he achieved was genuine and all his own.  No *claque* applauded him; no band of fellow-thinkers proclaimed and exaggerated his merits and demanded that he should be worshipped as the preacher of new truths. All that came to him was of his own unaided winning.

Dr. Holmes's New-Englandism, as the scope and field of his genius, is of course an entirely different thing from his Bostonianism, and yet the thought of the former naturally calls up also the latter.  In times past Boston has been a city which has stimulated the affection and the pride of New Englanders, perhaps even more strongly than Edinburgh used to inspire

the like sentiments in Scotchmen.  Off in a corner,
"side-tracked," out of the route of travel, as she is,
the old town has not only filled the hearts, but has
even satisfied the aspirations of her citizens.  Whether
she will continue to excite such loyalty now that her
children are no longer allowed to have her to themselves, but must be diluted or swamped by the swell-
ing current of dregs and sediment setting thither from
those trans-Atlantic regions which certain Americans
always speak of as "effete monarchies" and "worn-
out civilizations," though all the while welcoming
their worst scourings, is a question which the Bostonian would rather shun than answer.  Dr. Holmes,
contemplating this unsavory foreign flood in his later
days, and writing as an "inveterately rooted American of the Bostonian variety," expressed his "hope
that the exchanges of emigrants and re-migrants will
be much more evenly balanced by and by than at
present."  Happily during most of his lifetime he was
spared this painful spectacle.  The good old town had
its homogeneous population of pure-blooded Yankees,
whom he understood, and whose daily haunts he
dearly loved.  "I have bored this ancient city through
and through in my daily travels," he said, "until I
know it as an old inhabitant of a Cheshire knows his
cheese."  Of course the Autocrat's boarding - house
was in Boston, and it is pleasant to see that, little as
any of the local names and associations meant to the
rest of the world, Dr. Holmes found them quite good
enough for his use.  Boston Common is the favorite
scene in his drama.  The school-mistress takes the
"Long path" there.  Hard by was the Great Elm,
under which other lovers lingered.  Nay, the loyal
gentleman even writes of that small pool — so small

that it has thus far escaped the national mania for
vast names, and is still "the Frog Pond"—as if he
were talking of the famous Serpentine in the heart of
the world's great capital.  He recalls the days "when
there were frogs in it, and the folks used to come
down from the tents on 'lection and Independence
days with their pails to get water to make egg-pop
with."  Over it glittered the dome of that State
House, now tottering in decay and death, but which,
for Dr. Holmes, was ever "the centre of his little universe."  He creates "Little Boston" for the express
purpose of saying through him, as the Greek actors
through their masks, in a certain exaggerated or extravagant way, things which he *will* utter, but which
can only be wisely said in this manner.  Thus the
emphatic little man exclaims:—

"A new race, and a whole new world for the new-
born human soul to work in!  And Boston is the
brain of it, and has been any time these hundred
years!  That's all I claim for Boston,—that it is
the thinking centre of the continent, and therefore of
the planet."

"It's a slow business, this of getting the ark
launched. . . . I love to hear the workmen knocking
at the old blocks of tradition, and making the ways
smooth with the oil of the Good Samaritan.  I don't
know, sir,—but I do think she stirs a little,—I do
believe she slides; and when I think of what a work
that is for the dear old three-breasted[1] mother of
American liberty, I would not take all the glory of
all the greatest cities in the world for my birthright
in the soil of little Boston!"

[1] The unfortunate persons who do not know Boston may be
told that the city is, or was, built upon three hills.

Yet in spite of all his supreme satisfaction in Boston, it is not to be supposed, and it is not true, that Dr. Holmes resigned himself altogether willingly to such an out-of-the-way abiding-place for a lifetime, without occasional painful twinges at the thought of the great world without, of which he had had no glimpse since his youth, and could now know only by hearsay. He was not so narrow-minded as that! More than once in his letters to Motley and to Lowell he refers, not bitterly, but with something of regret and humility in his tone, to his own restricted "provincial" career and surroundings as compared with what they were doing and enjoying in those brilliant capitals, where all that was best in the world seemed to be brought together. Doubtless he felt that he too could win admiration in London society, and could drink deep — and with how great relish! — of its fascinations. "I have lived so long stationary," he wrote one day to Motley, "that I have become intensely local, and doubtless in many ways narrow. I should like to breathe the air of the great outer world for a while, but I am so sure to suffer from asthmatic trouble, if I trust myself in strange places, that I consider myself as a kind of prisoner for life, and am very thankful that my condemned cell is so much to my liking. There are some valuable qualities about an old provincial friend like me, to a cosmopolitan like yourself. He keeps the home flavor, a whiff of which from his garments is now and then as pleasant, I am willing to believe, as the scent of the lavender in which fair linen has been laid away in old bureau drawers. It is not the fragrance of the garden, but there is something which reaches the memory in it and sets us thinking of seasons that are

dead and gone, and what they carried away with
them."

To Miss Robins, a friend of his daughter, he vigor-
ously said one day, when he was over seventy-five
years old, that he should like to live another life,
[not this same life over again, but *another* life] of
equal length, and in it to do the things which he had
not done in this one; among these things he especially spoke of travel. "I don't want to leave the
world," he said, "before I have seen it." It was
somewhere near the same time that he wrote: "If in
a future state there shall be vacations in which we
may have liberty to revisit our old home, . . . I
think one of the first places I should go to, after my
birthplace, the old gambrel-roofed house, — the place
where it stood, rather, — would be that mighty, awe-
inspiring river," the Nile.

Yet though such disappointments occasionally made
the Doctor grave, they never made him discontented.
He stayed in his out-of-the-world home, hearing
rather than seeing the great mad torrent of life rush-
ing and swirling by through the nations, and he remained quite cheerful, partly because it was his temperament always to be so, partly because he had such
a multiplicity of interests that discontent could find
no chink to force an entrance amid his occupied
hours. No man, I believe, ever so refrained from
a murmur at any part of his lot in life as did Dr.
Holmes.

Having launched his barque upon *The Atlantic*,
and achieved so brilliant a trial trip thereon, Dr.
Holmes never afterward allowed himself to be lured
to tempting ventures upon strange waters. Profes-

*The Gambrel-Roofed House, Cambridge*

sional papers of course floated towards professional
publications; and I remember that he yielded to the
teasing persistence of kinship and friendship sufficiently to contribute two or three articles to *The Inter-
national Review*, when Henry Cabot Lodge and I
were trying in vain to keep that very heavy craft
afloat.   When *The Atlantic* went from the hands of
its projectors (whose business career was not prosperous) into the control of Ticknor & Fields, who had
formerly been Dr. Holmes's publishers, at that "Old
Corner Bookstore" which has been famous in Boston
annals, he stayed with the magazine, — part of its
"tackle, apparel, and furniture," in the phrase of the
admiralty courts.   The publishers of the magazine
were always his publishers, and his connection with
the successive firms remained ever cordial.   Relations
so long-maintained, so exclusive, and so friendly are
not of such frequency between author and publisher
that they do not deserve notice.   Mr. Fields was for
many years a next-door neighbor of Dr. Holmes, and
proximity and community of interests built up a considerable intimacy between them.   Dr. Holmes placed
great reliance upon the judgment of Mr. Fields, who
was well known to have rare skill in his calling.
Merely as a trifling example, here is one of the Doctor's notes, written to Mr. Fields : —


164 CHARLES STREET, February 7, 1870.

MY DEAR MR. FIELDS, — I send this letter to you
immediately on its receipt, because you are my best,
I may say my only literary adviser.

You have now plenty of young blood for *The Atlantic*, and it is a question with me whether others
cannot do better for you than I can.

I do not *at this moment* wish to undertake any new continuous labor, but my ambitions are not quite extinguished, and I love to cherish the idea that I may at some future time — not very remote, of course — make one or two more literary ventures.

My preference, I do not hesitate to say, is for *The Atlantic.* But if you think it might be worth my while to try a different audience one of these days — that is, if I could make a good thing of it — I should listen to your advice.

At any rate, I want a word or two from you with reference to this and any similar proposals.

Naturally Mr. Fields did not think it desirable that his contributor, who probably upon a purely mercantile scale of value stood at the top of *The Atlantic's* roll-call, should "try a different audience." Therefore somewhat later on in the same year came this: —

164 CHARLES STREET, *August* 18, 1870.

MY DEAR MR. FIELDS, — I am just beginning to clear the decks for autumn action. I think we had better *talk* the matter over any evening that you will appoint, either at your house or mine — any time after eight or half past eight, — inasmuch as we sit an hour or so after tea at the west window to enjoy the recollection of sunset, — which is premature nowadays, — and dig up the roots of remembrances that flowered and went to seed in the old summers and autumns.

Won't you come in any evening it suits you, and talk me into a fine frenzy of ambition and composition?

The connection continued unbroken, so far as was possible through some changes of firm make-up, and when Houghton, Mifflin & Co. emerged into ultimate and permanent occupancy, it was reëstablished with them and endured to the day of the Doctor's death, so that one of his last visits, if not actually the last, was made to the parlors of these publishers. In 1885 he manifested the closeness and sincerity of his interest in their affairs by interceding thus in their behalf with Mr. Lowell: —

TO JAMES RUSSELL LOWELL.

October 7, 1885.

MY DEAR JAMES, — Calling on Mr. Houghton this morning on business of my own, he expressed the strongest wish that you could be induced to write for *The Atlantic*. I told him that I supposed you had received, or would receive, liberal offers from the New York periodicals. He does not want to bid against other publishers; but, to use his own language, it would not be money that would stand in the way of your writing for *The Atlantic*. How much he or others would pay you I do not know, but I do know that Mr. Houghton has treated me very liberally, that he is an exact man of business, that he takes a pride in *The Atlantic*, which I suppose in a literary point of view is recognized as the first of the monthlies, and that he is very anxious to see you again in the pages of the old magazine you launched so long ago. I represent his wishes, and I need not say my own. You know your own value as an article of commerce — forgive me, I mean you know what the market will pay you for your writings, and of course must consult your own interests as well as your natural predilec-

tions in choosing a publisher.  Other things being
equal, you might perhaps prefer to publish in Boston,
and add to the prestige of the city and the University.  But it is not for me to strike the balance.  Mr.
Houghton did not ask me to *write* to you, — in a very
hesitating way he said he would like to have me *speak*
to you about it, seeming to doubt if I should be willing to do it.  I told him I should write, which seemed
to please him, and which cannot hurt you in any way,
as it does not oblige you to answer this letter or take
any special notice of its suggestions.

Only in making your plans please remember that
we have a first-class publisher here in Boston, whose
proposals may prove worth your consideration.  Please
lay this note by among the *faits pour servir* in deter-
mining where you will send your literary fruits to
market.

In June, 1890, when upwards of eighty years old,
he showed his spirit and vigor by suggesting to Mr.
Houghton that he should like to "enter into a new
written engagement for the next five years, or such
portion of that time as I may live."  In this letter he
speaks of their business relations as having "always
been so satisfactorily arranged," and goes on to
say : —

"I have written very briefly, simply, and frankly
to you, having entire confidence in your candor and
always kind consideration of my interests, where they
are involved with your own.  You have been my publisher for a long time, and I do not wish to listen to
any outside temptations, even when they come in so
attractive a form as that of *The Forum*.  My nature
is a very loyal one, and (in Prior's words): —

> ' I hold it both a shame and sin
> To quit the good old Angel inn.'

"Please think my letter over and write to me at your convenience."

These words lead to a reflection: that, apart from inferences as to the temper and character of the parties who so long dealt amicably together, the peaceful preservation of this sort of literary and publishing partnership was an indication of Dr. Holmes's sagacity in business affairs. There used to be a theory among his friends of the down-town regions that he was an absurdly helpless gentleman in the practical department of life, especially in what they vaguely but impressively called "money matters." It was altogether a mistake. He had a shrewd, Yankee capacity and a soundness of judgment for which he never received credit, chiefly because he never concerned himself with the prices of stocks and bonds, or the prospects of mills and railroads. Yet it was noticeable that he was never duped in such matters, and if he did not always know the best investment, he knew and selected the man who was best able to inform him concerning it. So in this matter of publishing his books, he had the good sense to avoid that jealous and quarrelling habit of authors, which leads them so often to the flattering fancy that their publishers are growing rich on the product of their brains, while they themselves are put off with a scanty paring of their just rewards. It was sound worldly, or practical, wisdom which made him believe, and consistently act on the belief, that in the long run he could do better by keeping the interests of the publishers and himself permanently united, than he could do by squabbling about payments or copyrights, by seeking competitive bids, and splitting up his allegiance, so that no one firm should have that sense of loyalty, good-feeling, and a common interest, which means more in business than is sometimes supposed.

# CHAPTER IX



BEFORE the Autocrat's second advent, Dr. Holmes, in his literary character, was known only as a writer of poetry; thereafter he was much better known as a writer of prose; and, indeed, he himself seemed to make his poems subsidiary by scattering them through the papers of the Breakfast-Table Series. It was in the fourth paper of *The Autocrat* that "The Chambered Nautilus" appeared, — "booked for immortality," said Whittier when he read it. The author himself and the critics are agreed that it is the best poetry that he ever wrote. It was his highest notch, his "record," as the sporting fraternity would express it; and the sporting fraternity understands distinctly, through long experience, that the only way to measure competitors is by their respective "records;" averages cannot be so accurately established.

Once, being asked whether he derived more satisfaction from having written his "Essay on Puerperal Fever," which had saved so many lives, or from having written the lyric which had given pleasure to so many thousands, Dr. Holmes replied: —

"I think I will not answer the question you put me. I think oftenest of 'The Chambered Nautilus,' which is a favorite poem of mine, though I wrote it myself. The essay only comes up at long intervals.

The poem repeats itself in my memory, and is very often spoken of by my correspondents in terms of more than ordinary praise.  I had a savage pleasure, I confess, in handling those two professors, — learned men both of them, skilful experts; but babies, as it seemed to me, in their capacity of reasoning and arguing.  But in writing the poem I was filled with a better feeling — the highest state of mental exaltation and the most crystalline clairvoyance, as it seemed to me, that had ever been granted to me — I mean that lucid vision of one's thought, and of all forms of expression which will be at once precise and musical, which is the poet's special gift, however large or small in amount or value.  There is more selfish pleasure to be had out of the poem — perhaps a nobler satisfaction from the life-saving labor."

Was, then, Whittier right, and was "The Chambered Nautilus," and of course Dr. Holmes with it, really starting on so long a journey into futurity? Moreover, is it always by his best verses that a poet reaches that moderately remote time which is, of course, intended by the word "immortality," a word inconveniently expressive in its accurate sense?  This may be doubted.  Is some of a man's work to be found in all the "Selections," all the "Anthologies"? Do the school-children learn his verses, and is it safe to quote them in a familiar way to the adult promiscuous public?  These are pertinent queries, upon this point of long survival; and some of Holmes's lyrics will stand these tests.  But among all that he wrote, if a gentleman of the betting fraternity were to propose placing a stake with me on "the favorite" in the race for the "Immortality cup," I should name — in spite of all the wise grooms in the stables of Art and

Poetry — not "The Chambered Nautilus," but "The Last Leaf." Edgar Allan Poe transcribed this with his own hand; Abraham Lincoln knew it by heart; the publishers selected it from all Dr. Holmes's poetry for printing by itself in an elaborately illustrated edition. Hundreds of persons can repeat every line of it. Such facts mean much.

Dr. Holmes himself was more ambitious to be thought a poet than anything else. The fascination of that word of charm had bewitched him as it has so many others. It implied genius, inspiration, a spark of the divine fire, — embellishments not regarded as necessary for the full equipment of the best man who ever wrote mere prose. It signified that he was one of a very small band. Moreover, it was pleasant to think that no true poet had yet been known to glide down the sloping road to oblivion. So beyond a doubt Dr. Holmes wanted to be esteemed a genuine *poet ;* and in the moments in which he pictured himself to himself in the most pleasing light, it was as a poet. He occasionally spoke of his manner of writing poetry, — to the effect that when he took his pen in hand, he knew not whither it would carry him; he became but a voice for the thought which was sent to him. Such is the formula for poetic inspiration. He who receives it is called a genius. Was there such inspiration for Holmes? Was he a genius? One can imagine his spirit awaiting with what supreme anxiety the answers which may come to these queries from one and another of his readers. Let, then, each of them make his own answer. I shirk the responsibility of guiding any one's judgment in so momentous a matter.

Sainte-Beuve once wrote: "The greatest poet is not he who has done the best; it is he who suggests the most; he, not all of whose meaning is at first obvious, and who leaves you much to desire, to explain, to study; much to complete in your turn." It is safe to say that Sainte-Beuve would not have ordered Dr. Holmes to a very giddy altitude on Parnassus. The Doctor was always entirely intelligible upon the first reading, — a very comfortable trait, surely, if not the most lofty. He was neither transcendental, nor mystical, nor a purveyor of sensations without ideas, like a fleshly form without a real skeleton. If his jolly fun, his wit, his humor, his not unkindly yet keen satire, his epigrammatic wisdom, his humanity, his genuine and tender pathos, failed to be apparent at once and easily to any reader, one can only say that really it was hardly worth while to have made that man able to read.

There may, therefore, be doubt whether or not Holmes was a great, inspired poet; but there is no doubt at all that he was a charming *singer*, according to a distinction which, it must be admitted, would affect the standing of some of the most delightful versifiers from the days of Sappho and Anacreon down to this current year. A song, half occult, but not less delicious for its lurking semi-concealment, nestled in a very large proportion of his short poems, — which means his best poems, since there can be no question that lyric poetry was his proper field. Truly the lyre was never far away from him in his happiest moods. His melody was absolutely perfect; he could take any form of rhyme ever devised by song-makers, and render perfect music with it. He was a consummate master of all that is harmonious, graceful, and pleasing in rhythm and in language. He played with measures with such light natural mastery as Hawthorne tells us that the Faun displayed in dancing.  In all respects his literary finish defied fault-finding.  His perfect taste could never be deceived.  He had more even than taste, or judgment, or discretion; he had a quality which must be called tact.  Is there in all literature a lyric in which drollery, passing nigh unto ridicule yet stopping short of it, and sentiment becoming pathos yet not too profound, are so exquisitely intermingled as in "The Last Leaf"?  To spill into the mixture the tiniest fraction of a drop too much of either ingredient was to ruin all.  How skilfully, how daintily, how unerringly, Dr. Holmes compounded it, all readers of English know well.  It was a light and trifling bit, if you will; but how often has it made the smile and the tear dispute for mastery, in a rivalry which is never quite decided!  It was the best, but not the only instance of his power in this way.  The like rare capacity may be seen, especially, in some of the later of the poems written for the meetings of the class of 1829.  It was the best proof of how truthful the Doctor's sensitiveness was, — so delicate and so unerring that it reminds us of some scientific instrument of the most exquisite mechanism.

That Dr. Holmes was easily chief among the writers of *vers d'occasion* will be readily admitted.  No matter what the occasion, he could meet it with a spirited poem in the note of perfect sympathy.  What a Poet Laureate he would have made!  Yet he was not wasted in a republic.  Such was his good nature that he did enough of this kind of writing, — for his own reputation almost more than enough.  "These ' occasional poems ' are fatal to any poet save Dr. Holmes," said Whittier ; and certainly there seems to be a popular suspicion that "occasional" poetry cannot be the best poetry. It rarely *is*, but there is no intrinsic reason why it *cannot* be. If all the "occasional" poetry were extracted from the *Odes and Epodes of Horace*, how the world would be robbed and the school-boys would rejoice! I do not mean to suggest an equation between Dr. Holmes and Horace; that, I fear, would hardly pass! Yet it may be justly said that Horace had not any very different *kind* of genius and inspiration from that of Dr. Holmes, of however much rarer quality these may have been in the Roman; and Horace has already lived some eighteen hundred years, and is not yet moribund, — a tolerably fair finite "immortality." [1]

That Dr. Holmes was quite conscious of the peril he was led into by his singular facility is made evident by the following letter: —

TO JAMES RUSSELL LOWELL.

*August* 3, 1865.

MY DEAR JAMES, — Here is the slipshod *jeu d'esprit* which you had a fancy to look at.

Please not let it get out of your hands, as I saw the other day a poem of mine in the papers which I had considered as a private manuscript, — I mean some lines read at a dinner given to Farragut, of which I gave a copy to Mrs. ——, and to nobody else that I remember.

It seems to me that I have done almost enough of this work; *too much*, some of my friends will say, perhaps. But it has been as much from good nature

---

[1] Among the numerous criticisms upon Dr. Holmes's poetry, one of the fairest is to be found in an article — in other respects also very good — which was published in the *Quarterly Review*, and reprinted in *Littell's Magazine*, No. 2643, March, 1895.

as from vanity that I have so often got up and jangled
my small string of bells.   I hold it to be a gift of a
certain value to be able to give that slight passing
spasm of pleasure which a few ringing couplets often
cause, read at the right moment.   Though they are
for the most part to poetry as the beating of a drum
or the tinkling of a triangle is to the harmony of a
band, yet it is not everybody who can get their limited significance out of these humble instruments.

I think, however, that I have made myself almost
too common by my readiness to oblige people on all
sorts of occasions.   At any rate, many of the trifles,
which served their turn with the bouquets and the
confectionery, ought to have withered and crumbled
with them.

But am I a woman, that I should fill eight pagelets
with less than nothing?


At this place, as appropriately as anywhere, may
be mentioned a little matter not altogether without
interest, in connection with the very attractive poem,
"Dorothy Q."

Dr. Holmes's sister, Mrs. Upham, had a son who
was named after his uncle, Dr. Holmes.   This gentleman, living at Salem, and marrying, became the
father of a little girl whom he named after the heroine of the portrait and the verses, Dorothy.   When
Dr. Holmes heard of this he wrote and sent to his
little grand-niece a couple of stanzas, which make a
pretty pendant to the original poem : —

> Dear little Dorothy, Dorothy Q.,
> What can I find to write to you?
> You have two U's in your name, it 's true,
> And mine is adorned with a double-u,

> But there's this difference in the U's,
> That one you will stand a chance to lose
> When a happy man of the bearded sex
> Shall make it Dorothy Q.+X.
>
> May Heaven smile bright on the blissful day
> That teaches this lesson in Algebra !
> When the orange blossoms crown your head,
> Then read what your old great-uncle said,
> And remember how in your baby-time
> He scribbled a scrap of idle rhyme, —
> Idle, it may be — but kindly, too,
> For the little lady, Dorothy Q. !

Here, too, is another scrap.  A gentleman, famous for a generation as "Tom" Appleton, wit, *raconteur*, and comrade of all the literary Bostonians of his day, in a lottery at a fair drew an album, of which the alternate sheets bore prettily painted flowers and foliage.  He passed it about to Longfellow, Emerson, Holmes, and the rest, asking each to select his page and write something upon it; and they, recognizing the claims of friendship, did so.  Holmes took a page bearing a cluster of wild autumnal leaves, and wrote : —

> Who that can pluck the flower will choose the weed,
> Leave the sweet rose and gather blooms less fair ?
> And who my homely verse will stay to read,
> Straying enchanted through this bright parterre,
> Where morning's herald lifts his purple bell
> And spring's young violet wooes the wanderer's eye ?
> Nay ! let me seek the fallen leaves that tell
> Of beggared winter's footstep drawing nigh ;
> There shall my shred of song enshrouded lie,
> A leaf that dropped in memory's flowery dell ;
> The breath of friendship stirred it, and it fell,
> Tinged with the loving hue of Autumn's fond farewell.
>
> BOSTON, *February* 22, 1874.

On one of the "occasions" at which the Doctor's

muse was invoked, quite a tempest was stirred up in the academic teapot of Harvard, of which the story is sufficiently told in the following letters. The University seal, it may be remarked, still bears the more modern motto, though popular opinion does not link the University and the Church in exceeding close comradeship to-day.

### TO WILLIAM AMORY.

296 BEACON STREET, *March 9th.*

MY DEAR MR. AMORY, — I enclose the two sonnets. If you will look in President Quincy's History of the University you will see that *Veritas* dates from 1643, and *Christo et Ecclesiæ* came in somehow towards 1700.

### JOHN O. SARGENT TO DR. HOLMES.

202 MADISON AVENUE, NEW YORK,
*January 24, 1878.*

MY DEAR WENDELL, — We have a Harvard Club here — numbering about two hundred members — and, for the want of an older man, I suppose, they made me president of it last week. Now we have an annual dinner, — and the next one is the 21st of February. I want to make it a grand success, so I propose to advise dropping the clergymen, who have generally been in the majority of the invited guests, and asking some representative gentlemen in the various careers for which men are educated at Harvard, or ought to be. Law, medicine, and priestcraft are not the only "liberal" professions nowadays, but we have "professional" architects, agriculturists, painters, sculptors, editors, and what not. I 've left out the poets! and don't mean to leave them among the

what-nots. Of course there will be great competition
to capture you for everything going on in the neighborhood of the 22d of February, but the Dining
Committee of the Harvard Club will send you an
invitation which I beg you to give the preference to.
President Eliot will be there as usual; but if you 'll
come, we 'll sink presidents of all sorts to their proper
level and make you the feature of the evening. You
shall represent just what you please, — only let me
know your selection of rôle. I believe pretty much
all your professors have been at our table, but I
think you have not yet honored us; so for the sake of
Harvard, if not for my sake, when you receive your
invitation formally from the committee, don't decline
it without first writing me in the premises.

TO JOHN O. SARGENT.

January 26, 1878.

MY DEAR JOHN, — You will not be surprised,
even if you should fancy that you are a little disappointed, when I tell you that I do not feel quite up to
the winter expedition you so kindly and warmly suggest. I only keep well by avoiding exposure, and I
am afraid of the risks I should run in the trip to New
York, mild as the season is and promises to be. It
is this fear of travelling about which has led me to
decline all lecturing invitations for some years and
content myself with my official work at the college in
Boston. I am more particularly cautious during my
lecture season, as I must keep well, and am apt to find
my duties, with the accidental labors, social and literary, which crowd upon me, somewhat fatiguing, —
something more so, let me confess, than they were
twenty or even ten years ago.

Another trouble is that I am tired out, completely, of getting on to my legs in response to a sentiment more or less complimentary, and turning the winch of that old hand-organ of which you remember some of the first discords.   I was asked to a dinner of one of the more recent literary associations here in Boston the other day, and I told them I would come only on one condition — no copy of verses or speech.   Oh, John, John, dear John!   I would almost crawl to New York to please you, old friend and constant friend as you are, but there are times when the "hopper-grass," as we country boys used to hear him called, is a burden, and I do feel just at this minute as if another cicada-song before the hyacinths are out would be more than I could carry on my old shoulders. Next June I have promised to go to Andover, where they have a centennial, and give them a poem of some kind or other.   Before that time I do not mean to be tempted.   The Sirens don't sing to me, confound 'em, but waggle their wings and tails and try to make *me* sing.   For all that I say, if I could just be popped down in the midst of the Harvard nurslings and see the faces of so many that I remember so well and hear their voices and shake their hands, and more especially sit somewhere near you on your throne as Master of the feast, how two or three hours — nay, four or five, for I am still up to so much on great occasions — would reel off into the infinite, staggering under their weight of enjoyment!

I have not been at New York since I had the great pleasure of meeting you there, and passed altogether a most charming week.   I hope I shall get there again some time or other, for it de-oxydizes and de-Bostonizes me, and I suppose I am as much of a

provincial in many of my ways and feelings and prejudices as one who lives in the centre of the solar
system can well be. . . .

February 19, 1878.

MY DEAR JOHN, — Here you are — letter and sonnets — may you have fifty better things to please your
company with! I would not have done this for any
other President of the Harvard Club, but it has been
a great pleasure to do my best, however small my
contribution, to help you through the evening. And
so God speed you, and may you wake up happy the
morning after.

BOSTON, February 19, 1878.

MY DEAR SIR, — I regret very much that I cannot
accept the polite invitation of the Harvard Club to
be present at their Annual Dinner on Thursday next.
To show my cordial interest in the Association and its
anniversary I send you a couple of sonnets, which I
should have read if I could have been with you, asking for them the indulgence which I feel sure would
have been granted to me personally had I been one of
the band of brothers gathered about the table.

As the construction of the sonnet often renders it
somewhat difficult to follow perfectly, when listened
to, I have had a few copies struck off, in case any of
the company should care to understand what many
of them may have heard with more or less dim perception of its significance.

A few words of explanation. At the first meeting
of the Governors of the College under the Charter of
1642, held in the year 1643, it was "ordered that
there shall be a College seale in forme following,"
namely, a shield with three open books bearing the

word *Veritas*. This motto was soon exchanged for *In Christi gloriam;* and this again shortly superseded by the one so long used, *Christo et Ecclesiæ.* The latter change took place, as President Quincy believed, "during the Presidency of Increase Mather, when a violent struggle was making to secure the College under the influences of the old established Congregational church." The date (1700), which I have assigned to this last motto, must be considered as only approximative.

The Harvard College of to-day wants no narrower, no more exclusive motto than Truth, — truth, which embraces all that is highest and purest in the precepts of all teachers, human or divine; all that is best in the creeds of all churches, whatever their name; but allows no lines of circumvallation to be drawn round its sacred citadel under the alleged authority of any record or of any organization.

This is what I mean to express in these two squares of metrical lines wrought in the painful prolixity of the sonnet, a form of verse which suggests a slow minuet of rhythms stepping in measured cadences over a mosaic pavement of rhyme, and which not rarely combines a minimum of thought with a maximum of labor.

May I venture to remind you, Mr. President, that it is nearly fifty years since you, as Editor of a College Magazine, gave a kindly welcome to the earliest printed verses known as coming from my pen? I was as a bird on the wing then, hardly knowing whither I was flying, with the morning sun behind me, with all the wide world and the unmeasured years before me. Now I am on my nest, and the evening shadows are fast falling around me. I am sure that you at least will be as indulgent to my failing as you were to my forming voice; and, for those around you, I will trust their hearts and their memories, for we are children of the same mother, and to-day we forget all else in the one feeling of brotherhood.

*February 26, 1878.*

MY DEAR JOHN, — Many thanks for your letter. It rejoiced me to hear that the dinner over which you presided was a success, as it ought to have been with you at the head of the table. It made me wish I could have been there; but I was quite right in staying at home, where I had a good deal to keep me besides my habitual great unwillingness to go anywhere in the winter season, — I had almost said at any season. I got two copies of the *New York Times* this morning, which I was glad to see, and read my own letter which I had pretty nearly forgotten. I was quite pleased with my description of a sonnet, — have n't we a right to like our own babies? I want very much to see the pamphlet, to know all that was said, and to live over in imagination that brilliant scene at Delmonico's.

It never occurred to me that any of our own people, even the oldest, would quarrel with the sentiment of my sonnets. I thought that possibly I might get a hit from some outsider, but inasmuch as *Veritas* is already sculptured over the door of Memorial Hall (if I remember rightly), I had a feeling that there was a willingness to return to the older motto. It seems that my bouquet was like the one I saw Modjeska smell of the other evening in Adrienne Lecouvreur — had some subtle poison in it — at least for certain idiosyncrasies. It will do no harm, though, and there is a good deal to be said in favor of truth, although it poisons some people who have lived too long upon the opposite kind of diet. You will send me the pamphlet as soon as it comes out, I know, and I shall look forward to it with great interest.

*March 6, 1878.*

MY DEAR JOHN, — I had no idea of my sonnets[1] making such a stir. It was rather with the idea that *Veritas* should be recognized as the understood motto of the College, than with that of having it cut upon a new die as the College seal, that I wrote the verses. It is only fair to say, in Mr. Quincy's words: "This is the only College seal which has the sanction of any record." I suppose it is a matter of expediency whether to make the change or not. Old habits are very tenacious, — you remember the old clerk's *mumpsimus* for *sumpsimus*, which he had hung on to so long that he would not change it for any Latin scholar.

As for O——'s talk, I do not think much of that. Of course he would rather have *Ecclesiæ* than *Veritas*, and so, perhaps, would a good many of the older and more clerical lot like him.

My dear John, I do not care very much which seal they have, provided it is understood that the *animus* of the College is with the grand motto which includes the other and everything else worth having. Eliot has not said anything about it to me, beyond the mere fact that O—— wrote him a letter. I should not think it worth while to quarrel over the seal, if it is a matter likely to excite much feeling. The Col-

---

[1] The sonnets referred to may be found in volume iii. of the Poetical Works, Riverside Ed., p. 77.

lege has taken such a firm stand and gone on so boldly with its changes, that I want it to settle itself firmly in the position it has reached, and not excite needless prejudices. If the majority of its well-wishers should be of opinion that the old seal is the *true* seal and restore it *on that ground*, I suppose the minority would acquiesce with a tolerable grace.

But my sonnets and my letter are all the contribution I expect to make to the matter in question.

"They have invented a new mode of torture, — readings from one's poems, by Dr. Holmes and me, for the benefit of charities of one kind or another. We bow our necks to the yoke like patient oxen, and leaning away from each other as oxen will, strive to retrace our ancient furrows, which somehow will not gleam along the edge as when the turf was first broken." Thus grumbled James Russell Lowell; but Lowell was apt to be somewhat impatient under the burdens which are laid upon the favorites in literature. Dr. Holmes, on the other hand, with good-natured satire, said: "Poets read their own compositions in a singsong sort of way; but they do seem to love 'em so, that I always enjoy it. It makes me laugh a little inwardly to see how they dandle their poetical babies, but I don't let them know it."

Betwixt lectures, and "occasions," and these numerous pressing invitations of charity-mongers and others, Dr. Holmes certainly dandled his poetical babies in public very often; partly because he was really obliging, and partly, perhaps, because he was conscious that he and his offspring appeared in company to much advantage. For he certainly read his own poetry very effectively, not at all after the fashion of the trained rhetoricians, but like a gentleman; that is to say, with much simplicity, yet with a sympathy of expression in voice and feature which was very charming. The music of his poems got into his reading; and he could be spirited, pathetic, or humorous by turns, with equal and certain mastery, being able to present upon the platform all the variety which he could conceive at his desk. He always carried his audience with him surely, easily, and entirely — and even in his old age, when he could hardly trust his voice, he still held a great deal of this power.

Nearly coeval in birth with *The Atlantic Monthly* was the beginning of the Saturday Club, — an institution very famous in Boston. Dr. Holmes says: "At about the same time [with the establishment of the magazine] there grew up in Boston a literary association which became at last well known as the 'Saturday Club,' the members dining together on the last Saturday of every month. The magazine and the Club . . . have often been thought to have some organic connection, and the 'Atlantic Club' has been spoken of, as if there was or had been such an institution, but it never existed."[1] The seed which thus sprouted was, he says, a trio, or quartette, consisting of Emerson and two or three of his admirers, who fell into a habit of dining together occasionally at "Parker's," an hotel which the Doctor rather fancifully calls the "Will's Coffee-House of Boston." This nucleus "gathered others to itself and grew into a club as Rome grew into a city, almost without knowing it." Mr. Underwood, in a letter to Dr. Holmes, took him to task for having somewhere spoken of the "Atlantic Club" as "sup-

---

[1] *Life of Emerson*, 221, where there is more on the same topic.

posititious."   "You remember," he writes, "that the contributors met for dinner regularly.  It was a voluntary informal association.  The invitations and reminders were from my hand, as I conducted the correspondence of the magazine.  I have hundreds of letters in reply, and it is my belief that the association was always spoken of either as the Atlantic Club or the Atlantic Dinner. . . . Your very decided statement seems to me (in the ordinary use of phrases) erroneous."  But the Doctor evidently thought that he knew as much as any one else did about the matter, and stuck to his colors very positively.  In his *Life of Motley*[1] he says: "The Club came into existence in a very quiet sort of way at about the same time as *The Atlantic Monthly*, and, although entirely unconnected with that magazine, included as members some of its chief contributors;" and these statements he never amended.  The discussion is of little moment unless perchance this Club shall become picturesque and interesting for posterity as did the Club of Johnson and Garrick and the rest, — which I fear will hardly come to pass.  Certain it is that nearly all the frequent (male) contributors to the magazine, who lived within convenient reach of the Parker House, were members of the Club, or doubtless might have been so had they desired; and that for a long while a multiplicity of nerves and filaments tied the magazine and the Club closely together.  Equally certain it is that from the outset a few members of the Club were never contributors to the magazine, and that all these nerves and filaments have long ere the present day been entirely severed.

Some outsiders furnished still another name for

_______
[1] Appendix A.

*Emerson*

*Motley*                                                            *Hawthorne*

*Holmes*

*Whittier*                                               *Lowell*

*Longfellow*

A Group from the Saturday Club

this much-entitled Club.  They called it "The Mutual Admiration Society," and sometimes laughed a little, as though the designation were a trifle derogatory.  Yet the brethren within the pale were nowise disturbed by this witticism.  "If there was not," says Holmes, "a certain amount of ' mutual admiration ' among some of those I have mentioned,[1] it was a great pity, and implied a defect in the nature of men who were otherwise largely endowed."  Possibly one or two of these gentlemen might have been criticised for admiring *themselves*, but it did seem hard to blame them for being sufficiently intelligent and generous to admire each other.  Would the scoffers have been better pleased to see them openly abusing or slyly depreciating each other?  There are enough such spectacles elsewhere in literature.

Outside the sacred *penetralia* which were shut within his own front door, nothing else in Dr. Holmes's life gave him so much pleasure as did this Club.  He loved it; he hugged the thought of it.  When he was writing to Lowell and Motley in Europe, he seemed to think that merely to name " *The Club*," was enough to give a genial flavor to his page.  He would tell who were present at the latest meeting, and where

[1] Besides himself, whom he did not mention, his list was: Emerson, Hawthorne, Longfellow, Lowell, Motley, Whipple, Whittier; Professors Agassiz and Peirce; John S. Dwight, Governor Andrew, Richard H. Dana, Jr., and Charles Sumner. The Club has also had among its members, President Eliot; Professors Felton, Norton, and Goodwin; William H. Prescott, T. G. Appleton, J. M. Forbes, J. Elliot Cabot, Henry James, W. D. Howells, T. B. Aldrich, William M. Hunt, Charles Francis Adams, Francis Parkman, James Freeman Clarke, Judge Lowell, Judge Hoar, George F. Hoar, Bishop Brooks, and many more scarcely less well known.

they sat.  He would recur to those who used to come,
and mention their habitual seats, — matters which his
correspondents already knew perfectly well.  But the
names were sweet things in his mouth; and in fact,
he was doing one of the deepest acts of intimacy in
thus touching the chord of the dearest reminiscence
which their memories held in common.  By this he
seemed sure that he would make his letter welcome,
however little else of news or interest it might convey.  In the later days there came to be something
pathetic about his attachment to that which still had
existence and yet was almost all a memory.  In 1883
he wrote in a letter to Lowell: "I go to the Saturday
Club quite regularly, but the company is more of
ghosts than of flesh and blood for me.  I carry a
stranger there now and then, introduce him to the
members who happen to be there, and then say:
There at that end used to sit Agassiz, — here at this
end Longfellow, — Emerson used to be there, and
Lowell often next him; on such an occasion Hawthorne was with us, at another time Motley, and
Sumner, and smaller constellations, — *nebulæ* if you
will, but luminous more or less in the provincial firmament.  We degenerate *laudatores temporis acti*,—
we or they, for I am getting patriarchal, and since
my son is ' His Honor,' I feel as if I belonged to the
past, — we or they must keep the Club up until you
come back and bring some fresh life to it."  There
are many passages in this same strain.

In 1885, when all the old faces save two or three
must have been gone, he wrote, in his vein mingled
of wit and pathos, to John M. Forbes: —

"I should like to see Tom Hughes at the Club; it
is a long while since I have met him.  *You* will

come, and if nothing hinders *I* shall be there; and, if *tres faciunt collegium, duo faciunt clubbum*."

Brilliant indeed must those gatherings have been, when, out of the dazzling bewilderment of London society, which he so dearly loved, Lowell wrote: "I have never seen society, on the whole, so good as I used to meet at our Saturday Club." But these were words of appreciation rather than of affection; and I fancy that few members of the Club felt towards it quite as Holmes did. Partly his sentiment was the result of the limited sphere of his life; had he ever travelled, seeing foreign lands, mingling with their distinguished people, and becoming in any degree cosmopolitan, the Club would have assumed proportions more accurately adapted to the universe in general. But in the little narrow Boston routine these monthly gatherings were like nuggets of glittering gold scattered in a gravel-field. The joy of such treasures sank deep into heart and memory.

Dr. Holmes could not, of course, say for himself what some of these "mutual admirers" magnanimously said for him: that of all who sat at that Saturday table he was by far the most brilliant talker. It is as impossible by any string of descriptive adjectives to convey the charm of his talk to those who never heard him at his best, as it is to place the tones and gestures of a dead actor before the mind's eye of those who never saw him. Therefore it is best not to try to tell how Dr. Holmes talked. Only it may be remarked that the pages of *The Autocrat* give some notion of it, for he talked in much the general fashion in which he wrote these papers. Yet he talked better than he wrote. *The Autocrat* held his talk crystallized, but those who heard it gushing fresh and fluid from his lips, liked it much better in this form than after the formative process had taken effect. For, however charmingly he might talk with his pen, the tongue remains the natural instrument for talking. He wrote, one day, to his friend, Thomas G. Appleton: "Of course your worst rival is your own talk, with which people will always compare whatever you write; and I do not know that I can say more of this book than that it comes nearer your talk than anything else you have written." It was his own case; *The Autocrat* came near to his talk, but did not reach it. Moreover, a man of his genial temperament was immensely aided by an audience present in the flesh, listening with pleased faces. Then talk seemed like throwing a ball against a wall, and striking it at each rebound until the game reached the highest pitch of lithe excitement. He was, I fancy, the first person to express a profound *respect* for talk. "Remember," he said, "that talking is one of the fine arts, — the noblest, the most important, and the most difficult, — and that its fluent harmonies may be spoiled by the intrusion of a single harsh note."

He had also a curious theory about his talking. "The idea," he said, "of a man's 'interviewing' himself *is* rather odd, to be sure. But then that is what we are all of us doing every day. I talk half the time to find out my own thoughts, as a schoolboy turns his pockets inside out to see what is in them. One brings to light all sorts of personal property he had forgotten in his inventory." And again: "Talk, to me, is only spading up the ground for crops of thought. I can't answer for what will turn up." But the wise men thought that this "spading" was more fascinating to witness than was the subsequent reaping of the crop in the shape of printed words.

Hoar

Agassiz

Appleton

Sumner

Andrew

Whipple

Fields

A Group from the Saturday Club

Sometimes he spoke of it more lightly: "People — the right kind of people — meet at a dinner-party as two ships meet and pass each other at sea. They exchange a few signals; ask each other's reckoning, where from, where bound; perhaps one supplies the other with a little food or a few dainties; then they part, to see each other no more." But the pleasantest incident on a voyage is to exchange greetings with another vessel; and those who met Dr. Holmes in his prime, in mid-passage, were likely to treasure the memory of few more delightful episodes.

Some persons used to charge him with talking too much, — a singular charge, for it was an unreceptive mind that could have too much of such talk. Still this was sometimes said, and he himself occasionally penitentially declared, after he had charmed a dinner-table for a whole evening, that he wished that he had been more silent and gathered more from his *convives*. In a letter to Dr. Fordyce Barker, speaking of having met Dr. Carpenter at the Saturday Club, he said: "He is a great talker, and I sometimes have to watch for my innings. I guess *he* has to, once in a while, for I have a tendency, myself, to *linguacity*." Mr. Edmund Gosse, however, brings good evidence for the defence on this point: "Perhaps no man of modern times has given his contemporaries a more extraordinary impression of wit in conversation. We are told that he never overpowered his companions, never held the talk in monologue, but that he listened as brilliantly as he spoke, taking up every challenge, capping every anecdote, rippling over with an illuminated cascade of fancy and humor and repartee." In fact, Dr. Holmes was of so eager, ardent, impetuous a temperament, that undoubtedly he did sometimes un-

wittingly monopolize conversation.  His thoughts, his
humor, his similes rose as fast, as multitudinous, as
irrepressible, as the bubbles in the champagne, and
nothing could prevent their coming to the surface.
It was in the nature of things that, if there were nine
men at table, Dr. Holmes would do more than a
mathematical ninth of the talking.  In his character
as *The Professor* he described himself with humorous truth: "I won't deny that sometimes, on rare
occasions, when I have been in company with gentlemen who *preferred* listening, I have been guilty of the
same kind of usurpation which my friend openly justified.  But I maintain, that I, the Professor, am a
good listener.  If a man can tell me a fact which sub-
tends an appreciable angle in the horizon of thought,
I am as receptive as the contribution-box in a congregation of colored brethren."

If his comrades gave him the stimulus of sympathy
and appreciation, if from time to time they interjected
the spur of clever interruption, they could make him
strike any pace that they chose. Yet he did not seriously think that it was always better to give than to
receive.  All who met him must remember the keen
expectant gaze with which he would fasten his eye
upon them, attentive to get the full value or beauty of
whatever they might seem about to say.  He greatly
liked the battledore and shuttlecock of talk, and could
play the game with skilful adroitness, keeping all his
marvellous quickness under perfect control.  But if
the other man was a bungler, the expert Doctor was
likely to find more enjoyment in keeping the feathered
cork climbing into the air without assistance.

Colonel T. Wentworth Higginson said once that in
his visits to London he had never met two men whose

talk was so habitually brilliant as that of Holmes and Lowell, but that they had not learned the London art of repression, and often monopolized the conversation too much; and he had a reminiscence of a dinner given to Dr. and Mrs. Stowe, at which Lowell endeavored to convince Mrs. Stowe that the best novel ever written was *Tom Jones*, while Holmes at the other end of the table was endeavoring to convince Professor Stowe (a clergyman) that all swearing owed its origin to the pulpit.   The story is as characteristic as it is amusing.

Here is an anecdote which may or may not be accurately true, but has, I believe, a substantial foundation.   The "Bohemian Club," celebrating a festal evening in San Francisco, chose Dr. Holmes to membership, and at once dispatched a telegram to notify him of the honor.   The message reached Boston in the dead of night, and no reply was expected.   What was the astonishment of the club when, before adjournment, a messenger boy brought the following responsive dispatch: —

> Message from San Francisco ! Whisper low —
> Asleep in bed an hour or more ago.
> While on his peaceful pillow he reclines,
> Say to his friend who sent these loving lines :
> "Silent, unanswering, still to friendship true,
> He smiles in slumber, for he dreams of you."

*February* 23, 1874.

He had a great admiration for Professor Agassiz, and used to call him "Liebig's Extract" of the wisdom of ages.   And once when the professor was away upon one of his scientific excursions among some remote, semi-civilized peoples, the Doctor said: "I cannot help thinking what a feast the cannibals would have, if they boiled down such an extract!" A gentleman once commented very unfavorably upon this little jest, explaining, with more than British gravity, that it was a poor one, because cannibals don't care for wisdom, and would only have relished Agassiz because he was plump!

He used to say that he always liked to listen to clergymen whose belief was stronger than his own, — a desire which it was probably not difficult to gratify.

In his old age he often fell asleep at church, and when a friend once poked a little fun at him *apropos* of such an occasion, he explained, with much earnestness, that it was out of no disrespect for the ministry that he had fallen asleep; and then, with a twinkle in his eye, he added, "But when I woke up, the clergyman was preaching very well."

It happened once that a considerable body of lion-hunters made an attack in force, so that it was by no means one of the ordinary occasions. The Doctor was asked whether he did not enjoy it. "Enjoy it!" he exclaimed. "Why, I felt like the small elephant at the Zoo, with a cheap excursion party on his back!"

It seems one of the grievous blunders of the order of things that the brilliant talker, pouring forth thoughts, comparisons, humor, and wit from an eternal horn of plenty, must become, like a great actor, a mere tradition. By and by, perhaps, some of the new word-catching machines will be stowed away in the corners of dining-rooms where the shining heroes of conversation are to be among the guests; but the day of our Agamemnon is past, and what is war without Agamemnon? With no better apparatus than tradition, there is as yet no means of measuring the talkers and the actors of one generation against those of another.   We do not know whether we are getting better things or poorer than those which fired the enthusiasm of our forefathers.   Yet there are actors, for example Garrick, whose equal few persons flatter themselves that they have seen in their own day and generation; and Dr. Holmes was a talker of this calibre and quality.   He gathered not the reputation which he deserved, because he stayed at home in a little out-of-the-way town, and talked only to his neighbors, and to the stranger who might occasionally stray thither.   But *we* know his height on the scale, *we* know that we were not deceived in our valuation of him; and we listen with tranquil faith when many competent judges, who met him and met the other best talkers of his generation, tell us that our Bostonian had no superior; and we agree when some of them declare that he had not even any peer.

Mr. Gosse hopes "that much of the Autocrat's priceless table-talk has been preserved."   Alas, that such is not the case!   No Boswell attended him, to hasten away from the display and jot down for posterity the rare things he had heard.   If Dr. Holmes's talk had been remembered in quotable shape anywhere, it would have been so in Boston, and if there were such reminiscences here, I think that I should be familiar with them; but I know of nothing of the sort.   His talk is remembered as the scenery of the clouds is remembered, a picture dwelling in the mind but never to be produced to eyes which looked not upon it.   How doleful this is no one appreciates more keenly than does the unfortunate writer of this memoir.   I know full well that readers have been expecting to find the pages of this volume sparkling with the hitherto unpub-

lished gems of Dr. Holmes's famous talk; they have
looked for choice new bits of his shrewd wisdom, for
some of his marvellous similes which they have never
heard before, for anecdotes embalming his exquisite
wit.   They have expected a fish, — nay, a miraculous
draught of many fishes, — but the net comes almost
empty.   Ah, disappointed reader, your disappointment
at not receiving these things is nothing in comparison with mine at not being able to furnish them to
you.   But they do not exist, — they have sunk away
and disappeared like the raindrops which fall into the
ocean; they are irrecoverable.   No! save the letters
herein contained, there is absolutely nothing left of
Dr. Holmes which is not in formal print under protection of the laws of copyright.

The sparkling current of the Autocrat's printed
talk, which flowed so spontaneously, so exuberantly,
seemed the outburst of an inexhaustible spring.
Twelve bucketsful bailed out of it in twelve months
for the use of *The Atlantic* were as nothing.   So forth-
with, that which every one was looking for appeared,
and the waters gushed afresh, only the new stream took
a new name, and it was now the Professor who spoke
at the Breakfast-Table.   Probably enough, the Doctor, who was ever buoyant and sanguine, did not, in
the bottom of his heart, feel much doubt that he was
going to score another success; but he began with a
delightful sentence which may be described as a sort
of modest compliment to himself: "The question is
whether there is anything left for me, the Professor,
to suck out of creation, after my lively friend (the Autocrat) has had his straw in the bung-hole of the
universe."   This newcomer did not talk quite in the

vein of his predecessor; he chose more serious topics, he was much graver, and exacted closer attention from his hearers; I think the "young man John" could hardly have been pleased at the change of dynasty. There was a great deal of discussion about creeds and tenets, which have been the subjects of religious controversy. Dr. Holmes said that he handled these matters "only incidentally." His readers will hardly agree with him, — they will think of the case of the tail wagging the dog. Of course the lively conversational style was retained, and the flashes of wit and humor were never far apart. By this means the Professor held many auditors who otherwise would have found him dull. But his hand was ever light, sprightly, and varied in its touch, so that no one fagged under it. Because the Professor was less entertaining than the Autocrat, he has been less famous, and less widely popular; yet, being more thoughtful and more profound, he has pleased some people better. After the first number was published, Lowell wrote to Dr. Holmes that he was "getting his second wind." "I like the new Professor better than the old Autocrat. . . . The ' Old Boston ' is an inspiration." Mr. Lowell doubtless meant " Little Boston," and every one will agree with his estimate of that spirited and original creation.

After the Professor became silent, eleven years elapsed before the landlady of the famous boarding-house had another boarder whose talk was up to the printing standard. Then, in 1871, the Poet took the vacant chair at the Breakfast-Table. He was a very charming fellow, yet not quite so agreeable as his predecessors had been. When the Doctor undertook to compete with himself he met a formidable rival.

He was like the great race-horses who come to the pole, matched to beat their own best time: he trotted gallantly, but his "record" was too much for him. If *The Autocrat* and *The Professor* had not been written, *The Poet* would have been esteemed a brilliant piece of work; but they had been written, and in the way of comparison their new comrade brought just a trifle of disappointment. The three volumes stand as the Breakfast-Table Series, like the three successive pressings of the grapes from an illustrious vineyard. The *premier cru* is the best; the second is very nearly as good; but by the third squeezing the difference in quality cannot escape notice, — still even then one says: "They were indeed grapes from a rare good soil."

Doubtless Dr. Holmes himself saw a difference, if not between the books, at least in the reception which they severally met with. In December, 1872, in a letter to Motley, he said (note the force of the *But* in the passage): —

"I have had some pleasant words in the *Spectator* and the *Examiner* about my new book, *The Poet at the Breakfast-Table*. But I wrote it to please myself (independently of the more vulgar motive) by saying some things which I should feel better for getting rid of. A man must talk himself into the current of opinion, or write himself into it, — I mean so as to let his individuality — his way of looking at things — tell in some way or other on its movement. I am curious about the future course of things. It looks to me as if my old formula of Rome or Reason was fast working itself out, and I think Rome and its offshoots are to be one of the main dependences of the coming generations. The anchor of the church is fastened in the mud of legend and superstition, but it will hold a good while yet, and our children or grand-children are going to need it, or they will see some grand overturn, and Caleb Cushing's ' Man on horse-back ' sitting on the heap of bloody ashes to bring order back again. The absurdity of my playing pro-phet to a student of the cycles and epicycles of the past, like yourself! Forgive me, and think instead of our warmest Christmas wishes which we send to you and all yours."

In point of fact he always did watch the symptoms of the age with close interest, and though he was dis-trustful of his capacity to read them aright, as being somewhat apart from his province, yet he occasionally ventured his forecast. I remember his saying to me that the vast fortunes heaped up by the "magnates" of oil and sugar, etc., seemed to him to involve the perils which might result in the destruction of modern civilization.

# CHAPTER X



No attentive reader of *The Professor* could fail to foresee what would be Dr. Holmes's next literary venture, for these papers held the skeleton of a story and some very well-drawn characters. Accordingly in due period *Elsie Venner* was born, wearing at first the title of *The Professor's Story*, but later taking her own name.

The critics — the trained professional ones, I mean — have dealt severely with the book. They admit that it abounds in brilliant passages, and that it is generously impregnated with New Englandism; they can hardly deny that local color was never shed upon paper with more truth and skill than in the description of the party at " the elegant residence of our distinguished fellow-citizen, Colonel Sprowle." But having said these things, some go on to say that the book has too much monologue by the author, — though in this Holmes sinned in the good company of Thackeray; and so good a critic as George William Curtis wrote: " This colloquial habit is very winning, when governed by a natural delicacy and an exquisite literary instinct." Others think that the characters are not real and lifelike, and that the incidents are but indifferent inventions. The crowning objection, taken by all alike, is, that it is that hybrid creation, condemned by the inexorable canons of literature, a novel with a purpose. Whether these canons are dogmas or truths, it is probable that a novel written for a purpose will rarely survive the elimination of the purpose from popular interest, either by its achievement or defeat. Certain it is, however, that whether Elsie Venner was or was not justly entitled to popularity, she enjoyed it, and for many years was widely read, and eagerly discussed, nor is it yet time to be composing an epitaph for her tombstone.

It was sufficient evidence of the popularity of the story that an effort was made to dramatize it. The scheme was hopelessly absurd, in view of the difficult moral purpose of the book, and the Doctor regretted that the attempt should be made. It signified utter incapacity to appreciate his work. It was tried, however, and the play was brought out in 1865 at the Boston Theatre; of course the result was absolute failure. There was published in the *Pall Mall Gazette*, in 1894, this account of an interview between Dr. Holmes and another person who seems to have revived the same project : —

" And so you want to put *Elsie Venner* into a play. Years ago, I remember, some one dramatized the novel. I went to see it. It was bad, very bad. I stood at the back of the box and watched it carefully. It was not *Elsie Venner* — my *Elsie Venner;* they had made it into a melodrama, and the psychology was not there.

" But times have changed, Doctor; the psychological drama is fast becoming popular —

" Oh, yes, I know that, though I don't often go to the theatre nowadays. I remember seeing Mr. Irving when he was here last time in ' The Bells,' which is a psychological play. I was greatly interested; it was

a wonderful performance, as wonderful as Booth in
'The Fool's Revenge.' But still (and he shook his
head), — but still I do not think a psychological play
with Elsie as its heroine would be more successful to-
day than it was thirty odd years ago. It was a great
shock to me, that performance, — a great shock. It
was the novel vulgarized, and I should not like to see
it again. You may imagine Elsie, with her strange
eyes and the snake look in them, but you cannot see
her on the stage: the illusion will not hold there;
and besides, it would not be easy to find an actress
who could look like her. The one who acted it in the
old days did not look like Elsie as I saw her. Nobody
could. No — no (in the softest voice imaginable),
Elsie was written as the outcome of a theory which
I held very strongly at the time; and I want to ask
you to let her remain where I put her — in the
book."

With the exception of the legend of Eve, *Elsie
Venner* is, *par excellence*, the snake-story of literature.
Yet in spite of the high and ancient precedent, some
people felt so repelled by this element that they declared it a fatal artistic defect. Dr. Holmes does not
seem to have anticipated this feeling. The snake was
not repulsive to him; while writing the book he was
so desirous to have the rattlesnake vividly present to
his mind as a living reptile rather than a mere bit of
natural history, that he procured a live one of pretty
good size from Berkshire County, and kept it for
many weeks at the medical school. He had a long
stick arranged with a padded kid glove at one end
and a prodding point at the other, and he used to
excite the creature, and watch its coiling and its striking, study its eyes and expression, its ways, its char-

acter. The result of the sort of personal familiarity thus established between himself and his prisoner certainly made itself felt in his book, where the rattlesnake sensation, so to speak, is marvellously, almost horribly lifelike, — no critic ever found fault with that!

His scientific research explored all printed knowledge concerning the reptiles and their venom. His friend Dr. Weir Mitchell was an authority on the subject, and Dr. Holmes gathered information from him, and wrote to him: —

"I received from the Smithsonian Institution your very interesting *Researches on the Venom of the Rattlesnake*. I have read a great part of it with singular interest, having kept one of these beasts during the past summer and watched his ways with great satisfaction.

"My fellow would not eat or drink. He killed a rat or two, but at last one killed him. I could n't find he took offence at the leaves of the white ash, according to the common notion."

The subject continued for a long while to interest both men, and ten years later the Doctor wrote: —

TO S. WEIR MITCHELL.

*May* 15, 1870.

DEAR DR. MITCHELL, —

.     .     .     .     .     .     .     .     .     .

I am reminded that I was questioned some weeks since, and again this afternoon, as to whether rattlesnakes are oviparous or viviparous. I was somewhat puzzled, and much inclined to compression, or *ovoviviparous*. Can you not tell me how it is from your experience? In your ophidian fold there must, or may, have been Crotalæ in an interesting situation, and upon whom the sacred obligations of maternity devolved while you were their shepherd. Dear little helpless innocent creatures! Did they come naked from their mother's womb into this cold and cruel world, or under the shelter of a calcified — an egg-shell, in short?

This is the question with which I wish to tax your knowledge, which I believe is more extensive and exact with regard to these interesting fellow-creatures of ours than that of any other living person.

A dozen years later still the same topic called forth further interchanges, and Dr. Mitchell sent to Dr. Holmes the skin of a rattlesnake of such vast propor-tions that it almost appeared to be the overcoat which some boa-constrictor might have taken off on an un-bearably hot day. These notes were a part of the transaction : —

*January* 13, 1883.

My dear Dr. Mitchell, —

．　　．　　．　　．　　．　　．　　．　　．　　．

I am mightily interested in your snake-experiments, and hope to have a full account of them by and by. Do send me that snake-skin you speak of, and per-haps I will wear it as a necktie.

Don't let 'em bite you! Remember poor Dr. Wain-wright, and how near you came to being crotalized into Hades by that fellow that turned round in his box. If you play any such tricks with your "worms," as Bacon calls 'em, I won't write your obituary for G. W. C.'s paper. Good luck to you and the var-mints.

March 1, 1883.

MY DEAR DR. MITCHELL, — I am reminded of Pope's line : —

> Pleased with a — rat*tler* — tickled, etc.

I don't think I have it quite right, but anyhow I am both pleased and tickled with my rattler's integument. It is magnificent, — not Tofana or Madame de Brinvilliers in all her glory of silks and satins was clad like one of these. But what a parlous worm it was, to be sure! I did n't know that pizon sarpents ever grew so big as that. He must have shed venom as a milch cow does her amiable secretion. I have got him hung up on my revolver (book-shelves, that is), and he hides a library of volumes. And when he rattled, how he must have waked the slumbering watch-men, if any such were within range! I should greatly enjoy a short biography of this individual specimen of a race which owes so much to your pious labors.

Well, well, — asps and vipers and copperheads, and cobras and rattlesnakes of reasonable dimensions I know, but a crotalus with the length and circumfer-ence of a boa-constrictor is a new acquaintance whose *bark*, if I may so call his integument, is much more welcome than his bite would be.

Always, and this time thankfully, yours.

March 15, 1883.

DEAR DR. MITCHELL, — I swallowed your little poison-pamphlet at a mouthful. There is something wonderfully fascinating about these venomous beasts, and I can never read too much about them.

Everybody admires the wonderful snake drapery. If my wife was a little taller I would have her wear it along the back of a cloak — the head coming up as

to a hood, — what a sensation it would make, to be
sure, as she walked along Beacon Street!

I am really very proud of it, and keep it displayed
in my library, where it is a great attraction.

I have thanked you for this most *piquant* and welcome gift before, but I hardly knew what an object
of curiosity and admiration it would prove to be both
to myself and others.  We all want to know where it
came from — I don't think you have told me.

*May* 11, 1883.

MY DEAR DR. MITCHELL, — Have I ever thanked
you for the *Preliminary Report on the Venoms of
Serpents?*  I read every word of it with the greatest
interest, and I want to know what comes of your further investigations.  It is a most fascinating subject
every way, chemically, biologically, and theologically,
— such a strange manifestation of creative animus.
The snake-skin continues to be admired, and the riddle to be read and praised by all whose eyes fall on
the great scimetar.

The possibility that Elsie's story might really have
a foundation in fact excited the imaginations of many
persons, and the Doctor had numerous letters of
inquiry.  He had, however, no instance to quote.
"I do not know," he wrote to Dr. Edwards, of Mon-
treal, "that such a pre-natal poisoning might not
affect the disposition, etc., but I do not assert it."
Yet he told a gentleman that he "was amazed afterwards to receive letters from two men of character
and position, one of them, I think, a Confederate
official, describing similar cases in their families, and
wondering how he had heard of them."[1]

<hr>

[1] *Lippincott's Magazine*, January, 1895, p. 110.

The book had been many years before the public when the Doctor wrote that he had never forgiven a "still cherished and charming friend" for calling his tale "a medicated novel." The witty word travelled fast and far, but it was, as the Doctor felt, not only an incorrect but an unfair description. The medical element was altogether secondary, a mere basis or introduction for a much profounder problem of theology. The possibility of pre-natal poisoning was interesting, but what Dr. Holmes had in mind was to raise the question of its effect upon the moral responsibility of the unhappy recipient of the envenomed instincts. To Mrs. Stowe, whose beliefs he might well fancy himself to be rudely shocking, he wrote this very interesting letter : —

TO MRS. HARRIET BEECHER STOWE.

*September* 13, 1860.

DEAR MRS. STOWE, — Your letter gave me great pleasure and encouragement. To have interested one who has made the world her own audience is in itself a reward for undertaking my perilous experiment.

You see exactly what I wish to do : to write a story with enough of interest in its characters and incidents to attract a certain amount of popular attention. Under cover of this to *stir* that mighty question of automatic agency in its relation to self-determination. To do this by means of a palpable outside agency, predetermining certain traits of character and certain apparently voluntary acts, such as the common judgment of mankind and the tribunals of law and theology have been in the habit of recognizing as sin and crime. Not exactly insanity, either general or partial, in its common sense, but rather an

unconscious intuitive tendency, dating from a powerful ante-natal influence, which modifies the whole
organization.  To make the subject of this influence
interest the reader, to carry the animalizing of her
nature just as far as can be done without rendering
her repulsive, to redeem the character in some measure by humanizing traits, which struggle through the
lower organic tendencies, to carry her on to her
inevitable fate by the natural machinery of circumstance, grouping many human interests around her,
which find their natural solution in the train of events
involving her doom, — such is the idea of this story.
It is conceived in the fear of God and in the love of
man.  Whether I am able to work out my delicate
and difficult problem or not is not of so much consequence.  A man may fulfil the object of his existence
by asking a question he cannot answer, and attempt-
ing a task he cannot achieve.  Still I can truly say
that the whole course of the story, and the resolution
of all its studied discords, is as clear at this moment
in my mind as the spires of Cambridge seen from
my window against the morning sun; — not all the
details, of course, but the disposal of all the characters, and the effects which are to harmonize all that
goes before.

I thank you very much for your kind hints.  I will
endeavor not to hurry, and to develop my leading
characters so that you shall know — I dare not say
remember — them.  Perhaps I can contrive to lengthen
my instalment somewhat, but I have a good many other
things to do besides writing my story. — I have stolen
this half hour from chapter xxi., which is not yet
begun, to thank you for your very kind and welcome
words, and to lift the lids of my story and of my heart

just enough to give you a moment's look into them.
I write the thoughts which are given me, by a kind of
necessity, and I cannot hope that you or any friend
will always agree with that which I must say, if I
speak at all.   But when I have the happiness of being approved in any aim by the woman who has taken
the world captive, and to whom it has been granted
more than to any other to reach the heart of the race,
colonizing her thought in all civilized and even half-
barbaric tongues, — it is indeed a deep delight.

I may not always please your taste or exactly meet
your judgment.   But one thing I am sure : I have, in
common with yourself, a desire to leave the world a
little more human than if I had not lived ; for a true
humanity is, I believe, our nearest approach to Divin-
ity, while we work out our atmospheric apprenticeship
on the surface of this second-class planet.

I may startle you some fine morning, when I am
strolling about Andover, by a knock or a ring, and
steal an hour of your time, for which posterity would
never forgive me, if indeed it happened to know of
my existence.

With my best respects to the Professor, I am, dear
Mrs. Stowe, faithfully yours.

Dr. Holmes allowed the public half a dozen years,
or more, to mull over the startling doctrines in this
"inartistic" story of *Elsie Venner*, and then gave
them another novel which moved along the same line
of moral speculation.   Properly viewed, this was a
step forward, because *Elsie Venner* had based its
problem on an abnormal, if not an impossible, instance,
and therefore had left open a back door, whereby one
could sneak away from giving a decisive answer to the

questions raised. But Myrtle Hazard's case was a simple one of heredity, as easy and natural a thing as a ghost to have in any family with ancestors. In a literary way, too, the second book far surpassed the earlier. If it was less weird and picturesque, — or shall we say fantastic, — it was also far more artistic. Evidently *Elsie Venner* is going always to be regarded as Dr. Holmes's most " important canvas," to borrow the language of the painter fraternity; but *The Guardian Angel* is much better work. In the earlier half every page sparkles with the gems of wisdom, wit, and humor; the reader is dazzled, and, however alert he may be, cannot look back without finding that he has missed something fine. Take a pencil, read carefully, and mark on the margin every striking sentence, and see how closely the marks follow each other; then you will have ocular demonstration of what the volume holds. It is true that the latter half is not quite so good as the beginning; but this is natural, for characters develop in the first half of a novel and plots in the latter half, and Dr. Holmes could draw characters but could not work out plots. As a picture of New England people at or shortly before the time when the book was written, nothing could be more graphic, and the *mise en scène* was worthy of the men and women who moved in it. The rural town of Massachusetts in the middle third of this century is as well drawn as the country society of England was drawn in the fascinating novels of Jane Austen.

It was not until 1884–85 that Dr. Holmes gave to the world his third and last novel, *A Mortal Antipathy*. He was then far past the creative age, and the book showed the fact too plainly. From Elsie Venner, with her mysteriously envenomed nature, to that absurd young man Maurice Kirkwood, who could not bear the sight of a young girl because his pretty cousin had caused him to fall from a balcony in his babyhood, the downward step was indeed a long one; and as for "The Terror" and "The Wonder" and the boat-race and the fire, and all the rest of the apparatus, human and other, these won't do at all. The problem, too, though akin to that of the other novels, was, in comparison, weak and uninteresting. The Doctor was "young for his years," but too old to do any more work in fiction. He himself seems to have been aware in a measure, though not fully, of the difference between this and his previous work.

TO ALEXANDER IRELAND.

April 5, 1886.

MY DEAR MR. IRELAND, —

.    .    .    .    .    .    .    .    .    .

I think you told me you had read my story, *A Mortal Antipathy*, and found something to like in it, and I was thankful to think that it pleased you. I had no exalted anticipations about it; in fact, I was a little afraid that it would be scouted as altogether beyond the bounds of credibility; and so I shored it up with scientific evidence of one kind and another. Oddly enough, whatever fault has been found with it, not one of its critics has accused it of improbability, — not one, so far as I have seen, at least.

*Dr. Holmes and Religion.* When his more famous books were publishing, these words would have headed the most important chapter of a memoir. To-day, prudent limitations of due proportion to the present interest of the topic must be respected. In this age

the questionings of one generation are the faith of the
next.   Yet, even knowing this, it is difficult to realize that a few still linger above ground of those who
used to call Dr. Holmes by any name of opprobrium,
from freethinker to atheist; and that people now in
middle life were, in their youth, forbidden to read *The
Autocrat of the Breakfast-Table*, because it was a
work of irreligious tendency.   None the less, these
things are, or were, facts; and when *Elsie Venner*
appeared there was an outcry as if this quiet gentleman, with the amiable face and kindly manner, were
the very Antichrist of old, deceptively averting suspicion by appearing in the coat and trousers of the
period.

Dr. Holmes loved medicine, and found deep pleasure in literature, but more than by either medicine
or literature he was attracted by theology.   His
thought, his talk, his writing, in whatever direction it
might set out, was sure soon to oscillate towards this
polar topic.   It was this which lent the dignity of a
persistent and serious purpose to his work.   His own
theories of heredity would indicate that this irresistible propensity might be attributed to that potent influence; but if so, it was a curious instance of what
must probably be called reactionary heredity; for the
Doctor made it his business to show that those beliefs
which his ancestors had held for a bunch of divine
keys to heavenly mansions were really a cluster of
instruments of torture fashioned by misguided human
intellects.

Every age and every nation makes its own religion.
Christianity has been the same since the days of
Christ.   But various communities in divers centuries
have called by its name the widely varying religions

which they have constructed to suit their own several and mutable, moral and intellectual, even political and social conditions.  The puritans of New England, not at the outset a collection of very gentle souls, placing themselves in moral and social antagonism with the established order of things in Europe, and in physical antagonism with the stern aspect of Nature in New England, naturally sought to strike a vindictive balance in their scheme for another world; it was to be expected, *a priori*, that they would make cruelty the corner-stone of their religious edifice, and they did so. In time they took Christ out of the Bible and put Jonathan Edwards in; they made a hell of immeasurable spaciousness and indescribable terrors, and over-crowded it; and they made Heaven hardly so big as a modern hotel.  They damned the heathen who had lived before the advent of Christ, and the later heathen who had never heard his name, and the poor babies who died before the minister could get to the bedside to baptize them!  They damned every one who did not agree with them, and they damned each other, too, pretty freely. Now all this is not very ancient history; for when Dr. Holmes fell first under the ban of the religious world, it was because he was laying his lance, or his pen, in rest against precisely this promiscuous damnation. He was one of the early comers in that period of broad *human humaneness*, now present, but which was only approaching during his youth and middle age. He was a singularly humane man, — kindly and gentle, though with virility and courage to fight for kindliness and gentleness.  It was these barbarisms, these grafts of thorns fastened by clergymen into the tree of Christianity, which he set himself to cut away.  " Any decent person," he said, and it was a favorite remark

with him, "ought to go mad, if he really holds such
or such opinions. . . . Anything that is brutal, cruel,
heathenish, that makes life hopeless for the most of
mankind and perhaps for entire races, anything that
assumes the necessity of the extermination of instincts which were given to be regulated, no matter
by what name you call it, no matter whether a fakir,
or a monk, or a deacon believes it, if received, ought
to produce insanity in every well-regulated mind.
That condition becomes a normal one, under the circumstances.  I am very much ashamed of some people
for retaining their reason, when they know perfectly
well that if they were not the most stupid or the most
selfish of human beings, they would become *non
compotes* at once."  Therefore it was the religion of
Orthodox clergymen, not the religion of Christ, that
he attacked; and the clergymen of course fought for
their own, and declared that Dr. Holmes was an infi-
del, when in fact he had only declared infidelity as
to certain inferences which they had drawn from the
Bible.  Yet the Doctor, a mettlesome man himself,
even while encountering them felt a certain admiration for these rigid, merciless, hard fighters of the old
theology.  "Whatever fault we may find," he wrote,
"with many of their beliefs, we have a right to be
proud of our Pilgrim and Puritan fathers among the
clergy.  They were ready to do and to suffer anything for their faith, and a faith which breeds heroes
is better than an unbelief which leaves nothing worth
being a hero for."

Thus endowed with inherited ecclesiastical pug-
nacity, — and the brethren of the church are so pugna-
cious that they have monopolized for their literature
the word *polemics*, which is only the Greek word for

war, as of course every one knows, so that it should not be mentioned except that it is so suggestive, — thus endowed, I say, the Doctor was not at all over-awed by doctrines and interpretations of the Bible which were of human origin and authority, and he conceived Jonathan Edwards to be no more infallible than the supreme Pontiff at Rome. Was not his, Dr. Holmes's, errand in theology as good as that of his colonist forefathers, who had made it their business "to diabolize the deity," as he expressed it? He wrote to Rev. James Freeman Clarke: "You are doing noble work in humanizing 'Theology,' which has been largely *diabology*. My testimony is not needful to you, who are the leader of a great wing of the Christian army, but it is a kind of pleasure to give it while we see so much that is shrivelling up and fading out among our contemporaries."

He believed that condition of change which had existed for eighteen centuries would continue, and that it was wholesome. He advocated discussion, and while he preached the new idea of humaneness, he did not even desire that every one should accept his teaching. He said: —

"What we want in the religious and in the political organisms is just that kind of vital change which takes place in our bodies, — interstitial disintegration and reintegration; and one of the legitimate fears of our time is that science, which Sainte-Beuve would have us think has destroyed faith, will be too rapid in its action on beliefs. So the doubter should be glad that he is doubted; the rationalist respect the obduracy of the dogmatist; and all the mighty explosives with which the growth of knowledge has furnished us should be used rather to clear the path for those who come after us than to shatter the roofs which have long protected and still protect so many of our humble and trusting fellow-creatures."

"We cannot fail to see," he said again, "that just as astrology has given place to astronomy, so theology, the science of Him whom by searching no man can find out, is fast being replaced by what we may not improperly call theonomy, or the science of the laws according to which the Creator acts." And again: "As if faith did not require exercise as much as any other living thing, and were not all the better for a shaking up now and then. I don't mean that it would be fair to bother Bridget, the wild Irish girl, or Joyce Heth, the centenarian, or any other intellectual non-combatant; but all persons who proclaim a belief which passes judgment on their neighbors must be ready to have it 'unsettled,' that is, questioned, at all times and by anybody, — just as those who set up bars across a thoroughfare must expect to have them taken down by every one who wants to pass, if he is strong enough." And still again he exclaims: "Besides, to think of trying to water-proof the American mind, against the questions that Heaven rains down upon it, shows a misapprehension of our new conditions!"

In the same connection may be taken this sentence: "Can any man look round and see what Christian countries are now doing, and how they are governed, and what is the general condition of society, without seeing that Christianity is the flag under which the world sails, and not the rudder that steers its course?"

But it was a question of considerable consequence what sort of a change he was introducing; was he making Hell hotter and more populous, or cooler and less crowded? So many excellent old-fashioned people believed that he was doing the former!

It was natural that many shook their heads very gravely when he talked, in language which seemed to them light and irreverent, of Americanizing Christianity.  Here are his words, which smote like blasphemy on many good little ears: "Our religion has been Judaized, it has been Romanized, it has been Orientalized, it has been Anglicized, and the time is at hand when it must be AMERICANIZED!  Now, Sir, you see what Americanizing is in politics; — it means that a man shall have a vote because he is a man, — and shall vote for whom he pleases, without his neighbor's interference."  And like unto the foregoing was this paragraph, which sounded terrible to the people who had not learned that the creatures fashioned their Creator as much as He fashioned them, though in a somewhat different sense, and only by making variations of the same prevalent image : " Every age has to shape the Divine image it worships over again, — the present age and our own country are busily engaged in the task at this time.  We unmake Presidents and make new ones.  This is an apprenticeship for a higher task.  Our doctrinal teachers are unmaking the Deity of the Westminster Catechism and trying to model a new one, with more of modern humanity and less of ancient barbarism in his composition."  Again: "Men are idolaters, and want something to look at and kiss and hug, or throw themselves down before; they always did, they always will; and if you don't make it of wood, you must make it of words, which are just as much used for idols as promissory notes are used for values."  In conversation, one day in his later life, he said: " Every age has its way of representing its idea of God.  Far back, it was the rude mass of metal, iron or bronze.   Then came the Greek with his finer ideal expressed in beautiful images of pure white marble. We select adjectives, the most beautiful and sublime in our language, and with these we make our God."

But matters were to reach a much worse stage than this.  In good season Dr. Holmes began to talk of the obligations of the Creator to his creations!   " If a created being has no rights which his Creator is bound to respect, there is an end to all moral relations between them."  Words were insufficient to express the horror of the religious world at this.  *The duties of God to man!*  Such audacious and awful profanity might tempt the Divine wrath as the rod tempts the lightning.   It seemed really dangerous to live in the age and nation where such words might well provoke the activity of One who could destroy!

When *Elsie Venner* came, the Doctor found himself in hotter water than ever before.  For "the imaginary subject of the story obeyed her *will*.  But her will obeyed the mysterious ante-natal poisoning influence."  In the book the Doctor set forth this cluster of opinions, any one of which was fuel for a martyr's fire.  We read that the liberal-minded clergyman " went so far in defence of the rights of man, that he put his foot into several heresies, for which men had been burned so often, it was time, if ever it could be, to acknowledge the demonstration of the *argumentum ad ignem*.  He did not believe in the responsibility of idiots.  He did not believe a newborn infant was morally answerable for other people's acts.  He thought a man with a crooked spine would never be called to account for not walking erect.  He thought if the crook was in his brain, instead of his back, he could not fairly be blamed for any consequence of this natural defect, whatever lawyers or divines might call it. He argued that, if a person inherited a perfect mind, body, and disposition, and had perfect teaching from infancy, that person could do nothing more than keep the moral law perfectly. But supposing that the Creator allows a person to be born with an hereditary or ingrafted organic tendency, and then puts this person into the hands of teachers incompetent or positively bad, is not what is called *sin* or transgression of the law necessarily involved in the premises? Is not a Creator bound to guard his children against the ruin which inherited ignorance might entail on them? Would it be fair for a parent to put into a child's hands the title-deeds to all its future possessions and a bunch of matches? And are not men children, nay, babes, in the eye of Omniscience? The minister grew bold in his questions. Had not he as good right to ask questions as Abraham?"

Neither, if Dr. Holmes's theory was true, could these pre-natal influences be wholly eradicated by education: "There are people who think that everything may be done, if the doer, be he educator or physician, be only called 'in season.' No doubt; but *in season* would often be a hundred or two years before the child was born, and people never send so early as that."

After allowing society to take care of itself by restraining the freedom or taking the life of any person whose pre-natal influences were so destructive of the social order as to call for such safeguards, Dr. Holmes stopped short. He seemed to shift the responsibility from that point onward upon the Creator, whose arrangements had brought about these conditions. A

just God, to say nothing of a merciful one, would of
course make it all right hereafter for the unfortunate,
involuntary victim.   He said : —

"It is very singular that we recognize all the bodily
defects that unfit a man for military service, and all
the intellectual ones that limit his range of thought,
but always talk at him as if all his moral powers were
perfect.   I suppose we must punish evil-doers as we
extirpate vermin ; but I don't know that we have any
more right to judge them than we have to judge rats
and mice, which are just as good as cats and weasels,
though we think it necessary to treat them as crimi-
nals. . . . Automatic action in the moral world; the
*reflex movement*, which *seems* to be self-determination,
and has been hanged and howled at as such (meta-
phorically) for nobody knows how many centuries, —
until somebody shall study this as Marshall Hall has
studied reflex nervous action in the bodily system, I
would not give much for men's judgments of each
other's characters.   Shut up the robber and defaulter
we must.   But what if your oldest boy had been
stolen from his cradle and bred in a North Street
cellar?   What if you are drinking a little too much
wine and smoking a little too much tobacco, and your
son takes after you, and so, your poor grandson's
brain being a little injured in physical texture, he
loses the fine moral sense on which you pride yourself, and does n't see the difference between signing
another man's name to a draft and his own?"

So, then, since no fallible man could ever be sure
just how far another man was under the control of
pre-natal influences, it became impossible to declare
any man to be a sinner.   Conceive an old-school
Orthodox clergyman deprived of this privilege!   Yet

lose it he must, unless he could give a negative answer to Mr. Langdon when that gentleman wrote: "Do you think there may be predispositions, inherited or ingrafted, but at any rate constitutional, which shall take out certain apparently voluntary determinations from the control of the will, and leave them as free from moral responsibility as the instincts of the lower animals? Do you not think there may be a *crime* which is not a *sin?*"

Without unbiassed freedom of the will, where was moral responsibility? Without moral responsibility, what became of sin? Without sin, what was the use of Hell? What a house-that-Jack-built this was! But the Orthodox religionists of the good old school clung with pertinacity to their belief in Hell, — there were so many people who ought to be there !

What made all these innovating arguments more distasteful was, that the sinner seemed to become actually an object of pity. It might be a necessity to punish him, but he was to be commiserated for having been made the victim of such necessity. This was logic, and Dr. Holmes was a clear-headed and inexorable logician ; so his humanity and his logic were compounded thus : —

" I don't deny that I hate *the sight* of certain people ; but the qualities which make me tend to hate the man himself are such as I am so much disposed to pity, that, except under immediate aggravation, I feel kindly enough to the worst of them. It is such a sad thing to be born a sneaking fellow, so much worse than to inherit a hump-back or a couple of club-feet, that I sometimes feel as if we ought to love the *crippled souls*, if I may use this expression, with a certain tenderness which we need not waste on noble natures."

It must be admitted that by this time Dr. Holmes
had a pretty big fight on his hands, in which it was
not altogether easy to array his own side.  In fact it
was the successor of an old contest, which had had
difficulties that logicians and theologians had never
been able to get into shape.  The impossibility of
reconciling "foreknowledge absolute" and "free
will" had kept the dialecticians by the ears for a
couple of centuries, till they had reduced to the commonplace everything which could possibly be said in
the disputation.  Now Dr. Holmes came along, leading science by the hand to take a place in the contest; and heredity, or pre-natal influences, were set up
as the new antagonists to continue the old warfare
against free will.  It is not settled yet, that unending
dispute, and probably it never will be.  Dr. Holmes
fought hard in it to the end of his life, and then died,
leaving it still furiously raging.  Indeed, how can one
make a chemical analysis of the motives which have
produced an action, or developed a character, and
allot so many ounces of free will, so many grammes
of heredity *per* the father, and other grammes of
heredity *via* the mother?  This is no place to enter
into the discussion; my purpose is only to show what
sort of things they were that Dr. Holmes said, which
caused him to live, for many years at least, under the
ban of the religious world, and to bear the character
of one teaching momentous innovations in the matters of established faith.

What was his own faith?  Many will think the
question interesting, and seek an answer.  But he
never formulated his beliefs, and no one has the right
to do it for him.  For the most part he sedulously
kept clear of any distinct commitments as to *religion,*

while speaking freely as to *creeds*.  Yet his writings
are full of disconnected, sporadic remarks bearing
upon the subject, and much more will be found in the
letters published in these volumes, notably in those to
Mr. Kimball and Mrs. Stowe.  I doubt if he could
ever have written down his *Credo*, at least in a shape
that would long have stood his own criticism.  What
he would have said on one day and in one mood, he
would have rejected, or greatly amended, on another
day and in another mood.  The things which he did
say are far from consistent with each other, far from
constituting a systematic whole.  Now his emotions
were in the ascendant, and anon his intellect held
domination.  He was a poet and a logician; what was
to be expected?  " Now you must know," the Professor says, " that there are a great many things which
interest me, to some of which this or that particular
class of readers may be totally indifferent.  I love
. . . old stories from black - letter volumes and yellow manuscripts, and new projects out of hot brains
not yet imbedded in the snows of age.  I love the
generous impulses of the reformer; but not less does
my imagination feed itself upon the old litanies, so
often warmed by the human breath upon which they
were wafted to Heaven that they glow through our
frames like our own heart's blood.  I hope I love
good men and women; I know that they never speak
a word to me, even if it be of question or blame, that
I do not take pleasantly, if it is expressed with a reasonable amount of human kindness."  His warfare,
be it remarked however, was always against the
glosses of Christianity, never against Christianity;
against clergymen, not against Christ.  He repudiated " the Deity of ecclesiastical commerce," as he

delightfully expressed it, but in the same paragraph delivered a strong appeal for faith in a kindly, parental God.  He was fond, his life long, of church-going. He says, again through the mouth of the Professor : " I am a regular church-goer.  I should go for various reasons, if I did not love it ; but I am happy enough to find great pleasure in the midst of devout multitudes, whether I can accept all their creeds or not.  One place of worship comes nearer than the rest to my ideal standard, and to this it was that I carried our young girl."  This was of course the old colonial King's Chapel, at the corner of School and Tremont streets in Boston, sometimes absurdly called the " Stone Chapel " (as being built of granite) by the people who were as much scared by the royalty in its proper title as if they were " jingo " politicians. Yet he went also to the " meeting-house " in Beverly Farms, about which certainly no associations of history or of antiquity cast any glamour ; for he found, as he said, that there was in the corner of his heart a plant, called reverence, which wanted to be watered about once a week.  He liked a good preacher, but he sat beneath a dull one contentedly, studying him perhaps as a character, since dulness is not dull to the observer of human nature.  He wrote thus to Bishop Brooks : —

TO PHILLIPS BROOKS.

296 BEACON STREET, May 23, 1888.

MY DEAR MR. BROOKS, — I had the privilege of listening to your sermon last Sunday forenoon.  I was greatly moved and impressed by it, and I came away very thankful that so divine a gift of thought and feeling and utterance had been bestowed upon one who was born and moves among us.

My daughter would be glad to have me as her constant companion, and of course it would be a delight to listen to such persuasive and inspiring exhortations as those which held your great audience last Sunday.

But my natural Sunday home is King's Chapel, where a good and amiable and acceptable preacher tries to make us better, with a purity and sincerity which we admire and love. In that church I have worshipped for half a century, — there I listened to Dr. Greenwood, to Ephraim Peabody, often to James Walker, and to other holy and wise men who have served us from time to time. There, on the fifteenth of June, 1840, I was married, there my children were all christened, from that church the dear companion of so many blessed years was buried. In her seat I must sit, and through its door I hope to be carried to my resting-place.[1] It is not any difference of creed which would keep me from following my beloved daughter, for I have been at times a regular attendant on the Episcopal service. This was at Pittsfield, where my son Edward's friend, Mr. Newton, is I hear doing admirable work in the most catholic, unsectarian spirit. I attend a Baptist church at Beverly, not rarely with edification, for my temple is a hypæthral one, and my church doors open very widely.

I am ashamed to ask you to pardon this letter. You know the language of sincerity from that of flattery, and will accept this heartfelt tribute in the spirit in which it is given.


Writing, in 1876, to Mr. James William Kimball, and speaking of hymns, he said : " It would be one of the most agreeable reflections to me, if I could feel that I had left a few worthy to be remembered after me."

<hr>

[1] So he was.

"Old realities have become shadows, but these shadows still torment me ; " thus wrote John Addington Symonds; and I think that Dr. Holmes was in the like case, and that he never got wholly away from the beliefs instilled into his mind in childhood.   He said once that he could never quite emerge from under the shadow of the old orthodox hell.   And he wrote : " We are all tattooed in our cradles with the beliefs of our tribe; the record may seem superficial, but it is indelible.   You cannot educate a man wholly out of the superstitious fears which were early implanted in his imagination ; no matter how utterly his reason may reject them, he will still feel as the famous woman did about ghosts, *Je n'y crois pas, mais je les crains,* — 'I don't believe in them, but I am afraid of them, nevertheless,' " — which quotation suggests what it is not altogether irrelevant to say in this connection : that the psychical, supernatural talk which became fashionable in the Doctor's later days interested him moderately.   A friend once sent to him an article concerning ghosts.   The Doctor, in his note of thanks, mentioned some singular occurrences within his personal knowledge, and closed thus : " I keep my cellar door open for ' Science,' and my attic skylights open for unclassed and as yet unclassifiable statements about the imponderable."   Though these words do not relate to the mysteries of religion, yet they indicate his general mental attitude towards all mysteries.

If Death knocked at the door of a friend, he gave not precisely the condolence of a Christian believer, and yet something not altogether removed from that. Here, for example, are three rather interesting letters, one to the old friend of his boyhood, Phineas Barnes, who had received his summons, another to a corre-

spondent whom he had never personally met, the third
to an acquaintance living in his neighborhood in
Boston.

TO PHINEAS BARNES.

March 10, 1871.

MY DEAR BARNES, — I just this moment received
your letter, which I feel impelled to answer, even if I
must do it hurriedly, on the instant. . . . Your letter
recalls me from myself and my own immediate family
interest to the tender recollections of an early and
pure friendship, which comes back to me as it was and
as it has always continued through a long period of
separation, in which we never lost sight of each other,
up to the present time, when your illness and the
fears, I hope less founded than you seem to believe,
have excited such anxiety in all who love you. You
may be sure I wish to help your sweet daughter in all
her untiring efforts to procure the best help and counsel our city could afford. . . . While I must hope
that you will find yourself permanently relieved by an
operation, if that is thought advisable, I admire, while
I am not surprised at, the calmness with which you
contemplate all possibilities. You are a philosopher
by nature, and something more than a philosopher
by faith. It is trust in something better and wiser
than we are, whether it comes to us in the inner light
which we believe is the direct gift of the infinite spirit,
or takes the human aspect in the person of him who
brings the Divine as it were face to face with us; or
whether with deeper than even Christian humility we
stretch our arms forth " like an infant crying in the
night," and implore the Being who gave us life to
give us even the crumbs of faith which fall from the
table of the triumphant and unquestioning believer.

To this, in one shape or another, we must all come, — if we have a Father, He will care for us and do what is best for us; and if He is as good as even our earthly fathers and mothers have been, will judge us not by our poor stumbling acts and short-sighted views, and pitiable shortcomings, but in the light of His own magnanimous, forgiving, loving nature. Add to this view of our weakness and His strength, of our imperfection and His all-perfection, of our need and His sufficiency, such a view of the manner in which His grace is imparted as we believe the Spirit of God has taught us, and we are ready, so far as our limitations will let us be, for all that may be sent us.

I thought you would like a few words from me of this general nature, far less for your sake than for mine, — for we must all soon cast anchor, if we have one, and mine is *Trust in God.*

### TO W. R. STURTEVANT.

BEVERLY FARMS, MASS., *September* 17, 1878.

MY DEAR SIR, — Your sad and tearful letter reached me at this seaside place, where I am spending the summer months — have spent them rather, and am still lingering among the autumn leaves, beginning now to fade and soon to fall. The flowers are many of them already withered — alas, for the sweet flower that has faded from your sight! How could I read that tender letter of yours without the deepest sympathy — how could I keep the tears from wetting my own cheeks, when I thought how yours and the heart-stricken mother's were flowing? I was three years old when a little sister of six died after a lingering illness. Her pallid face — the very posture in which she was sitting — her arms leaning on the arms of the little chair — never left me, and to this day I can never recall her without an emotion of tenderness which makes me akin to all grief in others. More than half a century had gone since her death, when I came upon a box carefully put away — it held her doll, and the sight of it made me a child again. Oh, no — I was not ashamed that it did. . . .

How can one "comfort" another under such an affliction as yours?   Not certainly by phrases — rather by those assurances of sympathy which all hearts ask in their supreme moments of trial.   Still, there are a few thoughts which it is not idle or ill-timed to recall.   There are no graves that grow so green as the graves of children.   Their memory comes back after a time more beautiful than that of those who leave us at any other age, because life has not had time to strip them of those " clouds of glory " which, as Wordsworth says so exquisitely, they come trailing with them "from Heaven, which is their home."   If no pang is sharper than parting with a beloved child, no recollection clears itself so naturally and perhaps I might say so early, of all but what is lovely to dwell upon.

There are two ways of accepting a grief such as you are now aching with.   Those who believe in a fixed order of things which goes on without regard to human welfare here or hereafter, according to inexorable laws which give no account of themselves to those who are under their dominion, and never will, must bear their trials as they best can with the aid of what is called "philosophy."   They have at least the consolation of feeling that there is no ill will in the blind forces which wreck their happiness.   The falling stone, the atmospheric poison, are not to blame for what they do. One must do his best to keep the natural laws on his side, and then take what comes to him. He can have no quarrel with a universe which cannot help itself. His best consoler is *Time*, which heals most wounds, though it leaves too many of the wounded cripples.

The other way of taking bereavements and misfortunes is to accept them as from the hand of One who will in due time explain to all His reasonable creatures the order of things in which their lives and welfare are bound up. All religions which do not treat men, women, and children as under the tender care of a Being who understands their natures, who knows all their griefs, who in allowing them to be born into consciousness — into intelligence and affection — took on Himself all the duties and obligations, and more than all, of the best of earthly parents, seem to me unworthy of the source from which they are pretended to be derived.

I hope you can accept your great sorrow as yet to be interpreted by the Divine wisdom and goodness. In the mean time be assured that the natural and outspoken expression of your anguish meets with my deepest sympathy, as I am sure it must with that of every feeling human heart.

TO MRS. JULIA C. R. DORR.

BOSTON, December 8, 1884.

MY DEAR MRS. DORR, — I write in the memory of a recent sorrow, which has fallen upon my own family, to express my sympathy with you in your great bereavement. It is not that words can do much to add to the simple phrase that says, — I sorrow with you and wish I could lighten your load of grief.

My loss is not only an affliction, but it is also a sad disappointment, for I had hoped and had every reason to hope for an honorable and useful and very happy career for my youngest son, who seemed to be just entering a new era in a life happy in all respects but one, — the want of health, which seemed to be returning to him when he was suddenly taken away.

I tell you my sorrow, but I am thinking now of yours. It is not for me to suggest the sources of consolation to which you must look in this hour of trial. A true woman's heart knows where to find its stay and support in those human affections which it has learned to lean upon, and in that higher trust which tells us that the source from which our earthly love derives its purest and warmest impulse must overflow with the same tenderness that belongs to our deepest emotions. I hope you find some solace in thoughts like these.

The extracts you send me show what a loss the community has experienced in the death of Judge Dorr. Your private grief is sacred, and I almost hesitate to send this note, but you will understand it, and perhaps be reminded by it of how many there are who mourn with you in your hour of trial.

These letters show the emotional, sympathetic side of the Doctor's nature. On the other hand, intellectually, as I have already so often had occasion to remark, he was a close and logical reasoner. He had learned that to take for granted a postulate which is essential and yet not known to be true, is only to court destruction and lead to a false conclusion in a vast majority of cases. The following seems to me a very striking letter concerning immortality ; it stands by

itself, solitary, so far as I know, amid all that he has
publicly or privately written : —

TO JOHN LINDLEY.

*Private — an impromptu answer.*

BOSTON, *December* 28, 1867.

DEAR SIR, — I should prefer to say that I *trust*
there will be a righting of this world's evils for each
and all of us in a future state, than say that I share the
unquestioning certainty of many of those about me.

The natural argument seems to me against the
supposition.  In the year 1800 I was not, to the best
of my knowledge.  Since that time my consciousness
has been evoked and my experiences have been accumulated.  I do not see that I have any natural
ground for claiming the future any more than the
past, — other than my conviction that it is or ought to
be so, — a conviction which is sometimes strong and at
other times weak, as in the experience of many others.

I have seen many human consciousnesses put together, like my own.  They were at one time represented by the unconscious life of *ova*.  By and by
they got sense, intellect, will, conscience, experience.

But I have seen many consciousnesses taken to
pieces also; they lost the senses to a great extent; the
intellect and of course the conscience, with the will,
were enfeebled, almost lost, and the experiences of life
so erased that the wife forgot her husband, the mother
her children.

The natural conclusion would be that this gradual
decay ends in extinction.  The question might well be
asked, whether the individuality, so nearly lost in this
world, is likely to be restored by the destruction of the

organism.  I *hope* and *trust* that my feelings are right, which tell me that this world demands a complement.

If the evidence of the New Testament is a *proof* (and not merely a probability of a certain value, variously estimated by different honest persons), there is no need of asking the question.

One thing seems to me clear, — that if the future life is to be for the bulk of mankind what the larger part of our pulpits teach, namely, a condition of hopeless woe, there is no reason why we should wish to have proof of another life.

The more I consider the doctrine of eternal punishment, the more it seems to me a heathen invention, which has found its way into Christianity, and entirely inconsistent with the paternal character attributed to the Deity.  (We must carry to any future sphere the characters we form here ; and these must influence, if they do not determine, our condition. Yet it seems in accordance with the paternal principle that any punishment should be reformatory and not vindictive.)

One thing is certain : it is impossible to *disprove* the reality of a future life, and we have all a right to cherish the hope that we may live again under more favorable circumstances, and be able to account for these preliminary arrangements, which, as a finality, are certainly unsatisfactory.

In connection with this letter it is interesting to read this passage from *Elsie Venner*.  Mr. Bernard Langdon, it will be remembered, had been lassoed by the too melodramatic villain of the tale, made unconscious, and narrowly brought back to life ; whereupon Dr. Holmes says : —

" There were some curious spiritual experiences connected with his last evening's adventure which were working very strongly in his mind. It was borne in upon him irresistibly that he had been *dead* since he had seen Helen, — as dead as the son of the Widow of Nain before the bier was touched and he sat up and began to speak. There was an interval between two conscious moments which appeared to him like a temporary annihilation, and the thoughts it suggested were worrying him with strange perplexities.

. . . . . . . . . . .

" A man is stunned by a blow with a stick on the head. He becomes unconscious. Another man gets a harder blow on the head from a bigger stick, and it kills him. Does he become unconscious too ? If so, *when does he come to his consciousness ?* The man who has had a slight or moderate blow comes to himself when the immediate shock passes off and the organs begin to work again, or when a bit of the skull is pried up, if that happens to be broken. Suppose the blow is hard enough to spoil the brain and stop the play of the organs, what happens then ? "

But Helen, the good New England girl, replies : —

" It is a strange experience, but I once had something like it. I fainted, and lost some five or ten minutes out of my life, as much as if I had been dead. But when I came to myself, I was the same person every way, in my recollections and character. So I suppose that loss of consciousness is not death. And if I was born out of unconsciousness into infancy with many *family* traits of mind and body, I can believe, from my own reason, even without help from Revelation, that I shall be born again out of the unconsciousness of death with my *individual* traits of mind and

body.  If death is, as it should seem to be, a loss of
consciousness, that does not shake my faith; for I
have been put into a body once already to fit me for
living here, and I hope to be in some way fitted after
this life to enjoy a better one.  But it is all trust in
God and in his Word.  These are enough for me; I
hope they are for you."

Here we have Dr. Holmes on both sides of the
debate, like the solitary domino player who pits his
right hand against his left.  I don't know which hand
the Doctor thought would win, — if he had a fixed
opinion.

There is another paragraph in J. A. Symonds's
Letters, which I feel tempted to quote before taking
leave of this topic: "It is possible for me to state
the mature opinion that my father typified an excep-
tionally interesting moment of English evolution.  He
had abandoned the narrow standpoint of non-conform-
ist or evangelical orthodoxy, but he retained what was
ethically valuable in the religious tradition.  He
opened his mind to every influence of knowledge and
of culture.  He relinquished nothing which affected
character and principle.  In this way he formed a
link between the past and the future, attaining to an
almost perfect harmony of conservative and liberal
ideas.  I, the product of a younger period, regard his
attitude with reverent admiration."  One would mod-
ify these words a little, not greatly, in fitting them to
Dr. Holmes.  It is interesting to note the movement
of an age by observing minds so far asunder in their
surroundings, yet advancing along parallel lines.

Thus much, then, is said as to Dr. Holmes's relations to theology, Christianity, and religion; too much,
from the point of view of present feeling and faith.

It is a peril threatening the longevity of his writings, especially his novels, that the lessons to which he gave so much space and emphasis have now been learned. He himself lived to see the beginning of the harvest from that seed which he and a few other co-laborers had planted, as their Pilgrim progenitors had been wont in the early days to put in their corn, with much hard labor and under the menace of barbarism. In 1882, in a preface to a new edition of *The Autocrat*, he was able to declare: "I can say without offence to-day that which called out the most angry feelings and the hardest language twenty-five years ago. I may doubt everything to-day if I will only do it civilly." In 1891, he saw "the tyranny of that dogmatic dynasty," against which Myrtle Hazard had revolted, "breaking up in all directions." He saw abundant "evidence that there is no such thing as an air-tight reservoir of doctrinal finalities." He beheld "the folding-doors wide open to every Protestant to enter all the privileged precincts and private apartments of the various exclusive religious organizations. We may demand the credentials of every creed and catechise all the catechisms. So we may discuss the gravest questions over our morning coffee-cups, or over our evening teacups. There is no rest for the Protestant until he gives up his legendary anthropology and all its dogmatic dependencies." "Some persons," he admits, "may even at this late day take offence at a few opinions" of *The Professor at the Breakfast-Table;* "but most of these passages will be read without loss of temper by those who disagree with them; and by and by they may be found too timid and conservative for intelligent readers, if they are still read by any." If this new condition was desirable, the credit was largely his ; though the truth doubtless is, that it was one of the natural, inevitable, glacier-like movements of mankind, wherein he happened to be conspicuously in the front, — one of the little group which made the cut-water, if glaciers may be imagined to need such an equipment.

# CHAPTER XI



### THE DOCTOR'S DISTASTE FOR PUBLIC AFFAIRS

As the story of Dr. Holmes's life moves on, one can hardly fail to notice how entirely it was that of the private citizen. Only by some sudden pricking of memory do we recall that this tranquil existence of the man of letters was running its peaceful course parallel with that momentous struggle, first political and then martial, equally fierce and spirit-stirring in both phases, which resulted in the abolition of slavery. The Doctor had no taste and felt no capacity for public affairs, or for any of that labor with organizations, societies, and what not, of a *quasi* public character, in which many persons so usefully interest themselves. Neither did his conscience compel him to do violence to his inclination, but permitted him to hold himself aloof from all these things, because he knew perfectly well that they could and surely would be done better by others. Politics, "movements," "causes," like factories and railroads, were to be handled by those who knew how; it would have been wastefulness for him to do such things badly to the neglect of other things which Nature had designed him to do well. He watched public affairs intelligently; he voted conscientiously; with this he conceived that he had fulfilled his duty. The position seems sound; yet it did not satisfy those of his friends who were of more militant temperaments, and who

were anxious to enlist him in their struggles for the
"good of mankind," little appreciating, what he so
well knew, that his abilities were not adapted to serv-
ing mankind in these special ways.  It is cause for
regret that a letter which James Russell Lowell wrote
to him cannot be recovered, but his answer puts his
case clearly.  The occurrence sank deep into his memory, and was referred to long years afterwards.

TO JAMES RUSSELL LOWELL.

BOSTON, November 29, 1846.

MY DEAR SIR, — I have read your letter, as I believe, in the same spirit as that in which it was written.  There is nothing in its frankness which offends
me; on the contrary, that is the very quality in it
which makes it valuable and acceptable.  I thank you
for it, and shall endeavor to make a wholesome application of whatever truth and wisdom it contains.

And now let me be frank with you.  If I have
endeavored to look at myself from your point of
view, to correct my observations by your quadrant,
will you be equally patient with me while I defend
and explain some of my own views in a very tedious
manner?

And first, my defence against certain specific grounds
of complaint which you have in a very mild and proper
way urged upon me : —

I am not aware that I have arrayed myself against
any of the " Causes " to which you refer, and I hardly
know where to look for the "many shrewd rubs " you
say I have given them.  First, War.  That old poem
you refer to had a single passage in which I used expressions which I think I should be unwilling to use
now.  But its main object was to show that war is one

of the most powerful stimulants in bringing out the
power of the human intellect.   Some years afterwards
I wrote a Canadian war song, which my better feelings prompted me not to print.   I own that I find in
myself a growing hatred and disgust to this mode of
settling national quarrels, and that in many points I
sympathized with Mr. Sumner in his Fourth of July
oration.   But I cannot shut my eyes to the beauty of
heroism and self-devotion which the battlefield has
witnessed.   I think our fathers were right in taking
up arms to defend their liberties, and I have even now
a mitigated and *quasi* kind of satisfaction in hearing
of the courage and constancy of our countrymen in so
poor a quarrel as we are engaged in.[1]   I believe there
is nothing in this last poem which would go farther
than defending our revolutionary struggle, and certainly I have a right to claim some credit for not
lugging in Major Ringgold and General Taylor.   If,
as you seem to think, silence in regard to any great
question is affording an incidental aid to its antagonists, then I administered a rebuke to the war party
in not alluding to our recent " glorious victories."

Secondly, *Slavery*.   I plead guilty of a thoughtless
verse delivered at the same time with my Φ B K poem,
meant in the most perfect good nature for a harmless
though a dull jest, and taken, to my great surprise, as a
harsh and brutal expression of contempt: " The abolition men and maids," etc.   Very certainly I should
not write such a verse now, partly because this party
has grown more powerful, perhaps, but partly also
because I now know it would give offence to many
good persons, whose motives and many of whose principles I hold in profound respect.   I believe my posi-

---

[1] The Mexican war.

tive offences under this head stop at this period —
1836 — with this one hardly-judged stanza.

Thirdly, *Temperance*. I have written songs occasionally for social meetings in which the pleasures of
convivial excitement were, perhaps, too warmly drawn.
Here is a verse from one :—

> The Grecian's mound, the Roman's urn,
> Are silent when we call,
> Yet still the purple grapes return
> To cluster on the wall ;
> It was a bright Immortal's head
> They circled with the vine,
> And o'er their best and bravest dead
> They poured the dark red wine.

I think I may say that it was from conscientious
motives, in part, at least, if not mainly, that I never
published the little poem from which this is taken —
though I had a fondness for it. This was written for
the Porcellian Club, many years ago ; but long since
that I not only wrote but printed a song of a very
different character for a temperance celebration in
New York, thereby showing, what is true, that my
sympathies, and in some humble measure my coöperation, were with the advocates of temperance. More
than this, I took two hundred and fifty dollars instead
of four hundred, rent, during the present year, for a
store on Long Wharf, which I manage for my mother,
rather than let it, like many of those about it, for a
grocery, knowing that rum would be retailed from it.
I mention this because it implies that I am not wholly
insensible to the significance of this particular reform,
and that, if needs be, I can make some little sacrifice
for it.

Fourthly, *The claims of the poor*. I believe I have
never treated them unkindly in any way. I am sure

that I feel a deep interest in all well-directed efforts for improving their condition, and am ready to lend my cordial support to such practical measures as furnishing them with better dwellings, and similar movements.

Fifthly and lastly, *Reform* in general, and *reformers*. It is a mistake of yours to suppose me a thorough-going conservatist; and I think you cannot have found that in my writings which does not belong to my opinions and character. I am an out-and-out republican in politics, a firm believer in the omnipotence of truth, in the constant onward struggle of the race, in the growing influence and blessed agency of the great moral principles now at work in the midst of all the errors and excesses with which they are attended. In a little club of ten physicians I rather think I occupy the extreme left of the liberal side of the house. The idea of my belonging to the party that resists all change is an entire misconception. I may be lazy, or indifferent, or timid, but I am by no means one of those (such as a few of my friends) who are wedded for better for worse to the *status quo*, with an iron ring that Reason cannot get away unless it takes the finger with it.

But you refer to a certain passage in my last poem as implying that I treat it as a matter of choice which side of the great questions of the day one shall espouse. You then accuse me of ignoring the existence of conscience in the spiritual organization. On the strength of this you indulge in nearly a whole page of ironical amplifications.

I was puzzled for a good while to conjecture what passage you referred to. At first I thought it was one with the lines, " Go to thy birthplace," etc. — Then I thought it must be one beginning, "Don't catch the fidgets," — but I finally concluded, no doubt correctly, that it was that which commences, "Does praise delight thee," etc.

Now, as I promised to be frank, I must say that your interpretation of this passage is perverse in the extreme. It is in the form of a precept, but it is in reality the explanation of a trick, which you must know is not an uncommon one. So, a little before, I said that a man who wants to get on fast in the world had better cultivate his elders, — but do you understand me as implying that to get on fast is the highest object of human nature? When I say

"Does praise delight thee," etc.,

I at once fancy the intelligent reader paraphrasing the sentence in this way : " If you act merely to secure the approbation or flattery of others (and this, everybody knows, is a mean and unworthy motive), the trick that people of this stamp find most effectual is to choose some ultra side," etc. Nor can I conceive without a good deal of effort how you could put the interpretation you do upon the passage. Besides, as if to render your ironical remarks still more gratuitous, I had devoted two long and elaborate paragraphs to the single point of illustrating the dignity, the sensitiveness, and the dangerous liability to debasement, of that very principle CONSCIENCE (as I had it in the text), which you say I would " expurgate altogether." My dear friend, this is not me whom you are criticising ; but some changeling of your own, whom you have put in my place. You speak of criticising from your own point of view, but what point of view is there if you will not open your eyes? What can you see with those organs if

> " So thick a drop severe hath quenched their orbs,"

or so fatal an obliquity has deranged the axis of
vision ?

And now let me drop these little points, which after
all are of small moment except as the index of the
state of the mind and heart, and speak more generally.

You blame me (kindly always) for what I do not
do.   I do not write poems or introduce passages stig-
matizing war and slavery.

As to war, I am perfectly willing to condemn it as
a barbarous custom, whenever I can do so with any
particular efficiency and propriety.   Probably, however, in the present state of my opinions I should not
go far enough to satisfy you — certainly not to meet
the views of Edmund Quincy.   But I saw no particular necessity to introduce war before my peaceful
assemblage at the Tremont Temple, very few of whom
could tell gunpowder from onion seed.

As to slavery, there would have been still less fitness
in introducing it.   No doubt the audience would have
applauded, — it would have been a popular thing to
do.   But I have in this place just two things to say :
1. Slavery is a dreadful business, but the people about
me are not slaveholders and generally hate it pretty
thoroughly already.   2. All the resources of language
have been so liberally employed upon this subject —
all the cloacæ of vituperative eloquence having of late
years found their freest vent just upon this very point
— that nothing is so flat and unprofitable as weakly
flavored verses relating to it.   Did you ever see a
volume of lines — not by you or me — that illustrated
this fact ?

Once more, I believe that at present you and I cannot prevent the existence of slavery.   But the catas-

trophe of disunion I believe we can prevent, and thus avert a future of war and bloodshed which is equally frightful to both of us in contemplation. Can you trust me that I really *believe* this, or do you confine all honest faith and intelligent judgment to those who think with you? *Mind this one thing,* — I give these as reasons why I did not feel specially called upon to introduce the subject of slavery in preference to many others, but I am glad there are always eloquent men to keep the moral sense of the world alive on the subject. I thought disunion the most vital matter at present.

I gave many lessons in my late poem on the most serious subjects. They were on points that most interested me. Most of all, I enforced as well as I could, in a long series of connected passages, the duty of religious charity. To vary my exercise, which was addressed to a young and somewhat mixed audience, I introduced many light passages, relating to trifling matters, every one of which was meant to convey some useful hint, if possible coupled with a pleasant thought. The consequence has been that one set of critics proscribe me for being serious and another for being gay, — you will take neither the one hand nor the other with a good grace, because I am not philo-melanic or miso-polemic enough to meet your standard.

I supposed that you, and such as you, would feel that I had taught a lesson of love, and would thank me for it. I supposed that you would say I had tried in my humble way to adorn some of the scenes of this common life that surrounds us, with colors borrowed from the imagination and the feelings, and thank me for my effort. I supposed you would recognize a glow

of kindly feeling in every word of my poor lesson —
even in its slight touches of satire, which were only
aimed at the excesses of well-meaning people.  I supposed you would thank me for laughing at that ridiculous phantom of the one poet that is to be, whose imaginary performances inferior persons are in the habit
of appealing to, to prove that you and such as you are
mere scribblers.  I am sorry that I have failed in giving you pleasure because I have omitted two subjects
on which you would have loved to hear my testimony.

If you have read as far as this, take courage, for I
have almost done.

I listen to your suggestions with great respect.  I
mean to reflect upon them, and I hope to gain something from them.  But I must say, with regard to art
and the management of my own powers, I think I
shall in the main follow my own judgment and taste
rather than mould myself upon those of others.

I shall follow the bent of my natural thoughts, which
grow more grave and tender, or will do so as years
creep over me.  I shall not be afraid of gayety more
than of old, but I shall have more courage to be
serious.  Above all, I shall always be pleased rather
to show what is beautiful in the life around me than
to be pitching into giant vices, against which the acrid
pulpit and the corrosive newspaper will always anti-
cipate the gentle poet.  Each of us has his theory of
life, of art, of his own existence and relations.  It is
too much to ask of you to enter fully into mine, but
be very well assured that it exists, — that it has its
axioms, its intuitions, its connected beliefs as well as
your own.  Let me try to improve and please my
fellow-men after my own fashion at present ; when I
come to your way of thinking (this may happen) I

hope I shall be found worthy of a less qualified approbation than you have felt constrained to give me at this time.

In Dr. Holmes's make-up, conservatism in things political and social was curiously compounded with the progressive tendency in religious thought. The abolitionists not only failed to secure his active coöperation, but it was very slowly and imperfectly that they got his sympathy. In his old age he explained, perhaps excused, himself for not falling in with them; he recalled that his father, living many years in Georgia, "came in contact with slavery in its best and mildest form; and, living among the best people, learned to look upon it with less abhorrence than if he had studied it from a distance. Though he rarely referred to it, I did not receive from him the strong feeling of hatred and opposition to the institution which many Northern children inherited from their parents. My maternal grandfather was the so-called owner of slaves received by inheritance, one of whom, by the way, was a witness to the Boston 'Massacre,' when a boy. The stories of the 'bobolition' ceremonies and processions were matters of popular jesting. So, when the negroes were excluded from the Common on artillery election day by general consent, it was natural that I should not have been so ready for sympathy with the abolition movement as those young boys and men who were differently educated. . . . While I was studying medicine and boarding at No. 2 Central Court, I met habitually at the table for a considerable period Mr. Knapp, the fellow-worker of Mr. Garrison on *The Liberator*, but I confess that I do not remember having any conversation with him on this subject. I was taken up with my professional studies to the exclusion of everything else."

In a word, abolition for a long while failed to interest him. Doubtless also there is truth in the suggestion of a writer in the *Quarterly Review* who says: "The same aristocratic and conservative attitude made him oppose some of the social and literary movements by which America was deeply stirred. It took many years for Garrison to convince him of the justice of the negro's claim. He half seriously attributes his reluctance to his perusal, as a child, in the southeast attic of his home, of a book called *The Negro Plot*. But the opposition came rather from his character than his reading, and there can be no doubt that the personal peculiarities of many of the abolitionists excited his keen perception of the ridiculous; the long hair of Charles C. Burleigh, the venerable appearance of Father Lamson, the wild gesticulations of Wright, outraged his strong sense of propriety. His opinion of the legitimate sphere and influence of women was cast in the Old World mould. Believing with Parson Wilbur that twenty *h*eresiarchs were nothing to a single *sh*eresiarch, he had little sympathy with Mrs. Abby Kelley Foster."

In 1856 he expressed the opinion that "we must reach the welfare of the blacks through the dominant race," — a notion abhorrent to abolitionists. Yet the struggle in Kansas aroused him to indignation, and he came out in a vigorous way for the free-state men. In 1858 he wrote to Rev. Samuel May: "Your note gave me *very* great pleasure. I told Edmund Quincy the other day that I valued the praise of the abolitionists because I knew it was honest." But the language indicates plainly that he was not one of the band.

When at last the war came, it found him, or made
him, as it did so many others who had previously felt
and talked in the conservative and moderate strain, a
strenuous, intense, often a greatly excited patriot, a
Unionist of course, and very soon an anti-slavery
man. His eldest son enlisted among the first; but
this incentive was not necessary to put the Doctor
in the right place. He wrote war lyrics with the
spirit of a Tyrtæus; if they did not take their places
among the camp songs, it was not because they had
too little fire, but because they had too much literary
finish; they were a trifle "over the heads" of the
soldiery. He watched public affairs with keen interest, and, in view of the fact that his previous pursuits
had given him scant experience in such matters, the
accuracy of his observation and the shrewdness of his
forecasts were remarkable. More than once he illustrated that the looker-on knows the game better than
the players do. All this need not be dilated upon;
it will be seen in the very interesting group of letters
which he wrote at the time to Mr. Motley, then in
Europe, — letters which are unquestionably the Doctor's best.

Nevertheless, while he wrote ardently in poetry and
prose, he could not be induced to come into working
organizations, in witness whereof is this letter to his
dear friend Rev. James Freeman Clarke, who could
have won him over if any one could have done so: —

TO REV. JAMES FREEMAN CLARKE.

*October* 24, 1862.

MY DEAR JAMES, — I received your circular for a
meeting of the "Protective War-Claim Association"
last week, and now I have a new one, which I feel
bound to answer.

I go very little to Society and Club meetings.
Some feel more of a call that way, others less; I
among the least.

I hate the calling of meetings to order. I hate the
nomination of officers, always fearing lest I should be
appointed Secretary. I hate being placed on commit-
tees. They are always having meetings at which half
are absent and the rest late. I hate being officially
and necessarily in the presence of men most of whom,
either from excessive zeal in the good cause or from
constitutional obtuseness, are incapable of being
*bored*, which state is to me the most exhausting of all
conditions, absorbing more of my life than any kind
of active exertion I am capable of performing.

I am slow in apprehending parliamentary rules and
usages, averse to the business details many persons
revel in; and I am not in love with most of the
actively stirring people whom one is apt to meet in
all associations for doing good.

Some trees grow very tall and straight and large in
the forest close to each other, but some must stand by
themselves or they won't grow at all. Ever since I
used to go to the "Institute of 1770" and hear Bob
Rantoul call members to order, and to the "Euphra-
dian," where our poor Loring used to be eloquent
about Effie Deans, I have recognized an inaptitude,
not to say ineptitude, belonging to me in connection
with all such proceedings.

"What if everybody talked in this way?" The
Lord arranges his averages in such a way that to
every one person like myself there are two or three
organizing, contriving, socializing intelligences, and
three or four self-sacrificing people, who have forgotten what they like and what they hate by nature, and

about a dozen good indifferent folks that will take part in anything they are asked to.

Now look at it, dear James, Father Confessor, Good Shepherd. I have just sent off a long article for the December *Atlantic*, and that puts off my introductory lecture — (which I promised to write for H. J. Bigelow, who was sick) — and on that lecture I want to be at work at 10.30 to-morrow, when your meeting is. I like to stir up my doctors with wholesome fresh thought; and to arrange that takes time, and as I have but a little over a week for it I don't want to go and sweat a forenoon away in doing what some of your committee will find a pleasant excitement, but what will vex and fret and drain my nerves more than to write an anniversary poem — which is itself a short fever.

This note is personal to you because I had a mind to tell you how alien associated action is to my tastes and habits, and because I knew you would take the trouble to read and understand it.

The only approach to public activity which I recall was his oration, delivered in Boston on the Fourth of July, 1863. I did not hear this, and do not know what oratorical capacity he may have developed; but as one reads it, it seems a speech of the highest order, instinct with stimulating spirit, almost fiery at times, honestly recognizing all the difficulties to be encountered, but with abiding courage to overcome them; expressing an appreciation of the cause, of all that was at stake for humanity and the nation, of the practical situation, the prospects, and of the temper which must be adequate to the trial. It is printed in the *Pages from an Old Volume of Life*. I dare say it is not often read nowadays, and in time will be forgotten.  But a country must be rich in patriotic eloquence which can afford to let such an address glide out of memory.  He had from Mr. Motley a letter of such admiration for this production that, after making the most liberal possible deductions on any supposable grounds of friendship and courtesy, there was enough of praise left to gratify any palate, however jaded with flattery.[1]

The interest in public affairs, which had been aroused in Dr. Holmes by the war, never afterward entirely died away.  Its vitality was assisted by his interest in the careers of his friends Motley and Lowell, and abundant indications of his shrewd observation continue to find place in his letters to them. He actually upon occasion wrote to the dignitaries in Washington concerning the latter.  In a note to him, December 13, 1884, the Doctor says: "Here is another case in which I have been meddling with your affairs.  Governor Cleveland, the President-elect, wrote a letter on my notorious birthday, so full of compliment and high estimation that I thought I had a perfect right to reply to it. . . . In writing to the President-elect, I told him I had no personal favors to ask, but that for the sake of the country I hoped he would consider the desirableness of retaining you at your post.  I gave him an outline of your special fitness for the place in terms that I fear would make you blush, and ended by saying that I did not believe there was a man in the country who could make your place good. . . . I have had slight, but pleasant, relations with Bayard, who is like to be Secretary of State (so they say), and have some thought of writing

[1] *Motley Correspondence*, ii. 141.

to him about keeping you in your position.  Of course
you can resign when you are tired of work and glory,
*lassatus et satiatus*, and we shall all be most happy
to get you back."  Again, April 6, 1888:  "Why
should not Cleveland send you back as minister?
When he was appointed, I wrote him a letter, telling
him he had better keep you, as we had no duplicates
of that coinage.  He may remember — who knows?"

This was not only very kind on Dr. Holmes's part,
but it also indicated that he felt an ingenuous distrust
of the injurious gossip which he must often have heard
about "practical politics."  His letters produced no
results.

His views and feelings towards the South after the
close of the war appear to have been reasonably but
not immoderately liberal.  He was neither vindictive, nor yet fancifully and romantically amicable; he
had a pretty clear view equally of what ought to be
and of what could be.  In his oration he had said:
"There is material power enough in the North, if
there be the will to use it, to overrun and by degrees
to recolonize the South; and it is far from impossible
that some such process may be a part of the mechanism of its new birth, spreading from various centres
of organization, on the plan which Nature follows
when she would fill a half-finished tissue with blood-
vessels, or change a temporary cartilage into bone."
But the plague of the "carpet-baggers," descending
upon that region to complete the waste of the war, did
not seem to him good medicine with which to restore
political or social health.

I find this letter, written apparently to the son of
one of his classmates at Harvard College, who was a
citizen of New Orleans: —

### TO ALEXANDER PORTER MORSE.

Boston, *January* 4, 1868.

MY DEAR MR. MORSE, — I find myself greatly embarrassed in writing to you now; the difficulty I find in separating two characters united in your person; namely, that of the son of my old friend and classmate, and that of an editor of a journal representing ideas which, as you know, must differ a good deal from those I entertain. I am going to speak to you in the first capacity to begin with, and reserve the pleasure of addressing you in the second until the last.

Assuming your paper to be a move in the right direction, I think it promises to be conducted with spirit and to find many readers in the Southern States, a few in each of the Northern States, collectively perhaps a number not inconsiderable. And just so far as it encourages a wide and liberal culture, and tends to unite the sections of a country which has failed to break into countries, I shall rejoice in its success. It is evident that there is a returning feeling of literary fellowship. I do not speak from a personal sentiment, for I have not received the number with the review of my book in it, though I have just got that of January 4th; but judging by the notice of *The Atlantic*, and the *Harper* advertisements, and from what I know personally of one of your contributors, Mr. Paul H. Hayne, with whom I have corresponded since the war. But you must remember that the "lost cause" is *to us* a crushed rebellion; that, *to us*, its true source was a great national wrong trying to perpetuate itself; that in this belief our children and friends have died, so that the whole North is still in mourning; and that *to us* such poems as "The Confederate Dead," such pieces as "The Confederate Flag," are only a reopening of all the old wounds, not profitable to any, but entirely unwelcome to those who want to make all whole again as soon as time will let them. I think, therefore, you must rely on your Southern friends for your support. A sectional literature does not seem to us to promise much, but it is a favorite idea with many of our Southern friends, and they must work it out successfully if they can. Whenever anything really deserving of high praise is accomplished, I very sincerely believe that none will more readily acknowledge its excellence than your Northern fellow-countrymen.

And now to you personally, son of my dear old friend Morse, I have nothing to say that is not full of all kindness and good wishes. I remember saying to him once, when we were looking vaguely forward to a possible conflict of sections, how our boys might yet face each other in the field. I wonder how near any of you three or more sons of his came to my first-born! He got three bullets from some of you, anyhow; two went through him — neck and breast, and one stuck in the bone of his foot; but he is as well as ever, and I forgive you if either of you did it. Your father always seemed to like me, and I always liked him; we could not help liking him. I wonder if you knew what a pleasant, amiable, lively, entertaining, witty, shrewd, original young man he was? Nobody was so free and easy, so companionable, so full of all kinds of agreeable talk. The only wonder was that he never seemed to make an enemy, so outspoken as he was, and so different in many of his notions from any of us. Well, his boys and mine had to fight; but if he had brought up mine in New Orleans, and I had brought up his in Boston, they would have still fought, only changing sides. I am sure I feel just as well disposed to you and all my Southern friends as before the war. I do not ask them to forgive and forget as easily, it is not in nature that they should. But old friendships like your father's and mine are hard to outgrow, and I cannot help feeling an interest in all the members of my old friend's family. I wish you would renew the expression of my lasting remembrance to your mother and your brothers, and be assured of my cordial regard, and my hope that I shall have the pleasure of seeing you whenever you visit Boston.

Another Southern correspondent called forth these remarks, and it is an amusing instance of the Doctor's caution that the earlier of these two notes is marked "*private:*" —

TO PAUL H. HAYNE.

BOSTON, *April* 11, 1877.

DEAR MR. HAYNE, — Your letter, with the poems it enclosed, reached me yesterday. I read both the poems carefully, and I wish I could say that I read both with pleasure. But it distresses me to hear, whether in prose or verse, of the wretchedness of a sister State. I could not call up the images which your poem pictured in words, the intensity of which showed how deep the feeling which prompted them, without a thrill of sympathy and an aching of regret, that my fellow-countrymen of your proud record and sensitive race should be doomed to such suffering — I will not say humiliation, though I fear many spirits

must have been broken down under the slow pressure
of these calamities. At last we may hope that the
dawn is showing itself. President Hayes means to do
justice, we all — or almost all — believe; and it remains to be seen if your people, left to themselves,
can right the wrongs under which they are groaning.
There is eloquence and force in your "South Caro-
lina" poem, and much beauty in the "Vision," which
strikes me as one of the best things you have done.

BOSTON, November 1, 1881.

DEAR MR. HAYNE, —

  .     .     .     .     .     .     .     .     .

I hope that the era of good feeling is at last inau-
gurated. First, between the different sections of our
own country, which were welded in fire and have now
been tempered in blood. We know each other better,
perhaps, than we could have done but for the fierce
embrace of conflict; and we may hope that the dread
lesson we have learned of what a civil contest means
for both parties will serve once for all to teach us the
meaning of E pluribus unum.

# CHAPTER XII



No sooner was Dr. Holmes famous than the countless jaws of that many-headed and voracious ogre, "the public," began to gnash for the new victim. The postman came weighed down with letters and parcels innumerable, all demanding reply, a few deserving it. The burden became very serious, and it grew always heavier. It was not simply the swarm of autographhunters, like mosquitoes rising from the limitless breeding-grounds of summer marshes; but people came with every conceivable and inconceivable request for advice and assistance, chiefly literary, of course, though by no means wholly so; for the variety and absurdity of the petitions addressed to him could only be equalled by the ingenuous prayers of childhood. In *Over the Teacups* he wrote: —

"For the last thirty years I have been in the habit of receiving a volume of poems or a poem, printed or manuscript — I will not say daily, though I sometimes receive more than one in a day, but at very short intervals. I have been consulted by hundreds of writers of verse as to the merit of their performances, and have often advised the writers to the best of my ability. Of late I have found it impossible to attempt to read critically all the literary productions, in verse and in prose, which have heaped themselves on every exposed surface of my library, like snowdrifts along

the railroad tracks, — blocking my literary pathway,
so that I can hardly find my daily papers."

Now this was all very flattering of course; like the
widening circles around the stone which falls into the
water, it showed what a big splash he was making in
the puddle of the world. But it placed him between
alternatives of which each was disagreeable. He
might leave the countless applicants unanswered; or
he might answer them. To choose the former he was
too kind-hearted; to do the latter was very distasteful. It resulted that from the beginning he elected
the task of replying to all, — or substantially so.
His rule, as he stated it, was: to answer "all letters
which are written in good faith, and where an answer
is like to be of any use or give any gratification."
No album or collection of autographs went without
his signature; he said once that, if it should retain
any value at all, at least it would be the cheapest
autograph on the dealers' catalogues. James Russell
Lowell, who pursued a different plan, grumbled at
him, because Holmes's amiable ways made it so hard
for the others. Yet autograph-writing was a trifling
part; there were countless more exacting desires,
of which many *could not* be gratified. For friends
sometimes presumed unduly upon friendship, and
many of the promiscuous horde of charity-mongers
had to take *No* for an answer, though little accus-
tomed to submit gracefully to the negative. Fortunately, however, the Doctor was a supreme master of
the art of refusal, and invariably did it with a singular combination of graciousness and decision. There
was no use in teasing him, and it was impossible to
be vexed with him.

As for the multitudes who asked for criticism, but

wanted praise, for their literary efforts; who prayed humbly for advice, but meant to get practical assistance; or those who frankly asked to have their effusions sent to some editor stamped with the approval of the Autocrat, — all these innumerable men and women, lads and lasses, the Doctor treated with an incredible kindliness and patience. He might have cut out some of the clever passages in *The Guardian Angel*, *à propos* of the literary aspirations of Gifted Hopkins, and have caused them to be printed upon postal cards, which would then have needed only an address to make them entirely satisfactory replies. But it was not in his nature to do this. "I have always tried," he said, "to be gentle with the most hopeless cases. My experience, however, has not been encouraging." Sometimes he received letters which were even abusive and insulting, from persons who were not pleased with the responses which their entirely unwarranted demands had brought forth. But the Doctor took these things philosophically, even if they pained him a little.

I once heard it said that he dispensed praise beyond what was deserved, because he loved praise himself and expected thus to secure it. The assertion was absurd and directly the opposite of the truth; for his advice and opinion were given with an honesty which is often amusingly blunt. Conscientious in all things, he was scrupulously so in advising, which he felt as a very grave responsibility, and performed under a sense of moral obligation.[1] Even in letters of thanks for

---

[1] So he himself says in *The Poet at the Breakfast-Table*, p. 156. "It is a very grave responsibility which these unknown correspondents throw upon their chosen counsellors. One whom you have never seen, who lives in a community of which you

books sent to him, if he expressed a good opinion of
their contents, he habitually stated with an accuracy,
which provokes a smile, just how far his reading or
investigation had gone.  No man ever strayed into
literature when he had better have kept out of it, and
thereby suffered loss or disappointment, because he
had received careless advice or disingenuous praise
from Dr. Holmes.  Persons who have had much experience in literature will appreciate how great credit
was due to him for his rule and his practice in this
very trying department of the literary man's gratuitous work.  Looking backward over these things,
when he was sitting over the *Teacups*, he wrote : —

"A great deal of the best writing the languages
of the world have ever known has been committed to
leaves that withered out of sight before a second sun-
light had fallen upon them.  I have had many letters
I should have liked to give the public, had their
nature admitted of their being offered to the world.
What struggles of young ambition, finding no place
for its energies, or feeling its incapacity to reach the
ideal towards which it was striving!  What longings
of disappointed, defeated fellow-mortals, trying to
find a new home for themselves in the heart of one
whom they have amiably idealized!  And oh, what
hopeless efforts of mediocrities and inferiorities, be-

know nothing, sends you specimens more or less painfully volu-
minous of his writings, which he asks you to read over, think
over, and pray over, and send back an answer informing him
whether fame and fortune are awaiting him as the possessor of
the wonderful gifts his writings manifest, and whether you advise him to leave all, — the shop he sweeps out every morning,
the ledger he posts, the mortar in which he pounds, the bench
at which he urges the reluctant plane, — and follow his genius
whithersoever it may lead him."

lieving in themselves as superiorities, and stumbling
on through limping disappointments to prostrate failure! Poverty comes pleading, not for charity, for
the most part, but imploring us to find a purchaser
for its unmarketable wares. The unreadable author
particularly requests us to make a critical examination of his book, and report to him whatever may
be our verdict, — as if he wanted anything but our
praise, and that very often to be used in his publisher's advertisements. But what does not one have
to submit to who has become the martyr — the Saint
Sebastian — of a literary correspondence!"

Sometimes, of course, there occurred the pleasure
of recognizing good work and encouraging men of
worth. It is a familiar story that Bret Harte, in his
youth, sent the manuscript of some of his early poems
to the Doctor, that the Doctor replied with decided
commendation; but that, since the communication
had been anonymous, he never knew whom he had
encouraged until one day when Bret Harte walked
into his library and developed the story.

At the famous Atlantic Breakfast, Mr. Aldrich
made some remarks to this point, in his wonted happy
vein, which I cannot resist transcribing: —

"I cannot, however, let this hour pass without
alluding to a certain characteristic of our honored
friend which no one has yet touched upon. I mean
his judicious and inexhaustible kindness to his younger
brothers in literature. In the midst of a life singularly crowded with duties, he has always found time
to hold out a hand to the man below him. It is safe
to say that within the last twenty-five years no fewer
than five thousand young American poets have hand-
somely availed themselves of Dr. Holmes's amiability,

and sent him copies of their first book.  And I honestly believe that Dr. Holmes has written to each of these immortals a note full of the keenest appreciation and the wisest counsel.  I have seen a score of such letters from his busy pen, and — shall I confess it? — I have one in my own possession.  Twenty years ago I printed a volume of boyish verse; the first copy that came from the binder's was dispatched to the Autocrat of the Breakfast-Table — as if he had been waiting for it.  In return I received the kindest letter ever written by a celebrity to an obscurity.  It virtually told me not to make any more verses unless I could make better ones.  It told me this, but with such delicate frankness of phrase that it seemed to me as if the writer had laid his hand in tender reproof upon my shoulder, as an elder brother might have done.  The fresh and subtle learning of the Autocrat, the humor and pathos of the Poet, that skylark quality of note in his lyrics, — he could not have perfected all these precious gifts, if God had not given him the most sympathetic of human hearts."

A gentleman has written to me stating his conviction that Dr. Holmes was, of course, a great "*epistolarian;*" another is of opinion that he must have been an "*affluent epistolater*," — singular and pleasing phrases, which would have amused the Doctor, who loved simplicity in language, and, when people spoke of "conversationists" and "conversationalists," asked whether *talkist* would not do just as well, and who told his students not to *ligate* arteries, but to *tie* them. But these judges probably spoke with little knowledge.  Certainly in his own family the Doctor was not considered an adept in letter-writing.  His wife used to say, in her lively way: "Oh, Wendell can't write a letter; he seldom knows what to tell, and never knows how to say it." He himself admitted that the task was not agreeable, or stimulating. To Mrs. Helen Hopekirk Wilson he wrote: "It always comes a little hard for me to put my thoughts on paper for a friend. It is so much slower than talking! *That* I am more at home in; and there is always so much more in the response of bright mobile features than in the blank stare of a sheet of white paper." He declared, however, to Mrs. Kellogg, his good friend of the Pittsfield days, that he was a "very good correspondent *as a reader* of letters" like hers. And to the same lady he said: "There is something in a live letter, just from the mail, like a hot cake just from the griddle. A book can give much, but the hot cake and warm letter have a charm all their own." In fact, though he said that he had "written a very large number of letters in his life," he really had had little occasion or even opportunity for sustained correspondence. His friends all lived within a few miles of the State House, and he saw them often enough to make letters needless. His intimacies were as locally circumscribed as was the rest of his life. It will be observed in the correspondence following this memoir, that there are only two considerable groups of letters, viz.: those written to John Lothrop Motley and those to James Russell Lowell, during their foreign residences; those to Mrs. Stowe may, perhaps, be added as a third but small group. Beyond these a few parcels of a score or so each, for the most part not very important, and detached letters on special topics or occasions are all that have been received by me. I may say to the reader that scarcely anything has been rejected, so that he will gather the extent as

well as the character of Dr. Holmes's correspondence
from what follows.

The condition of things which has been described
resulted in the Doctor becoming a great writer of
short notes.  His friend Dr. Mitchell well and wit-
tily said to him, that he "was not a man of letters,
but a man of notes."  He himself, in writing to Mrs.
Julia C. R. Dorr, said: "Not that I pretend to keep
up correspondence, for my unknown friends demand
all the time that I can spare, and more too, — so that
I furnish a hundred epistolary bites to a mob of
strangers instead of half-a-dozen decent meals to my
few intimates;" and, as he was then growing old and
feeling the burden of these things, he half complained
of "the quagmire of unanswered letters and unthanked-
for books in which" he was struggling.  He had remarkable facility and cleverness in this sort of literature, — for a kind of literature it really became in his
hands.  He might send off a page or only half-a-
dozen lines, dispatching it into space, as it were, to
some person whom he had never seen or known, a
mere name like any one of the thousands in a Direc-
tory.  But all the same the note was almost sure to
contain some bit of wit, some cleverly turned expression or happy simile, something which marked its
origin as different from the ordinary.  These notes
must have been sprinkled in myriads over the country, though not many have been sent in to me, —
doubtless because they have been considered too trifling for reproduction as "Letters," a phrase prog-
nosticating things more formal than such brevities.
This is true enough, but these small bits, fragments,
*jeux-d'esprit*, were so peculiarly characteristic of Dr.
Holmes, that a memoir of him which did not contain

many of them would be absurdly imperfect.  I therefore follow these remarks with a somewhat various and necessarily heterogeneous collection of such as have come to my hands.

The birth of his eldest son was announced to his sister by the following note: —

TO MRS. CHARLES W. UPHAM.

*March* 9, 1841.

MY DEAR ANN, — Last evening between eight and nine there appeared at No. 8 Montgomery Place a little individual who may be hereafter addressed as

—— HOLMES, Esq.
or
The Hon. —— Holmes, M. C.
or

His Excellency —— Holmes, President, etc., etc., but who for the present is content with scratching his face and sucking his right forefinger.

Long years afterward, when the elevation of this son to the bench of the Supreme Judicial Court of Massachusetts gave him a position more honorable than any of these merely political forecastings, the Doctor wrote to Mrs. Kellogg: "Thank you for all the pleasant words about the *Judge*.  To *think* of it, — my little boy a Judge, and able to send me to jail if I don't behave myself!"

His friend, Thomas G. Appleton, published a book called *A Sheaf of Papers*, and gave to it this dedication: —

" TO
OLIVER WENDELL HOLMES,

who has put the electricity of our climate into words, and been to so many a physician to the mind as well as the body."

A copy was sent to the Doctor by Captain Nathan Appleton, and called forth the following note: —

TO CAPTAIN NATHAN APPLETON.

May 2, 1875.

MY DEAR MR. APPLETON, — I have not had time to read all the papers which are bound up in the *Sheaf*, as I hope to in the course of to-day or to-morrow. But I have read enough of them to be quite charmed with their easy, bright flow of thought and fancy on just those very themes that I like to hear our famous talker discourse of.

I do not know whether I was more surprised or gratified when your brother told me he was going to honor my name by inscribing it, as he has done, on the opening leaf of his charming little book. Pleasantly as he had always spoken to me, I did not know that my pallid ray was more than barely visible to him in the corona of coruscations to which so eminently belongs the name "electric," which he has applied to my own mild phosphorescence. I can only thank him for one of the most pleasing tributes of regard and kindly feeling it has ever been my good fortune to receive.

TO THOMAS GOLD APPLETON.

March 19th.

MY DEAR APPLETON, — I have written a verse, not inappropriate, I hope, in the album. It only expresses in rhyme what so many have said of Kensett in prose. As to the Moore festival I have written at some length to Judge Daly. I can't meddle with it. My specialty is obituary notices, and inscriptions for tombstones. I have to say *No* to most of the urgent requests which are made to me, unless I wish my own epitaph to be speedily written, or to go over the river to Somerville.[1]  Lecturing all the time as I do, and literally buried in mortuary composition — I have Dr. Bigelow, and Dr. J. B. S. Jackson now on hand — I had rather face a loaded seven-shooter than an invitation to do anything in the way of writing or speech-ifying.  The Judge has been good and has not followed me up.  Why can't you sparkle yourself, on the Tom Moore occasion?

TO JAMES RUSSELL LOWELL.

*May 4th.*

MY DEAR JAMES, — Miss ——, here present, wants me to write to you, being afraid, she says, to write herself.  She says she sent to "Hon. James Russell Lowell, Boston, Mass.," her photograph and her sister's newspaper, which she edited in 1860 in Cleveland, Ohio, entitled the *Lady's Boudoir*, containing an article by "J. Russell Lowell, Reformist," from *Our Portfolio*, and a letter to her, ——, from Matthew Arnold.  She wants all these papers, badly, and sets me to badger and bother you about them.  Do not curse me by all the gods upper and lower, for here I am with the thumbscrews tight and the wedges in the boot, writing in durance and, as it were, in the inquisitor's chamber.  Of course you have treasured these things as the apple of your eye and can lay your hand on them in a moment, having nothing to do but take care of such treasures!  Please address any communication *not to me* but to Miss ——, S. D.

P. S.  She says President Arthur wrote her a beautiful letter, and *a fortiori* (*she* did n't say that) J. R. L. will answer her.

[1] The *locus* of a well-known asylum for the insane, near Boston.

The following was evidently written when Mr. Lowell was editor of *The Atlantic;* it enclosed the poem of a gentleman who was a friend of both, but who had seen fit to use the Doctor's intervention : —

TO JAMES RUSSELL LOWELL.

BOSTON, *March* 10, 1861.

MY DEAR JAMES, — I send you a letter and a poem from P—— B——, to which I invite your special attention. If you accept the poem I shall be glad for P——; if you do not, pray treat him gingerly and send it back to him with the politest of notes. P—— is an *enfant terrible*, and I don't want him to begin "blowing," as the boys say, at me.

I will write a recipe for you on the next page, to be administered to P—— in your note.

B Olei dulc.
Sacchari candati (vulgo *molasses*)
aa pp. equales.
ft. potio, cujus capiat
æger q. s.

This note, mind you, is to be sent at any rate, whatever you do with the poem. I have written and sent a reply to his letter, throwing off all responsibility, as I always do. I enclose stamps in case they should be needed, and also apologies for troubling you — but this is one of the cases that require tender handling.

TO THOMAS GAFFIELD.

*March* 15, 1861.

MY DEAR SIR, — I have just got a moment's rest after getting three books through — no, not quite through yet — the press. There is as much electricity in me as there is in a torpedo after he is made into a chowder. I don't want to do anything except

keep still and be let alone.  Don't think I am offended
at being asked to do anything; I am asked all the
time to do everything.  I shall have to stop payment
on autographs by and by, I am afraid.  Really, I
have my hands full in every way, and the kindest
thing my friends can do is just to let me carry what
I hold, and not ask me to take anything more at
present.

TO THE SAME.

*April* 24, 1862.

MY DEAR SIR, — Many thanks for your kind invitation to the Unitarian festival.  I shall not make
any promise to be with you, principally to spare you
any attempt at a speech, and partly because I do not
like to appear at public meetings.  The last is a matter of taste, in which a member of the silent profession has a certain right to be indulged.  I take a cordial interest in your meetings, whether present or
absent, and I rejoice that you are to have so noble a
representative of liberal and manly thought as our
true-hearted governor, — the only loyal pilot whose
hand was on the tiller when the black squall struck
the great fleet of the Union.[1]

TO G. W. KEMPER, M. D.

*August* 17, 1863.

DEAR SIR, — You are very welcome to my autograph, which I have given to a great many friends before yourself.  *Advice* is another matter; the request
is so general that I should not know where to begin.
You might almost as well ask me for a coat or a pair
of boots without sending your measure. . . .

---

[1] Governor Andrew, it is well known, had so far foreseen hos-
tilities as to have the State militia thoroughly equipped to take
the field for active service and leave the State instantly upon the
summons from the President.

This letter, I think, should be rescued from the oblivion of the newspaper in which I found it, with the explanation that it was "written in 1866, at the close of the war of the rebellion, in response to the request of Mrs. D. D. Tilton, lady manager of the Massachusetts table at the fair held in Washington, in aid of the Home for Orphans of Union Soldiers."

TO MOSES SWEETSER.

BOSTON, *June* 9, 1866.

DEAR SIR, — I must respond to your polite and flattering request by asking you to accept for the Fair two of my books, which contain some things in them more like to be read with patience, if not with pleasure, than anything I should write to order at short notice. To write a lyric is like having a fit, you can't have one when you wish you could (as, for instance, when your bore is in his third hour and having it all his own way), and you can't help having it when it comes itself.

If it had so happened a lyric attack had seized me just at the moment I received your letter, be sure that you should have had a copy of verses such as one finds written out and lying before him on his desk after the spasm has gone off. But having had a paroxysm three or four days ago, the nervous energy had expended itself, and I must therefore hold up a book in each hand as a shield against your friendly attack, hoping that they will not prove as impenetrable to any who may undertake to read them as to your attempts upon my importunate muse.

TO EDWARD EVERETT HALE, D. D.[1]

December 7, 1869.

MY DEAR MR. HALE, — I shall keep your note as a reminder that I hope some time or other to take up the pen which I have not cared to meddle with often of late. In the mean time you may be assured that nothing that one commits to paper is ever half so good as his great *unwritten article.*

Like an Easter egg, that unhatched production — its unbroken shell, I mean — is stained — by the reader — that-is-to-be's imagination I mean — with every brilliant hue of promise. Break it, and you have the usual albuminous contents, — keep it whole, and you can feast your eyes on its gorgeous color, and your mind with the thought that it carries the possibility of Phœnix.

Say, then, that you have the *promise* of an article from one of the most etceterable and etceteraed of our native writers, and it will be like a signed check with the amount left blank. Prophets and priests may desire it long and die without the sight, but will die saying, "When the great unwritten article *does* come — then — you will see" — and so turn their faces to the wall.

Let us leave it then unwritten for the present, and think how much more precious is an infinite series of undefined expectations than any paltry performance or transient fruition. In the mean time believe me always very sincerely and faithfully yours.

---

[1] At the time engaged in editing the magazine called *Old and New.*

TO PAUL H. HAYNE.

BOSTON, *January* 9, 1870.

MY DEAR MR. HAYNE, — I have sent your sonnet, which I liked much, to Mr. Edward Hale, who is best known to me among those connected with *Old and New.* I accompanied it with a note intended to draw his special and favorable attention to it, and then, in accordance with my rule in all cases, requested him to communicate directly with you with reference to his disposal of the poem.

You will see at once why I follow this rule. Editors have their own way of looking at contributions sent them, and I should too often have to write to my friends that their articles were to be returned to them. As I never know when this may happen, I make no exceptions, but always leave my friend the author at the threshold of my friend the Editor's *Sanctum.*

I trust there was no need of my doing so in this case except to maintain the principle, and I shall be most happy if any words of mine have helped you to get a foothold in the new Journal, which, I understand, begins with the best prospects of success.

TO EDWARD EVERETT HALE, D. D.

*March* 23, 1870.

DEAR MR. HALE, — You must excuse me from writing a critique — it is a kind of thing I dislike. I want to send you something, and, if I can work out a *motive* to my satisfaction, mean to do it one of these days. But I have been half sick through my whole lecture term, and am now very busy in some work I must attend to.

You are such a *polycephalous* and *polycheirous* producer that you hardly realize the limitations of a common mortal with only one pair of hemispheres and two hands.

I am delighted to hear that your Magazine is getting on well, and I shall not feel easy until I have "cut behind," as the boys say when they hang on to an inviting equipage.

TO MRS. CAROLINE L. KELLOGG.

BOSTON, *July* 16, 1872.

MY DEAR MRS. KELLOGG, — If I were not a pretty well-seasoned stick of timber you would have bent me to your purpose — would n't you?  Such a pleasant, lively letter from an old friend goes a good way towards breaking down a resolution; but it does not — I must say it — it does not go quite far enough.  It is not your fault — you have said all that can be said, with the seductive accents of a siren.  It is my fault, if anybody's.  I have got tired of appearing on public occasions.  I cut the Phi Beta Kappa and the Alumni meetings this year.  I did, it is true, take down my cornstalk fiddle for the Grand Duke; but I have refused every invitation since that time.  I have got enough of it.

> "Still must I hear ?  Shall hoarse Fitzgerald bawl
> His creaking couplets in a tavern hall ? "

says Lord Byron, and I feel about myself something as he felt about Lord Fitzgerald — if he was a Lord, as I think he was.

Now you must remember that I was not always obdurate — that I glorified the Ploughman and tried to help sanctify the Cemetery — to say nothing of random verses on less occasions.

I am now somewhat older than then, and I will not
say crosser — because I am not cross — only more set
in my ways, as I have a right to be.

I lectured steadily seven months from October to
May, and I have been writing for *The Atlantic* regularly since January, and I have promised a gratuitous
lecture to a "banquet" of ladies this autumn. It is
enough for me, and I do not want to plague myself
with pumping up patriotism and pouring it into stanzas. I want to get away as soon as I can and lay up
my heels and do nothing but read story-books.

"So easy! just sit down and write what comes into
your head." Tell that to the merinoes — (I adapt
the saying to the mountain district).

It costs sw**t; it costs nerve-fat; it costs phos-
phorus, to do anything worth doing.

No, my dear Lady, I adore you, but I'll bet you
can't coax me. I like your letter enormously —
though I was puzzled with the "Bucher fever" as I
read it the first time — Beecher, I discovered it to be.
But for all that, you must give me up as beyond even
your wonderful persuasive arts. Don't let anybody
get hold of this letter, which is written in great worry
of mind at saying *No* to a friend for whom I should
always like to have a *Yes* ready. Remember me
kindly to the Squire, and believe me

Faithfully yours.

TO MISS J. SHERWOOD, KIRKWOOD, MO.

*November* 11, 1875.

DEAR MISS SHERWOOD, — I am much obliged to
you for your very pleasant and flattering note, but I
am going to excuse myself from doing anything more

than thanking you and begging you to consider my answer as private. My hand aches with answering all sorts of invitations to do all sorts of things. Every one I accept makes it worse and worse, and I have at length to say *No* (wrapped up in the softest phrases I can clothe it in), to a great many friends I should be pleased to oblige.

My hands just now are very full, and as every note that is liable to be printed means a drop of blood from my veins and a spark of nervous force from my ganglions, I have to beg off from tasks that seem very slight to all but those who are already overburdened.

You will understand this — every woman knows what it is to have a stitch too many to take. If I do not look out I shall have to write, instead of "The Song of the Shirt," "The Song of the Sheet" (of paper), and draw tears from the eyes of everybody by my picture: —

> "With fingers weary and worn,
> With eyelids heavy and red,"
> A scribbler holding a used-up **pen**
> Sat racking his used-up head.

You would feel sorry for that, I know, so you will just keep this note to yourself and say no more about it.

TO JOHN COLLINS WARREN, M. D.

*March* 22, 1876.

MY DEAR DR. WARREN, — I *must* excuse myself. I have given what I could spare to the "Old South" Fund. I have written a poem, — some verses, at any rate, — printed in the *Daily Advertiser* under the title "A Last Appeal," to stir up people as much as I knew how to. And now I have ground my tune and taken my hand-organ on my back, I cannot make up my mind to come back to the same doorstep and begin grinding again. Seriously and absolutely, you must call some other street musician.

TO PROF. CHARLES ELIOT NORTON.

296 BEACON STREET, *June* 15, 1876.

MY DEAR NORTON, — Although I feel with the Archbishop that "mon esprit, grâce au ciel, n'a rien encore perdu de sa vigueur," and you are not playing the part of Gil Blas to me, I feel also the meaning of what Mr. Emerson said when he was younger than I am now: —

> " It is time to be old,
> To take in sail :
>
> . . . . . . . .
> There 's not enough for this and that,
> Make thy option which of two,
> Economize the falling river,
>
> . . . . . . .
> Leave the many and hold the few."

Pleasant as it is to be told we are not worn out and effete, I am so tired after my long winter course of lectures and all that has filled up their intervals, that I would give more for a few weeks of lotus-eating than for all the honors in the world.

I found the task of presiding at the business meetings very trying. I dreaded the mere matter of managing the dinner. When I gave up the presidency of the Alumni it was with a sigh of relief that Æolus might have envied. I have not heart to think of trying it again, if it were a conceivable thing that the office should be offered me.

I do assure you that in spite of all that is complimentary in the suggestion that I might be acceptable

once more to the Association, it made me ache all over
to read your kind note.   I have been so followed up
of late with requests, and urgent requests, to be and
to do so many things in so many places, that I feel
almost as nervous as Sydenham's male hysteric patient.   To-day I left town to get rid of two formidable friendly attacks, and came back to simmer
through an examination this afternoon of a candidate
for the degree of Phil. Doct.   To-morrow I am im-
paled by an Executive Committee; Saturday we
have a most tedious Faculty meeting; and early next
week sixty-nine books will be handed me for minute
examination of medical students for their degree.
And this is my vacation after seven months' lectures.
I was not made for so much work as I have been having — I cannot tell you half of it — and I know you
would not want to overdrive that poor old horse you
heard me tell of the other evening.

To —— ——.

December 4, 1886.

DEAR SIR, — I do not like to be asked to read
and give my opinion of manuscripts in verse or prose.
The critics of the magazines are the proper persons to
apply to, and they are commonly fair enough.   I fail
to see the distinguishing qualities in these verses
which would entitle them to a place in such a periodical as *The Atlantic*.   But I have nothing to do with
editing that magazine; and you can send your pieces
to the editor, if you have no fear of the waste-basket.
You have probably no conception of the vast number
of young persons who write passable, and even pretty
and pleasant, verse nowadays; it is a very common
accomplishment, if it deserves such a name, for it

leads many persons to write who have nothing in particular to say, and who are fascinated with the jingle
of their own verses.   I will not criticise your lines;
I do not see why you should ask me to.   Send them
to the magazines; and, if they all reject them, send
them to any newspaper that will print them, if you
think they are worthy of being made public; and
if they have any originality, any real merit of any
kind, you will soon be found out, you may depend
upon it.

P. S. You will ask me if I read these verses.   I
*did*, every one of them.


I find in *The Book-Buyer* this note : —


TO M. A. DE WOLFE HOWE, JR.

BEVERLY FARMS, MASS., *September* 22, 1887.

MY DEAR SIR, — For the first time since some
early date, whether A. D. or A. Mundi I hardly
know, I have got my harness off and am standing for
a month or two in the stall, so to speak.   In other
words, I have no literary work in hand at this moment, and am lolling in a rocking-chair at my autumnal fireside.

Now, as you know, my dear young friend, Dobbin
must be harnessed up just as much to carry one to
visit his neighbors as to go on a long journey.   To
continue my figurative manner of speech, I do not
wish to harness up, as I must do, even for the slight
excursion to the bowers of my Alma Mater.   For,
look you, I am what my friends the autograph-hunt-
ers call a "noted person," sometimes perhaps " notorious," but I am not quite sure of this.   They also
remind me that I am advanced in life, and not likely

to be good for autographs much longer, so that it
would be the civil thing in me to hurry up my signature before it is too late.   Under these circumstances,
being "noted," and also well-nigh the position of the
superfluous veteran, I have to be careful what I write,
as I often find it in print, sometimes to my great dis-
comfiture.   I cannot write even a careless note like
this without grave consideration.   The Interviewer
comes everywhere, and if a note happens to lie open
anywhere he will know what is in it, and it will be
served up in the next morning's paper.

So let me have my sweet do-nothing, as the Italians
say; and let poor old Dobbin stand in the stall with
his harness off, munching his hay and oats, and thinking when he is next to be trotted out, hoping it will
not be yet awhile.

TO WILLIAM H. POTTER, D. M. D., SECRETARY.

296 BEACON STREET, *December* 3, 1888.

MY DEAR SIR, — I am sorry to say that I shall
not be able to attend the meeting of the Harvard
Dental Association or take an active part in its proceedings.

I have a real interest in the welfare of a profession
to which so many of us ought to feel grateful with
every word we speak and every morsel we swallow.
Few persons have passed the age of threescore years
and ten, retaining their own self-respect and a proper
regard to appearances, whose mouths do not flash
with incisors which never knew what it is to grow
from a socket or to cut their way through a gum.   By
the thoughtful care and ingenious devices of the dentist, childhood is protected from the destructive pro-
cesses which threaten and tend to undermine the

structures essential to health and beauty; youth is rendered doubly charming, middle age comely, and old age presentable. We cannot be too grateful to our dental friends who do so much for us all, and it is pleasant to see them gathered together to use the organs in their own mouths in the important function to which the preceding hour has been devoted, and now to exhibit those same organs in the smiling amenities of social intercourse.

I am always pleased to hear of the success of the graduates of the Dental School, whom I had the pleasure of counting among the audience at my anatomical lectures. I will not refer to those established in our own city, who have filled and are filling so well the places once occupied by Dr. Flagg, Dr. Joshua Tucker, Dr. Harwood, and their more immediate successors. But I was glad to know that the son of my classmate, Dr. Horatio Cook Meriam, who bears his name, was prospering in a neighboring city famous of old for its witches and in later years for its bewitching daughters, whose most precious attractions are safe, I am sure, in his hands.

In my visit to Cambridge, England, two years ago, I met Dr. George Cunningham, one of the most intelligent graduates of the class of 1876, thriving and happy in a charming old residence under the shadow — the light, rather, of the great University.

In connection with this, here is a paragraph from an earlier letter concerning a dinner of the forceps-wielders which the Doctor *did* attend: —

TO JOHN LOTHROP MOTLEY.

*February* 15, 1873.

MY DEAR MOTLEY, — I got your letter of January 26th to-day, just as I was getting ready to go to a dinner at Parker's of our *Dental Faculty* — for you knew, or must know, that we have a Dental School now in connection with the University. I had to leave it unread, or I should not have been in season to hear the young man our professor got to come all the way from London to give the Anniversary Address. It was an awful kind of thought to sit down with a room full of tooth-doctors, gnashing their incisors and molars in concert; but I sat between President Eliot, for whom I have a fancy, and a white-headed old dentist from New York — Dr. Eleazer Parmelee, famous a generation or so since — worth four millions, somebody said, which fact seemed to cast a golden nimbus about his silver hair. So while you have been dining [with] dukes, I have been dining with dentists, — and to tell the honest truth I think we could get along better without the first than the second." . . .

TO JOHN CODMAN ROPES.

*February* 20, 1892.

DEAR MR. ROPES, — The time comes sooner or later when the muse has to say to her veterans: "Claudite jam rivos, *senes*, sat prata biberunt." I have written a great many occasional poems in my day, but I find the twilight of fourscore years and over less favorable to that kind of mental labor than the easier task of recording my recollections, with which I beguile the hours spared to me by my correspondence. I must therefore excuse myself from the honorable

office of Poet at the Gettysburg celebration, and if
any request comes in a more formal shape I will write
my apology in a more dignified and official fashion
than I have written this easy and familiar note.

P. S. I had forgotten the former letter you sent
and was thinking only of your note. I will answer
it, as I have said, in due season and dignified phrases.

*The Times*, of Trenton, published the following
reply of Dr. Holmes "to a young and ambitious literary aspirant who applied to him for a position as private secretary."

DEAR SIR, — I regret that it is not in my power to
direct you to any place of employment such as you
desire. In a city like this the crowding toward all
such employments is very great, and there are a few
situations to be divided among a great number of
applicants. As for myself, I am not (as I am often
supposed to be) an editor, and have no writing to do
which I am not competent to do myself, with a little
occasional aid from the members of my own family.

I regret not to be able to give you encouragement
as to employment in Boston, but the truth is, there is
next to nothing of the kind you mention, most of our
writers being as poor as rats themselves, and no more
able to keep an amanuensis than they are able to set
up a coach and six.

I do not even know how to advise you beyond this
simple counsel, which I have occasionally given to
young aspirants: If you think you have literary
talents, write something for the best paper or magazine you can get into; keep to one signature, and you
will be found out by a public which is ready to give

the highest price for almost every kind of literary ability.

I do not "turn from your petition with cold indifference," but it is utterly out of my power to do more than give you these few words of kindly advice.

Here is a short note, but probably as long as the recipient wanted : —

*May* 22, 1891.

MY DEAR SIR, — I have received your poem, "Heart of the Golden Roan," and read it all. There was enough in it to keep up my interest, and I paid an attention to it which I can rarely afford to give to the books I receive. I will not criticise it. I think some may find it obscure; but my eyes are not very bright, and my wits may be at fault when I think there is some difficulty in getting at your whole meaning. At any rate I thank you for what you have given us.

BEVERLY FARMS, MASS., *August* 19, 1882.

MY DEAR YOUNG LADY, — I know very little about the musical world of Boston, and am unable to advise you, etc., etc. . . .

As to your literary questions, I do not see how you can help yourself if an editor alters your papers, except by becoming so important to him that you can make it a condition of publishing your articles that they shall not be in any way tampered with.

I remember writing an article for the *North American Review* many years ago in which the editor *claimed his Editorial right* to change things to suit himself, and altered just *one word* — for the worse. I submitted. Long afterwards, when the article was reprinted, I altered it back again, as it was at first. I believe editors do claim that right until their contributors get too important to be interfered with, and I think all you would get by complaining would be to find the door of that particular periodical closed against you.

As to your literary prospects I can tell you very little. There is a great crowd of ready and agreeable writers, and it is neither more nor less than a "struggle for life" between them, and survival of the — fittest, sometimes — but it is safer to say survival of the — survivors.

Do your best, and you will find your market value in due time. I am afraid I can give no other counsel than this.

TO MRS. E. S. SINCLAIR.

*September* 16, 1882.

MY DEAR MRS. SINCLAIR, — I must begin by thanking you for your kind letter and the pleasant words it contains ; a word from Emerson, such as you have reported to me, is better than a page of eulogy from many very good people. I have read, and read carefully, the three poems you send me. Master Willie, your grandson, shows a poetical nature, and only wants training to do justice to it, but I am afraid he will want to do as most young writers of verse do, make a reputation by sending his immature productions to the literary market. Now he has a great deal to learn before he can present himself to the public; thus in "Man's Heritage," he makes "past" rhyme with "bequest" and "given" rhyme with "risen." I say "makes" them *rhyme*, but that he cannot do. He uses them as if they were rhymes. Most critics would instantly condemn a copy of verses to the waste-basket, which contained such errors as these. The verses might have merit, but such false rhyming would frighten them, and prevent their doing justice to the lines that held them. I do not commonly encourage young persons to write in verse. If they feel the impulse to do so very strongly, I advise them to take some signature and stick to it. The signature should not be a fancy name, or a boy's name like Willie, but initials; three are best, as they are less likely to have more than one owner. If the verse has any real merit the publishers will find it out, for they are always looking round for new talent. Mistakes in rhyme, rhythm, and even in spelling are very common in young writers. A young lady who is becoming known through leading periodicals, and writes very well, spells "absence" twice, in a letter she has just written me, "abscence." So the faults I have found with one of Willie's poems do not prevent my recognizing in them a poetic character, which may develop, with careful cultivation, to excellence. But writing verses is not the chief aim of man. It is a fascinating kind of labor and brings so much flattery and over-praise from friends, that it is too apt to engross more than its share of time and attention. The most assiduous study of the best models is one of the preparations for success. This takes time, which is an advantage; for if one publishes too hastily, as I did when a young man, he is liable to get a name for a certain cleverness or smartness which will be in his way when he aims at better work and a larger reputation.

August 26, 1863.

Dear Sir, — I have read your poem, or rather the extracts you have sent me, all of them carefully.

The composition appears to be of the nature of an Epic, a form of poem which has been successful only a very few times in the world's history. Southey tried it often, — you remember Byron's

"An Epic from Bob Southey every year."

Joel Barlow tried it and failed; Timothy Dwight tried it and failed. No living poet of repute, who writes in the English language, has ventured on such a task, that I remember. In the face of such facts it is, perhaps, more than you have a right to expect that I should prophesy success for your effort. I do not think it would prove profitable in a pecuniary point of view; on the contrary, I fear it might prove a losing enterprise. As to literary reputation, you must know what competition you would have to meet. I do not think your poetical training fits you to enter the lists against Tennyson and Longfellow and Browning, who are almost the only poets that write long pieces.

It is greatly to your credit that you have studied history and composition, while others have been wasting their time and talents. You have gained knowledge and happiness, with a certain degree of skill in working at your task. Still I cannot conscientiously advise you to print your poem; it will be an expense to you, and the gain to your reputation will not be an equivalent.

*November* 12, 1871.

MY DEAR SIR, — The instinct, perhaps as you say inherited, for writing verse needs long training and study, before it can produce rhymes that can be called poetry. The sonnet is a very complex and difficult form of verse, and hardly fit for a beginner.

It has been a good deal cultivated in this country, and many writers have become skilful in constructing it; perhaps your daughter may become so by practice, but I think she is too immature at present to wrestle with its difficulties. There is such a superabundance of verse in the literary market that with few exceptions it is a drug, a superfluity which sometimes brings a writer some slight reward in pay or in reputation, but it is for the most part a disappointment. Only one thing can be said to a beginner: "If you believe in yourself, try, try, and try again, until you succeed; or have failed so constantly that you had better try some pursuit that promises a better reward."

New York.

My dear Sir, — I receive great numbers of letters resembling that which you sent me. It pains me to say that I can do little, very little, to help the applicants. If you have the ability and the knowledge to write what the public wants, you will soon be found out. Write in any paper, in the obscurest village sheet in the country, and you will soon be known if you write with originality, force, beauty, scholarship of such a grade as the public demands. If you have not some, at least, of these qualities, you will find literature an unprofitable field. Any regular occupation — a clerkship, a mechanical employment — is better than writing prose or verse which is rejected by all the good paying periodicals, and only serves to fill up blanks in the columns of one of those papers I spoke of. You can *begin* with them, but if your productions attract no attention after a fair trial, it is not worth while to waste your strength in writing what does not bring reputation or profit. You see I have a good deal of confidence in the judgment of the reading public. It knows what it wants, at any rate, and pounces upon every new aspirant, who shows any mark of genius, with carnivorous avidity. The editors all want him, the public wants him — and he is soon dragged from obscurity. But both are intolerant of mediocrity, or at least indifferent to it, and the great majority of candidates for fame and money have nothing but mediocrity to offer — if they have as much as that.

You have got to save what powers you have — to show, not me or any friend, but the reading public and the editors. I have tried to help two men of real powers and accomplishments to a share of public favor, but I found I could do little, as the public will judge for itself. There is no royal road to reputation. The praise of friends is of no avail. The advice of experts is hardly needed by the youth of genius, and of no use to the ambitious young person who has no special gift.

As to suggestions how you shall write what will be acceptable, or how what you write may get the consideration of editors, I can only say that, if *you* do not know what you are to write upon, no stranger can tell you; and if you will do your best, you must take your chance patiently and cheerfully, as every one of us, who has had any measure of success, has had to do in his time.

Excuse my plain speaking. Your letter found me very busy, but I have answered it honestly and conscientiously.

No sooner had the Doctor's name acquired a merchantable value than certain of those persons who are politely called "sharp Yankees," signifying thereby persons who keep their practices just outside the statutes, sought from time to time to make use of him for their own personal benefit. But the Doctor was a wary and shrewd person, who generally thought twice, and cautiously too, before he acted, and who was not invested with that unfortunate quality of genius, — a stupid incapacity to take care of himself. Once, however, he got entrapped, and the result called forth this letter.

TO DR. SARGENT.

BOSTON, November 19, 1870.

DEAR DR. SARGENT, — You have hit it exactly. Five or six years ago, I received an elegantly bound volume, . . . and wrote as polite an answer as so unusual attention seemed to demand, . . . and though my letter is tolerably guarded, as you must see, considering it as a private communication, I said as complimentary things as the dedication, the rich binding and the gilt edges and the pages I examined would bear, much as one says "Your humble servant" at the end of a letter, not meaning that he will make his correspondent's pies or black his boots.

And now my innocently meant letter follows me about from town to town, and one professional brother after another writes to know how it was that I became the accomplice of this person, whom they all agree in denouncing as a charlatan.

I cut a large slice of humble pie and eat it, as Pistol ate his leek, before their eyes. I am eating a slice of it now. I ought to have seen the cat's ears and tail under the thin sprinkling of meal, but I did not. Worse than this, I have had a similar but more

ingenious trick to get my name played on me once
again since that. I am proud to say, however, that
a third attempt (this time from California), so admirably managed that it ought to have succeeded, found
me on my guard, and was met with fox-like astute-
ness under the cover of lamb-like ingenuousness.

So you see, my dear Dr. Sargent, that *I* am the
persecuted individual. Having the good or bad fortune to be known by name a little more widely than
the common run of doctors, it is an object to entrap
me for advertisements. It also happens that I receive
a great many letters, complimentary or otherwise,
from a distance, and I do not always study them as
carefully as I ought to, very probably, before answering them.

This is all I have to say. The ghost of that innocent letter will haunt me all my days. Indignant
remonstrances, severe sentences of condemnation, will
follow that apparition in endless relays. What can
I do? A newspaper battle between Professors ——
and Holmes will only make matters worse. You can
tell the story in your own words among your medical
friends. I have had to write in former years to ——
and ——, and I never know where he will turn up
next — but there is no peace for me.

Faithfully and sorrowfully yours.


The following little note is too clever to be lost: —

TO PROFESSOR ASA GRAY.

*May 21st.*

DEAR DR. GRAY, — You may remember that ——
brought me a note from Mrs. Gray, he being ap-

parently an acquaintance or correspondent of your own.

I have just received this letter from him, with the printed fragment, and it leads me to ask whether he is of sound and disposing intellect, or one of those people whose brains are slightly addled by a freak or phantasy? Shall I answer this letter? and if so, what shall I say to this man, who is stirring the infinite abysses with a toothpick? Please return the invaluable documents, with a hint as to whether it is worth while to answer the letter at all, except in a polite phrase or so. — I am disposed to leave the wearer of Mambrino's helmet in undisturbed possession.

Somewhere about 1872–73 the Massachusetts Medical Society undertook to expel those of its members who were avowed practitioners of homœopathy. The attempt was resisted; litigation resulted, and the court finally decided that the Society had the lawful right to make the expulsion. Of course feeling ran very high, and, apart from the legal conflict, discussion as to the wisdom and propriety of the proceeding was heated among the physicians and the community. Naturally enough the practitioners of the regular school (I hope the phrase is correctly used, though I speak with alarm upon the topic!), knowing the proclivities of Dr. Holmes, desired to enlist his trenchant pen upon their side. He, however, declined to enter the lists, and the following letter, in which he did so, is an excellent instance of the cool, shrewd judgment which protected him from many an error in life, though few persons appreciated the presence of the quality in his mental composition.

TO DR. JOHN COLLINS WARREN.

*April* 14, 1873.

DEAR DR. WARREN, — I have most carefully and patiently read all the documents you placed in my hands. I have thought the whole matter over deliberately, and am satisfied that the Society was entirely in the right in getting rid of the homœopathists as it did.

It is a question, however, whether it is worth while to stir the matter, since the Society has gained its point. The homœopathists would like a chance to answer an attack, and they would at once be lifted into notice by the article which was meant to finish them, especially if it were written in a way to attract the attention of the public.

There are two popular maxims which it is always well to bear in mind, when dealing with these *noli me tangere, quasi* scientific bodies: to "let sleeping dogs lie," and "to leave well enough alone." Where there is good evidence that public opinion is awake and active, with the impression that the homœopathists are a wronged and persecuted band of martyrs, when such opinion puts itself forward in a tangible shape, it may be proper to meet it with statements and explanations. Until such time the expediency of agitation appears to me questionable.

But, secondly, the result of the appeal to the Supreme Court has not as yet been made public so far as I know, and the publication of its judgment would seem to mark the proper time for taking up the general question, if it were to be taken up at all.

And, lastly, I am far from feeling certain that I should be the best hand you could call to the task of dealing with these people, in case it became necessary or was thought expedient to meddle with them. They know me of old, and they would know me in the domino of an editorial, you may be very sure. Now you know as well as I do that I have a certain kind of literary reputation which would make me a desirable antagonist to any impertinent upstart, who might want to advertise himself. When I published my lectures on "Homœopathy and its Kindred Delusions," in 1842, I had three formal pamphlets, besides miscellaneous newspaper squibs, launched at my head — from Boston, Providence, and Philadelphia. I am better known now than I was then, a great deal, and it would be a good thing for any of these obscure charlatans to have a chance to measure himself against me.

You must not mistake this for vanity, for I have had to learn by some very trying experiences that I must be very careful how I give the self-advertising classes any chance whatever to avail themselves of my name, which has been long enough before the public to have become available for their purposes.

The more I think of it the more I am convinced that, if anything at all is to be said in your pages, and whenever it may be said, a perfectly simple, dry, brief, impersonal article (not rhetorical, not brilliant, not popular in its tone) will be the best policy.

I must therefore return a "retaining-fee" of twenty dollars which has been sent me by Dr. R——, hoping that I have convinced you that I am right in preferring that some other person may be assigned the task.

I will return you the papers, which will go among the *faits pour servir* of the writer of any future articles, if such articles should ever be written.

A few of the short notes, though they hardly amount to very much, may be added, as specimens.

TO GEORGE ABBOT JAMES.

*June 20th.*

My dear Mr. James, — I have seen the bottom of a good many glasses in my time, but of none with more pleasure than of this which you send me. After having made many an old Roman tipsy in spite of his amethyst, the *cyathus,* or *patera,* or whatever it might have been called, is still ample enough, though it would hold but a few drops of Falernian, to carry a friendly pledge, which comes to me, glowing and fragrant, and for which please accept my most cordial acknowledgments.

Those who remember the famous Portuguese Grammar will enjoy this: —

TO DR. S. WEIR MITCHELL.

*April 29, 1863.*

Dear Mr. Sir, — I have to receive from you the past to-morrow the phrases-book of the Portugal language. Walking through the mail office to Cambridge, where I enhabit not, I am wanting it before the day next to this morning's hinder side. I find in it much rib movement. The English I discover to be very extraordinary pretty good. The London's native must have was a writer of the vermicular parts. I reflect the ditto well accommodated to the Portu-geese. To the Joseph Miller book much prefer I this, and thank the same for you with all my cardiac scrobicle.

Make believe I am faithfoolishly yours.

TO THE SAME.

October 4, 1882.

MY DEAR DR. MITCHELL, — I found the magnificent paper-scimetar on my table yesterday, and could not help thinking it was meant to remain there. Only it is too gorgeous — too grand — for such a humble literary work-bench. No matter; it shall stay there and divide the honors with the one Miss Thackeray sent me years ago.

The riddle on it is one of the best in the English language. I doubt if there are ten, or even five — I am not sure there are three, which can compare with it in finish and in the perfection of its graceful double-meanings. If you only left this, to consult me about whether it would be a fitting present — say for the Queen or the President — or Mr. Gladstone or Victor Hugo — why, I shall say certainly it is more than good enough for the best of them. If you meant it for me, I can only say I thank you most heartily for a gift of which any author might be proud, engraved with lines which he will never look upon without wishing he had written them.

The scimetar was an ivory paper-cutter, inscribed with this " riddle : " —

> " A simple go-between am I,
>     Without a thought of pride.
>   I part the gathered thoughts of men
>     And liberally divide.
>   I set the soul of Shakspeare free,
>   To Milton's thoughts give liberty,
>   Let Sidney speak with freer speech,
>   Bid Spenser sing and Taylor preach.
>   Though through all learning swift I glide,
>   No wisdom doth with me abide."

The following was to Mr. George W. Simmons, who had succeeded in making fruit trees grow upon the inhospitable soil of "Little Nahant."

21 CHARLES STREET.

MY DEAR SIR, — Mrs. Holmes desires to add her thanks to mine for the beautiful fruits and flowers.

I could not keep both those pears, and as Agassiz had asked me to dine with him on Thursday, I sent him the biggest, with the lines you will find on the next leaf.

> The Prophet for his thirsting flock
>   Bade streams of water flow ;
> The new enchanter smites the rock
>   And fruits of Eden glow.
>
> Like goes to like ; this beauty seeks
>   The great and good and fair,
> And finds at length, with blushing cheeks,
>   A second *matchless pair.*

TO DR. GEORGE C. SHATTUCK.

*September* 22, 1864.

DEAR DR. SHATTUCK, — You will be interested in this young man, Mr. W. M. F. Rounds, who wishes to begin the study of medicine. He is wide awake, full of good intent, and always *goes to your church* on Sunday when he is in town. He wishes to give his note for lecture fees, and I hope you will accommodate him in this and in such other ways as he may ask with reference to instruction, for he is a youth of promise and may do us honor by and by.

### TO WILLIAM C. WINSLOW.[1]

MY DEAR SIR, — I have read with great interest the accounts of the projected exploration of Zoan. I believe in the spade. It has furnished the cheap defence, if not of nations, yet of beleaguered armies. It has fed the tribes of mankind. It has furnished them water, coal, iron, and gold. And it has given, and is giving, them *truth*, historic truth, the mines of which have never been opened until our own time.

It seems to me that the whole Christian and the whole Hebrew world should be as much interested in the excavation of Zoan as the classic world is in that of Troy, or Mycenæ, or Assos.

My guinea-hen does not lay as many golden eggs as do the more prolific fowls of some of my neighbors, but one of them is at your service to hatch a spade for Zoan.

### TO FRANCIS BARTLETT.

*July* 29, 1879.

MY DEAR MR. BARTLETT, — My Doctor, O. W. H., M. D., has forbidden my going out evenings for the present, for fear of a return of certain troubles, which I believe I am getting rid of, but for which he is still treating me. I am very sorry that my respect for his opinion, founded on a very long experience with his patient, compels me to deny myself the pleasure of being with you and your guests on Friday evening.

In response to an invitation to visit Naushon, the far-famed Island Kingdom of "Governor" Swain, this note was written: —

[1] Concerning the "Egypt Exploration Fund," and the excavations at "Zoan," 1885.

TO JOHN M. FORBES.

September 12, 1851.

MY DEAR SIR,—I received a missive with the Seal of State a few days before yours. I do not pretend to rebel or repudiate — the authority is undisputed, and the command is one which it is the highest of privileges to obey. If therefore I should by ill chance be wanting among the faithful subjects, you may be sure I have entered into some private composition or coalition with the Governor. If it does not prove so, I will consent to be hanged (in any well-slung hammock), drawn (at full length in the Island Book), and quartered (in any room of the Gubernatorial mansion).

TO MRS. JULIA C. R. DORR.

BOSTON, November 1, 1889.

MY DEAR MRS. DORR, — The ivy has reached me in good condition, and if care and attention can make it live and grow, it shall flourish and spread until it begins to cut off the light of that study window which you remember. It is but a very little while ago that I was saying, "I must have some living thing in this room — a plant — a *plant* is what I want, — a live thing without nerves, that knows nothing of original sin and its penalties — of headaches and heartaches, — an innocent, delightfully idiotic being that is not troubled with any of our poor human weaknesses and irritabilities. . . .

Miss Kate Field is, I believe, responsible for this bit: "His reference in *Elsie Venner* to the ' twenty-seventh letter of the alphabet' so puzzled one lady reader, who was reading the story in company with a relative, that she wrote to the author, telling him that neither she nor her cousin Edward could make out his meaning."   His reply was: —

BOSTON, *March* 4, 1861.

MY DEAR MISS LAVINIA, — The twenty-seventh letter of the alphabet is pronounced by applying the lips of the person speaking it to the cheek of a friend, and puckering and parting the same with a peculiar explosive sound.   "Cousin Edward" will show you how to speak this labial consonant, no doubt, and allow you to show your proficiency by practising it with your lips against his cheek.   For further information you had better consult your *gra'mma*.

A Scotch gentleman who sent him a book called *Burns and the Kirk* had from him a note of thanks in which he said: "I find it full of interest, for it treats a question which has long puzzled me: how strait-laced Scotland could clasp her national poet to her bosom without breaking her stays."

A gentleman of the Jewish faith one day sent to the Doctor some wine from Jerusalem.   The note of thanks was: "Wine received.   Strong as Samson.   Sweet as Delilah."

Once, when a man of no great note died, his friends tried to get Dr. Holmes to "say a few kind words about the deceased which might be published."   But he declined.   "Do you see?" he said.   "They want to engage me in the embalming business!   But I cannot help to preserve this fly in amber."

In a letter he spoke of a learned gentleman as "not so much *stamped* with learning, as *stained* with it."

A newspaper preserves this story, which I believe

is correct: that at a country charitable fair he was
entreated to furnish a letter for "the post-office."
Placing a one-dollar bank-note between the leaves of
a sheet of paper, he wrote on the first page: —

> " Dear lady, whosoe'er thou art,
>     Turn this poor page with trembling care ;
>   But hush, oh, hush thy beating heart,
>     The one thou lov'st best will be there."

Turning the page in obedience to this injunction,
the one - dollar "greenback" was disclosed, and to
prove the truth of his assertion, the Doctor had written the following appeal on the opposite page: —

> " Fair lady, lift thine eyes and tell
>     If this is not a truthful letter.
>   This is the one thou lovest well,
>     And naught (0) would make thee love it better."

Half-a-dozen trifling anecdotes may perhaps find a
place here as fittingly as anywhere else.

Walking down Beacon Street one day, a physician
told Holmes of an amusing marriage, a "love-match,"
which had occurred in his family, wherein the bride
was eighty-eight years old and the groom a trifle
younger.  The Doctor was greatly amused.  Coming
to his house, he walked slowly up the steps, then suddenly turning, running down, and calling after his
companion, he said: "Of course they did n't have
any children; but, tell me, did they have any grand-
children?"

Here is a story told by Dr. C. B. Porter, of Boston.  "At the time of the Peace Jubilee I returned
to my office on Boylston Street one day, and I found
my slate in the hall covered with Latin words and
signed O. W. Holmes.  I immediately got down my

dictionary, for I could not translate it without; and I found out by my translation that he had been to the Peace Jubilee, had soiled his boots so thoroughly with the dirt there that he did not like to go down town in such a plight, and stopped and asked my servant for a boot-brush that he might clean up his boots, and he had dignified this rather menial performance by writing it all out in Latin and leaving it on my slate.   I do not doubt but that Dr. Holmes, with his keen sense of humor, was thinking of the trouble I should be put to in translating that Latin to ascertain the very commonplace thing which he had done." [1]

Mr. Howells, early in his career, introduced himself to Mr. Lowell; and thereupon Mr. Lowell took him into town to call on Dr. Holmes.  The handshakings being completed, the Doctor turned to Mr. Lowell, and said, "Well, James, this is something like the apostolic succession; this is the laying on of hands."

He said that he could not imagine a man falling in love with Mrs. Siddons; it would be like falling in love with the Pyramids.  On another occasion he remarked that, though a woman tempted man to eat, he had never heard that Eve had anything to do with his drinking; he took to that of his own motion.

[1] *Boston Medical and Surgical Journal*, vol. cxxxi. No. 24, p. 586.